THE DIVINE APPOINTMENT

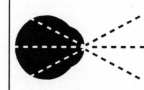

This Large Print Book carries the
Seal of Approval of N.A.V.H.

THE DIVINE APPOINTMENT

JEROME TEEL

THORNDIKE PRESS
A part of Gale, Cengage Learning

GALE
CENGAGE Learning

Detroit • New York • San Francisco • New Haven, Conn • Waterville, Maine • London

GALE
CENGAGE Learning

LIBRARY OF CONGRESS CATALOGING-IN-PUBLICATION DATA

Teel, Jerome, 1967–
  The divine appointment / by Jerome Teel.
    p. cm. — (Thorndike Press large print Christian fiction)
    ISBN-13: 978-1-4104-1148-8 (hardcover : alk. paper)
    ISBN-10: 1-4104-1148-6 (hardcover : alk. paper)
    1. Political fiction. 2. Large type books. I. Title.
  PS3620.E4355D58 2008
  813'.6—dc22   2008034784

Published in 2008 by arrangement with Howard Books, a division of Simon & Schuster, Inc.

Printed in the United States of America
1 2 3 4 5 6 7 12 11 10 09 08

In memory of my father-in-law,
Robert M. Jelks,
one of the greatest men I've ever
known.

ACKNOWLEDGMENTS

To those of you who called or wrote with encouraging words following the release of *The Election,* thank you. Your kind words were inspiring.

To my mother, Nona Teel, for your early critique.

To Ramona Tucker for your patient teaching and editing.

And, as always, to Jennifer, Brittney, Trey, and Matthew for your encouragement and support.

CHAPTER ONE

Brentwood, a suburb of Nashville, Tennessee
"I didn't mean for it to happen," Jessica Caldwell said. "This is the last thing I want in my life right now."

Jessica spoke into her wireless phone. It had been resting on the nightstand at the base of a brass lamp, beside the alarm clock, two unfinished books, and the remote control to the flat-screen television in her bedroom. Jessica had reluctantly answered after seeing his number on the caller ID. It was a conversation she dreaded, but it could be avoided no longer. There was no small talk between them. Their verbal exchange was an argument from the first word. That was more than fine with her.

"But it happened, and we've got to deal with it," Jessica said.

She sat in the middle of the bed in the upstairs bedroom of her Brentwood town house. Her legs and feet were still under the covers. The rest of her body was covered with a Vanderbilt University T-shirt. The glimmer from the half-moon filtered into the room through the venetian blinds of the second-floor window. The only other light was the glow from her digital alarm clock. It was 11:45 p.m. central time on Monday, the second week of May.

Jessica had arrived home after a late dinner, changed clothes, and watched late-night television before climbing into bed. It had taken a while to wind down. She had just fallen asleep when the phone rang.

"I *was* being careful," she replied to the biting comment from the other end of the phone. "I've been using birth control for years."

She felt agitated and scared at the same time. No one had ever talked to her like that. Shifting her legs, she crossed them under the covers. She held her head in her left hand, the wireless phone in her right, and closed her eyes briefly.

"I told you I didn't mean for it to happen. But it's not all *my* fault. It took both of us, or have you forgotten?"

Jessica ran her hand through her shoulder-length auburn hair and tucked it behind her ears. Tears welled up in her brown eyes, but she refused to let them escape onto her

10

cheeks. She refused to give him the satisfaction of making her cry. She had never loved the man on the other end of the phone, but during that conversation her feelings for him grew extremely close to hate.

No, she decided. *Hate isn't strong enough. I loathe him.*

"I don't want this any more than you do," she said. "I'm just beginning my career and —"

The male voice interrupted with yelling and profanity. He had never yelled at her during their relationship. He had always been polite and kind. The yelling and profanity were almost more than she could take. It was certainly more than she expected.

Then he said something that caused her heart to leap into her throat. She swallowed hard and spoke with determination. "I'm not doing that. I don't think that's right. And it's my body. I'll do what I want to."

The flood of harsh words intensified, angering and upsetting her even more. Jessica despised the day she had met him. She wished him dead.

"What?" she screamed into the receiver, punching the mattress through the comforter and sheets. "Tell your wife? Are you crazy? Of course not! Why would I do something like that?"

Jessica couldn't fight the tears any longer. The dam burst, and they began to stream down her face.

The man on the other end of the call continued to scream at her.

They'd had a comfortable relationship until then. It wasn't love, Jessica knew, but they had found pleasure in each other's company. Then one thing had led to another . . . and now this had happened. *He* had gotten what he wanted — her.

But no more. The physical relationship was officially over, Jessica vowed. She couldn't continue with him after this lashing, but they would always be connected. It was inescapable.

Like the relationship, the conversation needed to end as well. She was sick of talking to him. Jessica briefly held the wireless away from her ear and thought about simply disconnecting the call. She wiped tears from her cheeks with her free hand.

"I don't know how your wife found out," she finally screamed after she had endured the berating for several more minutes. "But I'm through talking about this. I'm hanging up."

The man's yelling continued as Jessica removed the phone from her ear again and pressed the End button. She turned off the power to the wireless phone and growled at it before slamming it down on the night-stand. She also angrily unplugged the land-line telephone cord from the wall. After she was certain she wouldn't be disturbed anymore by the telephone — any telephone — she extinguished the lamp, buried her face in her pillow, and wept. What sleep she experienced the rest of the night was rest-less.

The White House, Washington DC
President Richard Wallace left the two black-clad Secret Service agents in the hallway and entered the residential area of the White House. It was the only place in the world where he had any privacy. And privacy had become a rare commodity since his election to the presidency eighteen months earlier. He was a handsome man. Fifty-five years old. Brown and gray hair. Strong jaw. Rugged. He worked out almost every day in the White House gymnasium.

President Wallace made his way in the dark toward the bedroom suite he shared with his wife, Lauren, and removed his suit coat and loosened his necktie as he walked. It was 1:00 a.m. eastern time Tuesday, and he had been up since 4:30 a.m. the previous day.

He activated only one lamp in the sitting area adjacent to his and Lauren's bedroom — he was concerned that too much light might awaken her — and draped his coat over the back of a chair. He knew one of the housekeeping staff would find it at daybreak and have it dry-cleaned and back in his closet before he needed it again. He stretched and yawned before plopping down on the sofa in the sitting room. He knew Lauren was asleep in their bedroom, so he tried to be quiet. He didn't even turn on the television. He laid his head on the back of the sofa and closed his eyes.

Despite his efforts to keep from awakening her, Lauren opened the door to their bedroom and called softly from the doorway, "Are you coming to bed?"

"In a few minutes." He peeked at her through squinted eyes. "I just need to unwind. I didn't mean to wake you."

Lauren walked farther into the room. She wore navy silk pajamas and slipped on a matching robe as she moved toward her husband. Lauren, an attractive, slender brunette with a very elegant appearance even at one o'clock in the morning, was the same age as President Wallace.

"I haven't been asleep long," Lauren said.

"You need me to get you anything?"

"I'm fine. It's been a long day, with one crisis after the other." He scratched the top of his head and sat up straight. "I called Justice Robinson's family tonight. They don't think she'll make it another day."

Lauren sat on the sofa, rotated her body toward her husband, and tucked her legs under her. She propped her right elbow on the back of the sofa. He reached for her left hand.

"I hate to hear that." Concern flickered in Lauren's warm brown eyes. "I enjoyed her company on the few occasions I had to talk with her."

"Yeah, me too," he said sorrowfully. "I disagree with many of her decisions but respect her as a jurist."

"You have anybody in mind to replace her?"

President Wallace yawned. "Porter McIntosh and the general counsel's office have been compiling a list and background information for several weeks now. I'll probably start interviewing the leading candidates within the next week or so. The Supreme Court's term starts the first week of October. That's only five months away. So we don't have much time to work through the confirmation process."

15

"It's a big decision."

Describing it as a big decision was an understatement. Selecting a college or buying a house was a big decision. This decision was enormous. The magnitude of it was beyond description.

"It's probably one of the biggest, if not *the* biggest, decisions I'll make as president. I'm convinced this is one of the reasons God has placed me in this position."

"How difficult will it be, do you think, to have your nominee confirmed?"

President Wallace let go of her hand and stretched his arms over his head. He shifted in his seat. His shoulders ached. His exhaustion had finally caught up with him, and he could barely keep his eyes open. He twisted his head toward Lauren.

"The confirmation process will be one of the most politically vicious and brutal events that I can imagine," he told her. "The liberal-interest groups and senators from the left will ferociously attack any candidate I put forward. It won't be pretty, I can tell you that. But it'll be worth the fight if he or she is confirmed."

Reclining against the back of the sofa again, he closed his eyes. The aching in his shoulders eased, but only barely.

"Why don't you come to bed?" Lauren

16

insisted. "You look completely exhausted."

"I'll be there in a minute," he mumbled. "You go ahead."

Not hearing a response, he cracked his eyes open. Seeing the worry on her face, he gave her a reassuring smile.

Lauren returned the smile and kissed him on the cheek. She affectionately squeezed his hand and stood to leave. "Don't stay up too long. You have another long day ahead of you."

"I won't," he promised.

Lauren returned to their bedroom and closed the door.

President Wallace remained alone. He sat up on the edge of the sofa, lowered his head, closed his eyes, and whispered, "Lord, I know that you are in complete control of every situation. I pray for Justice Robinson and her family. Father, if it's in your will, I ask that you heal her body. Please comfort her. And, Lord, if she passes away, I ask that you comfort her family. I also pray for wisdom and your guidance in this most important decision that may now lie before me. Please provide strength and wisdom to me and also to the person you direct me to nominate to the Supreme Court. Please allow me to find your will. Amen."

President Wallace stood and rubbed his

droopy eyes. He entered the bedroom quietly. It was finally time for sleep, and he desperately needed it.

The Omni Office Center, Nashville, Tennessee

"I'm Elijah Faulkner, and I'm here for an afternoon meeting with Merrick Armstrong," Eli announced to the receptionist as he entered the Chandler & Spivey, PC law offices from the elevator that opened directly into the office lobby. The receptionist was protected from the common people by a five-foot-tall wall laden with hand-carved marble and an onyx granite countertop. Her enclosure was just one of the many posh appointments in the Chandler & Spivey offices that inhabited the tenth, eleventh, and twelfth floors of the Omni Office Center in downtown Nashville.

The receptionist smiled pleasantly. "We're expecting you. If you'll please go into the Walker B. Chandler conference room" — she pointed at a door across the lobby — "Mr. Armstrong will be with you in a few minutes."

Eli entered the conference room and placed his briefcase on the end of the long mahogany table near the oil painting of Walker B. Chandler, one of the founders of

Chandler & Spivey. Unbuttoning his gray pin-striped suit coat, Eli walked to the bank of windows that overlooked Centennial Park and the replica of the Parthenon. His six-foot-two frame and wavy black hair were reflected in the glass. The scene through the window was a view Eli witnessed each of the numerous times his law practice brought him to Nashville to do battle with one of the lawyers at Chandler & Spivey.

Although Eli knew well that the air outside was brisk, the park scene revealed that spring was, little by little, bringing life back to the vegetation that had hibernated through the winter. It was Tuesday, the second week of May, and the cold April showers had surrendered to warmer days. Buds covered the trees that lined the perimeter of the park, and sprouts of green were scattered throughout the otherwise dormant turf. He chuckled to himself at the irony. After years of virtual death at the hands of Merrick's ruthless client, his own client might begin to get his life back today as well.

"Mr. Faulkner," interrupted a young female voice. Eli pivoted toward the sound and saw a slender, attractive young woman standing in the doorway of the conference room. She was midtwenties, he guessed, with long blond hair and even longer legs that extended from a skirt that ended just above her knees. She presented herself in such a way that it was obvious she thought her likeness more fitting for the cover of *Vogue* than the inside of a law office. But there she was, at Chandler & Spivey, waiting to be discovered.

"Would you care for a cup of coffee or a soft drink while you wait for Mr. Armstrong?" she said with a warm smile.

"A cup of coffee would be great," he said patronizingly, and she dashed away to retrieve it.

After the model-in-waiting left, Eli sat down at the end of the conference-room table and spread the contents of his file in front of him. Soon the cup of coffee was delivered with a flirtatious flair.

His client, George Thornton, arrived shortly thereafter. He was several years older than Eli and was short and overweight. He had a large nose, long chin, and bushy eyebrows that matched his salt-and-pepper hair.

Eli had liked George Thornton from the instant he'd met him. He'd immediately seen in George the qualities he admired in a man — a hard worker, honest, and determined. They were the same traits Eli tried to emulate in his own life and legal career.

And there was something else that drew Eli to George. George was dedicated to his family. Eli had seen that loyalty clearly as he and George had become good friends over the last couple of years. The more their friendship had evolved, the more resolute Eli had become in attempting to right the injustice George and his family had suffered.

George joined Eli at the conference-room table and sat down in the chair to Eli's right. "Eli, where do you think this is going to end up?"

"Like I told you when I agreed to take this case," Eli responded, catching George's dark eyes with his own, "I'm a lawyer, not a magician. I can't magically put everything back the way it was before all of this started. But we've done a good job in building your case, and Armstrong is smart enough to realize that a jury could get excited and hit his client with a negative verdict and large punitive damages."

"Well, I want Rory Driscoll to pay dearly for what he has put my family and me through during these last three years. We've lived our entire lives in Jackson. I built Thornton Sportswear from the ground up, and Driscoll stole it from me. The people in town have looked down on us since my wife

21

and I had to file for bankruptcy." George took a breath.

Eli saw the familiar rage begin to build. He couldn't blame the man, but he needed George to be levelheaded during the meeting.

"I want him to *pay*," George continued through clenched teeth.

"I'm on your side, George. But you've got to be realistic. I hear Driscoll's having a difficult time of it financially, and may be about out of money. If they offer anywhere north of a million, you better think very seriously about it."

"A million dollars?"

Eli saw the disappointment on his client's face and heard it in his voice.

"I'm not taking a million dollars," George replied. "That's nowhere close to enough to compensate my family and me for what we've been through."

"From what I understand, there's not much left, George. I suspect that Armstrong has billed Driscoll for at least five hundred thousand dollars. The only reason they're talking to us now about a settlement is because Driscoll wants to avoid prosecution by the U.S. attorney's office. Otherwise, Armstrong would just keep on billing him. Our problem is that proving a violation of the RICO Act is only part of the game. Collecting the money from Driscoll is the other part. If Driscoll is in jail, I can't get you a dime." Eli studied George closely to make sure he understood. "So as I said, if they get to a million, we better take it."

Just then Merrick Armstrong and Rory Driscoll strolled into the conference room. Merrick was the older and led the two as they made their grand entrance. He wore a starched white shirt and a striped bow tie. He was slightly overweight, and it was more noticeable in his jowls than anywhere else. Aside from some graying black hair above his ears, he was completely bald. Rory was dressed in a tailored suit purchased, Eli assumed, with money he'd swindled from George Thornton. His black hair was neatly parted and slicked down close to his scalp.

Everything about Rory's appearance — and particularly his swagger — irritated Eli. The man was as slick as his hair. Eli had learned during the course of this case that George Thornton wasn't the first person Rory had swindled. It was just that, this time, he'd been caught. Helping a victim like George Thornton get justice against a swindler like Rory Driscoll was one of the reasons Eli enjoyed being a lawyer.

"Eli, Mr. Thornton," Merrick said crisply

as he entered and sat at the end of the table opposite Eli. He didn't shake hands with either man.

Eli and George nodded in the direction of the enemy to acknowledge its presence.

Rory didn't speak.

"I suppose you know why I asked you to come to this meeting," Merrick continued. "Mr. Driscoll and I would like to discuss a possible settlement."

Eli and Merrick haggled for the better part of the afternoon. Offers, counteroffers, and coy gamesmanship were all part of the negotiations. Two hours after the meeting began, Merrick said the words Eli had waited to hear.

"We can pay one million dollars," Merrick said. His face was rigid and firm. "And that's our final offer."

Eli relaxed back into his chair, stroked his chin thoughtfully, and exhaled. "Let me speak with my client in private."

He and George excused themselves from the room. Once they were safely where Merrick and Rory couldn't hear them, Eli spoke to George in a tone that was barely above a whisper, but forceful. "I think you should take it, George. My sources tell me that Rory is completely out of money, and may even file for bankruptcy. If he does that, then you can kiss good-bye all hope of recovering any money from him."

"I know." George looked dejected. "It's not as much about the money anymore as it is about punishing Rory. You can't imagine the times I've dreamed of my hands around his throat."

"A million dollars is pretty good punishment." Eli raised his eyebrows for effect. "I'll bet he despises the day the two of you met about as much as you do. Because of you, the federal authorities are investigating some of Driscoll's other businesses. And I can assure you that nobody likes having the FBI after them. Let's take the million and call it a day."

Eli could sense that George wasn't quite convinced, so he leaned in closer. "I know Merrick Armstrong, George. He may not be the best lawyer in the state, but he didn't get to be third on the letterhead at Chandler and Spivey because of his good looks. If we don't take this offer, he'll strike the best deal he can for Driscoll with the U.S. attorney, then Driscoll will file for bankruptcy. You'll be left out in the cold."

"All right," George conceded reluctantly. "But I want the money wired to your office this afternoon, before we leave. I don't want to risk his being able to renege on us."

In agreement, Eli and George reentered the conference room and announced that a settlement had been reached. By 4:00 p.m. Eli had obtained confirmation that his bank had received the money and that it was deposited in his escrow account. He and George signed the necessary settlement papers prepared by Merrick's office and departed.

As they left, George thanked Eli and genuinely appeared satisfied and relieved that the whole ordeal was finally over. Although Eli would receive a handsome fee for his efforts — one third of the total recovery — the appreciation from George meant as much or more to Eli.

CHAPTER TWO

En route to Jackson, Tennessee

Eli exited the parking garage behind the Omni Office Center in his charcoal gray BMW 760Li and merged into the westbound traffic on West End Avenue. Several cars and trucks and a handful of city buses cluttered his lane, so he zigzagged his way through the traffic. His BMW responded with little effort. Soon he was on the I-440 loop around Nashville, then headed west on I-40 toward his office and home in Jackson, Tennessee. Because he was slightly ahead of the afternoon rush-hour traffic, he hoped to be home by 6:00 or 6:30 p.m. at the latest.

As Eli drove, he loosened his necktie. His suit coat was already on the rear seat. He allowed his mind to relax. Finding a radio station that played songs from the 1980s, he sang along, off-key, with a few. After a couple of treasured minutes of solace, his wireless rang. The caller ID indicated that the call was coming from his office, and he activated the BMW's hands-free device to answer it.

"This is Eli."

"Eli, this is Barbara."

Barbara Lewis had been Eli's assistant for the last five years. In her midfifties, she was dependable, loyal, and a hard worker. She arrived at work on time, stayed late if Eli needed her to, and he paid her well to make sure she didn't look for another job.

"Did Mr. Thornton's case settle?" she asked.

Eli had spoken to Barbara on his way to Nashville that morning and had told her that a compromise was a real possibility. He knew she wouldn't be surprised by the outcome.

"The money's already in our escrow account. I'm on my way back to Jackson now."

"That's good news. I hoped it would be, and I bet Mr. Thornton is relieved."

"He needed some coaxing," Eli said. "But in the end he realized it was the best result we could hope for. Anything going on at the office?"

"Nothing that can't wait until tomorrow."

"What's my calendar look like in the morning?"

"It's clean. I scheduled an appointment

28

for tomorrow afternoon with Ms. Hawkins about her case, but the morning is clear."

"Good," Eli responded. "I'll be in later than usual." He liked taking some time off after a successful day.

"I guessed as much. Have a good evening."

The Faulkner residence, Jackson, Tennessee
Eli ended the call, and continued his trek toward Jackson. It was 6:15 p.m. when he pulled into the double garage and parked beside his wife's XJ7 red Jaguar convertible. Their house was a stately colonial in a gated neighborhood in north Jackson.

Eli put the car in park and grabbed his suit coat from the rear seat. The garage was immaculately clean, as always, and the reflections of the two automobiles glistened off the glossy concrete floor.

The aromas of pasta, Alfredo sauce, and garlic bread met him when he entered the house.

"How was your day?" Sara asked as Eli entered the kitchen where she was preparing supper.

"It went well. Finally got George Thornton's case settled."

Eli draped his suit coat over one of the kitchen-table chairs and walked toward

Sara. She rose up on her toes and gave him a welcome-home kiss, and the two embraced.

"I'm glad you're home," she said. There was love in her voice.

"Me, too. It's been a long day."

He smiled at her, and she returned the warm gesture. He took pleasure in holding her close. "You're still as beautiful as you were the first time I saw you." He brushed Sara's blond hair away from her face and gazed into her blue eyes.

"You're just saying that."

"I mean it." He held her for two or three seconds longer, until she gave him another kiss.

"You better let me go." She pushed at his arms, which were locked around her narrow waist. "Or we might burn dinner again."

Another quick kiss and Eli reluctantly released her. Sara resumed stirring the pasta noodles that were boiling on the stove while Eli began to set the table.

"George Thornton," Sara said.

Eli could tell from her probing tone that she was searching for the name.

"Is that the man who had the clothing-manufacturing business?"

"One and the same."

"You've been working on that case for

some time, haven't you?"

"Three years. I'm glad it's over, and I know George is. He really needs the money with two kids in college . . . but enough about George Thornton. What did you do today?"

"I went to the gym this morning," Sara replied, "and worked out until ten. I met Anne for lunch at the country club. After that I ran a few errands. I've been home most of the afternoon."

"How are Anne and Tommy?"

"They're doing fine. Anne was already lamenting how busy their spring will be with both Jack and Harry playing Dixie Youth baseball. And to top it off, Tommy is coaching both teams."

Eli removed a glass pitcher from the refrigerator and poured some sweet tea into two glasses he had filled with ice. "Better him than me," he commented honestly as he set the glasses at their appropriate places on the kitchen table.

Anne and Tommy Ferguson were the prototypical helicopter parents. They poured themselves into whatever their kids did. Baseball. Piano lessons. School plays. It didn't matter. If Jack or Harry was involved, so was Anne, or Tommy, or both. Eli could never see himself in that kind of life.

31

"Anne says he enjoys it." Sara shrugged. "I know she wouldn't miss one of the boys' games for anything in the world."

Sara removed the pot of noodles from the stove top and poured them into a metal colander in the sink. "Can you get the bread from the oven? Dinner's just about ready. The last thing is the tossed salad."

Eli slipped on an insulated mitt and opened the oven. The heat blasted him in the face. He removed the pan containing a small toasted loaf of French bread and set it on the counter.

"Eli, when are we going to have kids?"

Sara talked to his back. Her voice sounded timid, as if she were afraid to broach the subject.

Eli understood her reticence. He hadn't been very receptive in the past when the subject of children had been discussed.

"I'm ready for baseball games and parties at school and all those fun things Anne and Tommy do with their kids."

It was a running discussion between Eli and Sara. She wanted to have children. He wasn't ready. Sometimes the discussion was more intense than other times. They'd been married thirteen years, and she wasn't getting any younger, she often reminded him. He was in the prime of his career, he retorted. And he liked being able to go anywhere they wanted to . . . whenever they wanted to. Children would tie them down too much, he argued each time the subject came up.

"Don't start on that again, Sara." Eli pivoted and held his palms up toward her. "I've had a hard day, and I'm tired."

Sara abruptly turned her back to Eli and resumed preparing the tossed salad. "Why do you despise the thought of having children so much?" she demanded.

"I don't despise the thought of having children," he fired back. "I like kids. I'm just not ready to have any of our own right now."

Sara spun to face him and glared at him piercingly. "I don't think you're *ever* going to be ready." Her voice dripped with sarcasm. "Our friends' kids are already in elementary school. Some are even in middle school."

Eli knew how much Sara wanted children. It was growing harder to look into her eyes and say no. But he did. Time after time, he did. Their marriage was nearly perfect in every other way. They were regular attenders and faithful supporters of their church. They had no financial concerns. This one issue — whether to have children and when

— was practically the only one on which they disagreed. Any other differences had been minor and were resolved without difficulty. This issue lingered.

Sara didn't bring it up often. It wasn't as if she focused on it daily. But Eli knew how important having children was to her. Yet time and again he cut her off without fully discussing the issue . . . all the while knowing that his refusal to consider the possibility hurt her.

"I don't want to talk about this right now," he said firmly. "I'm hungry. Let's eat supper, and talk about this later."

Sara dejectedly spun away from Eli and placed the pasta Alfredo and the salad on the table. Eli had just closed the oven door when an image from the twenty-inch flat-screen television that sat on the kitchen counter caught his eye. He could barely hear the audio, but the image above the female news anchor's right shoulder was that of Lady Justice. Below were the words *Supreme Court.* He took the remote control from the kitchen counter and increased the volume.

"We have sad news to report tonight," the female anchor announced. "After a three-month battle with pancreatic cancer, Supreme Court Justice Martha Doyle Robinson has died. Justice Robinson was appointed to the Supreme Court by President Mitchell eight years ago and has been one of the most liberal justices to sit on the High Court . . ."

Eli decreased the volume and muttered, "That doesn't happen very often."

"What did you say?" Sara demanded from across the room.

"The news is reporting that Justice Robinson died today from cancer," he said defensively. Then he softened his tone before replying further. He knew Sara was still in a combative mood, so why agitate her further? "And I said that it doesn't happen very often that a new Supreme Court justice gets appointed."

Eli sat down at the end of the table and Sara sat to his left. The pasta was delicious, the iced tea refreshing, but the conversation between the two of them was nonexistent during dinner.

After dinner Eli changed into blue jeans and a T-shirt. He sat in his leather recliner in the den, surfing between baseball games. Marlins versus Cubs. Twins versus Orioles. Nothing too interesting. His favorite team, the Atlanta Braves, had the night off. He switched to Fox News and viewed several minutes of a segment about Justice Robin-son.

Sara gave Eli the silent treatment all evening and retired before he did. When he finally went to bed after the late news, she was asleep. Her back was to him, but he could see enough of her face through her sleek, shoulder-length hair to notice the red-ness around her eyes. She had cried herself to sleep, he realized.

He closed his eyes and sighed. A feeling of guilt washed over him. *Am I being too self-ish?* They had argued over whether to have children on numerous occasions, but he had never known her to be this upset. He bent over and gently kissed her on the cheek.

"I love you," he whispered. "Everything's going to be all right."

Avenue of the Americas, New York City
It was nearly 10:00 a.m. on Wednesday. Stella Hanover boarded the elevator and pressed the button for the twenty-seventh floor of the forty-floor building. The three other people on the elevator never made eye contact with her, and it was a good thing. She wasn't in the mood to be courteous to anyone. She tapped her foot anxiously as the elevator made stops at five separate floors with people exiting and boarding

before it reached her destination. When the elevator finally arrived at her floor, she stomped off in a huff even before the doors had fully opened. It was time to finalize battle preparations.

She knew it had to happen sometime. The justices on the Supreme Court were getting older, making a vacancy inevitable. She just hadn't thought it would be Justice Martha Doyle Robinson's seat. She was one of the younger members of the court, and one of Stella's favorite jurists.

Stella had hoped there would be no vacancies during the Wallace presidency. Even now she still couldn't comprehend how he had been elected eighteen months earlier. She detested Richard Wallace. He represented everything she opposed, and since the day after he was elected, Stella had been working day and night to ensure that he wouldn't be reelected.

But fate — and pancreatic cancer — had handed President Wallace an opportunity to change the shape of the Supreme Court, and Stella was determined to thwart him at all costs. Had one of the four conservative justices died, it wouldn't have been an issue. President Wallace could have appointed whomever he wished and Stella wouldn't have raised a hand. But Justice Robinson's seat was a different story altogether.

No legal scholar needed to speculate about how Justice Robinson would vote on certain cases or issues. Her opinions were very predictable — always to the extreme left of every issue. And Justice Robinson stood, unwavering, on the one issue that was of paramount importance to Stella — the right of a woman to choose to have an abortion. That's why Stella admired her so much.

Pushing her red-rimmed bifocals farther up from their resting place at the end of her nose, Stella dared anyone to cross her, particularly on this day. The National Federation for Abortion Rights — the largest pro-choice organization in the country — carried tremendous weight, and she was president. Her Avenue of the Americas office was the main war room for the campaign to defeat any conservative Supreme Court candidate nominated by President Wallace.

Stella made her grand entrance at 10:00 a.m., just as she did every day. Her employees scampered to hiding places when she entered, but she caught a couple in the break room before they could escape. She barked instructions at one of them and yelled at the other. After they ran scared from the room, she smiled to herself and poured a cup of hot coffee. Then she strode off to her office. She loved the power. Aides and staff all scurried to satisfy her demands. The NFAR office buzzed with the same noise and energy as a campaign headquarters during the last few days of an election. Justice Robinson had been dead less than twenty-four hours and Stella had her office ready for battle.

Once inside her personal office, Stella plopped down in her chair, reviewed her battle plans, and began making phone calls to senators' offices and news outlets. She demanded to be interviewed on CNN, NBC, CBS, ABC, and Fox so she could spew her venom at President Wallace and any nominee he submitted. Executives with every network and cable news station cowered and agreed immediately to whatever she wanted. Nobody dared to cross the heavyset, midforties redhead who was known for her cutthroat politics. Next Stella called the newspapers and demanded op-ed space in the *New York Times,* the *Washington Times,* the *Washington Post,* and the *Los Angeles Times,* to name a few. By noon all her demands were met, and she checked the media off her to-do list.

"Valerie," Stella called out from her chair

behind the desk. Covering the phone, cradled to her ear, with her hand, she peered over the top of her glasses at her assistant. "I need an updated list of every appellate court judge — state and federal — in the country who is a member of any right-wing legal organization. That's where Wallace is likely to look."

Valerie Marcom scribbled notes on a steno pad. She had been working for Stella for the better part of the last five years. She was of average appearance, with short, mouse-brown hair, and wore black-rimmed glasses. Stella kept her around because she did what she was told and never complained.

Valerie nodded. "I'll get some of the legal-clinic students to work on it right now."

Stella had more volunteers from the legal clinics of the law schools in New York City than she could possibly need. But she put all of them to work anyway. The more young, liberal minds she could foster, the better for her own future . . . and that of NFAR. Two dozen of them were currently scattered throughout the NFAR offices, eagerly awaiting instructions from Stella.

"That's a great idea," Stella replied. "And contact our largest donors. We're going to need at least twenty-five million dollars to fight this campaign in the media and in the

Senate." She paused. "Make arrangements for me to attend the memorial service on Friday."

"Have you heard who he'll nominate?" Valerie asked.

"Not yet, but it won't matter. Anybody he nominates will be unacceptable."

Washington DC

Jessica Caldwell had served two years as a law clerk for Justice Robinson. The news of her death on Tuesday was difficult to take. It wasn't unexpected, but that didn't make it any less difficult to stomach.

Justice Robinson's body lay in repose in the Great Hall of the Supreme Court Building on Lincoln's catafalque for two days before Friday's memorial service. Jessica arrived at Reagan National Airport from Nashville just after 10:00 a.m. eastern time on Friday. She flagged a cab to take her to the Washington National Cathedral and arrived just as the memorial service began.

For the past couple of days, she had gone back and forth about whether to attend the service. After all, she had memories of living in Washington DC for the two years during her Supreme Court clerkship. Many were pleasant memories, but others were downright awful. Those memories — the

41

awful ones, the ones that made her sick just thinking about them — had almost kept her away. But in the end she decided she owed more to Justice Robinson than a mere donation to the American Cancer Society.

After her black leather handbag was searched and a metal detector waved over her black dress and black shoes, Jessica entered the cathedral through a pointed-arch doorway and sat near the back. President and Mrs. Wallace sat in the front-left row with the Robinson family. Senators, congressmen, Supreme Court justices, and other Washington dignitaries filled the first twenty rows of each section of pews. Secret Service agents — some she could see, but she was certain others were blended in with the crowd and into the walls — were scattered throughout the church.

Jessica sat in a crowded pew between two other women also dressed in black and whom she didn't know. She smiled politely but didn't engage either in conversation. They were probably just well-dressed sightseers, she guessed. She crossed her legs at the ankles, sliding them under the pew and setting her purse nearby. She clutched a tissue in her left hand.

The organist played "Amazing Grace" as a prelude — which struck Jessica as odd for

Justice Robinson's memorial service — on the great organ. Jessica had never seen nor heard of Justice Robinson attending church, much less making any reference to God. Yet the priest spoke eloquently about Justice Robinson's life. His speech was followed by words from President Wallace, then a member of the Robinson family.

Jessica dabbed occasionally at the corners of her eyes during the hour-long service. She had admired and respected Justice Robinson for her intelligence and jurisprudence. When the great organ began to play the recessional, Jessica left the sanctuary and descended the concrete steps in the front of the building. She hailed a cab for the return trip to Reagan National. She had been back in Washington long enough.

Just as she opened the rear passenger door to the cab, someone grabbed her arm from behind.

"I need to talk to you," a voice said.

Jessica jerked her head around and faced the voice. Gradually she backed into the cab. The voice sat down beside her and closed the rear door.

"Just drive," the voice ordered the cab-driver.

CHAPTER THREE

The law offices of Elijah J. Faulkner,
Jackson, Tennessee

The building that housed Eli Faulkner's office was located one-half block west of the courthouse square in downtown Jackson, on Washington Street. Rays of sunshine were slowly chasing away the chill on Monday morning when Eli pulled into the alley between his office building and the First National Bank building and parked in his reserved parking space. The weekend had been pleasant, and he had played a rare round of golf on Sunday afternoon.

Now it was back to work. Eli entered the building through a rear door. He climbed the back staircase to a landing on the third floor that opened into the kitchen his employees used mainly for morning and afternoon breaks.

The building had been a very popular hotel during the late 1800s and early 1900s.

Several political dignitaries had occupied various rooms during those years — some for reasons that remained untold. The facility had been in a serious state of disrepair when Eli bought it at a foreclosure sale three years earlier. It had taken six months to rehabilitate the structure, but he was quite proud of the finished product. The old Otis elevator in the lobby of the building was still operational and serviced all three floors of the historic hotel. Eli had converted the third floor into an enviable suite of offices. The bottom two floors were likewise remodeled and leased for more than enough money to cover the mortgage.

"Good morning," Barbara said as Eli emerged from the stairwell. She was in the kitchen refilling her coffee cup. Even though her face was perhaps fifteen years past its prime, Barbara tried to look younger. Employees joked about her standing appointment at the beauty salon to replenish the dark red color in her hair at the first sign of a gray strand. She exercised regularly and had a steady boyfriend. He was a salesman or a truck driver or had some such occupation that kept him on the road often. Eli had met him at the office Christmas party last December but had immediately forgotten his name.

"It's a little cool outside for the third week of May, isn't it?" Barbara stirred her coffee and propped herself against the kitchen cabinet.

"It'll warm up soon enough." Eli lingered in the kitchen, preparing his own cup of hot liquid breakfast with caffeine, flavored creamer, and sweetener. "And" — he grinned — "we won't even notice because we've got a busy day."

Barbara nodded in agreement.

"Come into my office in a few minutes and we'll get our game plan prepared."

With that, he disappeared — coffee mug in hand — into the hallway that led to his office in the back of the building. The old wood floor creaked with each step he took.

A borderline perfectionist, Eli kept his office orderly. Every book was in its place, and his desk was free of clutter. His life was organized, too, and he liked it that way. The discipline had been instilled in him through high school and college athletics. At six feet two he wasn't tall enough to play professional basketball, but he had never lost his love for the game. He still played in an early morning pickup game at a local high school gym two days a week.

The office decor was minimal but tasteful. Frames with matted undergraduate and law school diplomas from the University of Tennessee hung on one wall of the room, next to his license to practice law. A settee and two leather wingback chairs formed a sitting area across from his most cherished piece of furniture: an antique partners desk. The desk occupied a prominent position in the middle of the room. The dealer from whom he'd acquired it had tried to convince him that it had been used by Supreme Court Justice Learned Hand. Eli wasn't that gullible, since he knew Judge Hand had never served on the Supreme Court. But Eli was convinced that the leather-covered top and oak drawers contained many personal and historical secrets that would never be discovered.

The whole room exuded success . . . for good reason. In his ten years as an attorney, Eli had risen head and shoulders above his peers. Now, at thirty-five, he was recognized as one of the best trial lawyers in Tennessee. He was at the point in his career where he possessed the two traits most important to a successful lawyer. He was old enough to have the necessary experience in handling difficult cases but still young enough to be hungry.

The legal business had been good to Eli. He had a nice home. Luxury cars. A large bank account. He had no complaints about where he was in life. And he knew exactly where he was going.

He and Sara had been high school sweethearts and had married as soon as they graduated from the University of Tennessee, in Knoxville. She had studied primary education. He had studied political science. He had gone on to law school, and she had supported them during those lean three years. Eli had worked for another law firm in Jackson for a couple of years, but since he'd started his own practice eight years ago, Sara hadn't worked outside the home.

Barbara entered Eli's office not long after he did, and the two of them spent the better part of an hour reviewing files and charting a course of action on each. Barbara made notes in a steno pad of the files on which she needed to prepare drafts of discovery requests and on which depositions needed to be scheduled. Armed with enough assignments to keep her busy for several hours — even days perhaps — she left Eli's office to return to her workstation.

"Hold my calls," Eli directed as Barbara left. "I've got some things I need to get finished this morning, and I don't want to be disturbed."

Barbara nodded and closed the door to

48

his office as she exited.

Eli removed several files from his credenza and stacked them neatly on his desk. He opened the first one and began dictating a letter to the opposing attorney about scheduling a date to conduct depositions of physicians who had treated his permanently injured client. But his mind wandered, and he laid the dictation recorder on his desk. He ran his fingers through his hair and stared across the room at nothing in particular. Losing concentration had become a common occurrence since his argument with Sara last week about having children.

He wasn't certain why that particular disagreement troubled him so much — especially since they had disagreed in the past about having children. But this time it had been almost a week, and he was still bothered by it. Was it because he'd violated the old adage of not going to bed angry? Or was it because Sara had cried herself to sleep? She had never done that before.

Eli sighed. Sara was a great wife. She didn't deserve to be upset about anything. He would make it up to her somehow . . .

The built-in intercom in the telephone on his desk rang, startling him. He punched the button to speak to the intruder.

"Your wife's on the phone," Barbara said

over the intercom before Eli had an opportunity to scold her for disobeying his instruction.

Eli picked up the receiver and pressed the blinking light to connect to the line on which Sara was holding. "Hey, honey. I was just thinking about you."

"Really?" She sounded surprised and pleased. "What about?"

"Just how wonderful you are. What are you doing for lunch?"

The Oval Office, the White House,
Washington DC

President Richard Wallace entered the Oval Office at precisely 5:30 a.m. on Tuesday for his therapeutic daily quiet time. It was never completely quiet at the White House, but this time of day was the quietest. A carafe of coffee, pastries, and fresh fruit were waiting for him when he arrived. The two Secret Service agents who escorted him from the third-floor residence assumed their post immediately outside the office door after he entered.

"Preacher is in the Oval Office," one of the agents said into the tiny microphone hidden in the sleeve of his suit coat. President Wallace liked the code name the service had assigned to him. He had overheard one of the agents using it not long after the primaries were over and had inquired about its origin.

"You act like one, sir," came the stiff reply. Whether it was meant as a compliment or not, President Wallace wasn't certain, but he decided to take it as one.

He had been elected to the presidency after two terms as the governor of South Carolina. The race was close. His opponent had more money as well as the backing of popular celebrities from both coasts. Liberal-interest groups ran television ad after television ad critical of Wallace's social conservatism, but that seemed only to fuel his own campaign. When the votes were tallied, he had won, and that was all that mattered. Now was the time to make good on his campaign promise.

President Wallace and Lauren had been married for thirty years and had two children. Thomas was in medical school at Duke, and Joann was a senior at the University of South Carolina in Columbia. Even though the demands of public service were great, he had vowed never to shortchange his children. And he had followed through on that vow. He had attended every athletic event, every recital, and rarely had missed an evening meal. He had also introduced each of them to Jesus Christ, the most important Person in his life. Best of all, his children were following through on their own commitment to God.

Before sitting down to his simple breakfast, President Wallace gazed around the room. He respected the Oval Office and had made sure when he took office that certain furnishings remained from prior administrations. The white marble mantel from the original Oval Office — constructed in 1909 on the south side of the White House — adorned one wall; the American and presidential flags stood faithfully on either side of his desk; and the presidential seal embossed on the ceiling presided over all meetings. President Wallace had chosen the resolute desk given by Queen Victoria of England to President Hayes in 1880 as his personal desk, although it was necessary to remove the two-inch base that President Reagan had added for his lanky frame in 1981. The paintings and prints that covered the walls of the Oval Office were of lighthouses and seascapes. They were on loan from museums throughout his native South Carolina.

After preparing a cup of coffee with a dash of half-and-half and two cubes of sugar, he settled in behind his desk for his morning

Bible study. Purposefully, he studied a passage from the fourth chapter of Esther in the Old Testament, focusing on the woman who was called by God "for such a time as this." President Wallace could relate. He felt certain, and humbled, that God had chosen to put him in the position he had and knew that he also was called to serve "for such a time as this." He prayed every day that he would be worthy, knowing that he never would be but accepting the responsibility that lay before him. And, like every day, when he had completed his Bible study, he spent time conversing with God.

Then he began to review the contents of a stack of manila folders that had been placed on his desk overnight. He began with the clippings of headlines and news articles from newspapers around the world and the translation summary that accompanied them. Media reports were rarely accurate, but it was important to digest what information was being disseminated to the world's population.

Next were intelligence reports. The Middle East was always boiling, but recently there were elevated concerns about terrorist cells in Sudan and the Philippines. One folder contained a report on North Korea's and Iran's nuclear production. He read through the reports briefly before placing them in the manila folder printed with the words *For the President's Eyes Only.* The national security advisor, secretary of state, and CIA director were scheduled for their daily briefing with him at 8:00 a.m., and he'd get a detailed overview from each of them then.

President Wallace laid his reading glasses to the side, stretched his legs, and refilled his coffee cup. With fresh coffee he began to work through the economic reports: consumer spending, durable goods orders, unemployment data. All seemed to indicate that the economic policy his administration had implemented was performing splendidly.

President Wallace closed the last of the manila folders and placed them in the stack for the morning file clerk to retrieve. He heard some stirring in the outer office and glanced at his watch.

"Already six forty-five," he mumbled to himself.

His daily meeting with his chief of staff was scheduled for 7:00 a.m. He sipped his coffee thoughtfully. Foreign and domestic policies were certainly important, but President Wallace had something else on his mind this morning.

There was a light knock on the door.

"Come in," President Wallace called, knowing his brief peace and quiet was gone for the day. He rose from his desk chair to greet Porter McIntosh as he entered the room.

Porter emerged with his right hand thrust at President Wallace in preparation for a handshake. With his starched white shirt, red-and-blue-striped tie, and leather briefcase, Porter looked as though he were going into a courtroom rather than the Oval Office.

"Good morning, Mr. President," Porter said as he entered.

"Good morning, Porter," President Wallace replied. "Would you care for a cup of coffee?"

"No, thanks. I've had my limit."

"How are the wife and kids?" President Wallace said, resuming his seat behind his desk.

Porter sat in a wingback chair across the desk from the president and set his briefcase at his feet. "They're doing fine, sir. Thanks for asking. I don't get to see them often enough, but they are doing fine. And Lauren?"

"Same here. Her schedule is almost as hectic as mine. Running the country sure is time-consuming, isn't it, Porter?"

"Yes, sir, it is."

Both chuckled softly at the understatement, but the humor didn't last long. A difficult and stressful decision lay ahead of them, President Wallace knew. History itself would measure their actions — *his* actions — and the weight of that thought dissipated their smiles.

"Sleep much last night, Porter?"

"Not much. Probably about three hours. Yourself?"

"Not much more."

President Wallace noted the creased forehead and exhaustion on Porter's face. The presidency was beginning to take its toll on Porter, too; he had aged from the stress and strain of working in the White House. President Wallace relied on Porter. *Perhaps too much,* he thought, realizing this. Porter had no streaks of gray in his sandy blond hair. No additional weight was noticeable through his tailored suit. But he simply looked tired. Haggard, really. Eighteen-hour workdays and crisis after crisis were catching up with him.

"You miss South Carolina, don't you, Porter?"

"I do sometimes, sir. Beaufort is a lovely place. I hope to one day return there with my family and live in one of her antebellum homes."

"We've got a lot of important things to accomplish before you can enjoy that Low Country lifestyle again."

"I know, sir," Porter replied.

"Let's go over the two possible candidates again," President Wallace said.

Aware of Justice Robinson's terminal illness, President Wallace had asked Porter to covertly begin the nomination process some three months earlier. With Justice Robinson's memorial service being last Friday, President Wallace wanted to nominate someone to replace her within the next few days. Porter and the White House counsel's office had begun with a list of ten jurists from around the country and had pared it down to two finalists for the president's consideration: Fredrick Lefler, the chief judge of the U.S. Court of Appeals for the Fourth Circuit, and Dunbar Shelton, the chief justice of the supreme court of Mississippi.

"Judge Lefler was appointed to the bench fifteen years ago," Porter said as he read from his printed report. His briefcase contained a complete dossier on each candidate. "He was elevated to the chief judge's position five years later. His written opinions have consistently held to conservative social and economic philosophies. He has consistently voted to interpret the Constitution as it was written. Strong supporter of Second Amendment rights —"

"What about Shelton?" President Wallace interrupted.

"You want me to finish the report on Judge Lefler?"

"Later, perhaps, but I want to talk about Shelton first."

Obediently Porter placed Judge Lefler's dossier on the corner of President Wallace's desk and removed the one on Judge Shelton from his briefcase. "He has served on the Mississippi Supreme Court for the last ten years and is as conservative, if not more so, as Lefler. His writings have restricted the reach of affirmative action. Like Lefler, he is a strict constructionist on constitutional issues. He has overturned excessive personal-injury awards. He —"

"I hear what you are telling me, Porter," President Wallace interrupted again.

He already knew every word in each dossier from memory. But it wasn't biographical sketches that interested him. It was philosophical and theological issues that concerned him. He wanted to know what each man thought about when he was alone in his own bedroom and stared at himself in the mirror. He rose from his chair and began to pace between the desk and the window that overlooked the Rose Garden.

"But you're not telling me what I want to know." President Wallace stopped pacing, thrust his hands in his pants pockets, and peered through the window at the garden that had yet to reach its full bloom. "What I want to know is where do they stand on *Roe v. Wade,* and can they be confirmed by the Senate?"

"I don't know, sir. I really don't."

President Wallace spun around from the window briskly and waved his arms out to the sides of his body. "Don't give me that, Porter," he chastised. "You're my chief of staff, and you worked for me when I was governor of South Carolina. I know you, Porter, and I know that you know the answer."

President Wallace shook the index finger of his right hand at Porter, and Porter squirmed in his chair. "You know it. You're paid to know it. It's your job to know it. President Mitchell knew that Justice Robinson would vote to uphold, if not extend, *Roe v. Wade* before he appointed her. She was the deciding fifth vote two years ago when the abortion issue was last before the court."

President Wallace rested the palms of his hands on the desk and leaned toward Porter. "I plan to appoint someone who will vote to overturn *Roe*. That's why I'm here, Porter. That's why I'm here. Now tell me which one."

Porter uncrossed his legs and crossed them again in the other direction. He averted his eyes from President Wallace. "You're not going to like the answer."

"Tell me," President Wallace ordered.

Porter crossed his arms in front of his chest as if he were already disappointed with his own words, which had yet to be spoken. He looked directly into President Wallace's eyes. "Shelton would vote to overturn, but you can't get him confirmed. You have a better chance at getting Lefler confirmed, but I'm not convinced he would vote to overturn."

"What do you mean?" President Wallace inquired as he finally returned to his seat behind the resolute desk.

"I mean that Lefler has been very careful over the years in what he has said both publicly and privately about the issue." Porter uncrossed his arms and gestured with his hands as he continued. "You may

60

find yourself with another David Souter."

President Wallace took another sip of coffee. It was cold. He set the cup down and pushed it away, to the side of the desk. "And you don't think we can get enough votes to confirm Shelton?"

"It's simple politics. Although the majority has only fifty-one votes in the Senate, they'll stick with Senator Proctor on this one. Those up for reelection this fall don't want to face their constituents and explain why they voted to move the Supreme Court to the right. I doubt you'd even be able to get Shelton's nomination out of the Judiciary Committee."

President Wallace detected concern in Porter's tone. That made him worry, too.

"Even if we get the nomination out of the committee," President Wallace mused, "we'll have a hard time on the Senate floor. Proctor will have one of his lieutenants filibuster the nomination."

"It will take sixty votes to put an end to the filibuster so that the Senate can even vote on the nomination," Porter said. "We don't have that many allies in the Senate."

President Wallace stood again and paced some more, thinking through the possibilities. Lefler wasn't right, he decided. It had to be Shelton. "We'll have to twist as many arms as we can to get Shelton confirmed."

"We can't twist enough arms to make it work."

President Wallace paced some more with his hands stuffed in his pockets. "But we've got to make it work. This is why I was elected."

Porter followed President Wallace with his eyes as he paced. "This is not the only reason you were elected. There are welfare reform and the economy and hundreds of others."

The president talked to the window again. "I know. All of those things are important. But this is the most important. Transforming the Supreme Court is the most important of all."

"Is it a political hill worth dying on?"

President Wallace turned and stared at Porter. "I'm not worried about getting reelected, Porter," he said in a grandfatherly voice. "If I'm supposed to serve another term, then things will work out. But you're missing the point. I know I was elected for this purpose, for this decision. I was elected for such a time as this, and we've got to fight on every political hill until we win."

"It'll be a bitter fight."

"I know. We'll have to cut as many deals as we can. I'm willing to play as many cards as I have to get the nomination confirmed."

"Is it that important?"

"It's that important."

"Any deal would have to be with Proctor, and my guess is that the stakes would be too high."

President Wallace sat down and reclined in his chair. He placed his hands behind his head, locking fingers together, and gazed at the presidential seal in the ceiling. He shifted in his seat. He evaluated the choices again, but only one was a real option. He knew that as soon as he said the word, Porter would work to make it happen. That's what Porter did best. He took care of things. And so Porter would be tasked with getting Dunbar Shelton confirmed to the Supreme Court, whatever it took. President Wallace couldn't take a chance on Lefler.

"You may be right, Porter," he conceded. "But I suspect the stakes are higher if we don't get Shelton confirmed."

CHAPTER FOUR

Brentwood, Tennessee

"Has she been dead long?" Lieutenant Mike Brantley asked as he ducked under the yellow crime scene tape between two uniformed officers, and into the town house of Metropolitan Nashville's latest homicide victim. The town house was part of an upscale complex in the southern Nashville suburb of Brentwood. Although the place was alive with police photographers snapping pictures, investigators dusting for fingerprints, and employees from the coroner's office examining the corpse, the finality of death struck Brantley as he entered the room where the body was found. It was an eerie feeling he'd experienced more often than he desired during his ten-year career with the Metropolitan Nashville Police Department.

"About eight to ten hours, I'd guess," Sergeant Lee Dodson responded from his crouched position beside the body on the living-room floor. The dead female was fully clothed, in red satin pajamas. "Her body is stiff. But the coroner should be able to give us a more exact time of death this afternoon." Dodson exhaled and shook his head. "It's a tough way to start a Friday."

Dodson stood as Brantley approached, finished making a few notes in his notepad, and tucked it back into the breast pocket of his blue blazer. The two watched as employees of the Davidson County coroner's office zipped the black body bag and loaded the victim onto a gurney.

"Do you have an ID on her?" Brantley asked.

"Jessica Caldwell," Dodson responded, retrieving his notepad and flipping through it. "Twenty-seven years old. Lawyer with McAllister and Finch, downtown."

Brantley studied the scene from different angles. Nothing was disturbed. Nothing appeared to be missing. The television, DVD player, and other electronic devices were visible and undamaged. A laptop computer was open on the kitchen table. It didn't appear that robbery was the motive.

"Lawyer?" Brantley responded as he walked and thought. "That should make for a long list of suspects."

"Not this one. She had only been working there three months. Not enough time to make a lot of enemies."

"Cause of death?"

"We don't know yet. Her secretary called the precinct and asked us to check on Ms. Caldwell when she missed an appointment this morning, and no one could get a response by phone or at her door. Two officers on first-shift patrol found her lying on the floor. No vital signs and no sign of forced entry. Medical examiner said it looked like strangulation, but he won't know for sure until the autopsy is complete."

As the death-laden gurney exited the town house onto the sidewalk, Brantley turned toward the glass table behind the sofa that was cluttered with photographs. He picked up one that was in a brass frame and stared at the smiling, auburn-haired, brown-eyed woman. "This her?"

Dodson glanced at the photograph. "That's her. Attractive, wasn't she?"

"I'll say."

"I've got a daughter a few years younger. Makes me sick to my stomach. You got any kids, Brantley?"

"Two boys. Ten and twelve."

"Hug 'em while you can," Dodson advised. "They'll be grown before you know it."

The detectives' philosophical moment was interrupted by one of the crime scene investigators.

"I've got two sets of prints over here, Detective," said the officer who was dusting the inside doorknob on the front door. "And another set on the outside doorknob."

"Good work," Dodson replied as he pivoted toward the front doorway. "Be careful when you lift them. We don't want any mistakes with this one."

As he left Brantley looked over his shoulder and spoke to Sergeant Charlotte Crossley, the investigator in charge of the crime scene team. Crossley was sharp. She'd been with the department for fifteen years, and had been the first African-American woman to earn the rank of sergeant.

"Sergeant, run those prints through both the state and FBI data banks and see if you come up with any matches."

Sergeant Crossley nodded her understanding and continued dusting the coffee table near where the body had been discovered. Brantley glanced around at the team of crime scene investigators who scurried about the interior of the town house searching for any clue that might lead to the arrest of, and hopefully the conviction of, the perpetrator of the murder of Jessica Caldwell.

"Y'all take your time in here, Sergeant," Brantley instructed. "Dodson and I are going to contact the girl's family and begin to interview neighbors and coworkers. Let me know if you find anything else."

Dodson and Brantley left Jessica Caldwell's town house to undertake one of the most difficult tasks a person could perform: telling parents that their child was dead.

Belle Meade, a suburb of metropolitan Nashville

The unmarked dark blue Ford Crown Victoria containing Lieutenant Brantley and Sergeant Dodson traveled the tree-lined thoroughfares of the exclusive Belle Meade area of greater Nashville before entering a residential area east of the famed Belle Meade Plantation. Their destination was the home of Jessica Caldwell's parents. Neither man relished the thought of this assignment, particularly Dodson. It hit too close to home. He couldn't stop thinking about how he'd feel if it was *his* daughter.

"How do you handle it, Dodson?" Brantley asked from the passenger seat when they were less than ten blocks from the Caldwells' residence.

"Handle what?" Dodson responded.

"You know," Brantley replied. He dragged out the rhythm of the word *know*. He motioned with his hands, as if Dodson should continue the conversation without any further prompting.

But Dodson refused.

Brantley pressed forward. "How do you tell parents that their daughter has been murdered?"

"Oh, that." Dodson nodded slightly as he thought through his answer before responding. "It ain't easy. I can tell you that for sure. Never is. But someone has to do it, and it might as well be me. You can't let your emotions get in the way. Is this your first time?"

Brantley appeared uneasy. He stared straight ahead and stretched his legs out on the floorboard as far as they would go. "Not my first," he said, shaking his head. "But I haven't had to do this very many times. Someone else involved in the investigation usually handled it."

"You'll be fine. Just don't cry."

Brantley eyed Dodson. "I'll try not to."

"This is the place."

Dodson pointed to a Tudor-style house that rested on a slight rise on the left side of the street. He drove the car into the gated entrance that was flanked by two gray stone pillars. The gate was already open, and Dodson steered the sedan to a parking area adjacent to the wood double-front door.

Jordan Caldwell peered through the large arched window of his dining room at the dark sedan as it approached. He shoved his hands in his pockets and dropped his head. He already knew that his daughter's whereabouts were unaccounted for and feared that the occupants of the approaching car carried news that he didn't want to hear.

Jordan looked up again to watch as two men exited the car and began to walk toward his front door. Their official appearance made him sick to his stomach. The passenger was the younger of the two. Dark hair. Dark suit. Starched shirt. His face showed signs of apprehension. The driver had a slightly disheveled appearance, but his hair — brown with gray around the edges — was maintained in a military-style crew cut. His face was firm . . . determined.

Anticipating the worst, Jordan moved toward the front door. When the bell rang, he opened the door.

Both men displayed badges and credentials for Jordan's inspection, then returned them to the inside pockets of their jackets.

"Mr. Caldwell," the younger man said, "I'm Lieutenant Mike Brantley from the Metropolitan Nashville Police Department, and this is Sergeant Lee Dodson. May we come in?"

"What's this about, Officer?" Even as he asked, Jordan feared he already knew the answer. He and his wife, Heddy, had grown concerned when Jessica's secretary called their house looking for her this morning. They had tried to reach her at her town house and on her wireless phone, to no avail. "Is it about my daughter?"

"I'm afraid it is, sir," Lieutenant Brantley responded. "May we come in?"

Jordan stepped back from the door and allowed the two officers to enter. "Please have a seat in there." He pointed to a sitting area to the right of the front door. "I'll get Heddy, my wife."

Brantley surmised that Jordan Caldwell was in his late fifties. Maybe sixty. He was six feet tall, slim, and his hair was mostly gray. There was an air of distinction about the man, even in the midst of a crisis, and that impressed Brantley.

"Nice place," Brantley muttered to Dodson as he turned to take in a panorama view.

"Yeah." Dodson sat on a leather settee

across the room from the arched opening where they'd entered. "But money doesn't impress me. It usually leads to problems."

Despite Dodson's obvious lack of appreciation, antiques and replicas of rare paintings adorned the interior, and the grounds outside were immaculately manicured. Persian rugs covered the floors. Even the settee on which Dodson sat was covered with Corinthian leather.

"Even so," Brantley replied, "this place is impressive. The antiques must be worth over a million bucks. Did you say the Caldwells were friends of the governor?"

"That's right. My friend at city hall told me Caldwell made his money in the highway-construction business. He got a lot of state contracts, if you know what I mean."

Brantley walked over and stood near where Dodson was sitting. "We better find a suspect quick, then," he murmured. "The press will be all over us on this one, not to mention the politicos."

Soon Jordan returned to the sitting room with an attractive, elegant woman. Brantley guessed her to be in her late fifties. She was about five feet four and maintained a shapely figure. Her hair color was similar to Jessica's, with a few strands of gray. But the one thing Brantley noticed most was the graceful way she entered the room.

"Mrs. Caldwell," Brantley said as she and her husband entered, "I'm Lieutenant Mike Brantley, with the Nashville Police Department, and this is Sergeant Lee Dodson."

"Is this about our daughter?" Heddy inquired immediately after the introduction. She glanced back and forth between the two men, as if desperate to read something, *anything,* from their faces.

"I'm afraid it is," Dodson replied sympathetically. "Why don't we sit down?"

Jordan and Heddy sank onto the settee Dodson had previously occupied, and the two officers sat in chairs across from the settee with their backs to the front door. A cherrywood coffee table covered with *Southern Living* magazines separated the settee from the chairs.

"I don't know of any way to say this," Dodson said in a solemn tone, "other than to just say it. I'm afraid your daughter is dead."

"No!" Heddy cried. "No! Anything but that!" She buried her face in Jordan's shoulder.

Pulling her close, into his arms, Jordan compassionately stroked her graying auburn hair. Tears streamed from his eyes, but he brushed them away. Brantley sensed that

Jordan knew he had to be strong for Heddy's sake. Perhaps there would be another time for him to mourn. Perhaps. But right now he had to be strong.

"How did this happen?" Jordan asked, still stroking his wife's hair as she sobbed on his shoulder. She refused to look at the two officers.

It was difficult enough to tell them that Jessica was dead, Brantley knew. But that was easy compared to what came next. He would rather tell them that she'd died in an accident. A car wreck perhaps.

But that wasn't true.

"We believe she was murdered," Brantley said.

"Murdered!" Jordan's head snapped around until he was looking squarely at Brantley.

Heddy raised her head from Jordan's shoulder and tried to wipe away the tears. "Did you say *murdered?*" Disbelief spilled from her voice.

"Yes, ma'am," Dodson replied. "I'm afraid so."

"Who would want to murder Jessica?" Jordan asked. "She didn't have any enemies."

"That's what we're trying to find out right now, Mr. Caldwell," Brantley said. "We're trying to determine who killed her, and why."

"How did it happen?" Jordan asked, his eyes focusing on the officers. "I mean, how did she die?"

Neither Brantley nor Dodson relished telling the Caldwells the specifics surrounding Jessica's death. It would be even more upsetting, Brantley knew. The truth was that Jessica probably had known what was happening and had been helpless to stop it. She may have looked into the face of her killer as she drew her last breath, unable to scream out for help.

"She was strangled, sir." Dodson's voice was calm and without emotion.

"Strangled!" Heddy screamed. "Oh, dear God!"

For a moment, Brantley thought Heddy would faint as she sobbed uncontrollably. He averted his eyes and felt a stabbing in his stomach. Jordan, although stoic, wept as well. He tried to hold his wife as the realization of their daughter's death, and the manner in which she'd died, slowly engulfed them. It was several minutes before either could speak.

It was Jordan who collected himself first. "Do you have any idea who did this?"

"We don't have any leads at this point,"

Brantley admitted. "We're hoping that you can help by telling us about Jessica. Names of friends and acquaintances. Things she liked to do. Places she liked to go."

"Sure." Jordan wiped his tears with a monogrammed handkerchief that he removed from his pants pocket. "We'll do everything we can to help."

"She was an attorney, you know," Heddy said proudly. She gradually regained her composure.

"Yes, ma'am," Dodson replied. "We're going to her office when we leave."

"She graduated first in her law school class at Vanderbilt," Heddy continued. Her voice was distant, and she gazed beyond the two detectives at an oil painting of Jessica at a young age on the wall over Brantley's right shoulder.

"She had been back in town only a few months," Jordan said. "She worked as a law clerk for Supreme Court Justice Martha Robinson after graduation from Vanderbilt two years ago. She went back to Washington last week for her memorial service." He hesitated. "Something seemed to be bothering her when she returned."

"Did she say what it was?" Brantley asked, intrigued by Jordan's last statement. He made a note of it in his notepad.

"No," Jordan replied. "After a couple of days, everything seemed to be normal, and we didn't ask her about it again."

"She had her whole life ahead of her," Heddy added, still staring at the painting on the wall. "I can't believe she's gone."

Brantley and Dodson visited with the Caldwells for fifteen more minutes before departing. During the conversation, they jotted down several pieces of information that might be useful in searching for the murderer. Armed with the information the Caldwells had given them, the detectives expressed their condolences again and departed. Their next stop would be the offices of McAllister & Finch.

CHAPTER FIVE

Downtown Nashville

"Let's get a quick lunch before going in," Dodson said.

He and Brantley exited their car in front of the multistoried office building on Commerce Street in downtown Nashville that housed the offices of McAllister & Finch. They parked on the curb beside a No Parking sign. The sign applied to everyone but them.

Dodson could smell the aroma coming from one of his favorite lunch places. "This street vendor has some of the best Polish sausage anywhere around." He motioned to a kiosk on the sidewalk near the front door.

They walked over to the kiosk and Dodson held up two fingers. "With everything," he said to finish the order.

Without speaking, the vendor removed two Polish sausages from his steaming grill and covered them with every condiment he had. Dodson handed him a crisp ten-dollar bill for the two sausages and two bottled sodas.

"What do you know about this law firm?" Brantley asked.

He and Dodson moved away from the vendor to eat their lunch. They rested against the side of their unmarked sedan. A stream of men and women in business suits, all in a hurry to get somewhere, passed them in both directions.

Dodson answered Brantley between bites of his lunch. "I know one of their lawyers worked me over pretty good on a drug case several years ago when I was working vice. We busted a congressman's son for dealing heroin, and his slick lawyer, a McAllister & Finch lawyer, got him off. They are what you would call an old-money law firm. My guess is that the senior partners charge five hundred bucks an hour, and their clients can afford to pay it."

"I take it that they aren't on your Christmas card list." Brantley chuckled. He downed the last of his soda and screwed the top back onto the empty bottle.

"No lawyers are, but especially these," Dodson replied as he finished off the last of his lunch. "You about finished?" he asked Brantley.

"Yeah." Brantley tossed his empty bottle into a nearby trash can. "You were right about that Polish sausage," he added as they passed the kiosk again on the way to the front door of the building. He took a deep breath and patted his stomach. "It *is* the best in town."

As they entered the building, Dodson noticed a wreath that hung on the tinted front door. *That's probably the only recognition they'll give her,* he thought as he held the door open so Brantley could enter before him.

"I can see why they charge five hundred an hour," Brantley said as he entered the building and moved toward the receptionist's counter.

Dodson followed.

"Everything is gold plated," Brantley added.

Dodson detected the sarcasm and smiled.

After they announced the purpose of their visit to the first-floor receptionist, Brantley and Dodson were ushered into the penthouse office suite of the senior partner, Reese Finch. He was a diminutive man, advanced in years. His half-lens spectacles, wispy white hair, red bow tie, and suspenders gave him a scholarly appearance. Reese's office was expansive, and it had the best view in the building. He shook hands with each detective and invited them to sit down.

"That's okay. We'll stand," Dodson said.

"Nothing like this has ever happened to an employee of our office," Reese said miserably. "My own grandfather was one of the founding partners of this firm. He's probably rolling over in his grave at the attention we're receiving as a result of this."

Dodson was immediately disgusted. The guy was obviously more concerned with the impact Jessica's death might have on his precious law firm than he was with apprehending the culprit.

"Is there someone in the office who can give us a list of clients who might have had contact with Ms. Caldwell in the last several days?" Brantley inquired.

"That is a very delicate situation, Officers," Reese explained as he sat down behind a desk that appeared to be too large for a man of his size. "We represent a clientele that expects us to maintain complete confidence, even to the point of not disclosing their names."

"We appreciate the confidential nature of your services, Mr. Finch." Dodson sneered, aggravated by the old man's lack of cooperation. He crossed his arms and glared at Reese. "But we've got an investigation to run. If you don't help us, you know we will be back in an hour with a search warrant, and we might stay here for days looking for information. Why don't you make it easy on all of us and let us speak with someone who can help?"

Reese stared at the detectives. Neither flinched. He tapped several times on the top of his desk with the end of an ink pen, then tipped back in his chair.

"That would probably be her secretary," Reese said, relenting after a couple of minutes. "And at this point I'm only willing to let you talk to her and no one else." His voice was methodical and stern. "If you want any more information, you'll have to get that search warrant. I'll have our office manager locate Jessica's secretary for you. I'm not sure who she is. We have over one hundred lawyers in our office, so it's difficult to get to know all of them, much less their staff."

Reese's secretary summoned Francis Morton, the McAllister & Finch office manager, who would escort Brantley and Dodson to Jessica's secretary. Before they left his office, Reese asked if the investigation could be kept as quiet as possible so as not to disrupt the operation of the law office.

"We'll do our best," Dodson replied, but he knew that was unlikely. A reporter for the local newspaper had been at the crime scene almost as soon as he arrived.

The trio of Brantley, Dodson, and Francis took the elevator to the fifth floor and arrived at the cubicle of Marion Barker just as she was returning from her lunch break. Francis introduced the two detectives to the startled midtwenties secretary, and Dodson began the interrogation. They stood outside her gray cubicle.

"Ms. Barker, do you know of any clients who might want to harm Ms. Caldwell or were angry with her?"

Marion Barker was modestly dressed and average in appearance — a stark contrast to the beauty and affluence of Jessica Caldwell. Marion appeared shaken by the news of Jessica's death. When she could finally respond to Dodson's questions, her voice trembled.

"I've been working for her only a month," she began. "I was in the office secretarial pool before then. I was just beginning to recognize the names of her clients, but I don't know of anyone who threatened her, if that is what you mean."

"Was she working on any cases where someone might have gotten upset with her?"

Dodson continued, pen and notepad in hand.

Marion rubbed her hands together and nervously rocked back and forth. "Nothing really stands out in my mind. If there was, she never mentioned it to me."

"Did you notice anything about her demeanor when she returned from Washington?" Brantley asked.

"Now that you mention it, she did seem a little preoccupied with something when she returned, but she never told me about it." Marion looked around, as if she were checking to see if anyone else could hear the conversation. "The staff and the lawyers don't socialize very much around here, if you know what I mean," she whispered.

"I guessed as much," Dodson quipped.

"What about her social life?" Brantley asked. "Did she have a boyfriend? Was she seeing anyone?"

"She didn't have a steady boyfriend. Not that I knew about, anyway. Some guy called her a couple of times. I may have his name somewhere on a phone message."

Marion entered her cubicle. The two detectives followed. Shuffling through a couple of stacks of documents on her desk, she retrieved a slip of paper containing a name and telephone number.

"Yeah, this is the guy," she said as she read from the message sheet. "Tag Grissom. He's a doctor — or something like that. I've got his phone number here if you want." She handed Brantley the phone message.

Brantley jotted the telephone number down on his notepad and returned the slip of paper to Marion. Both he and Dodson thanked Marion for her time and co-operation before leaving. They told her they'd call her if they had any other questions.

Brentwood, Tennessee
Todd Allen Grissom, M.D., was finishing with his tenth patient of the day at his Brentwood cardiology office when Lieutenant Brantley and Sergeant Dodson arrived and demanded to see him. Dr. Grissom had two partners, and their clinic occupied the entire third floor of a four-story medical complex next door to St. Francis Hospital. After making Brantley and Dodson wait five minutes, Dr. Grissom at last had his nurse escort them into his office.

"What's this about?" Dr. Grissom inquired arrogantly, then sat down nonchalantly in a chair behind his mahogany desk.

Dodson didn't like the doctor's condescending tone, and his cavalier attitude was infuriating.

Dr. Grissom propped his elbows on his desktop and looked down at Brantley and Dodson. "If it's about those overdue parking tickets, I'll get them paid before the end of the week."

As the officers sat in leather chairs across the desk from Dr. Grissom, Dodson's dislike of Dr. Grissom intensified. The cardiologist's appearance only served to fuel Dodson's — and he knew Brantley felt the same way — immediate abhorrence. The doctor's dark hair was slicked back. He wore black Gucci shoes, Armani slacks, a silk shirt, and gold-plated cuff links that protruded from under his starched white lab coat. He was a handsome man in his midthirties who clearly had a sizable income, most likely a large bank account, and he knew it.

Brantley and Dodson had previously decided to double-team Dr. Grissom. Dodson took the lead as bad cop and cut right to the chase. "We're not here about parking tickets, Dr. Grissom. What can you tell us about a young lady named Jessica Caldwell?"

"What about her?" A smirk emerged, revealing the doctor's bright teeth.

Dodson wanted to slap the smirk off the

doctor's face.

Brantley cleared his throat and took over the questioning. "Do you know her?"

"Yeah, I know her. What's this about, anyway? Is she saying I did something to her? Because if she is, she's lying."

Dodson glanced at Brantley, whom he knew was trying to measure Dr. Grissom's demeanor.

"Did you know she was dead, Dr. Grissom?" Brantley continued.

"Dead?" The doctor's eyes grew wide. "No, I didn't know that. Of course not." He straightened up in his chair and the smirk disappeared. "But what's that got to do with me?"

"How did you get that cut on your face, Dr. Grissom?" Brantley asked.

Dr. Grissom touched a small bandage on his left cheek. "I cut myself shaving this morning."

Dodson glanced at the photographs in Dr. Grissom's office. None of them contained any likenesses of Jessica Caldwell. But another attractive young woman appeared in several of the photos, including one of her in a wedding dress. He also noticed the gold wedding band on Dr. Grissom's left hand.

"Were you seeing Ms. Caldwell socially,

Dr. Grissom?" Dodson resumed the lead in the questioning. What he really wanted to do was drag the arrogant doctor down to the station for questioning on their turf, but he and Brantley didn't have enough evidence yet. Maybe later, Dodson hoped.

Dr. Grissom's vision shifted from Brantley to Dodson and he shrugged. "I've been to dinner with her a couple of times. That's all."

"Does your wife know about that?" Dodson continued.

"Now, just a minute!" Dr. Grissom shouted. The veins in his temples bulged, and his face grew red. "It's no concern of yours what my wife knows, or what she doesn't know." He gritted his teeth. "I think it's time the two of you left."

"Did you see Ms. Caldwell last night, Dr. Grissom?" Brantley pressed.

"I'm not answering any more questions, and I told you to leave. Don't make me call security."

"Don't threaten us, Dr. Grissom," Brantley responded tersely. He straightened his back and glared across the desk at Dr. Grissom. "You know that security's not going to do anything to us. Sergeant Dodson and I are going to leave, but I'm sure we'll be back. And when we do come back, we're not going to be as nice as we were this time."

Brantley and Dodson stood and walked toward the office door. Just as they were leaving the room, Dodson turned and fired one last question. "Dr. Grissom, can you tell us where you were last night?"

"Get out!" the doctor shouted from across the room.

The Vidalia restaurant, Washington DC
"How are things on the Senate floor?" Porter McIntosh asked. He and Cooper Harrington sat at a corner table in the swanky Vidalia restaurant on M Street NW, approximately five blocks northwest of the White House. Porter had vetted Judge Shelton's name with several friendly senators over the last couple of days. The time had come to approach Senator Proctor's office about the plan.

"Things are going great." Cooper scanned the lunch offerings, then laid the menu on the table. "Senator Proctor is getting his agenda through the Senate."

Porter recognized Cooper's intended message: that the Senate majority leader's agenda, not the president's, was getting pushed through the Senate.

"How's your boss doing?" Porter asked. "I heard his health isn't so good."

"Wishful thinking, Porter. He's fit as a horse and plans on getting re-elected this year."

Porter laid a cloth napkin in his lap and aligned the silverware beside his plate. Cooper took a sip of water and motioned for the waiter. The waiter was dressed in a white shirt, necktie, dark slacks, and a long white apron. He took Porter's and Cooper's orders promptly and disappeared.

Porter resumed the conversation. "As his chief of staff, aren't you worried that the good people of the state of Tennessee are tired of electing a liberal like Proctor? Bryan Edwards is running a great campaign, and that state's been leaning considerably toward the right in recent elections."

"Proctor will never lose in Tennessee. The senator, Mrs. Proctor, and I were in Nashville last night meeting with some of his key contributors. They're as excited as they've ever been to have him reelected. Do you seriously think that the son of the most popular governor in the history of the state is in jeopardy of not being reelected? Honestly, Porter, I thought you were smarter than that."

Porter chuckled softly and straightened his necktie. "You can't blame a guy for hoping, can you?"

Porter and Cooper were well into their conversation when the waiter delivered salmon seared in fennel for Porter and breast of duck for Cooper, refilled their crystal water glasses, and disappeared again. The employees of the Vidalia were trained well in the art of secrecy. The only time an employee of the Vidalia had spoken to a reporter about what he'd overheard he'd been immediately terminated. Porter knew that this waiter wasn't about to eavesdrop on a conversation between the president's chief of staff and the chief of staff of the Senate majority leader.

"Porter, I'm surprised you invited me to lunch," Cooper said. "We've never liked each other very much."

Porter took a bite of his meal and wiped the corners of his mouth with his napkin. Cooper was right, Porter knew. He didn't like the guy. Cooper had the reputation of being a playboy. The position of Senate majority leader's chief of staff provided Cooper with immense access to practically anything . . . and anybody he wanted. His good looks — blond hair over the collar, dark blue eyes, and year-round tan skin — only served to inflate his already large ego.

"I wouldn't be here if the president hadn't insisted that I open a dialogue with Senator

Proctor's office about the upcoming appointment to the Supreme Court."

"I hear you've struck out with practically everyone in the Senate." Cooper twirled his empty fork slowly and smirked. "And can't get enough votes lined up."

Porter bit his lip to keep from saying something that might hurt the cause. Cooper got under his skin, but he refused to let Cooper know it. Entering into a deal with the devil was the only choice the president had to get Judge Shelton's nomination through the Senate, and Porter hated it.

"The president's determined to have his nominee to the Supreme Court confirmed by the Senate," Porter replied forcefully, as if Cooper would roll over and immediately capitulate.

But Porter knew there was simply no chance of that happening. Cooper — or, more accurately, Senator Proctor — held all the aces in this game of poker.

"Tell me who's going to get the nomination and I'll tell you whether he has a chance at confirmation or not." Cooper sipped his ice water and peered at Porter over the rim of the glass.

"You know who it is." Porter's eyes met Cooper's.

"Who?"

Porter laid his fork and knife on either side of his plate and bent forward, toward the center of the table. He glanced around at the other patrons to see if anyone was listening. Satisfied that his and Cooper's conversation couldn't be overheard, he whispered, "Judge Dunbar Shelton."

"You're kidding." Cooper gave a loud, patronizing laugh.

Porter could feel his face flush. The people at adjoining tables glanced briefly at the two, in reaction to Cooper's outburst, before resuming their own chatter.

Cooper, obviously realizing that he had drawn attention to himself and Porter, also leaned toward the center of the table. "You're kidding," Cooper said again, only this time in a much softer voice. "It'll be a cold day in Hades before the Senate confirms him. He's much too conservative. The pro-choice lobby will have our heads on silver platters if he's appointed to the Supreme Court."

"That's who the president wants, and he's willing to do anything to get him."

Both men were still leaning into the center of the table. Their faces were less than two feet apart, speaking forcefully with tones barely above whispers.

"Anything?"

"Anything."

Cooper reverted to the upright position in his chair and narrowed his eyes. Porter, too, sat upright, and waited in silence for Cooper to make the next move. It took only two seconds.

"You know the price will be high."

"I know." Porter crossed his arms over his chest. He intentionally paused before continuing, for the dramatic effect. "And so does the president."

Cooper removed the cloth napkin embroidered with a script *V* from his lap, folded it, and laid it on top of his plate. "Let me talk with Senator Proctor." He pushed back his chair and stood to leave. "I'll get back to you in a couple of days."

The Hart Building, Washington DC

After leaving the Vidalia, Cooper went directly to the Senate majority leader's office in the Hart Building. It was the newest of the three Senate office buildings — the other two were the Russell Building and the Dirksen Building.

The Senate was on a lunch break between the morning and afternoon sessions. Cooper walked past the senator's secretary without waiting for her to announce him and entered Senator Proctor's opulent office with its sixteen-foot-high ceiling. Senator Proctor was sitting behind his oversize mahogany desk, watching the stock market on CNBC. He pressed a button on the remote control to lower the volume as Cooper entered.

"I just had lunch with Porter McIntosh," Cooper proclaimed. He plopped down in a wingback leather chair across the desk from Senator Proctor. He crossed his legs and smiled wide.

The senator was in his midfifties and a rather large man. To say he was robust would have been an understatement. His bushy black hair contained a hint of gray, and a full beard and mustache consumed his face. When his mouth was closed, which wasn't very often, his lips were barely noticeable among the dark facial hair. He had a very dominating personality, and a resonant voice that commanded attention when he spoke.

"Did he confirm that Wallace wants to nominate Shelton?" the senator demanded.

"Just like we thought."

"What did he offer?" Senator Proctor smiled.

Everything in politics was negotiable, Cooper had learned. He cocked his head back and spoke deliberately. "He said the president would do 'anything' it took to get

Shelton confirmed."

"Anything?" Senator Proctor asked rhetorically. He locked his fingers together over his corpulent stomach, and Cooper could sense the gears grinding in the senator's head. "Really," Senator Proctor said thoughtfully. "The president will do anything for this nomination," he repeated. He looked back at Cooper. "What did you tell him?"

"Only that I had to talk with you," Cooper responded proudly.

Senator Proctor stood and walked to the closet on the right-hand side of his office. "That's good, Cooper," he said, as if he were a schoolteacher complimenting one of his star pupils.

Cooper twisted slightly in his chair so he could watch as his master pondered the possibilities.

"Cooper, let's meet this evening after the Senate adjourns." The senator slid into the suit coat he removed from the closet and glanced at his wristwatch. "I've got to be back on the Senate floor in five minutes, but I think I know what I'll demand of the president, and I want you to be thinking about it, too. We have several senators up for reelection this fall, and three of them are quite vulnerable. Dawson in Wyoming,

96

Fleming in Kansas, and Martin in Kentucky. The president's been raising a lot of money for their conservative opponents. If we lose two of those three, then we lose control of the Senate, and we can't have that."

What Senator Proctor didn't say was that he would lose his Senate majority leader's seat if the balance of power shifted to the other party. He didn't have to say it. Cooper knew what he meant.

"So, I want the president to stay out of those races. I know he won't endorse our guys. But he can order the party chairman to pull their resources out of those three races. I think that's worth a Supreme Court appointment, don't you?"

"That's why you're the boss," Cooper said admiringly.

"I'll see you this evening," Senator Proctor said as he left Cooper sitting in awe in his office.

CHAPTER SIX

The medical examiner's office,
Nashville, Tennessee

"Do you have anything for us, Doc?" Lieutenant Brantley asked.

The question was directed at Dr. Morris Stephenson, the senior Metropolitan Nashville medical examiner. Lieutenant Brantley and Sergeant Dodson dispensed with the initial pleasantries. They were at the ME's office in downtown Nashville. It was Saturday — the day after Jessica Caldwell's body had been discovered. Murder investigations didn't stop for the weekend.

Brantley and Dodson were anxious to leave the coroner's office as soon as possible. The room reeked of the smell of death to Dodson, but it didn't seem to bother Dr. Stephenson. The doctor, in his midsixties, wore a lab coat with his name embroidered over the pocket. He was about six feet three and weighed about 280, Dodson guessed.

"You guys in a hurry or something?" Dr. Stephenson talked slightly out of the right side of his mouth. He glanced at the officers with an annoyed expression. "She's only been dead a little over twenty-four hours."

"We *are* in a hurry, Doc," Dodson replied. "We've got a killer to catch before the trail grows cold."

The medical examiner, in a huff, turned his back to the officers and began walking. "I'm retiring at year's end, and I won't have to put up with you detectives anymore."

Dr. Stephenson led Brantley and Dodson across the room to the table holding the body of Jessica Caldwell. The doctor's gait was a labored hobble. From other cases he'd worked with the ME, Dodson knew it was from two bum knees. He also knew — from experience and from reputation — that the doctor was rather cantankerous.

"Two tours with the navy and thirty years with you demanding detectives, not to mention the DA's office, is long enough for anyone."

"The sooner you tell us what we need to know, the sooner these two detectives will be out of your hair," Dodson said, pointing at Brantley and himself.

"Not much of that left either." Dr.

Stephenson rubbed his flattop, and began his report from memory. "The cause of death was asphyxia from neck compression. Do you see those marks on her neck?" Dr. Stephenson pointed to the neck area of the corpse and waited for Brantley and Dodson to acknowledge that they saw the markings. "Those are bruises caused by someone other than the decedent. She had hemorrhaging in the throat area, and her hyoid bone was fractured. Clearly strangulation."

"What's that bruise on her forehead?" Dodson asked.

"Blunt-force trauma, but that didn't kill her," Dr. Stephenson explained. "It probably dazed her, then the assailant finished her off by choking her to death."

"But it didn't happen when she fell to the floor?" Brantley inquired.

"No, she was clearly struck with something before she fell. She does have a small contusion on the back of her head from the fall, but again, that didn't kill her either."

"What was the time of death?" Brantley asked.

"Probably between twelve thirty and one thirty a.m. I can't get any more precise than that." Dr. Stephenson partially removed the drape that covered the torso of the corpse, so as to expose the victim's arms. "Defensive bruising on the inside of her forearm," he said, rolling the left arm so the detectives could see the bruises for themselves. He then walked to the other side of the table and rolled Jessica's right arm to likewise expose the bruises on the inside of her right forearm.

"She didn't go down without a fight." Dodson studied Jessica's gray, lifeless body. More than anything he wanted to arrest someone — and he hoped it was Dr. Grissom — for this murder. The woman — the *young* woman, Dodson reminded himself — had been struck on the forehead and strangled while she lay on her own living-room floor. Her life had literally been choked from her. Anything short of frying in the electric chair would be too good for her murderer.

"No, she didn't," Dr. Stephenson concurred. He hobbled to the counter located to the right of the examination table and retrieved a chart containing the complete report from the autopsy. Brantley and Dodson followed.

"I found skin tissue under the fingernail of the middle finger on her right hand," Dr. Stephenson said, flipping through several pages in the chart.

"Not hers, I take it," Brantley said.

"Nope," affirmed Dr. Stephenson. "Probably the assailant's."

Brantley and Dodson thanked Dr. Stephenson for his excellent work and returned to their car. Their investigation into Jessica's murder was moving rapidly.

"You remember that bandage on the side of Dr. Grissom's face?" Dodson asked as he opened the driver's-side door.

Brantley peered at Dodson over the top of the car. "Yeah, I do."

"I hope it's his skin Dr. Stephenson found under Jessica's fingernail."

"I hope you're right."

As they sat down in the car and closed the doors, Brantley's wireless phone chirped. "Brantley," he answered.

Dodson could only hear Brantley's end of the conversation. "Great," he heard Brantley say. "We'll be there in about fifteen minutes. Meet us in Captain Montague's office."

Brantley pressed a button on the telephone to disconnect the call and faced Dodson. "That was Sergeant Crossley. She has a match on one of the prints her team lifted from the crime scene. She's going to meet us in Captain Montague's office to see if we have enough to get an arrest warrant."

Sergeant Dodson and Lieutenant Brantley hastily returned to the police department headquarters downtown and met Sergeant Crossley outside the office of Captain Bill Montague. Captain Montague was a thirty-year veteran of the Metropolitan Nashville Police Department and was in charge of the criminal investigation division.

"What ya got, Sergeant?" Dodson asked.

The three detectives waited for Captain Montague in the hall outside his office. Dodson could see Captain Montague through the glass walls that separated his office from the rest of the department. He was standing behind his desk, talking animatedly on the telephone.

"We found a fingerprint match through the Tennessee Department of Safety for a handgun permit issued in 2001 to a Todd Allen Grissom." She handed Dodson the report.

Dodson scanned the report, then passed it to Brantley.

"Amazing." Brantley read the report and smiled at Dodson and Sergeant Crossley. "This investigation couldn't have come together any better."

"I like what I'm seeing," Dodson said.

Captain Montague looked up and waved the trio of officers in.

"I'll talk to you about it later," Dodson heard Captain Montague say into the telephone as they entered. "Bureaucrats," he muttered as he slammed the phone down and fell into the chair behind his desk. He locked his hands behind his balding head and looked up at Sergeant Crossley and the two detectives who had gathered at the front of his desk.

"I hope you've got something on the Caldwell murder. I'm getting a lot of heat from the mayor's office."

"How 'bout a suspect?" Brantley asked.

"Now we're getting somewhere. Give me the details."

Dodson took the lead. "It seems she was seeing a married man. A doctor from Brentwood. Sergeant Crossley matched a print from the scene with one on file for the good doctor with the Department of Safety."

Brantley handed Captain Montague the fingerprint report.

He scanned it and handed it back to Brantley. "Looks like you've got opportunity sewn up."

"It gets better," Dodson added. "Dr. Stephenson found skin tissue under her fingernail. Brantley and I noticed a bandage on Dr. Grissom's cheek. My bet is that the DNA matches."

"Sounds like he's our guy," concluded Captain Montague. "Go bring him in."

The Proctor residence, Washington DC

Hazel Johnson placed a cup of fresh coffee before Evelyn Proctor as she sat at the breakfast table of the Georgetown area brownstone she shared with her husband, Senator Proctor. Although Evelyn was rarely beaming with happiness, Hazel noticed that recently she appeared more sullen than usual. She was still dressed in her nightgown and robe, which was usually never worn outside her bedroom. Her salt-and-pepper hair was unkempt, and for the first time that Hazel could remember, Evelyn wasn't wearing any makeup.

Hazel wasn't certain as to what had caused this recent bout of depression that appeared to have reached a new valley this morning. It might have been the gray skies and May rain that pelted against the dining-room window, or it might have been something more disturbing. But whatever it was, it caused Evelyn not to speak as Hazel served her, and that was most unusual. Today Evelyn appeared to barely notice her presence in the room.

Hazel hesitated briefly at the swinging door leading from the dining room to the kitchen and glanced back at Evelyn, who remained virtually motionless at the end of the table.

"Mrs. Proctor doesn't look good this morning," Hazel told her husband, Albert, after the door that separated the kitchen from the dining room was safely closed. Although Senator Proctor and Evelyn rarely graced the kitchen with their presences, it, like the entire house, contained all the trappings befitting one of Washington's elite families. Only the best would do for the Senate majority leader and his wife.

"That's none of your business, Hazel," Albert reminded her. His voice was scratchy and hoarse. He was standing with his back to Hazel, near the stove, preparing breakfast for Senator and Mrs. Proctor. A cigarette smoldered in an ashtray nearby. "You stay out of that. You've got a job to do, and that's all."

"I know, Albert, but it kills my soul to see her suffer. She knows he's cheating on her, and it's eating away at her. I don't know how much more of this she can take. She's been depressed like this since she came back from Nashville Friday morning."

Albert and Hazel had been employees of

the Proctors for over ten years. They had first served the Proctors in their Nashville home, then had moved to Washington DC at the insistence of Evelyn five years ago. The Proctors were rarely in Nashville, Evelyn explained, and she needed their help in Washington. The Washington domestic staff was inadequate to handle the demands of the Senate majority leader and his wife. Albert and Hazel had hated the thought of leaving their native Tennessee, but the Proctors paid well and provided living quarters.

"It doesn't matter to us what goes on between the senator and Mrs. Proctor," Albert insisted. "It's their marriage, and you stay out of it, Hazel. You hear me?"

"I hear you, Albert, but it's —"

Hazel was interrupted in midsentence by the sound of Evelyn's voice in the adjoining room.

"What time did you come home last night!" Evelyn screamed as her husband entered the dining room dressed and ready for another day in the Senate chamber.

"Not that it's any of your business, but it was about two this morning." Lance sat down in a chair at the opposite end of the table and began reading the front page of the Monday-morning edition of the *Wash-*

"Who was she this time?" Evelyn demanded.

He held the newspaper in front of him, intentionally blocking Evelyn from seeing his face. It was a defensive tactic he had used on numerous occasions to aggravate her and to remind her that she was of little importance to him.

"I don't know what you're talking about, Evelyn," he replied from behind his paper shield.

"Don't give me that, you lying philanderer! You know exactly what I'm talking about!" She glared at him, burning a hole through the newspaper from the opposite end of the table.

She hated him. What was worse, she knew he didn't care. That was the way it had been for years. Thirty years ago they had been in love. But infidelity, lies, and mental abuse had a way of changing things. She was glad they didn't have any children. It would've been a terrible marriage to be born into.

"I need a cup of coffee, Hazel," he called out.

Hazel nervously entered the dining room with a cup and saucer and set it on the table in front of him. A small amount of the coffee sloshed over the rim of the cup and filled the saucer. Hazel hastily wiped the saucer and bottom of the cup with the hem of her apron before returning to the kitchen.

"Lance, look at me!" Evelyn yelled after Hazel left the room. Her frustration had reached a breaking point. She knew there had been other women with whom her husband had intimate relationships. How many she wasn't certain, but it no longer mattered whether it was one or one hundred. She had reached a point where their marriage wasn't worth salvaging.

Lance unhurriedly folded the newspaper at its creases and placed it to the right of his unused breakfast plate. He crossed his arms over his chest and returned her long, piercing stare. "What?" he said in a condescending tone.

"Who was she?" Evelyn demanded again. She banged her hand on the table, and the two china coffee cups rattled against their saucers.

"I don't know what you're talking about." His voice was calm.

Lance's calmness angered Evelyn even more. He was a liar and a cheat and had no remorse about either.

"You're lying, and I know you're lying!" she screamed. "You think I don't know about all of your other women? You think I enjoy having people come up to me and tell me that they saw you with someone else?"

"C'mon, Evelyn, you get as much out of this marriage as you put into it. We haven't loved each other in years. Do you honestly expect me to come home night after night to a loveless place like this?" He waved his arms at the walls around them.

"You may not love me," Evelyn cried, "but I've never stopped loving you."

"That's not true, and you know it. When was the last time you ever directed any affection to me?"

Awkward seconds elapsed. Evelyn opened her mouth to speak but had nothing to say.

"You can't think of anything, can you? That's because you don't love me. You're in love with being a senator's wife," he accused her. "You love the parties, the privileges, the lifestyle. Not me."

"You may have convinced yourself of that to ease your conscience about your infidelity, but despite what you may think, I've always loved you." Courage suddenly welled up inside her. She decided to risk saying the words out loud that she'd only been able to speak silently to herself before now. "But if that's the way you feel, then I want a divorce."

"Let me tell you something," Lance

growled.

Evelyn shivered at the rage in his face.

"You don't want a divorce. You know why? I'll tell you why. Because I'll ruin you, that's why. You'll get nothing out of a divorce. I'll make sure of it. You'll end up homeless and broke, without any friends. Is that what you want, Evelyn?" He paused briefly.

Evelyn knew the pause was to make sure she absorbed the fullness of his wrath and completely understood the consequences of her demand. She had seen it before in every argument they'd had.

"Do you want your little drug problem spread over the front pages of the news-paper?" Lance snatched the newspaper from its resting place beside his plate, waved it at Evelyn, and slammed it back down on the table.

Evelyn could feel the color leave her face, and her stomach lurched. Her heart began to race, and although she tried to hide it, she was certain her body was trembling. He had made his point.

"You didn't think I knew about that, did you?" he said proudly. "But I know all about it. I know about the doctor hopping so you can get more painkillers. I know about all of it. Now you listen to me." His voice was calm, but forceful, and he brandished a menacing finger at her. "Don't *ever* mention the word *divorce* to me again. I'll come and go when I want, with whom I want, and you won't complain about it. Do you understand me?"

Evelyn's body still shook. She was unable to form a verbal response to his question. She could only muster a slight nod.

"Good," Lance said as he rose from his chair. "Albert," he called toward the kitchen door, "I'll get something to eat at the office."

And he left the room.

Evelyn continued to stare at the empty chair where Lance had been sitting. It took minutes for the trembling to finally subside.

But it did subside. And there, in the midst of her fear, she decided she'd had enough.

CHAPTER SEVEN

Washington DC

Over the weekend journalist Holland Fletcher saw the AP wire-service report from Nashville on the death of Jessica Caldwell and the subsequent arrest of Todd Allen Grissom, MD. He made a few phone calls, got quotes, and used the wire report to write a crisp but short article that appeared on page fifteen in section A of the Sunday *Washington Post.* It wouldn't have otherwise been newsworthy except that Jessica had been Justice Robinson's law clerk. The article said nothing more than the facts: she was murdered, a doctor had been arrested, and she had previously served the late–Supreme Court justice. That story was stale by Sunday night, and he thought nothing more about it.

Holland was always telling his parents, his college fraternity brothers — and the few girls he could get to date him — with enthusiasm that he was an investigative reporter. He was twenty-eight and had gotten an entry-level job at the *Post* two years earlier, right after he'd broken a story of city government corruption while working at a weekly newspaper in a small town in Virginia. The editors at the *Post* had liked his writing and offered him $30,000 a year, a metal desk, and long hours. He'd jumped at the opportunity. Those same editors were still waiting for him to demonstrate the *investigative* part of being an investigative reporter.

Holland had thinnish red hair that lay flat against his scalp, got little exercise, and generally stayed out too late.

It was still dark when his phone rang Tuesday morning. He pulled the pillow over his ears and tried to ignore it. Four times it rang. Then the answering machine clicked on. No message.

He rolled onto his back. Within a minute the phone rang again. He managed to focus enough to see the clock: 4:30 a.m. He hadn't seen 4:30 a.m. from this direction since . . . since — He couldn't remember the last time he'd awoken at 4:30 a.m. The caller ID indicated that the call was from a restricted number.

He finally answered after the next ring.

"Fletcher," he mumbled.

"Is this Holland Fletcher with the *Post*?"

A woman's voice. Holland held the phone in his left hand and rubbed his bleary eyes with his right. "One and the same. Who is this?"

"I'd rather not say."

Holland sighed into the phone. The conversation barely kept him awake. He thought about hanging up. Any wacko playing telephone pranks at this hour of the morning deserved to hear the phone slammed in her ear.

"Well, Ms. 'I'd rather not say,' can you at least tell me why you're calling?"

"I saw your article about the Caldwell girl in Sunday's newspaper. That was real sad."

"Yeah, it was sad. Look, I need to get back to sleep. I have to be at work in less than four hours."

"There's more to her murder than you know."

Holland sat up on the side of the bed. "What do you mean?"

"I can't tell you right now. You just need to look deeper and you'll see what I'm talking about."

"You need to at least give me something so I know you're credible."

There was silence on the other end. Hol-

115

land thought the caller had disconnected the call.

"How about the name of President Wallace's nominee?" the female voice asked.

Holland was fully awake by this time and was up pacing in his pajama bottoms. He stopped and stared through the second-floor apartment bedroom window. Every talking head and print reporter was trying to get the name of the Supreme Court nominee. A short list had been talked about. It had been pared down to five through leaks from the White House and Capitol Hill, but nobody had identified the leading candidate.

"You know the name of the president's nominee?"

"Yes."

If this woman, whoever she was, had the name of the next Supreme Court justice, then she was on the inside. Deep inside.

"Who is it?"

"I'm not going to tell you unless you agree to investigate the Caldwell murder further."

"All right, I promise."

"You really promise?"

"I said 'I promise,' didn't I?"

"I know who you are, Mr. Fletcher. If you're lying to me, so help me God, I'll get even with you somehow."

Holland raised his eyebrows in the dark at

116

the threat and went back to pacing. "I said 'I promise,' and that's what I meant. Are you going to tell me or not?"

After another brief silence the woman said, "A judge from Mississippi named Dunbar Shelton."

"Dunbar Shelton?" Holland chuckled. There was simply no way a Southern judge could get appointed to the Supreme Court. "He's not even on everyone's short list."

"Whatever. I know he's the one."

"Assuming you're right about Shelton, where do you suggest I start in investigating the Caldwell murder? It happened in Tennessee, you know."

"She worked at the Supreme Court building. Start there."

With that the line went dead. Holland stood still with the phone in his hand for five or six seconds before placing the receiver back in its cradle. He shook his head. He was kidding himself if he thought he could convince his editor to run a story about Dunbar Shelton based on an anonymous phone call.

The Oval Office, the White House, Washington DC

Porter McIntosh paced anxiously as he waited for President Wallace to return from a Tuesday-morning meeting with the joint chiefs of staff. It wasn't good news that had brought Porter to the Oval Office, so what was only fifteen minutes of waiting time felt like hours.

At last President Wallace entered the Oval Office. "What's the matter, Porter?"

"Collins over in Justice told me he got a call from a cub reporter named Fletcher at the *Post.* He was trying to get Collins to confirm that Dunbar Shelton is the nominee."

The president hung his suit coat in the closet and sat down behind the desk. "Fletcher? I've never heard of him."

"Me neither, but I checked it out. There's a Holland Fletcher who's a reporter at the *Post.* Fortunately Collins is far enough down the ladder that he knows absolutely nothing about the background investigations or who rose to the top of the list. His denial was genuine."

Porter was still pacing. It was too soon for Judge Shelton's name to get out. And they wanted to announce it on their terms.

"Sit down, Porter," President Wallace ordered. "You're making me nervous."

Porter sat down in a chair across the desk from the president. He folded his hands into a little steeple under his chin.

They both sat in silence for a moment, thinking.

"Who do you think leaked it?" the president finally asked.

"I don't even know if it was leaked. The kid may be guessing, hoping to get a response. Shelton isn't on anyone's list."

"All the more reason to think it was leaked, right? If Shelton was on everyone's list, then the reporter would have a reason to be asking about him. But since he's not, then this Fletcher got information from someone who knows."

Porter had hoped that without confirmation Fletcher would go away. But he probably had enough to run the story already. "You're right," Porter relented. "There's a leak."

"Where are you with Proctor's office?"

"I hope to finalize the deal with the devil this afternoon. You sure you still want to do this? We could take control of the Senate if we take those three races."

Porter watched President Wallace as he thought briefly — very briefly — and smiled confidently.

"I'm sure, Porter. As sure as I am of my own name. Who do you think leaked it?"

Porter was back up pacing again with his arms rigidly locked together behind his back. "I don't know. I haven't talked to anyone other than the attorney general and Cooper. I don't think it would be anyone in the AG's office." He stopped and pondered. "It must've come from Proctor's office."

The president stood and walked to the window leisurely. "And if they're leaking, then they must plan on reaching an agreement with us on the nomination."

"Or they may be trying to embarrass us. They leak Shelton's name and then say there's no way Senator Proctor's going to support him. Too conservative, antiabortion, and all that. That would make us look like fools."

Porter kept pacing and the president continued to face the window. Silence reigned again in the room.

At last Porter spoke to the back of the president's brown-and-gray head.

"What if I call this Fletcher and feel him out? Pick his brain a little and see where he got his information? If he's bluffing, I'll know it."

"If you call him from out of the blue, he'll be suspicious," the president said to the window. "Then he'll know for sure that he's on to something. I think you leave it alone. If his best contact is a low-level staffer in Justice, then he doesn't have the right contacts. If he prints it and it gets out a little earlier than we wanted, no big deal. I'm going to nominate Shelton whether Proctor is onboard or not. The upside is, if you don't call him, maybe he won't print it."

Porter didn't like going into the confirmation battle without Proctor as an ally. *Ally? Is Senator Proctor really an ally?* But he knew the president was serious when he said Shelton was the nominee, with or without Proctor. As sickening as the thought seemed, Porter preferred to have Proctor as an ally in this process rather than an enemy.

"You're right. It's probably better not to call."

President Wallace turned from the window and faced Porter.

Porter stopped pacing. He was near the sofa.

"See if you can reach Cooper this morning and get the deal finalized," the president urged.

The Hart Building, Washington DC
Senator Proctor was behind his desk working the crossword puzzle in the *Washington Post* while Cooper was on the telephone with Porter McIntosh. He had only completed a couple of the answers in the puzzle.

He was stuck on thirty-two across. The senator didn't like Porter and made Cooper talk to him.

Cooper, wireless to his ear, was slouched on the leather sofa. Senator Proctor didn't pay attention to Cooper's exact words but noticed his big smile. Cooper victoriously pumped his fist in the air and nodded rapidly. He said a few more words before flipping his wireless shut and moving toward Senator Proctor.

"We've got a deal," Cooper announced excitedly. "The president will stay out of the races in Wyoming, Kansas, and Kentucky, and you'll support Dunbar Shelton's nomination."

Proctor lifted his chin. His seat of power was now completely secure. He had been only slightly worried about it, but now there was nothing to worry about at all. He was confident he'd rule for years to come.

"That's good news. It might be time to redecorate my office again, Cooper. By the way, what's a five-letter word for *discombobulated?*"

CHAPTER EIGHT

The law offices of Elijah J. Faulkner,
Jackson, Tennessee

Eli arrived at his office on Tuesday morning, the last week of May, just before 8:00 a.m. central time. As he exited his car, he noticed that the spring weather was quite pleasant. The rain and clouds that had draped Jackson overnight were gone, and the morning sun warmed his face as he walked toward the rear entrance of his office building. The brisk, wintry days were in the distant past, and the oppressive, humid days of summer were still two months away.

On days like this Eli wished he could abandon his law practice and spend a few hours on one of the local golf courses. One round of golf every two months wasn't nearly enough. But there was too much to be done at his office. There were too many clients who needed his services. Too many wrongs that needed to be righted. He was

123

passionate about his occupation. Many people despised what they did for a living, but not Eli.

Certainly there were times when the stress and pressure weighed heavily on him, when the countless hours of work kept him away from his lovely wife or precluded him from taking up a hobby or two. But it was his lifelong desire to help people that kept him going. Drove him, really. In brief minutes of frustration, he'd remind himself of the time he'd helped a young couple adopt a child. He'd remember representing the family who had lost their husband and father to a drunk driver. And he'd recall the times he had simply provided guidance and counseling to a husband and wife who were facing a financial crisis. Countless others had come to him in need, and he had been able to help.

Eli traversed his usual route into the office, up the back stairs, through the little kitchen, and down the hall to his private office in the rear of the building. Barbara delivered a cup of coffee as he settled in behind his desk for the ritual of sorting through the morning mail.

"Don't forget about your meeting at nine a.m. with Ms. Grissom," she reminded him.

"I saw it on my calendar. Do you know

why she's coming to see me?"

"I'm not sure I asked her. She called yesterday, and said she needed to see you as soon as possible. She said George Thornton told her to call. I worked her in this morning but told her you had only an hour before you had to finish preparing for this afternoon's deposition."

He nodded. "Let me know when she gets here."

After Barbara left the room, Eli meticulously opened each article of mail and organized the contents into three separate stacks: one for items he needed to respond to; one for items that needed to be filed away; and one for items that Barbara could discard.

It wasn't long before Barbara escorted Anna Grissom to Eli's office. She was a petite lady in her early thirties. She had chestnut hair, was stylishly dressed, and was attractive. But what struck Eli most were her eyes. It wasn't really even the color, a deep, dark brown. It was something else. Something he couldn't quite put his finger on. After a couple of seconds it came to him. They were kind. Anna Grissom had kind eyes.

Despite her engaging appearance, Eli recognized that Anna was troubled. After

Barbara introduced them, she gathered the mail from Eli's desk and excused herself from the office. Anna sat, legs crossed at the ankles, in a leather wingback chair across the desk from him. She and Eli exchanged small talk for a couple of minutes before Eli directed the conversation to the purpose for her consultation.

"What can I help you with, Ms. Grissom?"

Eli removed the top of his Mont Blanc pen. He found a clean notepad in the top-right-hand drawer of his desk.

"Please, call me Anna."

"All right, Anna. What can I help you with?"

Anna wrung her hands in her lap. "My uncle, George Thornton, tells me you're the best lawyer in the whole state, Mr. Faulkner."

What made her so nervous? Eli wondered. Aloud he said, "George is too kind. I hope I can live up to my reputation. And call me Eli."

"Okay, Eli. I hope Uncle George is right because my husband is in a terrible mess."

"What's your husband's name, Anna?"

"Tag," she replied through a forced smile. "We call him Tag, but his given name is Todd Allen Grissom."

After her first comments, Eli anticipated

that Anna wanted to pursue a divorce from her husband, and for that, Eli would politely refer her to another attorney. "Tag Grissom," he said as he wrote the name on the yellow notepad on his desk. "What kind of mess has Tag gotten himself into?" Eli continued to look at his notepad, prepared to write the response.

Two seconds elapsed without any noise from Anna.

Puzzled, he looked up.

Anna Grissom was no longer wringing her hands. She appeared to be barely breathing, and despair was etched across her face. She stared past Eli to some location beyond the walls of his office.

Two additional seconds passed before she apparently noticed that Eli was staring at her. When their eyes met, Eli saw the horror leaping from hers. Eyes that had once appeared kind now looked completely terrified.

"He murdered someone," Anna finally replied. Her voice was unemotional.

It wasn't often that Eli found himself speechless. It wasn't a good trait for a lawyer to possess. But this was such an occasion. He couldn't think of anything to say. He could only repeat the phrase back to Anna, but formulated into a question. "Murdered someone?"

"Well, not exactly," she explained. "The police say he murdered her, but I know he didn't do it."

Eli regained his composure from the shock that the husband of this polite, attractive woman was accused of murder. The only thing that might have shocked him even more would have been if Anna herself had been accused of murder. He replaced his pen in the pocket of his heavily starched shirt and focused his attention completely on Anna.

"You said 'her,' Anna. Who exactly is Tag accused of murdering?"

"A lawyer in Nashville named Jessica Caldwell."

Eli thought briefly as he processed the name of the decedent to see if it meant anything to him. He couldn't place it, so he continued his inquiry. "Why do the police think that he murdered her?"

The hand-wringing resumed as Anna told Eli as much as she knew. It wouldn't have been a surprise to her if Tag was having an affair with Jessica Caldwell, she explained. It wouldn't be Tag's first affair. She didn't question that Tag might have been in Jessica's town house the night of the murder. Eli sat on the edge of his chair as he listened to Anna recite the story of Tag's arrest at his office in front of a waiting room full of patients.

"But I know he didn't kill her," she stated adamantly and shook her head defiantly. She shifted in her seat, uncrossed her legs, and recrossed them with her knees pointing in the opposite direction from where they had been. "I know he didn't."

She sounded authoritative, as if she knew the truth and no one should question her about it. But Eli wasn't sure whether she was trying to convince him or herself of Tag's innocence.

"How can you be so certain that your husband is innocent?"

"I know my husband, Mr. Faulkner." She caught herself. "I'm sorry — Eli," she corrected. "I know he's a terrible husband and has been unfaithful to our marriage. But that's all he's guilty of." Anna removed a tissue from her purse and dabbed at the corners of her eyes.

"Was he with you the night of the murder?" Eli asked. He hoped that a credible alibi existed.

When Anna hesitated before responding, Eli knew the answer to his question.

"Would it help if I said that he was?" she pleaded. "It wouldn't be a complete lie. He *was* with me part of the night. I was by myself the other part. So no one could say otherwise."

"We can't do that, Anna," Eli responded delicately. He raised his hands slightly above the top of the desk, palms toward Anna. "We'll have to prove that Tag is innocent by using some evidence other than your testimony."

"I know," Anna admitted. She looked away from Eli and sighed. "I wouldn't make a good liar anyway. But I'll do just about anything to keep my husband out of jail."

A simple one-word question rose to his mind. It was a question that lawyers were taught in law school never to ask, and particularly never to ask unless you already knew the answer. But it escaped innocently from Eli's mouth before he could stop it. "Why?"

Anna's head snapped back to where her eyes met Eli's eyes again. The question caught her off guard. "Why what?"

"Why do you want your husband back?" Eli gestured with his hands as he talked. "You've already told me that he's an adulterer, and now he's accused of murder. It may turn out that he is, in fact, guilty of murder."

Genuine compassion was growing inside

him for this woman he'd only known for a few minutes. He gazed sympathetically at her and softened his tone. "Why do you want him back?" he asked again.

Anna dabbed at the corners of her eyes again. "Because he's the father of my unborn child," she responded through her tears.

Eli sat silently as Anna released several days of anger, sorrow, hatred, and confusion. The tissue Anna clutched in her hand was insufficient to capture all the tears that now streamed down her face, so Eli handed her a package of tissues he kept in the top drawer of his desk.

"I'm sorry," Anna said as she regained her composure.

"Don't be. I don't know how I would act if I were in your place."

"I didn't come here to bore you with our marital problems." She pressed a fresh tissue underneath her eyes, trying to remove the moisture that welled up. "I'm sorry," she repeated. "It's just that we've tried for so long to conceive, and I'm not about to let my child grow up without a father."

Eli saw the determination on her face and heard it in her tone. His earlier feeling of compassion evolved into admiration. Anna's fragile appearance was giving way to an inner strength that Eli suspected few people had ever seen. Any apprehension that he may have had about helping Anna and her ingrate of a husband subsided. He would represent Tag Grissom — but not because he thought Tag was innocent. He would do it because of Anna and her unborn child.

"Anna," he began, "I'll represent Tag, but on one condition."

"What's that?"

"You have to be present at every court hearing, regardless of what it's for or what it's about. I want the judge and jury to see you there, but more important, I want you to have full knowledge of everything that Tag has done. He'll have no way to hide from the truth in the courtroom, and I want you to hear every word of it, no matter how painful it may be."

Without hesitation she responded, "You've got yourself a deal, Eli." She smiled.

Eli and Anna spent the better part of an hour together as he gathered the necessary details regarding Tag's arrest and the charges against him. He decided that the final preparation for the afternoon deposition could wait awhile longer.

When he and Anna finished talking, Eli escorted her to the elevator in the lobby and stopped by Barbara's workstation on his return to his office.

"Will you see if Jill is in the building? If so, ask her to come to my office, please."

"She's here," Barbara replied. "I saw her a few minutes ago. I'll see if I can find her."

While Barbara went to get Jill, Eli retrieved a putter and four golf balls from the closet in his office. He could think better that way. He began putting at a plastic cup lying on the floor, across the room.

Five minutes later Jill Baker appeared in the doorway to Eli's office. Jill was four years removed from law school. After she had worked a year as a law clerk for Judge David Sawyer, senior judge of the United States District Court for the Western District of Tennessee, Eli had hired her as his associate. He had only employed one other associate over the years, and that employment relationship had ended less than amicably. Eli admitted he was demanding, and almost anyone would have a difficult time working for him. But he liked Jill. She was intelligent, quick on her feet, and deceptively demure. She was unmarried, unattached, and worked long hours for him with no complaints. Many who met her for the first time made the mistake of underestimating her. When Eli had interviewed her, he'd seen what he was looking for in an as-

133

sociate. Beneath her soft black hair and behind those hazel eyes was an intelligent, resourceful, and zealous lawyer. Another quality that he found enduring was that she liked the Atlanta Braves baseball team.

"Did you summon me?" Jill asked.

Eli tapped one of the balls toward the plastic cup and chuckled at the bad pun. He glanced up at Jill and back down at the floor. Using the head of the putter, he rolled another ball into his stance.

"*Summon* isn't exactly the right word," he replied. "But I do need you. Come in and sit down."

Jill obeyed and sat on the sofa against the back wall of Eli's office. She was safely off the makeshift putting green.

"What's up?" she asked.

"I just agreed to represent a doctor accused of murder over in Nashville, and I need your help on the file."

"Murder? I thought you weren't taking any more criminal cases."

Eli retrieved the golf balls again. All four had missed the cup, to the left. He walked and talked.

"I know, but I couldn't turn this one down. His wife is related to an old client of mine," Eli replied, masking the real reason he'd decided to take the case. "Anyway, I've

134

decided to take the case, and you'll need to do a lot of the legwork on this file."

"What's the guy's name, and where do we start?"

"His name is Todd Allen Grissom. His wife calls him Tag. He's a cardiologist in Brentwood. The first thing we need to do is hire Jimmy English — he's the best private eye I know. Tell him to find out everything he can about our client. We need to know the good, the bad, and everything in between. I'm sure the DA is doing the same thing."

Jill feverishly scribbled on the yellow legal pad she'd brought with her to Eli's office. She completed writing the last word from Eli and looked up, ready for the remainder of the assignment. "What else?"

Eli struck the fourth ball and propped himself on the putter to give her further instructions. "You'll need to go to Nashville in the morning and pull the court file. Get a copy of the warrant and anything else in the court jacket. Have Barbara prepare a notice of appearance to advise the court and the DA's office that we will be representing the defendant. A lawyer friend of the Grissoms in Nashville helped with the initial appearance, and Dr. Grissom made bail over the weekend. He's under house arrest, and

I'm going to meet with him Friday afternoon. The last thing is that you or Jimmy or both of you need to find out everything you can about the victim. I need to know who her friends were, who her enemies were, and what she did the night she was murdered. Ms. Grissom said the victim was a young lawyer in Nashville named Jessica Caldwell. See if you can find any lawyers in Nashville who knew her and would be willing to talk."

"Jessica Caldwell?" Jill replied. "I know that name. She was in her first year at Vandy when I was third year. I didn't know her very well, but I should be able to find some classmates who did."

"Good. That should give you a starting point. See what you can find out."

"I got it," Jill stated. "Anything else?"

"That's it for now," Eli replied. "Get back to me tomorrow afternoon on what you've found."

Jill stood to leave as Barbara entered Eli's office with a large expandable folder. Eli retrieved the golf balls again. Two were in the plastic cup and the other two had glanced off to the right.

"You haven't forgotten about your deposition this afternoon, have you?" Barbara asked Eli.

"I was just leaving," Jill assured her and

departed Eli's office to carry out his instructions.

"And I'll start preparing, but I need to call my wife first," Eli replied.

Barbara left the expandable folder with Eli. He pondered Anna Grissom's story as he putted the four balls again. All four clanked into the plastic cup and he propped the putter in the corner behind his office door. Before opening the file Barbara had left, he dialed home.

Sara answered after the second ring.

"I just took a case where I've got to be in Nashville later this week to meet with my client," Eli told Sara. "Why don't you plan to go with me, and we'll make a long weekend of it?"

"I don't know, Eli," Sara replied. "I've got so many things to do this week, I'm not sure it would be a good time to get away. And I'm scheduled to work in the nursery this Sunday at church."

"C'mon, honey," he pleaded. "We could go to the Loveless one night for dinner. I know it's one of your favorite places. Instead of a long weekend, we'll go up Friday morning and come home Saturday night. That way you can get everything done that you need to, and we'll be back in time for church on Sunday. What do you say?"

137

"The Loveless," she repeated with excitement in her voice.

Eli knew he'd placed a temptation before her that she couldn't resist.

"You've got yourself a date, Mr. Faulkner. When do we leave?"

CHAPTER NINE

The Rose Garden, the White House,
Washington DC

"Ladies and gentlemen," the president's crier said to the White House press corps gathered in the Rose Garden. "The president of the United States of America."

On cue, President Wallace exited the French doors that opened from the Oval Office onto the veranda and began walking toward a podium that had been erected in the Rose Garden for Wednesday's press conference to announce the president's nomination to the Supreme Court. Lauren Wallace, Dunbar Shelton, and his wife, Victoria, trailed closely behind President Wallace as he emerged from the veranda and into the spring sunshine. All four looked very solemn, but President Wallace knew that each one was screaming with excitement on the inside.

The *Washington Post* had been silent that

morning about the nomination. Despite lots of speculation inside the Beltway, there had been little talk of Judge Shelton and no article by one Holland Fletcher. The nation seemed taken by surprise.

The White House Rose Garden was bursting with deep reds, brilliant pinks, and whites as pure as the driven snow. The White House gardeners did a magnificent job of maintaining and manicuring the delicate shrubbery. The national flower couldn't have looked more beautiful than it did at that very moment.

The weather was perfect for this historic event, President Wallace thought. The blue sky was devoid of any clouds and the radiant sunlight chased away any hint of a shadow. It was as if the very heavens were smiling on the White House.

President Wallace approached the navy-and-gray podium with the presidential seal on the front of it and said, "Thank you," to the smattering of applause that rose politely from the White House press corps. He wore a blue suit, white shirt, and blue-and-red tie. Not a hair on his head was out of place. Everything had to be perfect, and was perfect, for the announcement of Judge Shelton as President Wallace's nominee for the vacant Supreme Court seat.

He opened the folder that had been placed on the podium by a member of his staff before the press conference started and began speaking to the small crowd of Washington and national media representatives. He glanced at his notes occasionally but mainly spoke without using them.

"Fellow Americans," he began. "Just over two weeks ago, we were saddened by the death of Supreme Court Justice Martha Doyle Robinson. She was a respected jurist whose voice was inexplicably silenced by a terrible and incurable disease. We will certainly miss her compassion, her forthrightness, and her wisdom. Our condolences continue to be poured out to her husband, children, grandchildren, and other members of her family. And even though her passing troubles us, we must move on. Justice Robinson would have had it no other way.

"Throughout the history of our great country there have been rare occasions when presidents were faced with the awesome responsibility of nominating a justice to serve on the Supreme Court of the United States. Today is one such rare occasion. It is a decision that must be carefully considered, and I have done so. It is a decision that will be debated by generations to come, but for me this decision is not about how history will judge it. For me, there is only one standard by which this decision must be measured. And that is whether it will pass the judgment of almighty God. The realization that the magnitude of this decision far exceeds any other decision I have made as president, or likely will make, has been quite humbling. It has caused many sleepless nights. That was, of course, until I reviewed the qualifications of Judge Dunbar Shelton and immediately felt at peace because he was to be the nominee."

President Wallace turned toward Judge Shelton, nodded slightly, and smiled. Judge Shelton returned the smile, and President Wallace continued his speech.

"Many of you are already familiar with Judge Dunbar Shelton and his contributions to our society, both as the chief justice of the Mississippi Supreme Court and as a person. But for those of you who may not be as familiar with Judge Shelton as others, I want to give you some of his biographical information."

President Wallace spent the next several minutes describing to the press corps the educational and professional pedigree of Judge Dunbar Shelton. He explained that Judge Shelton had done his undergraduate work at Mississippi State University and attended law school at Harvard. He talked about Judge Shelton's rise from a circuit court judge to a state appellate court judge to the Mississippi Supreme Court and then his appointment as chief justice of that state body. He even referenced several written opinions that Judge Shelton had authored, shaping the laws of the state of Mississippi.

"Without any further delay," President Wallace concluded, "I want to introduce you to Judge Dunbar Shelton and his lovely wife, Victoria."

President Wallace stepped back and shook hands with Judge Shelton. The clicking of the camera shutters had been barely noticeable during the president's speech. Now it reached a crescendo as the two men shook hands.

Then Judge Shelton approached the podium to a smattering of applause similar to that which President Wallace had received earlier and nodded his appreciation as the applause subsided. He wore a dark gray suit, white shirt, and striped tie. The White House staff had planned both his and the president's attire. Judge Shelton was about the same height as the president, but at fifty-eight was slightly older. He appeared stoic, dignified, scholarly, and fatherly as he stood behind the podium. It would be difficult to question his qualifications to fill the seat of trust that President Wallace had bestowed on him.

"Thank you, Mr. President." Judge Shelton opened a separate folder that had been placed on the podium for him and began his brief, prepared remarks. The words spilled from his mouth with ease and in a deep Southern drawl. "I, too, am humbled by what lies before us. It is with great awe and respect that I accept your nomination to serve on the Supreme Court of this great country. And I pledge to you, and to every American citizen, that I will do my best to be just and fair and right. So again I say thank you. I am looking forward to the confirmation process and sitting alongside the greatest judicial minds in the world."

Judge Shelton stepped back from the podium, and he and President Wallace shook hands again. The clicking from the numerous cameras in the Rose Garden reached another crescendo.

Then a female reporter with the Associated Press called out a question. "Mr. President, do you anticipate a difficult confirmation?"

President Wallace stepped to the podium before responding. "As with all judicial nominees, Judge Shelton will have to endure the gauntlet of the Senate confirmation process."

A few chuckles rose from the crowd of reporters.

President Wallace grinned. "But we're working closely with the Senate leadership to ensure that Judge Shelton's appointment moves through the Judiciary Committee and the full Senate as soon as possible."

"Can you tell us Judge Shelton's position on issues such as affirmative action and abortion rights?" the AP reporter continued.

"I think it would be inappropriate to discuss Judge Shelton's position on any issue." The grin evaporated from President Wallace's face. "His personal beliefs — and I believe Judge Shelton will tell you the same — are irrelevant. I haven't asked him to commit, nor would he commit, to a particular position on an issue that might come before him as a Supreme Court justice. What is important is Judge Shelton's judicial philosophy, and that is better left to the Judiciary Committee to inquire about than the press corps."

President Wallace knew it was time to end the press conference before other such intrusive questions were hurled at Judge Shelton and himself. The quartet of President Wallace, Lauren, Judge Shelton, and

Victoria circled and strode back to the Oval Office as a chorus of "Mr. President, Mr. President" rang out behind them. They stopped briefly as they entered the French doors they had exited from earlier and waved happily at the cameras in the Rose Garden for one last video clip for the evening news.

Porter McIntosh was waiting when they entered the Oval Office. He gave a confident thumbs-up when President Wallace looked at him. "I thought the press conference was perfect, Mr. President."

"I thought so, too. That reporter with the AP went a little too far with that last question and I decided to cut it off. You and Judge Shelton had better get busy preparing for the hearings. You both have a lot of work to do."

Both Porter and Judge Shelton nodded their agreement.

"We already have a series of mock hearings scheduled," Porter said. "And the general counsel's office is summarizing all of Judge Shelton's written opinions. Everything should be fine."

Avenue of the Americas, New York City
Stella Hanover screamed angrily at the image of President Wallace, Judge Shelton, and

their wives reentering the White House on the television in her Avenue of the Americas office. The battle was on.

"Valerie!" she yelled as she continued her glare at the television. By now it had switched scenes to a talking head who analyzed the president's nomination of Dunbar Shelton. Stella was no longer listening to the words that were being emitted from the television. She already knew everything she wanted to know about Judge Shelton.

The door opened slightly, and Valerie Marcom's black-rimmed glasses and mouse brown hair appeared.

"Yes," Valerie responded timidly.

"Get Senator Proctor's office on the phone," Stella growled.

The Grissom residence, Brentwood, Tennessee

Eli and Sara checked into the historic and recently renovated Hermitage Hotel on Sixth Avenue North in Nashville after lunch on Friday before Eli traveled alone to his meeting with Tag Grissom.

The Grissom residence was an opulent French-country-style home in the Governor's Club subdivision of Brentwood. Eli parked his BMW in the circle drive near the stone walkway that led to an arched entrance and wood front door, and exited with his briefcase in hand. His attire was business casual — no tie or jacket.

Anna Grissom met Eli at the front door. "I'm so glad you're here. Tag is in his study. I'll show you the way."

"You have a beautiful home."

Eli followed Anna through the palatial structure to a study adjacent to the den in the rear of the house. He took note of the professionally decorated interior with its expensive furnishings, lavish floor coverings, and art-gallery prints. But something was strange about the Grissom home. Although beautiful, the house felt cold.

"We may have a difficult marriage, but we've been fortunate to live rather richly," Anna said flatly.

Eli studied the back of her head as she walked in front of him.

"I thought at one time that having money would make our marriage better," she said softly, "but it hasn't."

Eli didn't respond to Anna's personal assessment. He realized that he couldn't repair their marriage. All he could do was try to defend Tag against murder charges. Anna and Tag would have to resolve their marital issues on their own.

"You look very radiant."

Anna patted her stomach and turned her head to smile back at Eli. "A little over six months to go." She opened the door to the study. "Tag's in here."

For the first time Eli saw Tag Grissom, sitting behind a mahogany desk. His dark hair was neatly parted and slicked down with a styling gel, but he looked like he hadn't shaved in two days. His skin was tan — too tan for late May — and it was obvious that he exercised regularly. Eli knew he'd have to work on Tag's appearance before a jury saw him. They wouldn't like him at all. Arrogance didn't breed sympathy. Tag had been reading a copy of the *Wall Street Journal* and placed it on the corner of his desk when Anna and Eli entered.

Like the rest of the house, Tag's study was lavish. Walnut wood panels covered the walls and expensive leather furniture occupied the sitting area. The custom-built bookcases that blanketed the rear wall from floor to ceiling were filled with medical books, novels, photographs, and mementos. French doors led to a veranda and beyond that to the seventeenth hole of the Legends Club of Tennessee golf course.

"Tag, this is Eli Faulkner," Anna said, introducing them.

Tag stood from behind the desk and approached Eli to greet him with a handshake. Tag's hand was soft — too soft. It gave Eli an odd feeling. *He's had an easy life.*

"Mr. Faulkner," Tag said. "It's a pleasure to meet you."

"Likewise," Eli responded. "And since we are going to be working together, how about you call me Eli and I'll call you Tag?"

"That's fine with me."

"I'll bring in some iced tea while you two get started," Anna offered. "I'm sure Eli has a lot of questions."

"Tea would be great." Eli sat on one end of a leather sofa and opened his briefcase while Tag resumed his seat behind the desk. Eli removed a notepad from the briefcase and placed it in his lap.

"Do you like it sweet or unsweet, Eli?" Anna asked.

"Sweetened, please."

"Great. I'll be back in a few minutes."

After Anna left the room, Eli turned to Tag. He got right to the point. "Your wife tells me that you've gotten into some trouble, Tag."

"That's an understatement. The judge ordered me to wear this thing on my leg." Tag propped his right foot on the corner of the desk and lifted his trouser leg to reveal an electronic monitoring device strapped to his ankle. "I'm a board-certified cardiologist, and I'm confined to my own house. My partners won't even let me back in the clinic."

"Your wife has hired me to help with that, but you're going to be my client. So I need to know that you want my help as well."

"Anna's uncle, George Thornton, recommended you highly, and I've checked you out on my own. My lawyer friend who helped me make bail over the weekend says you're one of the best trial lawyers in the state. But what I want to know is, can you get me out of this?"

It was a fair question. Most clients wanted to know the end result. But it was a hard question, too, one that Eli knew he couldn't answer. He responded honestly. "That depends on a lot of factors, most of which we don't know yet. I never guarantee success. What I do promise is that my office and I will do everything possible to provide the best legal representation we can. My staff has already begun to investigate, and as facts develop, I'll be better able to tell you where this case is going."

"Fair enough." Tag's reply was short, almost curt.

"The most important thing is that I need

to know everything, good or bad. I don't like surprises, and I can guarantee the district attorney's office is trying to unearth everything it can to convict you of this crime. Do you understand what I'm saying?"

"Completely. And don't worry. I'll tell you everything."

Eli listened to the words Tag spoke but wasn't completely convinced they contained the truth. There was something about Tag's abruptness that made Eli uneasy.

A soft rap on the door interrupted their conversation, and Anna appeared with a silver serving tray containing two glasses of iced tea. She set it on the edge of Tag's desk and handed Eli a glass and then one to Tag.

"Thank you," Eli said, but Tag expressed no appreciation to Anna.

"You're welcome." Anna gathered the tray. "I'll leave you two alone," she said as she exited and closed the door.

Eli sipped at his tea. "I assume you knew Ms. Caldwell."

"That's true. I knew her."

"Were you having an affair with her?"

Tag hesitated before responding, as if he were searching for an appropriate response. "Our relationship became physical," he said finally. A brief smirk appeared on his face.

Tag's lack of respect — both for his own marriage and for Jessica Caldwell — didn't sit well with Eli.

"But I didn't love her, by any stretch," Tag explained. "It was purely a physical attraction."

"Were you in her town house the night she died?"

Tag stiffened his jaw. "I was there, but she was alive and well when I left her. I had absolutely nothing to do with her death."

"Tag, let me explain something to you, and this may sound odd." Eli leaned forward on the sofa and propped his elbows on his knees. "As your attorney, my primary concern is not whether you murdered Ms. Caldwell or not. It's whether or not the district attorney has enough evidence, can get enough evidence, to convince a jury that you murdered her. And so far, it's not looking too good."

Eli returned to a normal sitting position and counted with his fingers as he continued his assessment of the case. "First, you had a relationship with her. Second, you were in her town house the night she died. I've already received a motion from the DA's office seeking to obtain a DNA sample from you to compare with tissue found under Ms. Caldwell's fingernail. If it matches, that could be strike three."

Eli noticed that Tag scratched at a small, healing wound on his left cheek. "So you see that we have our work cut out for us. The DA will easily be able to place you at the scene of the crime. Let's get started on trying to find a defense by you telling me everything you can remember about the night Jessica Caldwell died."

For the better part of an hour, Eli meticulously took notes while Tag described the evening, from the time he picked up Jessica until he returned home at 1:00 a.m. Periodically Eli asked follow-up questions, such as where they went to dinner and when they arrived at Jessica's town house.

"I even got a ticket in the mail for running a red light in front of her town house." Tag shrugged nonchalantly. "There must be one of those surveillance cameras at that intersection."

"Anything else?" Eli prodded. He could sense Tag's story was coming to a close.

"That's all I can remember right now."

"How long a drive is it from Ms. Caldwell's town house to your house?"

"Probably about fifteen minutes or so. Not very far."

"So you left her town house about twelve forty-five a.m.?"

"That seems about right."

"And what was Ms. Caldwell doing when you left?"

"She was asleep. I don't think she even knew when I left." The left corner of Tag's mouth turned up in what appeared to be a half smile of satisfaction.

Tag's facial expression caused a twinge of nausea in Eli's stomach. Were it not for his promise to Anna, he would have walked out. He was disgusted with Tag's cavalier attitude, but his commitment forced him to continue.

"You mentioned a traffic ticket. Do you still have it?"

"Yeah, I've got it in my desk." Tag opened the middle drawer of his desk and removed a letter-size piece of paper. "I guess this is the least of my problems now," he said as he handed the ticket and an eight-by-ten photograph attached to the ticket to Eli.

Eli scanned the ticket and the photograph. "It's time-stamped at twelve forty-eight a.m. That would be when you were leaving, correct?"

"That's right, and that's my car in the picture. I can even make out the license plate."

"You drive an Infiniti SUV?"

Tag nodded.

Eli scanned the ticket again, folded it, and placed it and the photograph in his briefcase. "I also need to ask you about your marriage. I suspect that the DA's office is looking for any dirt it can find to strengthen its claim that you were having an affair with Ms. Caldwell. How would you describe your marriage?"

Tag folded his arms and replied with little emotion. "Our marriage has been shaky from the beginning. I thought it was all right at the time we got married, but looking back on our wedding day, I don't remember it as a lightning-bolt experience. It was just okay and hasn't gotten any better since then. I don't know how much longer our marriage will last."

The finality with which Tag spoke troubled Eli. Clearly the man had no idea what true marriage was. Eli began to understand why he felt cold when he entered the Grissom house. There was no love there. Eli had represented a husband or wife in divorce many times, but it was easy to dislike the other spouse when he or she was the adversary. This was a difficult situation. He liked Anna Grissom. His sympathy for her was the main reason he'd agreed to take this case. But his client, the man he was supposed to defend against murder charges, the man to whom his duty, loyalty, and zeal were due, obviously despised his own wife. And she was pregnant!

"Anna tells me y'all are expecting a baby."

"Yeah, well, *she's* having a baby. It's due in December, but I'm not that excited about the idea. I'm too busy with my career to be tied down with children. There's too much I want to do and too many places I want to go. Children would be in the way. I pressed her to have an abortion early on, but she refused. We'll just have to deal with it when it gets here."

Abortion! The word screamed in Eli's mind. *And he's talking about the baby — his baby — as if it is some inanimate object.* The conversation began to make Eli feel even more sick to his stomach.

"Tag, I think I have about all I need for today. I have a lot of work to do, and I'll get right on it. The preliminary hearing is scheduled for a week from yesterday. My associate, Jill Baker, and I will meet you and Anna at about nine a.m. next Thursday. There is a parking lot two blocks north of the courthouse. Meet us there, and we can walk in together."

With that, Eli closed his briefcase and stood to leave. Tag stood as well, and they shook hands again.

"It was nice to finally meet you," Tag said.

"Same here."

The door to the study opened and Anna appeared almost on cue — as if she had been listening at the door. "I'll walk you to the door."

Once outside Eli sat briefly in his car before driving away. He scanned the manicured estate and thought about how perfect the Grissoms' house looked from the outside while the home on the inside was being ravaged.

How can God allow a child to be born in to this marriage? he thought.

Yet that was exactly what was happening. And Eli couldn't escape the feeling that even if he did manage to exonerate Tag, Anna and her baby would be abandoned by him.

CHAPTER TEN

The Loveless Café, West of Nashville, Tennessee

The nationally renowned Loveless Café was housed in the quaint, renovated office building of an out-of-operation roadside motel. It was located west of Nashville near the Natchez Trace Parkway and not far from the 1-40 exit for the sleepy town of Pegram. Eli and Sara loved its country charm and Southern cooking. Eli parked amid the dozens of other cars that filled the gravel parking lot, and he and Sara waited patiently on the front porch until their name was called for an available table.

The Loveless was frequented by Nashville and national celebrities. The allure of its award-winning country ham, Southern fried chicken, and made-from-scratch biscuits drew people from around the globe to its red-and-white-checkered tablecloths.

After they were ushered to a table near

the back of the main, but small, dining room, Sara ordered country ham and biscuits and Eli requested the fried chicken. Before long they were up to their elbows in homemade preserves, fried chicken, salt-cured ham, and laughter.

"How did your meeting go with Dr. Grissom?" Sara asked not far into their dinner conversation.

Eli spread strawberry preserves on a fluffy biscuit and took a bite before responding. He thought about what he'd seen in Tag Grissom. The arrogant doctor with an ego the size of Texas. A womanizer. Treated his wife like dirt. Not the kind of man Eli wanted to socialize with. But one word kept coming to mind: *client.* And to call someone a client meant something to Eli even if he didn't like the man.

"He's a tough guy to figure out. He says he didn't kill her, but he does admit he was in her town house the night of the murder. The prosecutor will easily be able to prove opportunity."

Sara took a bite of country ham and biscuit and sipped her iced tea. Eli stared at his plate, thinking.

"I wish you would stop taking criminal cases," Sara said. "They always weigh on you."

Eli looked up at Sara. He heard the concern in her voice and saw it on her face. "I know, and maybe I will. I wouldn't have taken this one were it not for his wife."

"You told me about her going to your office."

"I don't appreciate enough how wonderful it is being married to you. We may have our disagreements occasionally, but our marriage is solid. Those two don't know from one day to the next whether they are going to stay married or not. Anna wants to make it work because she's pregnant, and she wants her child to grow up with both a mother and a father. But I'm not sure about Tag. I think he could leave her and not think twice about it. He certainly doesn't like it that she is pregnant."

"That sounds a little familiar," Sara responded with a playful smile.

Even though Eli knew Sara was joking, the similarity between him and Tag suddenly struck him. Both were driven by their desire to succeed professionally, and neither wanted children to get in the way. He took a drink from his glass and swallowed hard. *How good a husband am I? And could I be a good father?*

"The difference," Eli defended, "is that I love you and he doesn't love his wife."

"I know you do," Sara replied affectionately. "And I suspect another difference is that neither Dr. Grissom nor his wife knows Jesus Christ."

Eli took a bite of his supper. Sara was right. The Grissom house was cold not just because it was loveless, but because it was without Jesus Christ.

"I'm convinced that's true," he said, reflecting. "Perhaps an opportunity will present itself when I can talk to them about their salvation."

"I'll be praying for that to happen. What does the pastor call it?" Sara asked. " 'A divine appointment'?"

Eli nodded thoughtfully. "Yeah. 'A divine appointment.' That's what I need — a divine appointment with Tag and Anna Grissom."

Not only am I to defend Tag against murder charges, he thought, *but the real reason Anna Grissom came to my office may be for me to lead them both to Christ. That was an awesome responsibility!*

"It'll work out," Sara said.

"I know it will. But they may be a tough couple to get through to. They barely talk to each other and never agree on anything so far as I can tell."

"Speaking of disagreements, have you

given any more thought to having children?"

"You never give up, do you?" Eli chuckled.

"Not easily."

"I've thought about it some more. Believe it or not, I'm warming up to the idea."

A contagious smile crossed Sara's face and soon was reflected on Eli's. The conversation improved to topics more pleasant than the marital difficulties of Tag and Anna Grissom. Before long their meal was concluded and they exited the Loveless arm in arm to Eli's car in the parking lot. As they rode quietly back to the Hermitage Hotel, Eli held Sara's hand and inwardly thanked God for his wonderful wife.

The Hart Building, Washington DC

"It's so good to see you, Stella," Senator Lance Proctor said as he entered his office, where Stella Hanover was waiting for him. He was followed closely by Cooper Harrington. It was the first Monday of June, and the senator's staff had alerted him to Stella Hanover's unrelenting demands for an audience.

"Don't give me that, Senator," Stella retorted. Her crisp Boston-accented words spewed rapidly from her mouth. She rose mightily from a leather chair and pounced on him. "I never like seeing you, and I know you can't enjoy seeing me either. Particularly when I'm this mad. I've been trying to get in to see you for days, and I finally had to just show up and make a scene before anybody would schedule me a time."

Her voice reached a crescendo, just below yelling. The husky clatter of her voice was like fingernails on a chalkboard. It made Senator Proctor cringe. He tried to give Stella a polite handshake but was met with a less-than-warm reception. He ambled toward his chair behind his desk, hanging his suit jacket in the closet on the way.

"Stella, just settle down, and Cooper and I will try to satisfy all of your concerns, whatever they may be," Senator Proctor said as he walked. His voice was calm and reassuring, with just a hint of Southern charm mixed in intentionally.

"I have one question for you, Senator. What are you going to do to stop Dunbar Shelton's confirmation to the bench?"

Senator Proctor knew exactly why Stella was in his office, and it was the very reason he had been avoiding her. That — and the fact that he really didn't like her.

"Now, Stella, you're all worked up over nothing. Sit back down and let's talk about it."

Stella returned to her seat while Senator

Proctor sat behind his desk and Cooper settled into a leather chair near Stella.

"Appointing a justice to the Supreme Court who will vote to overturn *Roe v. Wade* isn't 'nothing,' " Stella insisted.

"How do you know he will vote to overturn?" Cooper asked.

"That's a good question, Stella. How do you know?" Senator Proctor added.

"Because that Christian freak of a president would only nominate someone who would vote to overturn, that's why." Stella drew a long, slow breath. Her face showed surprise. She glanced at her two hosts and finally stopped her gaze at Senator Proctor. "I should've known," she mumbled.

"Known what?" Senator Proctor asked, playing with his beard.

Stella shook her head. "I should've known that Wallace had already struck a deal with you."

Senator Proctor saw her disgust. It didn't upset him in the least. "Stella," he began, "we're old friends. You've helped me in the past, and I've helped you —"

"You have, haven't you?" Stella interrupted, her voice rising again in anger.

"Hang on, Stella —" Senator Proctor tried to continue. He raised his hands defensively, and his voice rose to match Stella's.

"It's true, isn't it? Just tell me. It's true." Stella's voice again reached a crescendo just below yelling. Her pale face transformed to red, and her body trembled slightly.

Without Stella seeing it, Senator Proctor winked at Cooper. Then he said, "Cooper, please excuse us for a few minutes. I need to talk to Stella alone."

"But, but —" Cooper stammered.

"No buts, Cooper. Just do what I say. I need to talk to Stella in private. It'll only be a few minutes."

In dramatic disgust, Cooper stood and marched from the room. He closed the office door a little harder than normal. Senator Proctor stared at the closed door for five seconds. It was enough time for Cooper to make it to his office and activate the headphones.

Senator Proctor faced Stella. "Let me tell you something." His voice was soft but stern. "Don't you ever come in here again yelling at me and making demands. I've done countless favors for you and your organization over the years, and I think I deserve a little more respect than you've shown today."

Senator Proctor saw Stella clench her jaw. "And," he continued, "if I want to strike a deal with the president on this or any other issue, I will and you won't tell me otherwise."

Stella erupted from her chair more violently than she had when Senator Proctor first entered the room. "And let me tell *you* something. This fight isn't over! I'll spend every last dime we have to defeat this nomination and you at the next election."

Senator Proctor reclined in his chair and smiled. He knew Cooper was laughing his head off. "Don't threaten me, Stella," he said with a confident air. "I know you don't have the political connections in Tennessee to beat me. And besides, most of my constituents are against abortion. They'll hail me as a hero if Shelton is confirmed, and if in fact he's pro-life."

"Oh, he's pro-life," Stella said, no longer yelling. "No doubt about it. Wallace wouldn't have nominated him if he wasn't."

"How do you know? Do you have anything where he said he would overturn *Roe*?"

"You know I'm not going to find anything like that. Guys like Shelton and Roberts, they're careful not to say much on any subject. It's almost like they've been planning to be on the Supreme Court since grade school." She slumped back into her chair.

"Well, if you had something like that, I

might reconsider my position. Otherwise, I'm going to support Shelton, for confirmation."

"Just like that?"

"Just like that."

"You know I can't give up without a fight and that it'll get ugly."

"I know both of those things."

"All right." Stella's voice was calm for the first time since Senator Proctor had entered the room. But it was also determined. "And I know what I have to do."

With that, she stood and left without saying anything else to Senator Proctor. But she couldn't leave without conveying one last message to the senator by slamming the door harder and louder than Cooper had. Senator Proctor knew it had to hurt Cooper's ears.

The Washington Post, *Washington DC*

Holland Fletcher was at his metal desk at the Post headquarters on the corner of Fifteenth and L streets. His was one in a maze of cubicles in the expansive newsroom. Holland was dressed in his usual work clothes. Wrinkled khakis, three-button pullover short-sleeve shirt, and loafers, no socks. It was early afternoon, and he had finally found an opportunity to start on lunch — pastrami on rye — when the phone rang. He stuffed half of the sandwich in his mouth and chased it down with a Diet Coke. He mumbled something that sounded like hello into the receiver and dusted crumbs from his shirt.

It seemed that every reporter on staff was in the newsroom. They were trying to get an above-the-fold story together before the 10:45 p.m. deadline for the early city edition. The cacophony made it difficult for him to hear the woman on the other end of the phone. It was *her,* he finally realized.

"Don't even try to trace the call," she instructed. "I told you so."

Holland rolled his eyes. He didn't like being shown up. And he was still kicking himself for missing an opportunity to scoop everyone in town on the Shelton nomination. He took another swig of Diet Coke and swallowed hard. "That you did."

"Why didn't you run the story?"

"My editor wouldn't let me without corroboration, and I couldn't get any."

"At least now you realize that I'm telling the truth. Are you going to keep your end of the bargain?"

He remembered her threat. If she knew the nominee before it was announced, then she certainly had the resources to follow through on her threat against him. "I gave you my word, and I'm going to stick to it."

"That's good to hear, Mr. Fletcher. And you won't be sorry. The Caldwell murder will be a bigger story than Dunbar Shelton."

Bigger. He liked the thought of that. He set his feet on his desk and chewed on the end of his pen. "Are you going to give me your name now?"

"No. Not now. Maybe never."

"How am I going to contact you?"

"I'll give you my wireless number, but that's it. No home number. No address. You call, and I'll decide whether I want to answer or not."

He didn't like it, but they were her rules. If he was going to play the game, he had to play by her rules. He scribbled the number on a scrap of paper and stuffed it in his wallet. "I'll do it, but if I don't find something in a week, I'm giving up."

"If you're as good as you act like you are, you'll find something."

With that the line went dead, and Holland was left seething at the challenge.

CHAPTER ELEVEN

The Metropolitan Nashville–Davidson County Courthouse, Nashville, Tennessee

"There will probably be reporters waiting for us," Eli said as he, Jill Baker, Tag, and Anna walked along a sidewalk in downtown Nashville. All four were dressed in business attire. They had parked two blocks from the courthouse and were on their way to Tag's preliminary hearing on the first Thursday of June.

"If anybody says anything to them, it'll be me," Eli instructed. "But I doubt that I will allow interviews today. The trial hasn't even been set yet, and any potential jurors will forget what I say today by the time the trial begins."

Fifteen large granite columns greeted Eli as he and the others climbed the concrete steps that led to the criminal trial courts. The Metropolitan Nashville–Davidson County Courthouse was five stories tall and rectangular in shape, with entry points at each corner. Inside, a wide hallway ran along the outer part of the building, trapping the courtrooms — twenty in all — within its perimeter.

Eli and the others were stormed by the members of the print, television, and talk-radio media that littered the area outside courtroom 7. Eli ushered the Grissoms and Jill past the unrelenting demands for answers, through the bright lights from the television cameras and constant clicking from the photographers' cameras, and into the courtroom without providing comments or sound bites for the evening news.

The courtroom was small by most standards, but very ornate. Rich wood paneling, a high ceiling, and thick carpeting gave the room an elegant feel. The gallery area was only eight rows deep, and many of the reporters who had previously been in the hallway clamored for one of the few available seats. The entrance was in the rear of the courtroom, and Eli saw the judge's bench directly ahead as they entered. Although elevated, it wasn't as lofty as others Eli had seen.

Standing near the table on the right-hand side of the courtroom was the lead prosecutor, called the district attorney general in

Tennessee jurisprudence. In common parlance he was simply called the General. The General, Randall Dickerson, was a slender man of medium height. Eli knew that Randy was well connected politically. A man didn't get elected as district attorney general in Davidson County without knowing the right people.

"Randy, good to see you again," Eli said as the two shook hands.

"You, too, Eli. I'm a little surprised to see you over here on this case."

"Long story, but I'm sure you don't mind an out-of-town adversary every once in a while, do you?"

"Always glad to have a law school classmate across the table from me." Randy wore engraved gold cuff links, a dark gray suit, and black leather shoes that had recently been polished.

"I see you don't wear glasses anymore," Eli commented. "Contacts?"

"Lasik. Two thousand dollars per eye, but worth every penny."

"Since when does the district attorney handle preliminary hearings?" Eli asked.

"It's too important a case to allow for any mistakes. The victim was the daughter of one of the mayor's closest friends." Randy nodded toward a distinguished older couple sitting in the courtroom.

Eli hadn't noticed them before now but realized they must be the parents of Jessica Caldwell. *Jordan and Heddy Caldwell.* The names came to his mind from reading them in Jill's report. Eli's eyes met Jordan's, and Eli could sense the pain and the anger that Jessica's parents must be experiencing. He returned his gaze to Randy.

"I'll be lead on this case," Randy continued. "I can't delegate responsibility for it to one of my assistants."

"All rise," the slightly overweight bailiff in the Metro Nashville PD uniform commanded as she entered the courtroom from a door, to the right of the judge's bench, that led to the judge's chambers. There was no doubt she was to be obeyed. Everyone in the courtroom who wasn't already standing leaped to their feet.

The bailiff was closely followed by Judge Russell Blackwood, who bounded to his position on the bench. He was of average height and weight, with a freshly starched shirt and an orange-and-white-striped necktie under his black robe. His hair was brown with a hint of red, and his face was clean shaven. He settled into his leather chair behind the bench and nodded at the bailiff.

"Please be seated," she said.

Eli and Randy separated, each to his respective table, and sat down — Randy to the table on the right facing the judge and Eli to the one on the left. Tag sat between Eli and Jill. Eli had yet to talk to Tag about his arrogant appearance, but there was still time to work on that before the trial. Anna sat in the first row of the gallery behind the bar. She looked sympathetic — just like Eli wanted. Everyone was in their respective places as the preliminary hearing in the case of the *State of Tennessee v. Todd Allen Grissom* began.

Sometimes lawyers waived the requirement of a preliminary hearing and moved to the next stage of the case. But Eli knew that he could use the preliminary hearing as an opportunity to discover some things about Randy's case against Tag to which he might not otherwise have access.

"Mr. Faulkner," Judge Blackwood began, "do you waive the preliminary hearing?"

"No, sir," Eli responded, partially rising from his seat and then sitting back down.

"All right, then. General Dickerson, are you ready to proceed?"

"We are, Your Honor." Randy stood from his chair, buttoned the top two buttons of his coat, and strode to the podium between the two tables.

"Call your first witness."

"The state calls Lieutenant Mike Brantley."

The bailiff opened a side door to the courtroom and Lieutenant Brantley entered — blue blazer, dark red tie, and khaki pants. After being placed under oath, Lieutenant Brantley sat in the witness chair that was located to the right of Judge Blackwood and slightly lower.

"Lieutenant Brantley," Randy began. "For the record, will you please tell us your name and your occupation?"

Randy opened a three-ring notebook and placed it on the podium. He checked off each question as he went. The process was methodical and uneventful. He had used this script hundreds of times, Eli knew. Lieutenant Brantley was also comfortable in his seat. He angled toward the microphone in front of him without being instructed to do so.

"My name is Mike Brantley, and I am a lieutenant in the homicide division of the Metropolitan Nashville Police Department."

"Lieutenant Brantley, in your capacity as a lieutenant in the homicide division, have you had the opportunity to investigate the

176

death of a woman named Jessica Caldwell?"

"I have. I was the lead detective."

"And what did your investigation determine?"

"We determined that the decedent, Jessica Caldwell, was murdered by strangulation."

Randy backed away from the podium a couple of steps and rested against the rail that separated the actors — the lawyers, judge, defendant, and witnesses — from the audience. He spoke clearly and loudly so the members of the media in the gallery could hear.

Eli watched the act and smiled.

"Lieutenant Brantley, tell us how you arrived at the conclusion that Dr. Grissom was the perpetrator of this crime."

Lieutenant Brantley spent the better part of five minutes reciting how the police officers had discovered Jessica's body, the condition of the body, and the other physical evidence at the scene of the crime. His mannerisms weren't as smooth as Randy Dickerson's, but he was effective. Eli could hear paper from the reporters' notepads ruffling behind him. Lieutenant Brantley then described the discovery of Tag's fingerprints in Jessica's town house, the revelation of a relationship between Tag and Jessica Caldwell, and the skin under Jessica's fingernail.

"Thank you, Lieutenant Brantley," Randy said when Lieutenant Brantley finished his answer. Randy turned toward Judge Blackwood. "I'll pass the witness to Mr. Faulkner." He unbuttoned his coat and sat down.

"Mr. Faulkner, any questions?" Judge Blackwood inquired.

"Just a few, Your Honor." Eli rose from his chair. He buttoned the top two buttons of his gray pin-striped three-button suit coat and moved to the podium between the two tables. "Lieutenant Brantley, I'm Eli Faulkner, and I represent Dr. Grissom." Eli gestured toward Tag, sitting behind the table. "Were Dr. Grissom's fingerprints the only fingerprints you found in Ms. Caldwell's town house?"

"No," Lieutenant Brantley admitted. His body language and his voice indicated that he did so reluctantly.

"Who else's fingerprints did you find?"

"Obviously the decedent's fingerprints were there, and there was another set of prints that we were unable to identify."

Eli's eyebrows rose at Lieutenant Brantley's response, and he glanced over his shoulder to make sure Jill was taking notes. He could hear Randy shifting position in his chair. That was a good sign. He would later request the full transcript of the hearing from the court reporter.

"Where were those prints located?"

"We found them in two locations. One was on the inside of the doorknob and the second was on a glass table near the couch in the den."

"And you ran those prints through the NCIC and FBI databases?"

"We ran them through all the databases, and no matches."

"One last question, Lieutenant Brantley. Was there any sign of forced entry?"

"No. There wasn't any forced entry."

Eli looked at Judge Blackwood. "Those are all the questions I have for Lieutenant Brantley."

"Lieutenant Brantley," Judge Blackwood said, "we thank you for your time today. You may step down."

Lieutenant Brantley stepped down from the witness chair and the bailiff led him out the same side door he'd entered earlier.

"Call your next witness, General," Judge Blackwood told Randy.

Randy stood again, walked to the podium, and began act two. His part in the play was second nature. "The state calls Dr. Morris Stephenson."

Soon Dr. Stephenson emerged from the same side door Lieutenant Brantley had recently exited. Eli noticed a limp as Dr. Stephenson ambled across the courtroom. After being placed under oath, he sat down in the witness chair to the right of Judge Blackwood. Dr. Stephenson filled more of the witness chair than Lieutenant Brantley had. Eli also noticed that the doctor's brown tweed jacket with leather elbow patches was about one-half size too small for him, and he wore an out-of-date brown knit necktie.

"Dr. Stephenson," Randy began, "you are the medical examiner for the Metropolitan Government of Nashville and Davidson County — is that right?"

"That's right. I am." Dr. Stephenson spoke in a matter-of-fact fashion and primarily out of the right side of his mouth.

"And in that capacity, have you had the opportunity to examine the body of Jessica Caldwell?"

"I did," Dr. Stephenson replied unemotionally. Eli assumed that Dr. Stephenson had testified at preliminary hearings and trials hundreds of times. He was very comfortable.

"As a result of your examination, did you prepare a report of your findings?"

"I did."

"State's exhibit number one, Your Honor," Randy said as he approached the court reporter to have Dr. Stephenson's report labeled as the first documentary evidence in the preliminary hearing. As he walked toward the court reporter, Randy gave a copy of the report to Eli.

Eli thumbed through the several pages in the report, then handed it to Tag. "Glance through this," he whispered. "You're probably more familiar with some of the terminology than I am. When you're finished, pass it to Jill for the file."

After the court reporter labeled the report, the bailiff handed it to Dr. Stephenson.

Randy returned to his position behind the podium. "Dr. Stephenson, what was the cause of death?"

Dr. Stephenson removed his reading glasses from his inside coat pocket and put them on. They were half lenses and rested near the tip of his nose.

"Asphyxia from neck compression," Dr. Stephenson read from the report. He then looked over the top of his glasses at Randy. "She was strangled to death."

While Randy continued questioning Dr. Stephenson, Tag nudged Eli on the arm. Eli looked over at Tag, and he pointed at something in the report.

"Ask him about this," Tag whispered.

"What is it?"

"It shows that there was HCG in her blood."

"What's that?"

"Just ask him," Tag directed, almost in a commanding tone.

Eli moved a little closer to Tag and whispered in his ear. He was more forceful than usual. "I'm not asking a question I don't know the answer to. What's HCG?"

"It means she was pregnant," Tag said.

Eli moved away from Tag and searched his face. All he saw was the same insolence he'd noticed during their earlier meeting.

"And I can't be the father."

Tag seemed so sure, but how could he be? Eli wondered.

"Those are all the questions I have for Dr. Stephenson," Eli heard Randy say.

Randy's voice disrupted Eli's focus on Tag's expression. Eli faced the front of the courtroom and stood. Randy sat down.

"I have a few questions for Dr. Stephenson, Your Honor," Eli said.

"Mr. Faulkner, you may proceed."

Eli took the medical examiner's report from Tag and, rather than stand behind the podium, eased around to the front of the table and began his questioning of Dr. Stephenson. It was like leading a horse to water.

"Dr. Stephenson, how long have you been with the medical examiner's office?"

Dr. Stephenson smiled slightly and removed his glasses. "I've been with the medical examiner's office for over thirty years, and chief of the office the last fifteen."

"And in those thirty years, Dr. Stephenson, you were trained to fully examine every part of a body that has been a victim of homicide, is that correct?"

"Of course it's correct, Counselor." Dr. Stephenson's voice was agitated but forceful. "We do a very thorough job."

"And before you finalize your report on this or any other homicide, you make certain that every part of your report is absolutely accurate? That every part will stand up under the scrutiny of the best medical experts that an enterprising defense attorney like myself might hire? Isn't that right, Dr. Stephenson?"

Dr. Stephenson smiled even more broadly. "Mr. Faulkner, in thirty years I haven't had one of my reports refuted for any reason. If I put it in my report, you can bet money on it being accurate."

"Good, Dr. Stephenson. That's good, and that's what I thought your answer would be. If you will, Dr. Stephenson, please turn to page three of your report." Eli waited while Dr. Stephenson replaced his glasses on his nose and located page three as directed.

"On line twelve on page three, Dr. Stephenson, what does that say?"

"That her blood was positive for human chorionic gonadotropin, commonly referred to as HCG." Dr. Stephenson peered over his glasses at Eli.

"What does that mean?"

"It means she was pregnant."

Eli eyed Randy. He could tell from the look on Randy's face that he already knew what Eli had just discovered but was uninterested. The information wasn't important to Randy. The fetus was likely too young to support a prosecution for another death.

Eli then looked at Mr. and Mrs. Caldwell and immediately recognized that this was the first time they'd heard their daughter was pregnant.

He also heard the reporters in the gallery flipping pages in their notebooks, trying to scribble down every word.

"Can you tell me from this test how long she had been pregnant?" Eli asked Dr. Stephenson.

"My office didn't test the value or level of HCG. We were only concerned with whether her blood tested positive or negative for

HCG. When it came back positive, we opened the uterus and measured the fetus."

"And were you able to determine the gestational age of the fetus by measuring it?"

"I can't be precise, but my best estimate is that the fetus was about twelve weeks old."

"Those are all the questions I have for Dr. Stephenson," Eli concluded and headed for his seat. As he rounded the end of the table, he noticed Tag again. His earlier arrogance had changed to something different. Momentarily he looked inquisitive. As Eli returned to his chair, Tag lifted his chin with an air of resolve.

"What is it?" Eli whispered.

Tag's gaze was focused. He spoke in a low but unwavering voice. "I can't be the father," he told Eli again.

Just then Judge Blackwood spoke. "Dr. Stephenson, you're excused."

After Dr. Stephenson left the courtroom, Judge Blackwood turned to Randy. "Call your next witness," he directed.

"Those are all the witnesses we're calling today, Your Honor."

Judge Blackwood then eyed Eli. "Any witnesses, Mr. Faulkner?"

Eli faced Judge Blackwood. He knew that

Randy had carried his burden of proving probable cause and that he wasn't going to get the murder charge against Tag dismissed. There was no need to give Randy free discovery by calling any witnesses to testify.

"No witnesses," Eli replied. He then rested his back against his chair as he waited for Judge Blackwood's ruling.

"The court finds that the state has demonstrated sufficient probable cause for the case against Dr. Grissom to continue," Judge Blackwood stated. "That doesn't mean Dr. Grissom will ultimately be found guilty of any crime but simply means that the state has sufficient evidence to present to a jury regarding Dr. Grissom's involvement with the death of Jessica Caldwell. The court also finds that Dr. Grissom should continue to remain free on bail pending the trial of this case. Mr. Dickerson and Mr. Faulkner, my office will be in touch with you in the next several days to schedule a trial. With that, the court will stand adjourned." Judge Blackwood banged his gavel and stood.

"All rise," the bailiff said as Judge Blackwood left his bench and disappeared through the door to his chambers. "Court is now adjourned," she concluded.

The reporters in the gallery immediately

began to clamor for Eli and the others to answer questions. Eli grabbed Tag by the arm and led him through the horde of reporters. Anna fell in line as well, and Jill brought up the rear of the quartet. Randy Dickerson stayed behind and answered as many questions as the reporters had.

As soon as Eli and the other three exited the courtroom, two Davidson County sheriff's deputies appeared and directed them toward the building's back entrance. It was used often by litigants who desired an escape from the building without having to battle the media.

"Mr. Faulkner," one of the deputies said, "if you'll have someone bring a car to the portico at the rear of the building, we can get the four of you out through the back door."

Eli removed his car keys from his pocket and gave them to Jill. He motioned for her to do as the deputy had suggested, and she left the group to retrieve Eli's car.

"You can wait in here until she gets back." The deputy pointed to a conference room at the end of the hall.

Eli, Tag, and Anna entered the room, and Eli placed his briefcase on the table. The deputy closed the door behind them.

"You're pretty confident that you can't be

the father of Ms. Caldwell's child," Eli directed at Tag. "But when I met with you at your house the other day, you told me that you had been intimate with Ms. Caldwell."

"We had been," Tag admitted without looking at his wife.

The admission was in a conquering, bragging tone. Eli glanced at Anna and noticed a stiff upper lip as she peered straight ahead, not looking at either Eli or Tag.

"Then how can you be so confident?" Eli demanded.

Tag glanced at Anna, who returned the glance.

Was that an inquisitive look on Anna's face? Eli wondered.

After a couple of seconds of eerie silence, Tag responded, "Because I'm sterile."

CHAPTER TWELVE

*The Oval Office, the White House,
Washington DC*

"Am I interrupting?" Porter asked as the president's secretary admitted him to the room. It was just before noon on Thursday.

"I was just finishing." President Wallace closed his tattered Bible and slid it into the top-left-hand drawer of his desk. "A few minutes with God every day does wonders for the soul, Porter."

"I agree, sir."

"Come in and sit down." President Wallace waved for Porter to come farther into the room. "What's on your mind?"

Porter sat in a leather chair near the front of the president's desk. "I thought we should talk more about the Senate Judiciary Committee hearings for Judge Shelton."

"I trust everything is still on track with Senator Proctor's office."

"Everything is still on track. I spoke with

Cooper Harrington yesterday afternoon, and he confirmed that they are lining up enough votes for Judge Shelton."

"Good. Sounds like everything is going according to plan, then."

"Everything except Stella Hanover."

President Wallace noticed the anxiety on Porter's face. Stella Hanover made Porter nervous.

"Stella Hanover? Why am I not surprised? She gave us quite a fight during the election because of my position on abortion. What is she up to?"

"Rumor is that she made an appearance at Senator Proctor's office on Monday and gave him an earful over Judge Shelton's nomination."

"But you've talked to Cooper and our deal with Proctor is still in place, right?"

"That's right, but I'm worried about Stella. She's tenacious and will do anything she can to derail the confirmation. She has demanded a meeting with every senator who was supported by her organization in the last two elections. I've also heard that she has hired a team of private investigators to uncover everything they can possibly find on Judge Shelton."

President Wallace reclined in his chair and thoughtfully considered the ceiling. He rubbed his chin with his right hand. "We may need to get the committee hearings moved up so he can be confirmed before Stella's people have time to do any damage. I'm confident, based on our own investigations, they won't find anything on Judge Shelton, but there's no reason to make any mistakes at this point."

"That's exactly what I was thinking. I talked to Cooper about that yesterday. He said the earliest the committee could begin is the last week of this month. But they'll have to adjourn for the Fourth of July. Several committee members will be traveling to their home states for parades and other events where they can be seen by their constituents."

"I'd hate for them to miss a baby-kissing opportunity," President Wallace said sarcastically.

Porter chuckled politely. "If things go well, we could get to a vote on the Senate floor before the August recess. But any delays will put the vote into September."

"Let's get everything arranged to make it easy on the committee. We need to have the vote before the recess."

"I agree," Porter replied. "I'll continue to work on it."

"How's Judge Shelton performing in the

mock committee hearings?"

"He's doing great. He can quote the Ginsburg rule with ease — no hints, no forecasts, no previews."

En route to Jackson, Tennessee
They had been driving for fifteen minutes, and Jill could no longer tolerate the silence. Eli hadn't said good-bye to either Tag or Anna when they'd deposited them at their waiting car in the parking lot near the courthouse. And he hadn't said a word to her since then either. His lips were pressed together and his jaw was flexing rapidly. Jill now wished she had remained in the driver's seat after she retrieved the car. But Eli had insisted — *demanded* — and she had moved to the passenger seat. She could see anger in his body language. He even gripped the steering wheel with both hands so tightly that his knuckles turned white.

She had seen that look before. Not often, but she had seen it. The last time she recalled seeing it was when a client had lied to him. Jill could tell that Eli was mad and the gears in his brain were grinding.

"Okay," Jill said. "What's wrong?"

When Eli shook his head, she knew she'd have to drag it out of him. But she had to be careful. He was her boss, and she didn't need his anger directed at her.

Delicately, she prodded further. "Obviously something happened while I was gone to get the car. What was it?"

"I don't want to talk about it." The words barely escaped through his clenched teeth.

"Well, are we still working on this case or not?"

When Eli finally exhaled deeply, Jill knew he wouldn't stop talking until he had told her everything. She twisted her head and studied the side of his face.

Eli continued to watch the interstate ahead as he spoke. "Do you remember when Anna came to the office and I decided to take this case?"

"Sure. I remember."

"What did I say was one of the reasons I agreed to represent Tag?"

"Because Anna was pregnant and didn't want her child to grow up without a father."

Eli relaxed his death grip on the steering wheel and made an emphatic up-and-down motion with his right hand. "Exactly!"

"And?"

"And today I found out that it is impossible for Tag to be the father." The volume of Eli's voice escalated through his statement.

Jill stared at Eli and then through the front

windshield. She tucked her sleek black hair behind her ears and looked back at Eli again. She was confused. She sat quietly for several seconds as Eli steered the car into the left-hand lane and sped past a semitruck and trailer. She didn't know what to say and her brow furrowed.

"I don't understand," she finally admitted.

"When the coroner said that Jessica Caldwell was twelve weeks pregnant, Tag was confident it couldn't be his. I confronted him about it while you were getting the car because I knew their relationship had been physical. But when I questioned him, Tag told me he's sterile."

"Sterile? If he's sterile, how can Anna be pregnant?"

"That's what I asked."

"And they said what?"

"They said nothing."

"Nothing?"

"Nothing. Neither of them explained how Anna could be pregnant and Tag could be sterile. I saw an odd look on Anna's face after Tag said he was sterile, but I can't decide if it meant he was lying or if she was surprised he told me that. Maybe both."

"If he really is sterile, then obviously someone else is the father of Anna's baby."

"I questioned Anna about an affair, and she denied it. I couldn't tell for sure from the look on either of their faces whether she was lying or not. And Tag didn't say anything."

Eli loosened his necktie and unbuttoned the top button of his shirt. He stretched his head from side to side and front to back as if he were trying to release the tension in his neck.

"Does Anna look pregnant to you?" he asked.

"Not really, now that you mention it. Has she told you when the baby is expected?"

"When I was at their house the last week of May, she said something about the due date being a little over six months away, but that's all."

"I don't know anything about being pregnant," Jill admitted. "But I think it's possible to be nearly three months pregnant and for it to not be very noticeable."

Eli ran his hand through his hair in anguish. "I guess you're right. But I still don't like being lied to."

Jill knew that Tag's revelation was only part of the thoughts spinning in Eli's mind. The other part had to be the formulation of a plan. "What are you going to do?"

"I threatened to withdraw from the case.

When I first met with Tag, I told him that I needed to know everything, and he assured me he would tell me everything. I reminded him of that again this morning . . . but still no explanation."

"Are you going to withdraw?"

"I doubt Judge Blackwood will let me out this far into the case. We've already had the preliminary, and the trial will be scheduled in a couple of months."

"This certainly puts a new light on things, doesn't it?"

"It certainly does." He frowned. "And to think that I premised my agreement to represent Tag on a lie."

The Hart Building, Washington DC
"I talked to Porter McIntosh earlier today," Cooper Harrington said as he entered Senator Proctor's office. The Senate was finished for the day, and Senator Proctor was enjoying his pipe and a glass of Scotch.

"What did he want this time?" Senator Proctor was tired of hearing from Porter McIntosh. The man always seemed to need something, and that irritated the senator. He held the pipe in his right hand with his teeth clenched around the mouthpiece. Tiny puffs of smoke rose from the pipe's wooden bowl as he spoke.

Cooper stood and rested his hands on the back of a chair across the desk from Senator Proctor. "The president wants us to move the committee hearings up. They're worried about Stella."

"Stella?" Senator Proctor chuckled. "Did you tell Porter that we're not worried about Stella?"

"I did, but President Wallace wants a vote on the Senate floor before the August recess."

Senator Proctor took a sip from his glass of Scotch, leaned back in his chair, and resumed smoking his pipe. What a waste of time the conversation was. The president was kidding himself if he thought confirmation could be rushed.

"That may be difficult. Some of the senators may want to pacify Stella by delaying the vote until after the recess. She can be pretty . . . what's the word I'm looking for?"

"Ruthless?"

"Yeah, that's it. She can be ruthless."

"I know," Cooper replied. "She made herself very clear the other day."

"Walk the idea around with some of the Senate leadership and see what their thoughts are about moving the hearings up."

"Move the hearings up?" Stella said when Valerie Marcom gave her the news. "They can't move the hearings up. Who ever heard of that? I've heard of them being delayed before but never moved up."

"That's the word I got from one of my friends who works with the Judiciary Committee. Cooper Harrington is floating the idea around with the Senate leadership and the Judiciary Committee members to see if anyone is opposed. He's telling them that Senator Proctor wants an up-or-down vote in the Senate on Judge Shelton before the August recess."

Stella didn't like the thought of that at all. *Move the hearings up? Preposterous!* She couldn't let that happen.

Stella paced for a few steps before pivoting to face Valerie. "Something's up, Val. This isn't coming from Proctor's office. He's carrying Wallace's water on this one. And Wallace wants things sped up. There must be something we're missing about Shelton, and we need more time."

Stella paced further before she continued talking to Valerie. Senator Montgomery was the chair of the committee. She'd start there, she decided.

"Val, get me Senator Montgomery's number and all the numbers for the other committee members. I can't let the hearings be moved up. We're still turning over stones and looking for skeletons."

CHAPTER THIRTEEN

New York City
Stella Hanover ducked into McClanahan's
Bar & Grill on the corner of Forty-sixth
Street and Madison Avenue just before
midnight on Friday. It was only a few blocks
from her Avenue of the Americas office and
a short taxi ride to her apartment on the
east side of Central Park. She had been
working late — like every other night since
Judge Shelton's nomination — trying to
find some way to derail the inevitable.

She had talked to all the committee members several times since yesterday, when
she'd first heard that the president wanted
to move more quickly on Judge Shelton's
nomination. She wasn't confident she had
convinced them to hold the hearings as
scheduled. Senator Montgomery was on her
side, as well as six others. At least eight
wanted to move them up because Senator
Proctor — *President Wallace,* she reminded

herself — had asked them to. That left three fence riders, and she wasn't certain on which side of the fence they would fall. Desperate times demanded desperate measures.

Stella hadn't anticipated the rain. She'd left her umbrella at home that morning. So she located a copy of the *New York Times* in the lobby of her office. She used it to deflect the June drizzle while dashing from the front door of her office building to the taxi and from the taxi to the door of McClanahan's. Two seats were empty at the end of the bar, and she sat in the next to last one.

"Glass of chardonnay," she said as the bartender approached.

She laid the damp newspaper on the bar and draped the strap of her purse over the back of the bar stool. After drying her hands with a cloth napkin the bartender provided, she nibbled at some pretzels from the nearby bowl. Soon she was sipping thoughtfully on her glass of wine.

Stella stared at herself in the mirror behind the bar. She liked the image she saw in front of her even if no one else seemed to. Unmarried, she had dedicated her entire adult life to women's issues and the last fifteen years to NFAR. She had been instrumental in defeating legislation in several states designed to limit the accessibility and availability of abortions. Even when a law passed that restricted abortion rights, her organization successfully challenged the law in the federal court system. She knew, however, that any tilt in the balance of the Supreme Court could deteriorate over thirty years of successes on that issue. That's why defeating Judge Dunbar Shelton's nomination was so vitally important to Stella.

Stella had been to McClanahan's several times but didn't consider herself a regular. She took another sip from her glass and glanced around the room. It was about half full, but no one was present that Stella recognized.

A middle-aged man of Italian descent — strange for a place called McClanahan's — entered through the front door. Black hair. Leather jacket. Black denim jeans. He looked out of place, but he matched perfectly the description she had been given. He was without an umbrella and dry, so it must have stopped raining.

The man sat on the stool beside Stella at the end of the bar and ordered a drink. Stella finished the last of her wine, paid her tab, and stood to leave.

"Are you finished with your newspaper?" the Italian man asked. "I haven't had a chance to read it today."

Stella looked at the man and lifted the newspaper from the bar. "It's a little wet, but you're welcome to it." She handed the newspaper to him, grabbed her purse, and departed.

After Stella exited, the man unfolded the newspaper, revealing a white oversize envelope inside. He lifted the flap of the envelope and smiled at its contents: $25,000. He would wait until later to count the money, but he knew it was correct. His clients knew better than to stiff him for even one penny. And there would be that much again when the job was finished.

He refolded the newspaper, laid a ten-dollar bill on the bar to cover his drink, and within five minutes after Stella's departure, he, too, was on his way.

Washington DC

Holland Fletcher drove his ancient camel-colored Toyota Camry to the Supreme Court building and parked two blocks away on First Street NE. He hadn't washed the car in years. The floorboard was gritty and the dashboard dusty. The car had two hundred thousand miles, dents in both fenders, and fading paint, but it still got him where he needed to go.

It was barely past 8:00 a.m. on Tuesday. He was up earlier than usual, and he didn't like it. He reminded himself that this was why he wasn't a morning person. He looked as if he'd slept in his clothes.

He'd tried over the course of the last week to find something about the Caldwell murder that wasn't right, but he had uncovered nothing. He read online the articles from the *Tennessean* that covered the preliminary hearing of Todd Allen Grissom, MD, and it certainly appeared that the authorities had the right man. Although he'd lost interest in the case, he decided he at least needed to go to the Supreme Court like *she* had suggested. He didn't want her to think he hadn't obeyed. He was scared of her . . . whoever she was.

He entered through the public entrance, walked through the metal detector, and was issued a visitor tag. The security officer told him to discard his cup of café mocha from Starbucks that was only half empty. That made him mad, but the officer had a gun and a badge, and Holland didn't. So he complied. His first stop was the administrative office, where he demanded to see Jessica Caldwell's personnel file.

"Those records are confidential, sir," the

lady behind the counter said. She was polite but firm. She was old enough to be his mother and addressed him as if she was.

He decided he'd demonstrate how smart he was. He was an *investigative* reporter, after all, and investigative reporters were smarter than everyone else in the world. He smiled and placed the palms of his hands on the counter.

"Haven't you heard of the Freedom of Information Act?" he asked and spoke slowly when he said "Freedom of Information Act."

He then stepped back and anticipated that she would dash off to get the file and whatever else he needed. *She might even ask if I want a cup of coffee,* he thought.

But several seconds elapsed, and she didn't move. She simply glared at him with indignation.

So Holland raised his eyebrows in a way that meant *hurry up.*

Still nothing. Finally she waved him closer. He leaned over the top of the counter.

"Mr. Fletcher, personnel files are exempt from the Freedom of Information Act."

"Exempt?"

"Exempt."

"You mean that I can't see her file?"

"That's correct."

He stood up tall and spoke in a very serious voice. "You know I'll get the *Washington Post* to file a lawsuit and force you to give it to me."

She snickered and covered her mouth. "I'm sorry. I don't mean to laugh, but if that is what you want to do, then please do so. This is the Supreme Court, after all."

She continued to smile. She'd had this conversation before, Holland realized. He wasn't getting anywhere. He decided it was time to bring in the big guns.

"What if I said 'please'?" Holland smiled.

Another giggle. "That won't work either."

Defeated, Holland turned to the door. "Thanks anyway."

Maybe now the mystery caller would leave him alone.

When he spun around he bumped into a young lady he hadn't seen earlier. She was in her late twenties, slender and attractive, with curly, sandy blond hair. She was dressed professionally in a beige business suit and white blouse and carried a stack of expandable folders. Holland almost knocked them from her arms.

"Excuse me," he said and caught a couple of the folders before they fell to the floor.

After he made sure she was all right, he

exited the administrative office and hurried down the hallway.

She followed him. "Were you asking about Jessica Caldwell?" she asked to his back.

Holland pivoted abruptly. "Yes, I was. Did you know her?"

"I knew her. We shared a town house."

Finally this investigation was getting interesting. He had discovered a beautiful woman who knew Jessica Caldwell. Maybe there was a hope of a front-page story after all. Or at least a date.

"I'm Holland Fletcher." He extended his hand.

She shifted all the folders she was carrying to under her left arm and shook his hand. "I'm Tiffany. Tiffany Ramsey."

Holland reluctantly released her hand. "Nice to meet you, Tiffany. Did you say you roomed with Jessica Caldwell?"

"The last year she clerked for Justice Robinson was the first year I clerked for Justice Crawford. We shared a town house in Georgetown. Why were you asking about her?"

"I'm an investigative reporter with the *Washington Post.* It's not often that a Supreme Court law clerk is murdered. I was thinking about doing a human-interest-type story about her." Holland waited and pondered his next question. "Is there some place where we can get a cup of coffee?"

Tiffany nodded. "The Supreme Court cafeteria. Let me put these files away and we'll go."

After Tiffany took care of the files in a room that Holland was forbidden from entering, she emerged and the two headed toward the cafeteria. Once there, they walked between the metal railings that formed a short maze. As they waited in line, they chatted about things other than Jessica Caldwell before reaching the cashier. Holland ordered a cup of coffee and a cinnamon roll. Tiffany ordered just coffee. Holland paid for both, and they sat at a table in a corner of the room.

"Several of the law clerks flew to Nashville for Jessica's funeral. It was terrible . . . and so soon after Justice Robinson's death."

"I'm sure it was tough on all of you," Holland said sympathetically. He blew on his coffee and took a sip. The coffee was mediocre at best. "What can you tell me about her?"

Tiffany sat back from the table slightly and crossed her legs to the side. It appeared to Holland that she didn't plan on letting him get too close.

"I'm not sure I like talking to a reporter

about my friend. All I can say is that she was a good roommate, a good friend, and a brilliant lawyer."

Holland smiled. "That was a nice company line. Did the justices circulate a memo through the building that told everyone what to say about Jessica Caldwell?"

Tiffany looked at him over the top of her paper coffee cup. Her green eyes were intoxicating. "Of course not. It's just that I'm uncomfortable talking about her. I don't want what I say to end up in some newspaper article. That's all."

Holland finished the last of his roll and coffee. "Do you think the doctor got her pregnant?" He watched Tiffany's face and body language closely. They told something different from what came out of her mouth.

"I don't have any reason to think otherwise. Why?"

Tiffany knew something. Just what, he wasn't certain, but she knew something. Otherwise, why would she stop him in the first place when she knew he was asking about Jessica? And why would she agree to come get a cup of coffee with him? He knew it would take more than a cup of coffee to get her to show him her cards.

"No reason. I'm just looking for a story."

"That doesn't seem like a human-interest

story to me." Her eyes narrowed.

"You got me there." Holland smiled and removed a business card from his wallet and handed it to Tiffany. "If something comes up that you want to talk about, give me a call. I'm going to work on this story for a few more days. How can I reach you if I want to talk to you again?"

"You can call the operator here in the building and she will connect you." She glanced at her watch. "I really need to get back to work."

He had hoped for a home number, but no such luck. They stood and walked to the exit that opened onto First Street. Holland departed for his dented Camry and hoped Tiffany didn't see him in it.

Holland drove back to the *Post* headquarters and told his editor he was working on something big. He changed clothes at his apartment, put on a baseball cap and sunglasses, and was back on First Street by 2:30 p.m. He grabbed some lunch along the way. He parked one and a half blocks from the Supreme Court employees' secure parking lot and waited.

And waited.

At about 4:30 p.m. he saw her. She was unmistakable. A cover girl.

When he was in college, Holland and his

fraternity brothers had used a ten-point scale to measure the appearance of girls on campus. It was shallow and chauvinistic, he knew, but it gave them something to talk about. Holland continued to use the rating system and had tried to date women who were at least a seven. But most of the time he found himself with a five or a six. He decided that Tiffany was at least an eight. She exited the Supreme Court building through the employees' entrance and waved good-bye to the security officer. The officer followed her with his eyes — evidently he liked what he saw — until she sat down in a dark green Volvo C70 convertible.

Holland's Camry had difficulty following her. She drove fast and dangerously, west on Constitution Avenue, then Virginia Avenue NW. Her dark blond hair blew in the wind. He lost her briefly on Twenty-third Street, but the red light at the Pennsylvania Avenue intersection saved him. He was stopped four cars behind her, and she didn't see him. When the light changed to green, he stayed close but not too close as she zigged and zagged along M Street NW and then Wisconsin Avenue. She finally parked in front of a town house on tree-lined Thirty-seventh Street NW, closed the top to the convertible, and used a key to enter through the front door.

After Tiffany was safely inside, Holland drove past the front of the building and memorized the number on the door of the town house. One-half block northwest of Tiffany Ramsey's town house a black Mercedes-Benz S65 pulled away from the curb and fell in behind him. He glanced at it in his rearview mirror. The windows were tinted, and he couldn't see the driver clearly. That made him nervous. It trailed him for six blocks until he turned right on Van Ness Street and the Mercedes turned left. He exhaled deeply.

"You're being paranoid, Fletcher," he told himself.

The Shelton residence, Vicksburg, Mississippi
During the two weeks after his nomination, Dunbar Shelton made the rounds on Capitol Hill and the obligatory handshaking with all the senators. He met individually with each one. It was less than pleasant but necessary. One of the hazards of being nominated. He spent the next week in mock Judiciary Committee hearings orchestrated by Porter McIntosh. He hadn't been home since the Rose Garden press conference. His wife had been home once and then

returned to DC, but he had stayed in Washington.

It was Wednesday, the second week of June, and he was glad to be on his way to Vicksburg for some rest and relaxation before the confirmation hearings began. Life was much slower in the Mississippi delta than in DC.

Judge Shelton performed well during the mock hearings and would go through another round of simulated questioning before the real hearings began next week. But he needed to get away from Washington for a few days to recover.

He and Victoria — Vicki, he affectionately called her — flew on a chartered Gulfstream jet from Reagan Washington National to Jackson International Airport in Jackson, Mississippi. A limousine was waiting to take them to Vicksburg. Two FBI agents met them at the airport and escorted their limousine on the fifty-mile trek. Judge Shelton and Vicki were both exhausted from the whirlwind of activities that went along with the nomination. He dozed during the flight, and neither said much during the ride from the airport. But it was a comfortable, relaxing silence.

They arrived at their house on Fayette Street about 9:30 p.m. The sky was completely dark except for the stars glistening overhead. The FBI agents parked at the curb across the street from the Sheltons' house.

The house had been in Judge Shelton's family for generations. It was only six blocks from the court square. When he had been in private practice, he'd walked to his downtown office some days. He and Vicki had reared their four children here: three daughters and a son. Vicki had aged well despite four kids. She was five feet six and slim. Her black hair held only flecks of gray. Margaret, their oldest daughter, practiced with a one-hundred-lawyer firm in Jackson, Mississippi. John Edward, named for Judge Shelton's paternal grandfather, coached high school football in Hattiesburg. Vivian and Melissa — the family called her Missy — were sorority girls at Mississippi State University.

Judge Shelton and Vicki exited the car and entered the house. The driver carried their luggage and set it inside the door. Their part-time housekeeper, Florence, had stacked the mail and copies of the *Vicksburg Post* on the solid-oak kitchen table. Judge Shelton scanned the headlines while Vicki thumbed through the mail.

"That's a tragedy," Judge Shelton commented. He held up the previous day's edition of the newspaper and read the full article.

"What's that, dear?"

"It says Trooper Rusty Jones was shot and killed Monday night during a traffic stop on I-20 near Clinton. I knew him."

"Does it say what happened?"

"Just that he was killed and the motorist fled." He put down that newspaper and picked up the next day's edition. "Today's *Post* says that the authorities are still trying to find the motorist who shot Trooper Jones. I hope they catch him or her, whoever did it. Rusty was a good man."

"You want me to send flowers to the funeral?"

Judge Shelton had by now flipped to the obituaries in the back of the newspaper. "The obit says that a college fund for his children has been established at First National Bank. Let's make a donation to that instead of flowers."

"I'll do that tomorrow. Let's go to bed," Vicki urged. "I'm exhausted. Florence left a note that Billy Ray is coming to get your car in the morning for its regular servicing. He thought that might be easier than your driving it to his garage. The note said to leave the keys under the mat, and that way he won't have to disturb us in the morn-ing."

Judge Shelton laid the newspaper on the kitchen table and yawned and stretched. "That sounds like a good idea. And I'll tell the guys out front to be expecting him."

CHAPTER FOURTEEN

The Shelton residence, Vicksburg, Mississippi
The next morning at 7:00 a.m. Agent Brian Cole and Agent Fred Michaels sat across the street from the Sheltons' house in an unmarked, dark-colored sedan. Agent Cole was in the driver's seat. The sun was still low in the eastern sky, and clouds were nowhere to be seen. The two FBI agents were drinking coffee and eating doughnuts delivered by a patrol officer with the Vicksburg City Police.

A dented white Chevy pickup approached and parked at the curb in front of the Shelton house. A sign on the driver's door of the truck read BOLTON'S GARAGE. A middle-aged, wiry man with closely cropped red hair exited the truck wearing a grimy uniform of navy blue pants and a gray-and-blue-striped shirt with buttons down the front. He waved at the FBI agents.

"That must be Billy Ray," Agent Cole said

and gave a stiff wave back.

Agent Michaels held a chocolate-glazed doughnut in one hand and a steaming cup of coffee in the other. His mouth was too full to respond verbally, so he nodded his agreement.

Billy Ray walked up the driveway to the carport where Judge Shelton's Lexus LS was parked beside Vicki's Cadillac STS. He opened the driver's-side door and bent over to look for the keys under the floor mat. Then he eased himself into the driver's seat and closed the door.

The explosion knocked both Judge Shelton and Vicki from their bed. He landed face-down. He was dazed but not unconscious. He didn't know what had happened but knew that something was terribly wrong. He was quickly aware of the heat and billowing smoke.

"Vicki!" he called out. "Vicki!"

"I'm over here." Her voice was faint.

He lifted himself onto the side of the bed. "Where?"

"On the floor by the bed."

He crawled over the top of the bed and peered down at her lying on the floor. She was in peach-colored silk pajamas and the bedcovers were tangled around her. He slid off the bed onto the floor beside her. The room was filling with thick, black smoke.

"Are you okay?" he asked anxiously.

"I'm not sure," she mumbled. "What happened?"

"I don't know, but we've got to get out of here. Can you move?"

"I think so," she said and tried to sit up.

"Judge Shelton!" an anxious voice yelled from somewhere in the house. "Judge Shelton!"

"We're in here!"

He was trying to untangle Vicki from the bedcovers when Agents Cole and Michaels crawled into the room.

"We've got to get you out of here," Agent Cole said. "But stay on all fours. The smoke will rise to the ceiling."

"I'm not leaving without Vicki."

"Michaels will take care of her. C'mon."

Agent Cole grabbed Judge Shelton and practically dragged him toward the front door. Judge Shelton could hear sirens wailing at him from a distance. The closer to the front of the house he got, the hotter the air felt. He could hear a popping noise and smelled fire. It seemed like an eternity before he and Agent Cole finally reached the front door. The fresh air felt good.

"Can you walk?"

"I think so. Where's Vicki?"

"They're right behind us, sir."

Judge Shelton got to his feet with assistance, and Agent Cole grabbed him by the elbow. He stumbled through the door onto the porch and then into the yard. He supported himself against Agent Cole. Vicki and Agent Michaels were on their heels. Two ambulances screamed to a stop in front of the house, and paramedics raced to Judge Shelton and Vicki. Red and white lights flashed from both vehicles and sirens blared. The first fire truck came to a stop behind the ambulances and firemen scrambled in all directions.

The paramedics placed Judge Shelton in the rear of one of the ambulances and Vicki in the other. His burgundy-and-white-striped pajamas and face were covered in soot, and his left arm and hand were covered in blood. Agent Cole stood beside the open rear door of the ambulance. He stared toward the house.

The paramedics put an oxygen mask over Judge Shelton's face and began to examine him. The female paramedic wrapped a blood pressure cuff around his right biceps. She sterilized the contusion on his forehead and bandaged an abrasion on his left forearm. His knees were bruised, and he could feel them begin to swell.

"I think you're going to be all right," the female paramedic said. A stethoscope was draped around her neck. She looked into Judge Shelton's eyes and breathed a sigh of relief. "You and your wife are very lucky."

Judge Shelton finally looked back at his house and saw it engulfed in flames. The once majestic oaks behind the house were ablaze, and the one-hundred-year-old magnolia tree in the front yard was stripped bare. Firefighters ran in all directions, pulling fire hoses and spraying water. He could hear instructions being yelled. The carport was completely destroyed. The two cars were nothing more than burning metal frames. The Lexus was upside down on top of the Cadillac.

Judge Shelton pulled the oxygen mask down to his chin. "What happened?" he asked Agent Cole.

Agent Cole blinked before he shifted his gaze from the house to Judge Shelton. "I don't know for sure, sir, but it looks like a car bomb."

The law offices of Elijah J. Faulkner, Jackson, Tennessee
"Judge Blackwood called," Eli told Jill as their planning session on the Grissom case

221

began on Thursday. They were meeting in the front conference room of Eli's office and had the file contents spread over the table. "He scheduled the trial for the third week in August."

"That doesn't give us much time," Jill replied. She sat across the table from Eli, reviewing the transcript from the preliminary hearing.

"Eight weeks, to be exact. We've got a lot of work to do, and Judge Blackwood ordered us to have Tag available next Monday so a vial of blood can be drawn. The state crime lab is going to compare his DNA with the DNA found in the skin fragments under Ms. Caldwell's fingernail. Can you call him later to arrange it?" Eli shuffled a stack of papers and stacked them neatly to the side.

"I don't mind calling," Jill said, "but have you talked to either one of them since the preliminary hearing?"

Eli spoke without looking up from the document he was reading. It was a background check on Todd Allen Grissom prepared by Jimmy English. It contained a criminal-background check, a credit report, and a job history. Most of the information was easily obtainable from the Internet. Some was harder to retrieve, but none of it revealed anything that intrigued Eli about Tag.

Todd Allen Grissom was the only child of a single mother who was now deceased. He went to a private prep school in Nashville, did his undergraduate work at Vanderbilt, and his medical degree came from Emory University in Atlanta.

How was a single mother able to pay for that type of education? Eli wondered briefly.

Tag had never been arrested. He paid his debts. There was nothing in his background for Randy Dickerson to get excited about, Eli reasoned.

"Anna called last week and begged me not to withdraw from representing Tag. She said she would tell me sometime all that is going on, but she couldn't right now. She assured me that it wouldn't have an impact on the case. I think she's lying, but I hope she's right. I don't like surprises."

"Me neither," Jill commented. "What's next?"

"Get Jimmy English back on the case. I want him to dig up everything he can on the investigating detectives and the coroner. If there is any way to attack their credibility, I want to."

Jill took detailed notes on a yellow note-

223

pad before looking up at Eli. "I got it. What else?"

"Let's get discovery requests out to Dickerson's office. We need to see everything they have on this case, particularly the detectives' investigative notes."

"Is that it?"

Eli had thought about his next move long and hard over the last few days. He had acquired a certain dislike for his own client, which was a weird feeling. But he finally came to the realization that he had no option. To properly represent Tag — despite his dislike of him — he had to establish that he wasn't the father of Jessica Caldwell's fetus.

"What do you think about asking Judge Blackwood to order the body exhumed?"

"To do what? Run DNA tests on the fetus?"

Eli stood up and stretched his legs. He peered through the window in the conference room at the three-story concrete county courthouse building across the street. "Exactly. I think I've got to prove that Tag didn't father the child. That would give us an opportunity to argue that someone else had a motive for killing Ms. Caldwell."

"That'll be very disturbing to the Caldwell family."

"I've thought about that and I'm sure it will be, but I can't worry about it. If we're going to do everything we can to exonerate Tag, we've got to obtain DNA from the fetus."

Eli turned and eyed Jill. He could see from the determined look on her face that she was running through all the possibilities in her head. He waited for her to process them all.

"What if Tag's lying and the DNA matches?"

"I've thought about that, too," he said, "and it's a chance I've got to take. And if it matches, it matches. I'll know then that Tag was lying about being sterile and it'll make it harder to defend him. Not impossible . . . but certainly harder."

"If that's what you want, I'll start drafting a motion and call Dr. Grissom."

The Grissom residence, Brentwood, Tennessee

Anna could tell from Tag's end of the conversation only that the call was from either Eli or Jill. Tag was mostly listening and talking very little. After several minutes, Tag hung up the receiver on the phone in the kitchen and faced Anna.

"That was Jill," he said. "Judge Blackwood has ordered me to submit to DNA testing, and Eli is going to ask the judge to exhume Jessica's body so that he can get a DNA test on the fetus."

Tag appeared anxious. He began to pace through the kitchen with his face down toward the floor. He appeared to be thinking.

"What are you upset about?" she asked. "Eli already told you that Judge Blackwood would likely order you to submit to testing."

"I'm not upset about that."

"You think exhuming the body is a bad idea?"

Tag had his back to Anna and didn't respond.

She asked again. "Wouldn't that prove that you're not the father?"

Again, no response.

"Tag, did you hear me? It would prove that, wouldn't it?"

Tag finally turned to Anna, and his face was as pale as death.

Anna raised her hand to her mouth. Her voice was barely audible from behind it. "Oh, no. It can't be."

Vicksburg, Mississippi

It rained FBI agents in Vicksburg on Thursday. Within two hours of the explosion, one hundred agents had descended on the port city. They were inspecting every square inch of the burned wreckage that had been the Sheltons' automobiles. What could be found of Billy Ray's body was taken to the state medical examiner's office in Jackson. Forensic investigators with the FBI took control of the body fragments. The neighbors were evacuated, and pieces of the Shelton home were found as far as two blocks away.

The White House, Washington DC

At 10:00 a.m. President Wallace summoned FBI Director Leslie Hughes to the Oval Office. Director Hughes was five feet eight inches tall, bald on top, and thick in the middle. It was impossible for him to button his suit coat. He entered the office with two of his five assistants in tow. The three of them against the president and Porter. Porter liked the odds. The president was perched behind his desk looking very presidential and Porter was standing like a sentinel at his side. The door wasn't closed completely before President Wallace was on his feet.

"Les, your guys can't protect Dunbar

Shelton? I want to know what's going on, and I want to know right now."

Porter knew that Director Hughes didn't like being referred to by his first name, even by the president. It was Director Hughes or Mr. Hughes, but not Leslie and certainly not Les. That's why Porter had encouraged the president to use it.

Director Hughes maintained his composure, though. He stood near the sofa and his bodyguards flanked him on either side. He spoke without emotion. "Mr. President, we're doing everything we can to find out what happened and how. We have a hundred agents —"

President Wallace cut him off with an angry look and a dismissive hand. He marched to the front of his desk, where he was closer to Director Hughes. Porter maintained his rigid sentinel's post.

"I don't care what you're doing now, Les. I'm sure you will investigate, and that will take weeks, if not months."

"I assure you that it will not be months," Hughes interjected.

"Don't interrupt me when I'm talking!" the president shouted.

Director Hughes looked irritated. The bodyguards recoiled from the president's yelling. Porter grinned to himself.

President Wallace continued talking. "You almost killed the next Supreme Court justice and one innocent man was blown to pieces. Do you understand that, Les?"

"We had two agents on-site," Director Hughes began, talking both with his mouth and his hands. "They pulled Judge Shelton and his wife from the house before the house was fully in flames. They probably saved their lives, not almost killed them."

President Wallace sat on the edge of his desk. His arms were folded over his chest. The contempt with which he held Director Hughes was clearly expressed on his face. "If you had two agents on-site, how did someone get this close?"

"We don't know yet," Hughes admitted. "Our guys swept the area before the Sheltons arrived. The bomb must've been planted earlier in the week. We're interviewing neighbors, sanitation workers, and everyone else we can find to see if anyone saw anything."

President Wallace circled his desk and sat in his executive chair. His demeanor was calmer now. "This was a professional, Les," he said in a grandfatherly tone. "You know that no one saw anything."

"You're probably right, sir, but if I may. We do have one lead."

President Wallace looked at Porter with surprise and Porter returned the look. *A lead!* One of the bodyguards produced a manila folder and gave it to Director Hughes. He stepped forward and timidly laid it on the president's desk.

"That's good news," the president said. "Let's see it."

As President Wallace scanned the contents folder, Director Hughes spoke to no one in particular. "If we can have that video now."

One of the twenty-five microphones hidden throughout the Oval Office picked up his voice. All the microphones terminated in a communications room on the third floor of the White House.

Within seconds, a panel in the wall across the room from President Wallace's desk descended to reveal a four-by-six-foot plasma monitor. The lights in the Oval Office dimmed. Porter finally broke his stance and moved to where he had a better view of the screen.

Director Hughes began the presentation. "This is a video from a Mississippi state highway patrolman's dash-mounted camera during a traffic stop near Clinton, Mississippi. Clinton is west of Jackson, Mississippi, on I-20, toward Vicksburg. Trooper Rusty Jones is the patrolman you will see in a minute. He was wearing a lapel microphone that recorded onto the tape in the dash camera."

The video showed the gray hood of Trooper Jones's patrol car and a Lincoln Town Car with Alabama plates. The blue lights from the patrol car reflected off the Town Car and the pavement. After a few seconds Trooper Jones was seen walking from his car toward the Town Car.

"Increase the audio," Director Hughes spoke into the room.

The volume increased, and Trooper Jones's voice could be heard. "You're going a little fast, aren't you, buddy? Where's the fire?"

"It's been a long day, Officer," a voice from inside the car said. The contrast between Trooper Jones's Southern drawl and the Northern accent of the driver was discernible. "I was just trying to get to Jackson and perhaps was going a little too fast. It won't happen again, I promise."

"I'm sure it won't. I need to see your license and registration, please."

"If you could just let me go this one time, I promise it won't happen again."

"Sir, either give me your license and registration or step out of the car."

"You're making a mistake, Officer."

231

Trooper Jones placed his right hand on the handle of the nine-millimeter pistol strapped to his hip and took two steps back.

Porter, glued to the screen, hardly blinked.

"Step out of the car!" Trooper Jones ordered.

The blast of a gunshot reverberated through the speakers in the Oval Office. Both President Wallace and Porter jumped. Porter watched as Trooper Jones's head snapped back and his body crumpled to the ground. The Lincoln Town Car sped away and the video continued to show Trooper Jones's lifeless body lying on the pavement. His nine-millimeter pistol was still in the holster. The screen went black.

Director Hughes walked toward the screen. "State police were on the scene in seven minutes. Roadblocks were set up throughout the area, but the guy slipped through somehow. The car was found abandoned near Ridgeland, Mississippi. It had been reported stolen two days earlier in Tupelo. The tags were stolen from a junkyard near Culman, Alabama."

"What's that got to do with the bombing at Judge Shelton's house?" the president asked.

"We think this is the guy who planted the bomb."

President Wallace and Porter shot another look at each other. Then the president turned his attention back to Director Hughes. "If that's the guy and you can catch him, I'll take back everything I said earlier and what I said before you arrived."

Director Hughes smiled. "Bring up the close-up," he said into the room.

The screen flickered again and an image appeared.

"This is an enhancement of the driver's-side mirror," Hughes explained. "The driver's face appeared in it briefly. Probably less than half a second, but that was enough. We were able to get enough of the face to make an identification, although not a hundred percent."

"Who is he?"

"We think it's Joe Moretti, a made member of the Italian Mafia with the Colombo family in Brooklyn. You have our file on him there in front of you."

The image disappeared and the lights became brighter. Porter rapidly blinked to adjust to the light.

President Wallace picked up the folder and scrutinized its contents. "You think? When will you know for sure?"

"We're analyzing the voice from the driver with known recordings of Moretti. We should know later today if there's a match."

President Wallace straightened in his chair, and Porter returned to his position beside him. "Can you find him?" the president asked.

Director Hughes nodded. "We can find him. It might take some time, but we can find him."

"Well, don't just stand there. Go find him," the president ordered.

President Wallace and Porter watched Director Hughes and the bodyguards leave. All three looked very confident.

"You know he won't find him, don't you?" Porter asked.

President Wallace rubbed his forehead in anguish. Porter shared his concern. They were prepared for political battles over Judge Shelton's nomination, but an assassination attempt had been beyond their wildest thoughts. And they were relying on Director Hughes, of all people, to find the culprit.

"You're probably right. He's an imbecile, and I probably should fire him. But he did get this video. He might stumble onto something else. We'll give him some time."

CHAPTER FIFTEEN

The White House, Washington DC

President Wallace relaxed in the sitting room of the living quarters on the second floor of the White House and completed his morning devotional. It was Friday, the day after the Shelton car bombing. He was still shaken. He had tossed and turned all night. Two people — fathers, sons, husbands — were dead because someone didn't want Dunbar Shelton on the Supreme Court. The president had spoken with Judge Shelton yesterday afternoon by telephone. He said he was all right but didn't sound all right.

The sitting room had been only slightly redecorated when the president and Lauren moved into the residence. Former President Mitchell's wife had completely redecorated the entire living area, and the Wallaces didn't think it was a wise expenditure of the people's money to remodel it again. So they had made only a few modifications to personalize the White House living quarters.

President Wallace had already showered, shaved, and dressed for the day. Dark blue suit, white starched shirt, and a navy-and-white-striped tie were his attire, although he hadn't yet put on his suit coat. He usually conducted his devotions in the Oval Office, but today for some reason he was inclined to spend time with God before going downstairs to the West Wing. So, while Lauren was preparing herself for her busy schedule of First Lady activities, President Wallace sat on the cream-colored sofa in the sitting room and studied a familiar passage from Jeremiah 29. Even though he had read the passage dozens of times, it took on a new meaning today.

Before long President Wallace found himself praying aloud, on his knees, by the sofa. The room was completely silent aside from his voice.

Awe flooded through him as he spoke directly to God. "Your Word says that you know the plans you have for me, and that gives me great peace and at the same time great humility. But I don't know what's happening. Two men are dead, and Dunbar and Vicki were almost killed. How can that be in your plans?

"Lord, I pray for the families of Rusty Jones and Billy Ray Bolton. Love and comfort them. Hold them in the very palm of your hand and protect their hearts and minds. I also pray for Dunbar and Vicki. I pray that you will heal their bodies and their minds.

"Father, your Word also says that you cause all things to work together for good to those who love you. I stand on that promise and believe that something good will come from these terrible events.

"I know that you have placed me in this position of trust for some purpose, and my desire is to be completely in your will. I pray that the decisions I make will be guided by your hand and will fulfill your purpose for this great country. I pray for wisdom and discernment. And I pray that you will restore this great country to the God-fearing nation it once was."

President Wallace continued to pray — praising God, thanking God, and worshipping God — for the better part of thirty minutes before being interrupted by a knock on the door by one of his security detail.

The Faulkner residence, Jackson, Tennessee
Eli arose earlier than normal on Friday and slipped on a pair of blue jeans and a white

T-shirt before tiptoeing from the bedroom to the adjoining study. It was still dark outside — daybreak was at least an hour away — and Sara was sleeping. He softly closed the door that connected the bedroom to the study and triggered the lamp on the top of his desk. Stretching back in his leather desk chair, he propped his feet on the desk and clasped his hands together behind his head. It was a sitting position he used often — particularly when a case was eating at him.

The Grissom case had begun to weigh on him over the last several days, and he'd hardly slept last night. Sara was right. Murder cases always burdened him, but this one was beginning to make all the rest pale by comparison. He felt as if he had been deceived by Anna into taking the case.

But was it really deception? Had he made the assumption that Tag was the father of Anna's unborn child — if she *was* pregnant — without asking the correct questions? *It doesn't matter now,* he tried to convince himself.

The other troubling part was exhuming Jessica Caldwell's body. Disturbing an interred body just didn't seem right. It would upset the Caldwell family, but that couldn't be helped. It might prove that Tag was, in fact, the father, but that was a risk Eli was willing to take.

Eli lowered his feet to the floor, closed his eyes, and crossed his arms. *Why does this case bother me so much?*

As soon as the words passed through his mind, he recalled his and Sara's conversation at the Loveless Café. Perhaps it wasn't the case itself that was weighing on him. Perhaps it was a burden for the souls of Tag and Anna Grissom. At that moment, a yearning to share the gospel with them began to grow. It engulfed much of the space that his self-pity, from their perceived deception, had. His disgust and distrust didn't totally disappear, but now he had a renewed focus.

The River Region Medical Center,
Vicksburg, Mississippi

Judge Shelton's hospital room at River Region Medical Center was dimly lit. After he was cleaned up and examined from head to toe, the medical personnel decided his injuries weren't very serious. That was a relevant term. They were serious to him, but not life threatening. But as a precaution, his treating doctor had admitted him to the hospital for observation the previous night and had prescribed continuous oxygen because of his extensive smoke inhalation. He told Judge Shelton that he could leave later that day. He had showered and put on clean navy blue pajamas and was resting in his hospital bed. The tubes running to each nostril aggravated him, and he tugged at them repeatedly.

Two FBI agents stood guard outside the door to his room and a dozen others were either in the hospital or patrolling the parking areas. One attempt on his life was one too many. There couldn't be another. There was a soft knock at the door and then it opened. His son, John Edward, entered, followed by Judge Shelton's three daughters.

"Hey, Dad. How are you feeling today?" John Edward asked.

Judge Shelton was glad to see them and glad they looked like their mother. They all had her deep black hair, with the exception of Missy, who had somehow acquired a blond-hair gene from his side of the family. He pressed a button on the bed railing that raised the head of the bed to more of a sitting position. The children gathered around and took turns giving their father a hug.

He squeezed each one tightly. "I'm doing fine," he said. "A little sore, but that's about it. They're going to let me leave this afternoon. Have you checked on your mother this morning?"

Margaret spoke up. "She finally fell asleep a few minutes ago, the nurse said, and we didn't want to wake her. She couldn't get comfortable last night with that cast on her left arm, so she didn't get much rest."

"She might need to stay another day or so," Vivian said.

"How's the house?" Judge Shelton asked.

The siblings looked at each other.

After two or three seconds, John Edward answered. "It's gone, Dad. Completely destroyed."

"Everything?"

"We might find a few things to salvage, but not much."

Judge Shelton felt sick to his stomach. *A lifetime of memories gone, just like that.* "Did you talk to Billy Ray's widow like I asked you to?"

"I did," John Edward replied. "She was very grateful that you offered to pay for the funeral. They don't know yet when the FBI will release his body."

Again there was an uncomfortable silence. The siblings eyed each other again. Margaret nudged John Edward.

He spoke with hesitation. "Dad, we've been talking. We want you to withdraw from this Supreme Court thing."

Judge Shelton shifted position in the bed and grimaced. He ached all over, but his physical pain paled in comparison to the fear he had for his and Vicki's safety. His kids were scared, too. Concern was evident on their faces, and with good reason. Somebody out there wanted him dead, and none of them would rest easy until he or she or they were apprehended.

"Why do you want me to withdraw?"

"This was too close," Margaret said. "We don't want to risk losing you or mom." She sounded like a lawyer.

But he wasn't a quitter. His father had taught him to see through to the end whatever he started, no matter how tough the going got. *Would Dad say the same thing about this?* Judge Shelton was certain he would.

"I lay awake last night thinking about that very thing," he said slowly. "Part of the night I wanted to quit, and I almost called the president. But the more I thought about it, the more I realized that if I withdraw, then whoever did this wins. They get exactly what they want."

"But, Dad," they protested in unison.

He held up his hand to stop them from continuing their protest. "When your mother is awake, I'm going to talk to her about this. If she is against my continuing, then I'll reconsider. But I don't plan on letting them — whoever they are — win."

The law offices of Elijah J. Faulkner, Jackson, Tennessee

Eli was back to his putter to think. It was Monday morning, the third week of June. Sara had surprised him with an automatic ball returner for his birthday, but it worked only if he made a putt. He still had to walk across the room to retrieve the balls that rolled past, and that happened more often than not. He kicked his black leather loafers to the side and aligned his next putt. His necktie dangled, in the way.

Eli had thought about Tag's case most of the weekend. It had drained him. He hadn't been able to work much on any other project in the last two weeks. Other files were piling up and he didn't like it, and some of the clients regularly gave Barbara an earful. Sara commented again about the pressure she could see he was under.

Things were weird. Tag claimed to be sterile, but two women he had a relationship with — Anna Grissom and Jessica Caldwell — were both pregnant. Or at least Anna claimed to be pregnant. There was no proof of that fact other than her and Tag's word, and Eli wasn't convinced he believed either of them. The pieces of the puzzle didn't fit. The *clink* of the putter head tapping a golf ball was audible but didn't break his thought process. No wonder he was missing so many putts.

Jill knocked softly on the door frame in the middle of his backswing and entered his office. The putt sailed wide right.

"I hope I'm not interrupting anything." Her voice was full of mockery.

"Not anymore. You just caused me to lose the Masters."

Jill smiled. Her black hair was pulled back and held in place with a plastic hair clip. She wore a beige skirt, white blouse, and high heels. "I thought you would like to see these." She handed Eli a stack of documents.

Leaning the putter against the wall, he carried the documents to his desk and sat down in his executive leather chair.

"Our PI was able to get copies of the investigative file from the DA," Jill continued. "That's the first set of documents. But I think you will find the second set more interesting. It's the follow-up report on Tag Grissom."

Eli deposited the top stack of documents on his desk and began to read through the second stack. He read two pages and looked up. Jill stood at the front of his desk.

"Interesting," he exclaimed. "This case gets weirder all the time."

"I thought so, too."

"This says that Tag's mother died mysteriously not long after he finished medical school."

"It was a one-car accident, and the authorities thought it was suspicious. But nothing ever came of it."

Eli studied the report again. "Her car went over the side of a cliff, but no skid marks. That makes me think she either wanted to die or the brakes failed."

"The police could never conclusively determine whether the brakes were tampered with or not. And Tag, being the next of kin, asked them to drop the investigation."

Eli wrinkled his nose. "It doesn't quite pass the smell test, does it?"

"No doubt there's something weird about it. Your mother dies under suspicious circumstances and you don't want the authorities to investigate? When my parents died, I wanted the guy who hit us to rot in jail. And my parents died in an accident, not something that was intentional."

Eli frowned. "And another thing. I remember thinking about it when I found out, but I didn't consider it important at the time. How did Tag's mother — a single mother at that — send him to a private school, Vanderbilt, and Emory? That's a very expensive education on a single parent's income."

"Family money?"

"The PI's report doesn't reflect any significant family wealth," Eli said. "Tag earns a handsome salary as a cardiologist and puts some of it away. But that's it."

"He's hiding something."

Eli drummed his fingers on the desktop and exhaled. "I'd say that he and Anna aren't just hiding *one* something but a *bunch* of somethings."

The James S. Brady Press Briefing Room, the White House, Washington DC

President Wallace's staff arranged a news conference in the James S. Brady Press Briefing Room of the White House on Monday afternoon at 1:00 p.m. eastern time. The president hated meeting with the White House press corps more than anything else. He didn't trust them. But he'd decided it was time to address the media and the country regarding Judge Shelton. A podium was erected with a blue top and a gray trunk. A dark blue drape covered the wall behind the podium and a large plaque of the White House hung in front of the drape.

White floodlights beamed from the ceiling in all directions and washed over the platform. A shadow didn't have a chance. The room was filled with representatives of all the major news outlets. The president and his entourage entered from behind the platform, and President Wallace bounded up to his place behind the podium amid rapid *click*s from camera shutters. The remainder of his entourage, including Porter, stood to the side, stage right. President Wallace wore a dark blue suit and a red tie. He wanted to look presidential and in charge, and he did.

"I want to thank all of you for coming today," the president began. He glanced down occasionally at the statement prepared by his speechwriter. The pace of his words was slow and deliberate. "As you know, four days ago there was an attempt on the life of Supreme Court nominee Judge Dunbar Shelton and his wife, Victoria. Their lives were spared, but an innocent man was killed. I've spoken to Billy Ray Bolton's widow and told her that the federal government will do everything it can to bring to justice the individual or individuals who committed this horrible crime."

President Wallace slid the top sheet from his prepared remarks to the right-hand side of the podium and began to read from the second page. "It has been a very difficult time for the Shelton family. Judge Shelton is a faithful public servant. His only desire is to serve the people of this great country in any way he can. He was nominated by me to fill a seat of honor, and his reward was an attempt on his life."

The speech had been written by one of his favorite speechwriters. Porter liked her, too. The words in the speech directed him to pause for dramatic effect at this point, and he did before continuing. He looked directly into the television cameras and banged his fist on the podium.

"His attacker or attackers will not go unpunished. I have spoken to Judge Shelton many times over the last several days, mainly to check on his well-being. But I also offered to allow him to withdraw his nomination to the Supreme Court. No man or woman should live in fear of his or her life simply because they desire to serve the public good."

President Wallace shifted his weight from one side to the other and moved to page three. "Judge Shelton contacted me this morning. He, his wife, and his children have discussed what is best for their family. They have prayed earnestly. And after much prayer and discussion Judge Shelton informed me that he desires to go forward with the confirmation process. I told him how much I admired him and that his country greatly appreciates him."

"Because of the injuries sustained by Judge Shelton and Victoria, it will be impossible to begin the confirmation hearings next week. They need time to recuperate and to deal with insurance and other logistical things that necessarily follow an event such as this. I have asked the Senate leadership and the chairman of the Senate Judiciary Committee to delay the hearings until the week after the Fourth of July break. Senator Proctor and Senator Montgomery concur in my assessment. We have agreed that the confirmation hearings will begin the Monday after the Fourth of July."

President Wallace shuffled his speech together and scanned the crowd. "I'll be glad to take any questions."

A female reporter with the AP who was seated in the front row raised her hand.

The president pointed to her. "Yes, Olivia."

"Mr. President, do the authorities have

any suspects at this point?"

He didn't particularly like Olivia Nelson. She tried to burn him in her reporting every chance she got. But she was one of the senior members of the White House press corps, and that meant she was entitled, on a rotating basis, to ask the first question at press conferences. He had known this question would be asked. But he also knew he couldn't answer it — yet.

"Olivia, it would be imprudent for me to talk about the investigation at this point. The FBI is following up on every lead, and Director Hughes has assured me that his office will do everything it can to apprehend the person or persons responsible for this attack as soon as possible."

President Wallace scanned the crowd again. Hands went up everywhere, and pleas of "Mr. President, Mr. President" echoed through the room; it sounded like kindergarteners trying to get the teacher's attention. He pointed to a male reporter from NBC who sat on the third row, left side.

"Mr. President, will this delay in the confirmation hearings change your strategy in any way?"

The president placed his hands on either side of the podium and tilted his head toward the microphones. "I don't think it will have any impact on the confirmation process whatsoever. We expect that Judge Shelton will receive a fair up-or-down vote in the Senate and that he will be confirmed."

President Wallace glanced at Porter, who gave him the sign that it was time to end the press conference. "That's all the time I have for now. Thank you for your attendance and patience."

He stepped down from the platform and was ushered through the door behind the platform by Porter and other members of his staff. The *click*ing from the camera shutters resumed and intensified, and a chorus of "Mr. President, Mr. President" rang out until the exit door completely closed.

CHAPTER SIXTEEN

The Metropolitan Nashville-Davidson County Courthouse, Nashville, Tennessee

"All rise," the bailiff called out as Judge Blackwood entered the courtroom and assumed his position on the bench. Judge Blackwood's docket had been backlogged, and it had taken several days to schedule a hearing after Eli's motion to exhume Jessica Caldwell's body was filed. But the hearing had finally arrived. Eli, Jill, Tag, and Anna were in their respective chairs from the preliminary hearing. Eli still had yet to change Tag's appearance to a more likeable one. Randy Dickerson was there, too, looking very important at the prosecution table.

The room was crowded again with reporters and media types. Eli and the others had been accosted in the hallway by a larger throng than at the preliminary hearing. A request to exhume a body was rare, and this was a high-profile case. The combination created nothing short of a media frenzy.

Jordan and Heddy Caldwell were there, too. Eli noticed them when he entered. There was someone else with them today, and Eli recognized him as Reese Finch of McAllister & Finch — Jessica Caldwell's previous employer. Reese's appearance hadn't changed in years: half-lens spectacles, wispy white hair, and a bow tie. Every time Eli had seen Reese Finch he was wearing a bow tie.

"Mr. Faulkner," Judge Blackwood began. "We're here on your motion to exhume the decedent's body. I'll be glad to hear from you at this time."

Eli stood and approached the podium that stood between the defense table and the prosecution table. He opened his three-ring notebook on the top of the podium and skimmed his notes as he began.

"Your Honor, we appreciate the court hearing us on such short notice. But the court has scheduled the trial in this case for the third week of August. That is less than two months away, and we didn't think we had time to delay seeking a ruling on this matter much longer."

"I'm aware of the time constraints, Mr. Faulkner, and the court is glad to accommodate. But let's get to your motion."

Interruptions by Judge Blackwood weren't unusual.

Eli returned to his notes unfazed. "If it pleases the court, we're asking for an order that Ms. Caldwell's body be exhumed so we can obtain DNA testing on the fetus to determine whether the DNA matches that of my client. The state has already obtained a blood sample from my client to compare against skin fragments found under the decedent's fingernail. So —"

"Do you even know whether the fetus is still available?" Judge Blackwood interrupted. "Most of the time the internal organs are thrown into the incinerator during the autopsy."

Eli wasn't easily rattled, even by judges who didn't know what they were talking about. "The coroner's report doesn't indicate that the organs were destroyed during the autopsy, but we have subpoenaed Dr. Stephenson to today's hearing to clarify that point."

Eli could hear Randy rise from his chair and pivoted to look at him.

"Your Honor," Randy said without acknowledging Eli, "the state isn't opposed to Mr. Faulkner's motion. In fact, we're in support of it. We believe that the DNA will match the defendant's."

"But we're opposed to it," came a voice from the gallery.

Eli and Randy both turned and saw Reese Finch standing in the front row of the gallery.

"May I be heard?" Reese asked Judge Blackwood.

"It's highly unusual, Mr. Finch, but step forward."

Reese stepped through the swinging gate in the bar that separated the area of the courtroom reserved for lawyers from the parties in the gallery and approached the podium. Eli stepped away from the podium.

"I'm Reese Finch, with McAllister —"

"We all know who you are, Mr. Finch," Judge Blackwood said. "Tell me why you're here."

Eli noticed that the back of Reese's ears became red at being interrupted by Judge Blackwood.

"I represent Mr. and Mrs. Caldwell, the parents of the decedent," Reese said in a wounded tone. He pointed back at Jordan and Heddy Caldwell, who sat in the front row of the gallery. Heddy dabbed lightly at her eyes with a tissue, and Jordan placed his arm around her.

"My clients are opposed to the request of defense counsel to exhume Ms. Caldwell's body. It will be very traumatic to my clients to have their daughter's grave desecrated at the request of the very man who killed her." Reese's voice rose as he spoke. Now he pointed a menacing finger at Tag. "He's already done enough. Why can't he just leave her body alone?"

Eli had heard all he could stand. He approached the podium. "May I speak again, Your Honor?"

"Go ahead."

"I certainly recognize how disturbing the possibility of an exhumation is to the Caldwell family. I struggled with that before ever filing our request with the court. But the truth is that Mr. and Mrs. Caldwell don't have the standing to oppose the motion. They are not parties to this litigation. And my client has his Sixth Amendment right to be confronted with the witnesses against him and to be assisted by counsel. To effectively assist Mr. Grissom, I believe we have a right to know who fathered Ms. Caldwell's unborn baby."

"And, Mr. Dickerson, does the court understand you to say that the state is not opposed to having the body exhumed?"

"That's right, Your Honor."

"Mr. Finch, I'm afraid Mr. Faulkner is correct. You don't have the standing to oppose the motion. But before I rule on Mr. Faulkner's request, I'd like to hear from Dr. Stephenson."

With that, Dr. Stephenson was escorted into the courtroom. He hobbled to the witness chair, was sworn in, and sat down. Eli, Randy, and Reese all returned to their respective seats as well.

"Dr. Stephenson," Judge Blackwood began. "I have a couple of questions. Were Ms. Caldwell's internal organs destroyed during the autopsy?"

"No, sir, they weren't. In a lot of autopsies the organs are destroyed, but in this case the cause of death was strangulation. We opened the uterus and measured the fetus, but otherwise the organs were left intact."

"Tell me this, Dr. Stephenson. Is it medically possible at this point to obtain a credible DNA sample from Ms. Caldwell's fetus?"

Dr. Stephenson scratched his head through his flattop and winced ever so slightly before looking at Judge Blackwood again. "Forensic science has come a long way in the last several years, Judge. Yeah, I think so. In fact, I'd say that it is just not possible, but *probable* that reliable DNA tests can be run on a tissue sample from the fetus."

"If I order the body exhumed, how long do you think it will take your office to conduct the exhumation, obtain the tissue samples, and reinter the body?"

"Let's see," Dr. Stephenson said as he began to calculate days in his head. "This is Wednesday, and I think we can have that done by the end of next week."

"Thank you, Dr. Stephenson. You may step down."

Dr. Stephenson left the witness chair and exited through the same door he had entered. Eli had leaned back in his chair during the colloquy between Judge Blackwood and Dr. Stephenson but now sat up straight in anticipation of Judge Blackwood's ruling.

"Mr. Faulkner, I'm going to grant your request and order that the body be exhumed. The coroner's office will be directed to obtain samples to be sent to the state crime lab and samples to be sent to a lab of your choosing." Judge Blackwood then focused on Reese Finch and the Caldwells. "Mr. Finch, I know that isn't what your clients wanted to hear, but I think the law requires me to do whatever is necessary to ensure that Mr. Grissom receives a fair trial."

Judge Blackwood returned his attention

to Eli and Randy. "Anything further, gentlemen?"

"No, sir, Your Honor," both Eli and Randy replied almost simultaneously.

"All right, then. The court will adjourn."

Judge Blackwood banged his gavel, and the bailiff commanded, "All rise," as the judge left the courtroom. Eli could hear Heddy Caldwell crying softly in the gallery behind the prosecution table.

Eli turned to Tag and Anna. "Jill has some research she needs to do while we're in town. Can I come out to your house while I wait for her? There's something I want to talk to you about."

Anna and Tag exchanged a look before Anna nodded at Tag.

"Sure," Tag replied. "In about an hour?"

"That would be great. I won't stay long, I promise. See you then."

The Grissom residence, Brentwood, Tennessee

Approximately an hour after the court hearing, Eli arrived at the Grissom residence and Anna greeted him at the front door. She escorted Eli to the den, where Tag waited.

Anna couldn't refer to their house as a home. It had become nothing more than a place to live. But it was a very rich and lavish place to live — the den had high ceilings, a hand-carved marble mantel, and the finest of imported furniture.

Anna would have traded it all if it would have made her marriage to Tag stronger and better.

"I thought the hearing this morning went well," Eli said. He parked on the leather sofa while Tag settled into one chair and Anna into the other. Eli had left his suit coat in his car and had loosened his necktie.

The television was off, so other than Eli's voice, the room was strangely quiet. It wasn't often that Anna didn't have some audible noise in the house — the television, the stereo, or something else — because there usually was very little conversation between her and Tag to fill the void. But today there was something different about the quietness. Instead of something to be avoided, it seemed rather peaceful.

"What do you plan on doing with the DNA results?" Tag asked.

Anna knew Tag was concerned about the results but would never tell Eli that he was or why.

Eli crossed his right leg over the left at the knee. "In the movies or on TV, you might hear a lawyer refer to it as plan B. When all of the hard evidence points toward your client, you look for someone else at whom to point the finger. Based on what you told me the other day, the fetus's DNA *can't* match your DNA. We would then have someone else to point our finger at — even if we don't know who it is. That's plan B."

"What's plan A?"

"Plan A is to prove you didn't do it."

"I like plan A better."

"Me, too," Eli said. "But that's not why I wanted to come by and talk to you."

Anna noticed some nervousness in Eli's body language. She had never seen that in him before. He had always appeared very confident. Eli's nervousness garnered her attention.

"I feel led to talk to you about something," Eli began. "And it may seem odd coming from me, your lawyer. But I'll just come right out and say it. Do either of you know whether you would go to heaven if you died?"

Tag appeared startled. He flung a glance at Anna. "That's an odd question. I'm sure that we both will. But what does that have to do with my case?"

"It doesn't have anything to do with your case. As a Christian, I believe that I should talk with other people about whether they are Christians or not. And I wanted to talk with you about it as well. That's all."

"Well, don't worry about us," Tag assured Eli. "We're Christians."

"How do you know for sure?"

Anna sat quietly, her vision fixed on Eli. Her heart began to race. There was something about the way Eli spoke. His words had a different tone to them from what she had heard from him before. They weren't carefully measured. He didn't sound like a lawyer. She knew when she had talked with Eli before that he was genuine and honest and cared. But this was beyond mere professional concern. He seemed more like a friend who was worried about her and Tag's well-being, but there was nothing wrong with them, was there? Out of the corner of her eye she saw Tag change position in his chair.

"I don't understand," Tag said. "Know what for sure?"

"How do you know for sure that you're going to heaven if you were to die?"

"Isn't everybody?" Tag shot back.

"Not exactly," Eli responded. "Only those who have accepted Jesus Christ as their personal Lord and Savior." He shifted his gaze back and forth between Anna and Tag.

Anna studied Eli. Now he looked comfortable and at ease . . . confident in what he said.

"Have each of you done that?"

Eli's words were direct and unavoidable. His question caused a chill to run along Anna's spine. The inside of her mouth became dry and she couldn't speak, even if she'd wanted to. Her hands grew clammy. She rubbed them together and hoped that neither Eli nor Tag noticed.

Anna had rarely been to church. Even when she was a child, her parents took her only on special occasions, such as Easter and Christmas. She had heard the name of Jesus Christ but had never had anyone ask her the questions that Eli now asked. This strange mix of anxiousness and desire and emptiness all rolled into one was inexplicable to her. She had never felt anything like it before. Her eyes darted back and forth between Eli and Tag.

"Look, Eli," Tag said. "We appreciate your concern, but you don't have anything to worry about. I have no doubt that both Anna and I will be in heaven when we die. One way or the other."

"But I don't think you understand how it works," Eli pressed. "People don't just end up in heaven without —"

Tag cut Eli off in midsentence. "We understand completely, and I don't want to talk about this anymore."

Anna wished Tag had kept quiet and allowed Eli to continue. Something inside her yearned to hear more of what Eli had to say.

Eli relented. "I won't bring it up again, but if either of you ever want to talk any more about it, I'll be more than happy to talk to you."

Eli stood to leave and thanked Tag and Anna for listening to him. He said goodbye, and Anna escorted him to the door. She wanted to grab his arm and beg him not to leave. But he left anyway. She stood in the doorway and watched him drive away.

When she returned to the den, Tag was still there.

"What did you think about what Eli said?" she asked.

"I'll tell you what I think. I think we have a Jesus freak for a lawyer. That's what I think."

The Faulkner residence, Jackson, Tennessee
"Tell me how your visit with Tag and Anna went," Sara requested as they sat down for dinner. Eli detected an excitement in her voice that he'd unfortunately have to dispel. Both of them had been praying for an op-

portunity for Eli to share Jesus Christ with Tag and Anna. He wasn't interested in his meal. He was still bothered by his meeting with Tag and Anna.

"Not very well. They didn't want to hear anything I had to say. It was strange. I don't recall ever being in a more awkward situation, where I was talking about something that no one else in the room cared anything about."

Sara passed him a roll and filled his water glass. "I hate to hear that. I really thought that this was going to be the divine appointment we talked about. But that just goes to show that we don't get to decide when the Holy Spirit will move."

Sara always knew what to say and spoke with wisdom. God did have a plan. He had a plan for Sara and him and for Tag and Anna. Eli needed to find it, rather than trying to make God follow his.

He smiled. "You're right, and I'm not going to worry about it anymore. I'll just keep praying for them. Some people sow and others reap. Maybe a seed has been planted that someone will harvest later."

"At least you tried. Not everyone who claims to be a Christian is bold enough to share their faith with others."

Chapter Seventeen

The Greenhills Memorial Garden,
Nashville, Tennessee

A steady drizzle pelted Jill Baker's umbrella. Some of it splattered against the sleeve of her hooded blue raincoat. The ground beneath her waterproof Timberland boots was soggy. It was a miserable Friday morning, and under her breath she complained that Eli had made her come. But someone needed to be present when the body was exhumed to make sure everything went correctly, and it made more sense for that somebody to be her instead of Eli.

At least that's what he'd said.

She watched as the employees from the coroner's office unloaded a backhoe from its resting place on a flatbed trailer, and soon the grass and earth that covered Jessica Caldwell's grave were being removed rapidly. The coroner's office employees were soaked and muddy. Time constraints necessitated that the exhumation be conducted that day, regardless of the weather. It was a short week the following week because of the holiday, and Dr. Stephenson had promised Judge Blackwood to have Jessica Caldwell's body back in the ground by the next Friday.

Greenhills Memorial Garden was not far from the Caldwell residence in Belle Meade. Jordan and Heddy Caldwell were both standing nearby, watching the violation of their daughter's grave. Jordan wore a maroon, long-sleeve pullover and held a blue-and-white golf umbrella large enough to protect both himself and Heddy. Heddy wore a blue raincoat similar to Jill's and had her hands in the pockets. Jill noticed the epitaph on the grave marker: OUR LOVING DAUGHTER. She wondered what Jordan and Heddy thought as they watched the coroner's office employees unsealing Jessica's grave.

Jill didn't like cemeteries. They caused too many bad memories to surface. There were only two funerals she had forced herself to go to since her parents had died fifteen years ago. One was her grandmother's and the other a college sorority sister. Her grandmother had reared her and her brother after their parents had died in a car wreck while

the family was vacationing in the Gatlin-
burg area of the Smoky Mountains in
eastern Tennessee. She had been fourteen,
her brother sixteen. They had survived the
accident, but their parents were buried in
the family cemetery in Springfield, Tennessee. She and her brother were left with only
$150,000 each from insurance. After their
grandmother died, her brother had moved
to the Florida Keys to work on a shrimp
boat. His money was gone. Jill's was safe
and growing. Her family was now at the law
offices of Elijah J. Faulkner.

Randy Dickerson was at the cemetery
also. He made Jill's skin crawl. He was
dressed like a Chicago criminal-defense
lawyer. His pin-striped suit was getting
soaked under his small umbrella, and that
pleased her. He sloshed over to where Jill
was standing. The soles of his wingtip shoes
were covered with mud and wet grass.

"I see Eli sent you to do the dirty work,"
Randy said.

"He was afraid he might melt but knew
that neither of us would."

Randy smiled. "You don't like me very
much, do you?"

"Don't flatter yourself. I don't like you at
all."

Randy stopped smiling. They both directed their attention to the men working at Jessica's grave site.

"You know you can't win this one, don't you?" he said patronizingly.

The rhythm of the drizzle intensified on Jill's umbrella. Randy was getting wetter, and that pleased her more.

"If anybody can, it'll be Eli."

"Not even Eli." Randy spoke confidently. "You know your client's DNA matched the skin fragments under the decedent's fingernail, don't you?"

"Eli told me the report was back, and there was a match. But it doesn't matter. We're still going to win."

Randy chuckled. "You're not going to win, and this certainly isn't going to help." He pointed at the men who were unearthing Jessica's grave.

By now Jill was mad. She was also worried about the DNA testing on the fetus and couldn't tell whether Randy knew more than he was telling or not.

"Whoa, that's enough," one of the coroner's employees yelled.

He must be the foreman, Jill thought.

The employee held his hand up at the backhoe operator as a sign to stop. "I can see the top of the vault. You guys climb down in there and shovel the rest of that out by hand."

He waved at two other employees who slid down the muddy embankment and began tossing scoops of mud onto the large pile already created by the backhoe operator. Jill watched as the two men fully exposed the top of the concrete burial vault. After several more minutes, the top of the vault was removed, and straps and chains were attached to the coffin inside. As delicately as possible, the coffin containing Jessica's decomposing body was removed by a hydraulic lift and placed in the back of a box van waiting to carry it to the coroner's office. The lid to the concrete vault was replaced to keep water, mud, and debris out of it until the coffin could be returned.

Jill saw Heddy Caldwell turn her head and bury it in Jordan's shoulder as the coffin crested from the burial vault.

"I hope this is worth it, Eli," Jill whispered to herself.

The van drove away with the coffin secured inside. Mud, water, and grass splattered from the tires until it reached the pavement of the narrow driveway, then left the cemetery grounds.

Jill walked the few steps back to her car without saying good-bye to Randy. She sat in her car with the engine running. The windshield wipers cleared away the drops of rain almost as quickly as they fell. She watched the Caldwells as they miserably made their way to their car.

To her surprise, they returned to Jessica's grave. In the rain they set fresh flowers on the top of the tombstone.

For the first time Jill read the entire inscription on the marker. The day the coroner's office employees removed her body from the grave would have been Jessica's twenty-eighth birthday.

Jill rested her forehead on the steering wheel and felt miserable.

The Grissom residence, Brentwood, Tennessee

"I forbid you to go," Tag said to Anna.

That angered her. She wasn't a child. She would make her own decisions. "Tag, I'm going. And you can't stop me from going."

Anna was standing in front of the dresser mirror in their bedroom, putting on her pearl earrings that matched her necklace and double-checking her hair. It had been so long since she had been to church that she had forgotten what women wore to church. She just wanted to look her best, so that's what she wore — her best summer dress. It was white, embellished with flow-

271

ers, and comfortable.

Tag had been complaining since Anna finished her shower. At first it was just a low murmur, but as she continued to get ready, it grew louder. He finally used the word *forbid,* and she still wasn't unnerved. She was going, and he wasn't stopping her.

Tag stood, growling, behind her as she put on the finishing touches to her wardrobe. She could almost feel his hot breath on her neck. She glanced at his image in the mirror.

"Why now? Why all of a sudden do you want to go to church? It's because of what Eli talked about the other day, isn't it?"

Anna had been unable to shake the feeling she had when Eli mentioned the name of Jesus Christ. It had been four days, and that pain in her stomach was still there. It was Sunday, so she had decided she would find a church — any church — today with or without Tag. Just thinking about church eased the pain in her stomach.

She felt excited. Tag wasn't going to forbid her. "Why don't you come with me?"

Tag stomped around the foot of their bed flailing his arms. "You know I can't leave the house. And because I don't need church or anything it offers. And you're not going either!"

His antics didn't deter her. Anna slammed her hairbrush on the dresser and glared at Tag. His temples were pulsing. Clearly, he was angry. Anna couldn't care less. He had too often told her what she could and couldn't do. But not today.

"I'm going, and you're not going to stop me. What are you going to do, Tag? Lock me up?"

Clutching her purse, Anna marched past him and to the garage. Tag yelled at her the entire way. She ignored him, got in her car — a black Infiniti FX SUV — and backed out of the garage. She nearly scraped Tag's white Saab convertible.

Tag was still screaming as she pulled into the street. And she still ignored him. Anna pressed the button on the remote clipped to the sun visor, and he disappeared behind the garage door.

Anna exited the Governor's Club subdivision. She didn't know where to go and didn't care. She just wanted to find a church. *Any* church. Soon she remembered seeing a church on Concord Road the many times she had driven that way. She decided to go there. It took her less than ten minutes to reach it. The medium-size church looked inviting from the street. It wasn't large enough to be intimidating. It had stained-glass windows, dark red bricks, and a steeple with a cross.

The sign read NEW HOPE BAPTIST CHURCH. Anna had never noticed the name before. She parked in a space reserved for visitors. She glanced around at the few people who were walking toward the church building and inhaled deeply. Rousing her courage, she left her SUV and began to walk toward the building. The sky was clear, the sun brilliant, and the temperature pleasant. A breeze ruffled the hem of her dress. It was a beautiful day for a new beginning. As she walked, the church began to draw her like a magnet. She had never wanted to get anywhere as fast as she wanted to right then. Her legs tried to run, but her judgment prevented it.

She entered the front door and was greeted warmly by men and women she didn't know. They talked to her like she was an old friend and they were glad to see her again. One gentleman handed her a brochure and escorted her to a vacant seat on an otherwise crowded pew in the middle of the sanctuary.

When she sat down, Anna looked at the brochure the man had given her. It read like a program for a play. At the top were printed the words *Order of Service.* Men and women of different ages sat in the pews around her. They spoke to her and she felt at ease.

Soon a choir marched in with all its regalia and filled the chairs in the loft in the front of the sanctuary. Words appeared on two big screens on either side of the choir. Musical instruments began to sound. The people stood and sang, and Anna sang with them. She didn't know why. But her mouth opened and the words flowed out. She enjoyed singing.

After a few minutes a gentleman began to speak from the podium on stage. The Order of Service said he was the pastor of the church — Dr. Graham Frazier. He was tall, and Anna guessed he was in his midforties. He had thick black hair and his suit had been pressed recently. White starched shirt, necktie; and his black leather shoes sparkled. His voice was deep and soothing. She didn't remember everything he said, but he talked about the need for a relationship with Jesus Christ. His words were similar to those spoken by Eli, she realized. The time went by too quickly.

Before she knew it, Dr. Frazier concluded his sermon — that's what the Order of Service called it — and invited anyone and everyone to come and speak with him at the front of the church. The piano and organ played. The people sang again. She saw people walk to the front of the church. A young couple with a toddler. A middle-aged man wiping tears from his cheeks. Anna felt a yearning to speak to Dr. Frazier, but her feet were nailed to the floor. Her heart raced and she wrung her hands. Soon the music ended, Dr. Frazier prayed, and the people started to leave. She didn't want to go but fell in line and exited the sanctuary.

Before Anna knew it, she was back in her car and staring at the front of the church building. It seemed as if it was only a minute ago that she had parked her car, but an hour and fifteen minutes had passed. The event had been like a whirlwind. She had never before experienced anything like it. It took five minutes for her to make herself start the car and drive away. She told herself that she would have to come back.

Washington DC

Holland Fletcher tried to find out who owned the town house Tiffany Ramsey lived in — the one she had previously shared with Jessica Caldwell. But the deeper he dug, the more confused he was. All he discovered from the District of Columbia public records was an elaborate maze of limited partnerships, subchapter S corporations, and dead ends. Somebody wanted to hide the ownership of the town house and had succeeded.

Holland was playing by *her* rules again and he didn't like it. It was like a bad spy novel. Untraceable phone calls. No name. Coded messages. All that was lacking was a Russian defection. He was tired of it.

"I've been working on this for over a month, and nothing. I'm through."

It was early morning on the Fourth of July. Holland was in his apartment on the telephone. He held the cordless phone from the den and strolled incessantly around and between the furniture.

"My editor is screaming at me to show some results or I'm fired. And I don't want to be fired."

"You won't be fired, I assure you," she said. "This will make your career."

"I won't have a career in about a week."

"I've got some information for you, but you've got to do exactly what I say."

He stopped by his threadbare plaid couch. "Here we go again. I did exactly what you said last time and found absolutely nothing at the Supreme Court building."

"You found Ms. Ramsey, didn't you?"

Holland stared at the wall. A lump formed in his throat. He hadn't mentioned meeting Tiffany Ramsey to anyone. Not to his editor, his parents, his friends. No one.

"How do you know about her?"

"She's a beautiful young lady who lives on Thirty-seventh, right?"

Holland went back to his walking trail around and between the furniture.

"Do I have your attention again?" she asked.

"I'm listening."

Holland parked his old Camry in a parking lot off Fourteenth Street NW, near the Ellipse. He put on an army green military jacket and a red Washington Nationals baseball cap. He preferred a New York Yankees cap, but again, they were *her* rules. He paid the attendant ten dollars for one hour of parking and berated her about the cost. He said it was highway robbery, but she threatened to have his car towed if he didn't pay. So he paid and walked away mad. He stomped off onto Fourteenth Street NW toward the National Mall. It was 7:30 p.m. on the Fourth of July.

The Mall was thick with people — men, women, and children — who were there for the fireworks scheduled for 8:00 p.m. over the Reflecting Pool. Holland shoved his way through the crowd and said, "Excuse me," several times. Some people refused to move and he detoured around them. A few fathers cursed at him for almost knocking their children to the ground, and several more yelled at him.

"Bud, you don't have to get any closer," one man said. "You can see the fireworks fine from here."

Undeterred, he kept moving. Her instructions were specific. Stand under the Washington Monument on the west side at precisely 8:00 p.m. He had complained about the jacket. It was hot and humid in Washington in July, he'd said.

But she hadn't wavered. He would be the only one with a red cap and a military jacket and would be easy to spot.

When he finally reached the monument, he was out of breath. Sweat dripped from under his baseball cap and he wiped it away with his hand. He glanced at his watch: 7:55.

The fireworks would begin in five minutes. He scanned the crowd in all directions but knew he wouldn't recognize her even if he saw her. Five minutes later the fireworks began, and the crowd cheered and pointed.

Two minutes after the fireworks started he

felt something hard in his back. He had never felt the business end of a pistol, but if this wasn't it, he didn't want to feel the real thing. A chill ran over him.

"Don't turn around," a voice said near his right ear.

It was a man's voice and raspy. It was the gravelly rattle a voice made after years of smoking cigarettes. It was a voice that he wouldn't forget. Holland's heart raced, the sweat poured from all parts of his body, and he almost wet his pants. But he didn't turn around. He didn't move. He didn't even blink. He barely breathed.

"I'm going to place an envelope in your coat pocket and leave. Count to ten before you move, and remember, we're watching you."

Holland felt a hand in his pocket. Then the voice and the man were gone.

Holland counted to ten and jerked around. He breathed easier and looked at and over the crowd. Nothing. There were white faces and black faces and brown faces, but he didn't see anyone looking at him. He felt something in his pocket as he fought his way through the crowd until he broke free. When he was finally back on Fourteenth Street, he began to run. He could feel the nausea rising up through his esophagus. A block and a half from his car he couldn't fight it any longer. He propped himself against a brick wall and heaved. Once his stomach was empty, he stumbled to his car. Throwing the army jacket in the rear seat, he sat down in the front. He was breathing hard. He was scared. Maybe he wasn't cut out for being an investigative reporter. Things were completely out of his control.

CHAPTER EIGHTEEN

Washington DC

Cooper Harrington's limo eased along the Beltway that encircled the capital area. It was the day after the Fourth of July. He reclined in the back of the car, sipping at a bottle of sparkling water. He wasn't in any hurry. FBI Director Leslie Hughes sat across from him. He had refused Cooper's offer of a bottle of water or another drink. The soundproof glass separating the driver from the rear of the car was closed. It wasn't the first time Cooper and Director Hughes had met like that.

"We just want you to delay in finding Moretti, that's all."

"Is this officially coming from the senator's office?"

Cooper saw right through Director Hughes. He wanted some cover, some protection, and Cooper couldn't provide it. Not this time. There was only so much he was willing to do for Stella Hanover — and particularly without Senator Proctor's knowledge. Talking to Director Hughes about it was one thing. Providing official cover was another and completely out of the question.

Cooper smiled and drummed his fingers on the leather seat. "Les — I'm sorry — Director Hughes, you know that nothing is ever official. There won't be any memo or letter. I'm just telling you that the senator wants this investigation to go as slowly as possible."

Director Hughes glanced through the window at the automobiles that sped past. "You know the president's breathing down my neck. Moretti almost killed his precious Supreme Court nominee."

"But he didn't, and that's the important thing."

"It's not going to be easy to keep the president at bay. And Moretti killed two other people. What about them?"

"I'm not saying you don't ever bring Moretti in. Just not right now. Give it a couple of weeks. That's all I'm asking for. A couple of weeks. And if you say yes, there'll be a nice surprise in your Panama bank account in the morning."

Cooper's voice was smooth and convincing. He showed his white teeth again. Money always bought loyalty from Director Hughes. And Cooper didn't mind spending as much of NFAR's money as necessary. It was Stella's problem, not his, and she would have to pay to correct it.

"Two weeks, Cooper, but that's it. I'm already looking bad enough that I haven't caught him before now."

Cooper's limo exited the Beltway onto River Road and soon entered the parking lot at Congressional Country Club. It stopped beside Director Hughes's waiting limo. Several other cars were scattered around the parking lot. The director departed Cooper's limo. Cooper shook his hand, patted him on the back, and thanked him for helping.

As soon as the door closed, Cooper breathed easier and was on his wireless with Stella Hanover. The limo pulled back onto River Road, toward the District. It moved with a little more haste than previously.

"He said two weeks," Cooper said. "You better tell Moretti to disappear."

Cooper listened and ran his hand through his long blond hair. His brow furrowed. Just talking to her caused a headache to begin at the base of the back of his head, and it rose over the top to his forehead. He grimaced and pinched the area between his eyes with his index finger and thumb.

"No, I haven't talked to Senator Proctor about it. He's not to know anything, Stella. If this thing goes bad, he'll be in the clear. And I'm not going down either. You understand me, Stella. This is all on you. I can't believe you were stupid and desperate enough to try to assassinate a Supreme Court nominee."

Cooper listened again.

"He's still going to be confirmed," Cooper replied after a minute. "This hasn't changed anything."

Cooper said good-bye to Stella and rode quietly in the rear of his limo back to the Hart Building. He finished the last of his water and laid the empty bottle on the seat. At least now Stella had one less marker to cash in on him.

Director Hughes settled into the back of his limo. He was all alone. He gave the driver instructions, then the driver raised the soundproof glass. The car began to move, and soon it, too, was on the Capital Beltway. Director Hughes removed a tape recorder from his breast coat pocket. It squawked as he rewound it a short distance and then pressed Play. Cooper's voice was crystal clear.

"I'm just telling you that the senator wants this investigation to go as slowly as possible," Cooper's voice said.

Director Hughes pressed the Stop button and rewound the tape to the beginning. The statement about the Panama bank account would be erased later, he decided. The tape would be labeled and placed in the safe in his office with the other hundred or so similar ones. There was only one real rule in Washington: always cover your back.

The Faulkner residence, Jackson, Tennessee
Eli and Sara spent the Fourth of July holiday in Anne and Tommy Ferguson's backyard. There were three other families at the cookout. Tommy grilled hot dogs for the kids and steaks for the adults. Eli admitted that he ate too much but took pleasure in it. There were eight kids in all, and they spent the better part of the afternoon splashing around in Anne and Tommy's swimming pool. Tommy set off an arsenal of fireworks at dark. All the dogs in the neighborhood howled, but only one neighbor complained and threatened to call the police. Tommy told the neighbor that his lawyer — Eli Faulkner — was at the party, and he wasn't afraid of the police. The

286

police never arrived, and the five men laughed all evening about how tough Tommy had acted.

All during the afternoon, Eli caught Sara gazing at the eight kids. She stood and talked with the other ladies, but Eli saw her glance in the direction of the children often. At least one time he saw her standing near the swimming pool, watching. Eli stopped and watched Sara as she watched the children. He could see that look in her eyes.

That had been two days ago, but Sara hadn't said anything about it.

When Eli arrived home from work, the lights were dim. Candles flickered on the dining room table, and their places were set with fine china. Romantic music played through the house's stereo system. He caught the aroma of his favorite meal just as Sara appeared from around the corner. She wore a black cocktail dress, a strand of white pearls, and her blond hair brushed the tops of her shoulders. She was incredibly beautiful, and her appearance made Eli weak in the knees.

"What's going on?" Eli asked.

"I thought we'd have a quiet, romantic dinner at home tonight."

She took his hand and led him to the dining room table. Sara's hand was warm and soft, and Eli loved holding it.

"Is there an anniversary or birthday that I forgot about?" Eli quipped.

When Sara cut her eyes at him, he knew that meant to stop being coy. He pulled a chair out for Sara to sit in and then took his seat at the end of the table. Sara sat to his right.

"No." Sara smiled. "It's not an anniversary or a birthday. I just thought it would be nice to sit down and have a candlelight dinner."

"I think it's a great idea. I've been working late every night. It's nice to sit down and relax."

The meal was delicious, and the ambience even better. Eli and Sara sat and talked and laughed more than they had in weeks. He had been working too much, he admitted. The Grissom case was always demanding. And other files had piled up from neglect. She knew he worked too hard, she said. But she also knew that what he did for other people was important.

Eli kissed her hand and gazed into her lovely blue eyes. He was reminded again of how much he loved her and the many reasons he had married her.

"I love you," he said.

"I love you, too."

Eli released Sara's hand and sipped from

his water glass. "You're still thinking about having children, aren't you?"

"I haven't thought about it much since we were in Nashville, but being at Anne and Tommy's the other day made me think about it again."

Eli rested his water glass on the table and looked into Sara's eyes again. "I was watching you."

"What are you talking about?"

"The other day at Tommy's. I was watching you as you were watching the kids playing in the swimming pool."

Sara averted her eyes from Eli's gaze. "I wasn't watching —"

"You don't have to deny it. I thought it was wonderful the way you looked at them. You'll make a great mother."

Eli knew that Sara wanted children. He knew how much Sara wanted to be a mother. But he also knew that she worried about it. She worried about whether she could do all the things a mother did.

She needn't worry, Eli told her.

"The real question is whether *you've* thought any more about it. This is an important decision that we both have to make," she said.

He lifted his chin. "I have thought about it."

"And?" She appeared to be holding her breath.

"And I can't wait."

Eli and Sara laughed and talked into the evening. They enjoyed each other's company. Before long, the dishes were put away and the candles were extinguished. The music continued to play softly from the ceiling speakers in each room of the house. And Eli and Sara quietly disappeared into their bedroom.

The Fletcher residence, Washington DC

The white envelope had been perched on the kitchen counter in Holland's apartment ever since the Fourth of July. He had walked by it often and had even picked it up and looked at it on three separate occasions. But he had always tossed it back down. He just couldn't bring himself to open it.

He'd thought about the possibility of running it through the shredder and forgetting about it. And when *she* called again, he would tell her that he was through. Finished. She could take whatever information was in the envelope to someone else. He didn't want it. He was convinced that he was a pawn in a game he knew he didn't want to be in.

Or he could be brave and open it. But he

didn't feel very brave. In fact, he still felt very scared. He didn't like having a pistol — he was convinced it was a pistol — stuck in his back. Maybe bravery wasn't the right motivation.

Holland had had that conversation with himself many times over the past several days. But he decided that today, Saturday, was the day he had to either fish or cut bait. No more talking with himself about it. Either open it or shred it. He finally decided that if he was going to be a reporter — an *investigative* reporter — he had no choice but to open it. He owed it to his employer, the public, and to himself to find out what was inside the mysterious envelope.

So without any ceremony he slid his finger under the flap and ripped the top out of the envelope. He removed five sheets of paper folded together and laid them on the coffee table.

Holland skimmed the first page, then the second, and so on. He digested only bits and pieces of information on any page. But it was enough. He realized that on the pages he held in his hands were the keys to deciphering the maze of limited partnerships and subchapter S corporations regarding the ownership of the town house where Tiffany Ramsey, and previously Jessica

291

Caldwell, lived.

He retrieved his previous research from his bedroom and began comparing the public records with the information supplied by the woman with no name. After several minutes of drawing flow charts and comparing names, he came to a conclusion.

"Senator Proctor," he mumbled to himself. "What have you gotten yourself into?"

Brentwood, Tennessee

Anna Grissom went to New Hope for the second Sunday in a row. She couldn't rid herself of the inexplicable feeling she'd had last Sunday, nor did she want to. And she couldn't stay away. She had driven past the church several times during the week. She had a thirst that she couldn't quench. Twice she had entered the parking lot, circled through, and exited again. Those brief jaunts only served to whet her appetite more. Sunday couldn't arrive soon enough.

Tag yelled at her again as she got ready, but not as much. She ignored him again, and it was easier the second week. The allure of New Hope was stronger than her fear of Tag, which was diminishing. She still hoped he would go to New Hope with her sometime. She was certain that Eli could obtain permission from Judge Blackwood for Tag to attend church. But Tag didn't want to go, so there was no need to ask.

Anna parked her Infiniti SUV in the church parking lot and entered through the front door. She was again greeted warmly by members of the church as she entered. She sat in a similar location in the sanctuary as the previous Sunday, and those seated around her told her they were glad she was back.

When the congregation sang again, Anna sang along from words displayed on the screens in the front of the sanctuary. She didn't know what the words meant, but the singing was beautiful and she couldn't stop herself.

Soon Dr. Graham Frazier stood behind the podium and began to speak. His voice soothed her and his words captivated her. He read poetically from the Bible. Dr. Frazier said it was from chapter fourteen in the gospel according to John, whatever that meant. The words he read were displayed on the screen in front of her and she followed along as he read. After he finished reading he peered out into the congregation.

"Friends," Dr. Frazier said, "listen to me closely."

It felt to Anna as if Dr. Frazier was not

only looking directly at her but speaking directly to her as well. She couldn't divert her eyesight from him or prevent herself from listening. She readily obeyed his instruction.

"There is only one way for a person to get to heaven, and that is through a personal relationship with Jesus Christ."

Anna recognized those words. They were virtually identical to the ones Eli had spoken. The words she had been unable to get out of her mind. She knew she didn't have any relationship with Jesus Christ. She barely knew who he was. Did that mean she wasn't going to heaven?

Dr. Frazier continued to speak, but the remainder of what he said was a blur to Anna. Thinking about his first statement consumed her. She had more questions than answers.

Soon — too soon — the service was over again. The piano and organ played, and people stood and sang. Dr. Frazier invited anyone and everyone who wanted to speak privately with him at the front of the sanctuary to meet him there.

Anna's heart raced, and her palms grew clammy again. *Why do I feel like this?* She held on to the pew in front of her and her knuckles turned white. She wanted to speak with Dr. Frazier, but she couldn't move. After a few minutes, the opportunity passed and the yearning eased. And just like last week, the music ended, Dr. Frazier prayed, and people began to exit.

"We hope you'll come back again," an elderly lady said to Anna as she was leaving.

Anna smiled politely and nodded. *Don't worry. I can't stay away.*

CHAPTER NINETEEN

The Hart Building, Washington DC
Porter McIntosh waited in the expansive hallway outside room 216 for the beginning of the confirmation hearings. Judge Shelton had recovered physically, and Senator Proctor's office had been singing his praises for the last two weeks. All the talking heads and editorials said how shocked they were by Senator Proctor's support of Judge Shelton. But Porter was still worried. He didn't trust Cooper Harrington or Senator Proctor one iota.

Porter and President Wallace prayed regularly for a speedy and uneventful hearing process. The end couldn't arrive soon enough. Porter looked at his watch. The confirmation hearings for Judge Dunbar Shelton were scheduled to begin at 1:00 p.m. eastern time. It was the Monday after the Fourth of July. Two weeks later than the president wanted, but it couldn't be helped.

And there was still time to get Judge Shelton confirmed before the Senate's August recess, but there couldn't be any more delays.

Porter shook hands with several people in the hallway and made small talk. He saw Cooper Harrington across the hall near the entrance to room 216, and Cooper gave him a slight nod. *I can't believe all hope lies with you and Senator Proctor,* Porter thought. He returned the acknowledgment and quickly diverted his eyes from Cooper. He didn't want anyone to see him make eye contact with Cooper.

Porter moved toward a window that overlooked Constitution Avenue. The police had blockaded the area in front of the building, and Constitution Avenue was blocked off from traffic between First and Second streets. To the right Porter saw dozens of people behind the barricades carrying signs supporting Judge Shelton's confirmation. But to the left, and to Porter's dismay, there were not just dozens but *hundreds* of people, perhaps as many as a thousand, behind the barricades protesting the confirmation. Even from this distance Porter saw that the leader of the protestors was Stella Hanover, bullhorn in hand.

"Stella," Porter whispered to himself.

"Why don't you just give up?"

Outside the Hart Building, Washington DC
"We can't let them steal the Supreme Court from us," Stella screamed into the bullhorn. She was only steps from the marble facade of the Hart Building. The raucous crowd holding DEFEAT SHELTON and SAVE ROE and other similarly worded, premade signs echoed back its approval. Stella's staff had worked days putting the signs together. The voices from this crowd easily overpowered the predominately passive supporters of Judge Shelton's confirmation. And the television cameras that covered the protests were focused only on Stella and her minions.

"We've got to let the senators know that confirming Judge Shelton would be devastating to our country," Stella screamed to resounding approval. Her face felt red from the exertion.

Soon the crowd was worked into a frenzy. Stella began moving her arms like an orchestra director as rhythmic chants rose. The cacophony from the pro-abortion protesters suffocated any noise being made by the pro-life supporters across the way. Stella stared up at the second-floor windows in the Hart Building and raised the bullhorn to her mouth.

"We will never give up!"

The Hart Building, Washington DC

Porter McIntosh entered and sat in the front row of the gallery seating in the austere chamber that was room 216 as the Senate Judiciary Committee opened its hearings on the confirmation of Judge Dunbar Shelton to the United States Supreme Court. Directly ahead, at a large mahogany table, sat the isolated figure of Judge Shelton. Judge Shelton's back was to Porter and a single microphone was set in front of him. Immediately behind him was a row of aides, advisers, and attorneys who were assisting Judge Shelton. Porter referred to them as Judge Shelton's handlers. They had all been carefully selected by Porter and President Wallace.

Judge Shelton's wife, Victoria, was in the chair immediately behind his right shoulder. Her left arm was in a cast and sling. Porter glanced around the gallery area and saw that it was crammed with news reporters.

FBI and Secret Service agents blended in with the walls. Judge Shelton's security detail had gone from two to fifty overnight, after the bombing. They were in the hearing room. They were in the hallway. They had the building surrounded, and a helicopter was on standby in case Judge Shelton needed to be evacuated. Every security risk had been eliminated. Porter felt more at ease. He was back to only having to worry about getting Judge Shelton confirmed, not protecting him.

Scattered on the floor directly in front of Judge Shelton were photographers from all the major newspapers and wire services — Senate aides called them "shooters." Televisions were mounted in several strategic locations in the room to assure that every word, movement, and facial expression of Judge Shelton's was captured for all of America to see.

Beyond the photographers, and slightly elevated behind the dais, sat the members of the Senate Judiciary Committee. They were a righteous bunch. Senator Franklin Montgomery, the senior senator from the state of New York, sat in the middle and chaired the committee. He was the most righteous. To his left sat nine members of his political party and to his right sat eight members of the opposition party — President Wallace's party. Immediately behind each senator were several members of their respective staffs armed with, among other things, biographical information about

Judge Shelton, copies of articles written by him, and copies of Mississippi Supreme Court opinions he'd authored. All looked intent on unlocking the mystery of Judge Shelton's judicial philosophy.

Porter crossed his legs and stared at the arrogant Senator Montgomery. His thinning white hair was parted from left to right and slightly toward the back, and his dark eyes seemed to pierce through everything caught in their gaze.

Porter knew that Senator Montgomery fought bitterly against President Wallace's initiatives at every turn. Cooper Harrington had assured Porter that Senator Proctor had obtained Senator Montgomery's support for Judge Shelton, but looking at him now, Porter was unsure.

The chatter and other noises in the room dissipated as the time for the hearings to begin drew near.

Senator Montgomery peered over the top of his reading spectacles at Judge Shelton below as he called the hearing to order. "And now we'll begin with opening statements. Each senator will have ten minutes, and please hold your comments to ten minutes each." When he looked up and down the row of senators like a schoolteacher, each senator grinned. Laughter and smiles emerged briefly from all corners of the room. Everyone present knew that it would be impossible for any member of this pompous group to limit listening to themselves talk to ten minutes.

"Judge Shelton," Senator Montgomery continued, "I know I speak for all of the committee members when I say this, but we are terribly sorry for what happened to you and your family."

All of the committee members nodded. Judge Shelton nodded back in appreciation.

"We're all glad you stayed the course. There are extreme factions in our society who try to manipulate the efficient operation of government through threats and violence. I trust you agree that we cannot allow those extremists to interfere with our responsibilities."

"I do, Senator," Judge Shelton replied respectfully.

"Judge Shelton, this is a very unique hearing. It is the first hearing on the confirmation of a Supreme Court justice in over eight years. I'll reserve my opinion about your confirmation until the conclusion of the hearings. But I firmly believe that there ought not to be partisan politics in the confirmation process of a Supreme Court justice, whether Republican or Democrat.

We all have a responsibility to ask probing questions to determine an individual's qualifications to serve on the Supreme Court, and we must look beyond academic and professional accomplishments."

Porter liked what he heard, even if he didn't much care for Senator Montgomery. He released the tension in his back and exhaled quietly. Senator Montgomery appeared to be on the bandwagon.

"And I further believe that a candidate shouldn't be asked questions about how he or she might decide on a particular issue. The judiciary should have the necessary independence to make decisions without the fear of keeping promises made to secure confirmation."

Porter relaxed further as he listened to Senator Montgomery complete his opening remarks — twelve minutes after he began. Each committee member in order of seniority also gave their opening remarks. Nearly three hours after Senator Montgomery called the hearings to order, the opening remarks were finally over. Porter was bored to tears and wondered about Judge Shelton. He had noticed Judge Shelton shifting in his seat several times, but for the most part he remained tall in his chair. Victoria appeared uncomfortable the entire time.

"That concludes the opening remarks from the committee members," Senator Montgomery said. "We'll recess for the day. The hearing will resume at nine a.m. tomorrow and we'll begin with Judge Shelton's opening statement."

Porter exited with Judge Shelton, Victoria, and their entourage. All requests for comments from the media were refused. Dinner, a final dress rehearsal, and a good night's rest were awaiting Judge Shelton.

The Oval Office, the White House, Washington DC

President Wallace again summoned FBI Director Hughes to the Oval Office. It had been over three weeks since the bombing at the Shelton residence and still no Joe Moretti. The president was furious.

Director Hughes, hat in hand and with his bodyguards, entered the office. They stood erect in front of the president's desk. Director Hughes pled his case to deaf ears. Porter stood beside the president's desk and gloated.

"Are you sure it was him?" Porter asked.

Porter knew Director Hughes didn't like conversing with him, and he didn't care. Director Hughes thought he was too important to talk to anybody less than the president himself. That was precisely the reason Porter had initiated the conversation.

"Yes, we're sure," Director Hughes shot back at Porter. He looked at President Wallace as he answered instead of at Porter. "The voice analysis returned a perfect match."

"But you can't find him?" President Wallace used his grandfather voice again.

"It's like he evaporated."

"People don't evaporate. Do you have any leads? We're in the middle of confirmation hearings. If anything were to happen now —"

Director Hughes raised his hands in defense. "Nothing's going to happen. We have around-the-clock security on Judge Shelton."

"Les, what have I told you about interrupting me? I don't like it. I don't like it at all." The president's voice was still calm and collected, but had taken on a stern edge.

Porter grinned. The grandfather voice was lecturing, and Porter liked it. Especially when it was directed at a guy like Director Hughes.

"You find this man, and you find him soon," President Wallace ordered. "Or I'll find someone who can. Do you understand me, Les?"

"Yes, sir," Director Hughes replied through clenched teeth.

Director Hughes and his bodyguards stormed from the room. President Wallace and Porter looked at the closed door.

"You want me to start getting some names together?" Porter asked. He watched as President Wallace pondered the question.

The president didn't think about it for long. "Yeah, it's time for a change. I've been looking for a good reason to get rid of him, and this is it. He's been here since the last administration."

"I don't like him very much either."

Porter knew the president meant it was time for a new FBI director. But Porter also decided it was time to find Joe Moretti. It had been long enough.

CHAPTER TWENTY

Washington DC

It was after midnight. Porter drove his own private car — no government plates, no limo — down Seventh Street NW, near Mount Vernon Square in Chinatown. He parked on the curb in front of a renovated warehouse that housed an art studio on the first floor. He carried a manila folder when he exited his car. An African American with a barrel chest, a four-button suit, and a matching tie appeared from the shadows and walked toward him. Porter recognized the man and nodded. The man nodded back, moved closer, and stopped by Porter's car. Porter knew his car was safe and would be intact when he returned.

Porter climbed the five concrete steps that led to the entrance to the studio. He glanced above the door to the hidden television camera. A buzzer reverberated, and the door opened without any effort from Porter. The studio was dark. Only a couple of floor lamps lit his path. He walked through the studio, out the back door, and up a flight of stairs. Again a buzzer sounded, and another door opened without Porter's assistance.

Two more bodyguards met Porter as he entered. One was Caucasian, the other African American. He recognized them both, but no one spoke. The Caucasian bodyguard opened a third door, and Porter stepped into the offices of Simon Webster. Their meeting would be brief.

"I've been expecting you," Simon said.

Porter wasn't surprised by the statement. He knew Simon kept his ear to the ground. Simon sat behind a large desk. He was intimidating. Even sitting, he looked tall. Muscular. Rough, tan skin. Thick, black hair and mustache. And he had a scar under his chin that ran from one ear to the other. It was the closest Simon had ever come to dying, it was said. No one had ever found the body of the man who did it. Simon had made sure of it.

Simon was ex-CIA, ex–Navy SEAL, and current mercenary. His walls were covered with photographs of him with pro-democratic militant groups from all corners of the world. He had the only copies. Porter kept Simon on retainer through various unregulated political-action-committee accounts but kept the knowledge of his existence from President Wallace. The president's hands couldn't be soiled if Simon's identity were to be discovered. FBI Director Hughes denied Simon existed. And he didn't exist. His official file said he was killed when his unit parachuted into Iraq over the Turkish border during the first Gulf War.

"I need you to find Joe Moretti."

Porter was all business and ready to leave. There weren't many people in the world who intimidated Porter, but Simon was one of them. If Simon wanted to, he could make Porter disappear without a trace. Porter knew it — and that scared him. Porter tossed a folder on Simon's desk. Its contents were from the FBI's file on Joe Moretti that Director Hughes had left with President Wallace.

Simon took the folder and flipped through the pages. "Shouldn't be hard. Two-bit Mafia wiseguy."

"I need him in one piece, and soon."

An evil smile appeared under Simon's mustache. He had one gold tooth right in front, and the overhead light glistened off it when he smiled. "One piece might be a little difficult, but we'll see what we can do."

Porter didn't laugh or smile. The assignment was delivered, and he wasn't staying for the jokes. He turned and vacated Simon's office.

Retracing his steps, he found his car intact, with Simon's bodyguard still protecting it. Less than ten minutes after his arrival, Porter left Chinatown and was on his way to his house and family in Bethesda, Maryland.

Amelia Island, Florida

Myron Carlson and his wife, Dorothy, lived in an antebellum home off North Fletcher Avenue in the Fernandina Beach area of Amelia Island near Fort Clinch State Park. The majestic home with its four large columns was set on a small point and overlooked the expansive Atlantic Ocean. A narrow, nondescript dirt-and-gravel driveway a quarter mile long led from the home to North Fletcher Avenue. The view from the street to the house was so obscured by dense trees that hardly anyone other than Fernandina Beach locals even knew of the house's existence. Myron and Dorothy valued the seclusion, away from tourists and vacationers.

"Dot, did you see where Dunbar's going to begin his questioning today?"

Myron sat in his wheelchair at the breakfast table, his legs covered with a quilt. He read from an article below the fold on the front page of the *Florida Times Union* that lay beside his plate of fried bacon, scrambled eggs, and white toast. A glass of orange juice and a cup of coffee — black — were nearby.

"I saw it, dear," Dot replied. "I'm glad he and his wife are safe. That was just terrible what happened to them. Terrible. I don't know why people act like that sometimes."

"Because politics makes people crazy. That's why."

"You want to watch some of the confirmation hearing later?" Dot sat in a wooden chair to the right of Myron. She was skimming through the lifestyles section of the paper.

Dot and Myron were both in their eighties. Dot's hair was a blue-gray, and she wore glasses that hung from a chain around her neck. She was plump and in remarkable health for a woman her age. But Myron looked frail. He had wispy white hair, bristly white eyebrows, and eyeglasses with thick lenses. But they still lived independently. A nurse from a home health agency checked on them twice a week.

They had moved to Amelia Island after Myron retired from Harvard Law School nearly twenty years earlier. Neither could tolerate the brutal Boston winters any longer. And there was nothing to keep them in Boston. They had tried to have children, but after two miscarriages and one stillbirth neither had the desire to try again.

Despite his poor health, Myron liked waking up early. He savored the stillness of the early morning. Dot, too, delighted in the serene mornings. As the sun slowly rose over the calm waters of the Atlantic Ocean, she would prepare the same breakfast for Myron that she had for the last sixty years.

"Bah," Myron grunted. "No, I don't want to watch. There's nothing in the Constitution that requires confirmation hearings for judicial appointments. Advice and consent, that's what it says. Advice and consent."

"Don't get upset, Professor," Dot warned. She called him "Professor" when he acted like one, which was often. "You don't have to watch if you don't want to."

"Don't professor me. It's the most ridiculous circus in the world." He took a bite of toast and drank from his glass of orange juice. "A bunch of politicians asking unintelligent questions of a constitutional scholar about constitutional law. That's just ridiculous."

Dot sipped her coffee while Myron ranted.

"All they should do is take a vote on the floor of the Senate," Myron continued. "That would satisfy the requirements of the Constitution."

"You don't think Dunbar can handle the questioning?"

"He can handle it. Dunbar was one of the best constitutional students I ever had. He'll eat those senators for lunch. But they'll probably try trapping him on *Roe.* He'll have to be careful even though *Roe* really is bad law, despite what people may think about the morality of the subject."

"I know, I know." Dot's voice was patronizing. "Penumbras and emanations and all that. I've heard it a hundred times before."

"And you're going to keep hearing it until the Supreme Court justices stop being judicial activists. Judges are no better qualified than the average American to decide moral issues. They need to leave the lawmaking to state legislatures."

Myron finished the last of his coffee. "Penumbras formed by emanations," he mumbled. "I wish someone would show me where that is in the Constitution."

"That's enough, Professor," Dot said as she carried the dishes to the kitchen. "Let me get the dishes finished, and we'll go out to the pier. I bet the dolphins are out this

313

morning."

The Hart Building, Washington DC

On Tuesday morning Porter looked through the second-floor window at the mass of people. The pro-life group had grown, but the pro-choice protesters had at least doubled overnight. Maybe tripled. Now thousands of people were chanting and yelling. A sea of DEFEAT SHELTON and SAVE ROE signs floated over the crowd. Porter didn't like what he saw.

And then there was Stella. The sight of her made him shake his head. A makeshift stage had been erected overnight, and Stella stood in the middle of it. A bullhorn was no longer sufficient. Large speakers flanked either side of the platform, amplifying Stella's voice for all to hear. Two or three Hollywood celebrities stood with her and waved to the crowd. The roar intensified. A dozen television cameras recorded the whole scene.

Porter left the window and strolled to the door that led to room 216. The Tuesday session — the second day of confirmation hearings — was scheduled to begin. He had seen enough through the window, and what he saw made him mad. He entered room 216 and sat in the seat he'd sat in the day before. All the same players were present.

Senator Montgomery called the hearings to order and asked Judge Shelton to stand and be sworn to tell the truth. A faint yellowish bruise was visible on the judge's forehead, but no other physical evidence of the bombing was noticeable. He wore a dark suit and navy blue tie. After taking the oath, Judge Shelton returned to his seat and gave an opening statement. His notes were on the table in front of him, but he spoke without using them.

Porter listened intently.

"Let me begin by thanking President Wallace for nominating me. I am very humbled by the trust he has placed in me. As you know, the past few weeks have been very trying for my family and me. But as my father used to tell me, once you start something, you can't give up."

Judge Shelton eyed each senator individually as he spoke. He didn't look over their heads or at their staffs. He looked the senators directly in the eye. Some pretended to be listening. Others turned their heads and chatted with staffers. Their inattentiveness irritated Porter, but it didn't seem to bother Judge Shelton. He simply continued on. He told about his childhood and those who had influenced him. He mentioned Professor

Myron Carlson as one of his mentors.

"I have no agenda," Judge Shelton said firmly. "If I am confirmed, I will evaluate every case with an open mind. And as I've done on the Mississippi Supreme Court, I will work to make sure the United States Supreme Court upholds the rule of law. I don't make any promises other than to fairly and impartially consider cases that come before the Court."

Judge Shelton concluded his opening statement and handed his unused notes to a handler behind him. The mahogany table was clean.

The first volley of questions for Judge Shelton was to come from Senator Montgomery, the committee chair. He shuffled some papers that were handed to him by a staffer and spent three agonizing minutes with an opening monologue to his question. He liked hearing himself talk, Porter knew. Finally the question came.

"Judge Shelton," Senator Montgomery began. His Northern accent was nasal and annoying. "Do you think that the Constitution contains a right to privacy?"

The question was one that had been covered in Judge Shelton's mock committee hearings. Porter could almost recite Judge Shelton's answer before he gave it.

"I do, Senator. My reading of the Constitution and the precedent of the Supreme Court indicates that there are privacy rights in the Constitution."

But, Porter knew that didn't mean that in the Constitution there was a right to an abortion. And that was the crux of the matter.

"And what about precedent, Judge Shelton? Can a decision such as *Roe v. Wade* be overturned?"

The room fell silent and Judge Shelton shifted in his chair. Again, a question for which Judge Shelton was prepared.

"Senator, not all precedents are created equal. Some vary in strength, and overruling a weaker precedent might be merited in some instances. As to a specific case, it would be inappropriate for me to comment on whether a previously decided case should be affirmed by the Court or overruled. That same issue might come before the Court again, and I cannot ethically discuss it in these proceedings."

Porter liked the answer. And it didn't alarm anyone in the room. A murmur of noise resumed. Judge Shelton's answer was exactly the way they had practiced. No hints, no forecasts, no previews. That was the way the game of Senate confirmation hearings was played, and Judge Shelton played it well. Porter was pleased.

Washington DC

After he had finally opened the envelope, Holland Fletcher left several messages for Tiffany Ramsey on her voice mail at the Supreme Court building. He left his home number, his wireless number, and the direct line to his desk at the *Post.* He had tried to reach her all day Monday. All messages had gone unreturned. He had driven by her town house several times over the weekend but had never seen her car parked in front. One reason he wanted to talk with her was simply to hear the sound of her voice. But more important, he had questions for her about Senator Proctor and Jessica Caldwell. He called again, but this time added something extra to his message.

"Tiffany, this is Holland Fletcher with the *Washington Post.* Please call me back on my direct line. I have some information about Senator Proctor I want to discuss with you."

Within ten minutes the phone on his desk rang. It was Tiffany.

"You really need to stop calling me," she said.

Holland had a pen in his hand and a notepad on his desk. Like all good reporters, he was prepared to scribble down whatever Tiffany said. It didn't matter so much whether he correctly recorded what she said so long as at least part of it was right and it fit into the article he was writing.

"If you had returned my earlier calls, I wouldn't need to keep calling. I'm just trying to write a story."

"I told you before that I don't want to be interviewed for your story. Jessica was a friend —"

Holland cut her off midsentence with his first question. "Do you know that Senator Proctor owns the town house you live in?"

Silence. No words, no sound, no breathing. There was complete silence from Tiffany's end of the telephone.

"Tiffany, did you hear me?"

"I heard you, but what does that have to do with anything?"

"Did you know it?"

"Not really." The tone of her voice wasn't very confident.

She knew something and Holland was determined to get it out of her. He pressed further. "What does that mean, 'not really'? Either you know or you don't know."

"Look, Holland. It's dangerous for you to be calling me and for me to be talking to you. Please stop calling me."

Dangerous! "Why is it dangerous?"

"I'm not talking to you anymore. Good-bye, Holland."

Holland heard her disconnect the call. He listened to a dead line for several seconds and then a dial tone. He finally hung up and stared at his empty notepad. He wrote the words *Senator Proctor* and *dangerous,* but he didn't know what they meant.

CHAPTER
TWENTY-ONE

The law offices of Elijah J. Faulkner,
Jackson, Tennessee

Jill Baker knocked on the frame of Eli's open door, and he glanced up from behind his desk. He waved her to the sofa in his office. It was Wednesday, the second week of July. Eli and Jill had been working on Tag Grissom's case for six weeks. Eli could tell the case was really beginning to get to Jill.

"I called the lab to get the status on the DNA test," she said. "They received the tissue samples from the fetus last week from the coroner's office."

Jill's voice was detached. He knew she was still troubled over exhuming Jessica Caldwell's body. Eli didn't like it any more than she did. But it had to be done. His choice was either to seek DNA testing on the fetus or only halfway represent Tag Grissom, and the latter wasn't an option. If he took on a case, then he had to do everything possible to win. Even if that meant exhuming a body, and even if he didn't want to.

"How long before they'll have any results?"

Jill sank into the sofa in Eli's office. Her face was blank, and her voice distant. "Probably about two weeks. Maybe sooner, but not likely. They're pretty backlogged."

"I'd like them sooner, but two weeks will be fine. That'll give us about two or three more weeks before the trial starts. We've got our work cut out for us with Eli's DNA matching the skin fragments under Ms. Caldwell's fingernail. I hope these new tests have a different result. We need a break."

"I know. Randy made me mad the other day at the cemetery."

Jill still looked miserable. Her countenance was downcast. Eli knew what she was going through. It was the gut wrenching that came from handling murder cases. It was the reason he had quit taking them . . . until this case. And there were times when he wished he didn't have this one.

"You can't let it get to you." Eli spoke with concern and understanding. And he spoke from experience. "This is a tough business, and sometimes we have to do things that aren't pleasant."

"I know, but this has been really difficult.

I don't have a mother and father, and now Jessica's parents no longer have a child. Life is weird and unfair sometimes. And we made her family endure the whole emotional roller coaster again by exhuming Jessica's body."

Jill's despondency was only partially about the Caldwell family, Eli realized. The rest was about her own life. She had no family. No mother. No father. And it was the same as if she had no brother. He was worthless. That had to be a difficult way to live. Jill was an attractive young woman, but to Eli's knowledge she didn't have a boyfriend and rarely even dated.

"Have they buried her body again?" Eli asked.

Jill flicked away a wisp of hair that had fallen into her face and turned her face from Eli. "Yeah, last Friday. I didn't go back. I couldn't. One time at that cemetery was enough for me."

Eli felt compassion for Jill. She had worked for him for three years. But the relationship had always been employer and employee. Now he saw a side to her that he'd never seen. She wasn't all business. She had emotions and felt pain like everyone else, and she was reliving some of her worst memories. Memories that no teenager should have to create. But she had been forced to because of that accident and her parents' death, and this case had caused them to come racing back. Even worse was the fact that Jill didn't have anyone to lean on when she was troubled.

"It'll all be over soon," he consoled. "And you know you can talk to me about anything at any time."

"I know, but I'll be fine."

The Hart Building, Washington DC
Same song, third verse. And Porter hoped it was the last verse. The senators had gone through two rounds of questioning the previous day and Judge Shelton performed perfectly. One more cycle of questioning had been scheduled for Wednesday. Judge Shelton danced delicately and unscathed around such controversial issues as abortion, executive powers, and racial quotas. The media — as much as it hated to — was already christening Judge Shelton as the next Supreme Court justice.

Porter smiled when he watched the morning news programs. He smiled even more when he read the morning editorials. He felt as though the confirmation was on the downhill slide. If the committee finished today, then there could be a committee vote

324

by the end of the week and on to the full Senate by the end of next week.

Porter walked tall in his freshly polished shoes as he entered the Hart Building. His shirt was starched, his suit was clean and straight from the dry cleaner's, and his tie was knotted perfectly. He was confident. Very confident.

He breezed by the windows in the Hart Building that opened onto Constitution Avenue with barely a peek. It didn't matter that the pro-life group had diminished in size from the previous day or that the pro-choice group had doubled in size again. They had had no impact on the hearings up to this point.

But in that fleeting look he noticed something unusual: no Stella. It took two steps past the window for that fact to register with Porter. He stopped, retreated to the window, and looked again. Still no Stella. He couldn't find her anywhere.

"Maybe she's finally given up," Porter mumbled to himself.

Amelia Island, Florida
"Mrs. Carlson," the woman at the door said, "I just need a minute of your time."

"Who is it, Dot?" Myron called out from the back porch. He and Dot had converted the house's veranda into a screened-in back porch. It kept the insects out during the summer. It was just after 9:00 a.m. eastern time on Wednesday. After finishing breakfast, he had rolled himself to the back porch to watch the ocean waves crash onto the beach. It was a very relaxing activity.

Dot had cleared the table and cleaned the kitchen before they heard the knock at the door.

Dot had gone to answer it. "It's a reporter with a newspaper in Washington," she called back to Myron. "She wants to talk to you about Dunbar."

"A reporter? I don't want to talk to a reporter."

"That's what I'm trying to tell her."

Myron could hear the conversation between Dot and the woman at the door continue, so he rolled his wheelchair from the porch into the house and toward the front door.

"It'll only take a few minutes. I have a couple of questions for Professor Carlson that I need in order to finish my article, then I'll be on my way."

Myron rolled his wheelchair to where he could see the woman at the door. Red-rimmed glasses. Overweight. Rust-colored hair. He immediately disliked her.

Dot tried to close the door on her, but the woman blocked it with her foot.

"What kind of questions?" Myron said. His voice was gruff.

Dot opened the door slightly more but not enough for the woman to enter completely. The woman looked at Myron through the opening. She seemed surprised and tried to force the door open wider. But Dot held firm.

At last the intruder gave up and spoke to Myron from the threshold "Professor Carlson, I didn't see you there. I'm Cynthia Wellington with the *Washington Times* and I have a few questions for you concerning Judge Shelton's confirmation hearings."

"I think it's a big waste of time, that's what I think. There. I answered your question, now leave." Myron liked being crotchety at times and was quite proud of himself for being short with this reporter.

Dot began pushing the door closed again, but the woman wouldn't move her foot.

The woman pressed against the door with her shoulder. "Do you think he would vote to overturn *Roe v. Wade*?"

Myron was leaving the room and was almost where he could no longer see the intrusive woman. But he stopped and looked back at the door. It was a weird scene. Two women were standing at the same door. One was trying to close it while the other tried to keep it open. It made him laugh inside. And he was always glad to tell a living, breathing soul what he really thought about the *Roe* decision. Even greater pleasure came from being cantankerous about it.

"I hope so!" Myron yelled. "It was a terrible decision. Dunbar dissected it point by point in a research paper when he was a student of mine. It was one of the greatest pieces of writing I ever saw. I get it out and read it all the time. There is absolutely no way to support the *Roe* decision under any provision of the Constitution."

The woman finally removed her foot, and Dot managed to close the door.

"Thank you," Myron could hear the woman say from beyond the door.

"Bah," Myron grunted, then rolled himself back to the screened-in porch.

Dot followed him. "I wish you hadn't talked to her. It'll only get your blood pressure up."

"I've never felt better. I was just glad to yell that at someone other than you. It's about time somebody else listened to me."

Myron watched and listened to the waves crashing against the shoreline and smiled.

He was quite proud of himself. It had been too long since he'd been able to lecture someone. He preached like that to Dot all the time, but he knew she never listened and only patronized him. But now one more person knew exactly what he thought about *Roe v. Wade* and that pleased him. Maybe that reporter would print what he said in her newspaper, and thousands more would know the truth. The thought made him smile even more.

Stella Hanover returned to her car, parked in the driveway of the Carlson home. It had taken five hundred dollars to discover the house's location from some of the locals, but it had been worth every penny — she hoped. Professor Carlson hadn't provided much information, but maybe it was enough. It was all she could get. As she began to drive away, she dialed a number on her wireless.

"He's got something," Stella said. "He mentioned something about a research paper. See what you can find and then you need to disappear for a while."

The Hart Building, Washington DC
"Judge Shelton," Senator Montgomery began. "The committee thanks you for your

graciousness in sitting through three days of hearings and answering our questions. I must say that I thought you were one of the best, if not the best, candidate I've had the privilege of questioning."

"Thank you, Senator," Judge Shelton replied.

"The committee will stand in recess and will reconvene on Friday to deliberate and take a vote on whether to recommend confirmation to the full Senate or not." Senator Montgomery banged his gavel.

There were only four or five senators still present as the hearings concluded. Those who were present exited hastily after Senator Montgomery adjourned the hearing. Senate aides and staffers vacated the premises hurriedly as well, and reporters and photographers dashed for the exits in an attempt to file a report for the evening news or meet a deadline for the next morning's newspapers.

Porter approached Judge Shelton from his first-row seat. They shook hands, and Victoria joined them just behind the mahogany table that had been Judge Shelton's perch for the last three days.

"You did a great job." Porter smiled broadly. He felt a sense of relief.

Judge Shelton and Victoria were smiling

also. Porter could see the relief on Judge Shelton's face.

"Thanks, Porter. I owe it all to the rehearsals I had with you and the general counsel's office."

They both laughed. It was a laugh of satisfaction. It was a laugh that could only come at the end of the confirmation hearings when all the worry and anxiety were gone. It was up to the Judiciary Committee and the full Senate now. Porter and Judge Shelton had done their part.

Porter faced Victoria. "When do you get your cast off?"

"In two weeks, and I can't wait."

"I bet. Just so long as it's off in time for the swearing-in ceremony, right? I know you'd hate to have your picture taken in that." Porter casually pointed at Victoria's arm.

She smiled and nodded in agreement.

"Let's not get ahead of ourselves," Judge Shelton cautioned. "There're still a couple of votes that need to take place."

The Oval Office, the White House, Washington DC

Porter left the Hart Building and his limo transported him on the short ride from the Hart Building to the White House. A separate limo carried Judge Shelton and Victoria to their accommodations for the week. They were exhausted and needed rest. President Wallace had already heard the news that the hearings were over and was waiting for Porter in the Oval Office.

"Good work, Porter." President Wallace smiled as Porter entered the room.

Porter appreciated the compliment, but President Wallace smiled and Porter knew that that was about the extent of the excitement he would see from the president. He also knew that he had only done what was expected of him and nothing more. His job was to obtain confirmation of Dunbar Shelton's nomination to the Supreme Court. And the job wasn't completed yet. There was still work to be done. "Thank you, sir. But Judge Shelton did all the work. He was magnificent before the committee."

President Wallace waved Porter to a chair in front of his desk before returning to his chair behind the desk.

"Even still. You were tasked with this assignment, and you've done an excellent job. We can't celebrate yet, but I'd say we're well on our way. When's the committee vote?"

"They're voting on Friday and hopefully the full Senate will vote by the following Friday. If that happens, then Judge Shelton can be sworn in before Congress takes its August recess."

President Wallace's nominee to the Supreme Court was on his way to being confirmed. The president was pleased, Porter saw. And that pleased Porter.

"Porter, I like it when a plan comes together."

The law offices of Elijah J. Faulkner,
Jackson, Tennessee

It was late in the afternoon on Wednesday, the second week of July. Most of the staff was gone. Eli was working on the preparation for the Grissom trial. Wedged between two files stuffed in one of the many expandable folders he discovered the photograph Tag had given him from the traffic surveillance camera. Eli had forgotten about it. He was studying the photograph when Barbara knocked on his door.

"I'm going home," she said. "Do you need anything before I go?"

"I'm fine, but would you see if Jill is still here before you go?"

Barbara left and Eli resumed his study of the photograph.

Soon Jill was in his office.

"I forgot about this photograph," Eli said. "Tag gave it to me when I met with him the first time. It was taken from a surveillance camera mounted on a traffic light near Jessica Caldwell's town house. Take a look."

Jill stood in front of Eli's desk. He handed the photograph to Jill and watched her expression as she viewed it.

"You've had this the whole time?"

"The whole time. Tag told me that he was there the night Ms. Caldwell was killed and that he got this photograph from the police department a couple of days later. He told me it was his car in the picture, and I didn't question him about it. I only glanced at it that day before putting it in my briefcase."

"I thought he drove a convertible."

"He does."

"But this is an Infiniti SUV."

"I know. It's not his car. It's Anna's."

Eli watched Jill as she studied the photograph again.

She tucked her black hair behind her ears, then looked at Eli. "But why would he give it to you? Was he trying to implicate his own wife?"

"I don't know why yet. It still may be him driving her SUV. I can't make out the driver in that photograph. But I'm going to ask them about it."

"You want me to see if the police department has any other photos?"

"Yeah. See if there are any that show the driver of this vehicle. And check with the police department to see if there are any other photographs like this one taken at any intersection near her town house on the night of the murder."

CHAPTER
TWENTY-TWO

The Fletcher residence, Washington DC
The phone rang in the middle of the night again in Holland Fletcher's apartment. It was early Friday morning, and he was asleep.

On the third ring he cracked his eyes enough to look at the digital clock on his nightstand: 2:30. It had to be *her*, and he didn't want to talk to *her*. But he knew *she* wouldn't stop calling until he answered. He dragged the cordless receiver into bed with him and spoke into his pillow.

"Hello," he mumbled.

"Is this Holland Fletcher?"

It was a woman's voice, but much too young to be *her* voice.

"This is Holland. Who is this?"

"Tiffany Ramsey."

Her last name was barely out of her mouth before Holland was sitting on the side of the bed, fully awake. He listened hard and shook the sleep from his voice. "Tiffany? Why are you calling me at two thirty in the morning?"

"I don't really know. I'm scared, and I don't know who else to talk to."

Holland was in his pajama bottoms, walking back and forth around his bed with the cordless telephone. It was dark in his bedroom, so it took a few seconds for his eyes to adjust.

"Why are you scared?" he asked.

There was a brief silence on the other end of the phone. Then, "Because I know something about Jessica Caldwell and Senator Proctor."

Holland stopped at the foot of the bed. The room was deathly quiet. He could see Tiffany in his mind . . . sitting on her bed with her knees pulled up under her chin, whispering into the telephone. She even looked scared.

"What exactly do you know?"

The quietness from the other end of the call was nerve-racking. Holland held his breath, hoping Tiffany would simply blurt out the secrets she kept buried.

She continued to clutch them. "I'm almost too scared to say it."

"I'm not going to pressure you. You can tell me when you're ready."

"You're right about the town house, you know. Jessica told me not long before she moved out. I can't believe it's been almost six months since she left."

Holland could tell that she was talking merely for the sake of talking. She was avoiding what she really wanted to say but trying to build her courage to say it.

He sat back down on the edge of the bed and tried to set her mind at ease. "Were the two of you friends?"

"We weren't close friends. We didn't have much in common. She went to Vanderbilt. I went to Princeton. But sharing a place to live forced us to find a few things in common. And we did. We just didn't socialize together very much. She had her friends and I had mine."

"Did her friends include Senator Proctor?"

"Jessica was quite the partier. She liked going to all of the social events in town. And she met Senator Proctor at one of them. He called the town house a few times. He never said who he was, but I recognized his voice. Who else has a voice like that? I mean, once you've seen him on television it's hard not to put the face with the voice."

"So they knew each other, and he called and talked to her. That doesn't sound like

338

much of a relationship."

Another pause. This one longer than the previous two. Holland realized that the truth was about to come out. The secret — the skeleton — she had locked away was about to escape.

"There's one other thing. I came home from work one day in the middle of the afternoon. I was working on a file and had left it at home accidentally and needed it. When I entered the front door, I could hear Jessica laughing upstairs. I was surprised that she was home and almost called out her name. Then I heard Senator Proctor's voice, too. I retrieved my file and slipped out again. They never knew I was there."

"When was this?"

"Just a few days before she moved to Nashville."

Holland gazed at the floor. He held the phone in one hand. "But you never saw them and don't know exactly what they were doing?"

"Be serious. They were in her bedroom in the middle of the afternoon, giggling. What do you think they were doing?"

"I guess you're right."

"And then three months later she died. She was murdered. And it turns out she was pregnant."

"When was the last time you saw Jessica?"

"She came back to town for Justice Robinson's memorial service. I saw her at the cathedral, from a distance. I tried to find her after the service, but she left hurriedly. When I got to the door of the cathedral, I saw her getting into a taxi with a man."

"Was it Senator Proctor?"

"No. It was someone I didn't recognize."

"What did he look like?"

"He was handsome. Blond hair. Tan. But I didn't know him."

"You just described about a million men."

"But how many would have attended Justice Robinson's memorial?"

"That's true. Do you think you could identify him again if you saw him?"

"I think so. I didn't get a real good look at him, but I think I would recognize him again if I saw him."

Holland thought for a moment. There had to be a way to determine who had attended Justice Robinson's memorial service. Video clips. Interviews. Did the *Post* have any photographs from the service? He pondered his next question, then cautiously asked it. "Did you ever tell Jessica you knew about her and Senator Proctor?"

"Are you crazy? That wasn't any of my business."

Holland stood and paced again. He was quiet for several seconds, thinking.

"What are you thinking about?" she asked.

"I'm just thinking."

"You know you can't publish any of this."

He stopped pacing. That was exactly what he'd been thinking about. He had to get a story out of this information somehow. "Why not? That's what I do. I write articles for the *Post.*"

"Because you can't, that's why. If you mention any of this in the *Post,* Senator Proctor will know I talked to you. I'm too scared for that to happen."

"Do you think Senator Proctor killed her?"

"I don't know what to think anymore. The facts in the newspaper in Nashville sure point to the guy they arrested. But I don't know. How'd you find out about the town house?"

Holland wasn't sure it was a good idea to tell Tiffany. But she had opened up to him. He felt he at least needed to reciprocate.

"There's this mystery woman who keeps calling me. She's led me around by the nose for weeks. She gave me some information that made the connection."

"Who is she?"

"I don't know. She won't tell me her name

341

or how to contact her. She only calls me. Her rules."

"Now I'm really scared."

Holland remembered the night by the Washington Monument. A man with a raspy voice and a gun in the small of his back were hard to forget. They didn't teach him how to handle such things in journalism school.

"I'm a little scared, too," he admitted.

"You're not going to publish any of this, are you?"

Holland relented. "No. I can't yet. I need more corroboration."

"That's good."

Holland sensed that the conversation was coming to a close. He didn't want it to end. Even though they were talking about things that scared them both, he didn't want to stop. He liked hearing her voice.

"I think I'm going to hang up," Tiffany said. "I'm getting sleepy finally. Thanks for talking with me."

Holland could hear the tiredness in her voice and knew that her appreciation was genuine. "Don't mention it. I now realize why you said it was dangerous the other day. You need to be careful."

"I will."

"And, Tiffany?"

"Yes."

"You really need to find a new place to live."

"I'm already working on it."

Holland hung up the phone and lay back down on the bed. He and Tiffany had been talking for thirty minutes. He closed his eyes and tried to go back to sleep, but it was useless. There wouldn't be any more sleep for Holland that night.

The Hart Building, Washington DC

In the closet in Senator Proctor's office in the Hart Building a digital line-activated recorder went into sleep mode after the conversation between Holland Fletcher and Tiffany Ramsey ended. The call was time stamped and date stamped. It was added to the listing on the LCD screen and would be easily retrieved later in the morning. Their words were recorded in crystal clarity.

The Oval Office, the White House, Washington DC

Wallace watched the plasma television monitor across the room as the Judiciary Committee voted on whether to recommend to the full Senate that Judge Dunbar Shelton be confirmed to the Supreme Court. The committee was back in session at 9:00 a.m. eastern time on Friday. Judge

343

Shelton and Victoria, as well as Porter and Lauren, were in the office with him.

It was a surreal feeling when each committee member voted aye as their name was called. President Wallace recalled his time as a state legislator and then as governor of South Carolina. He remembered when he decided to run for president, and the burden of responsibility he felt when he won. There were still many issues — both foreign and domestic — that needed tackling, but watching the committee members vote made him realize that one thing he desired more than all else was close to being accomplished . . . even though the full Senate had yet to vote.

As the last committee member cast his vote, Judge Shelton hugged Victoria and President Wallace hugged Lauren. Porter gave a confident fist pump and shook hands with the president.

"We're almost there," Porter said.

President Wallace and Porter smiled at each other. They were smiles of relief and satisfaction.

"Almost," President Wallace replied. "I think we're on the downhill, Porter."

"I can't imagine anything getting in the way of confirmation now."

Georgia Mathis had worked for Fernandina Home Health for twelve years. For the last two she had been checking on Myron and Dorothy Carlson — mainly Myron — twice a week. She made sure Myron's medicine was regulated and helped him with thirty minutes of physical therapy. Myron generally complained the entire time.

Georgia, just turned forty-five, arrived at her usual time of 9:00 a.m. eastern. She smoothed her bleached blond hair, pink blouse, and the white polyester uniform she hated. She rang the doorbell beside the front door and waited.

No response.

She rang again.

Still no response.

That was odd, since Dot and Myron were usually so prompt.

Georgia knocked and listened but didn't hear anything inside. She stepped back from the door and squinted toward the end of the house, where Dorothy's car was usually parked. It was there.

Maybe they're on the back porch, Georgia thought and walked around the house. She climbed the steps to the screened-in porch but didn't find Myron or Dorothy.

She knocked on the back door.

345

Still no response.

She cupped her hands around her eyes and peered through the window in the door . . . and gasped. The den was in complete disarray. Some of the furniture was toppled over, and books were strewn everywhere. Seeing Myron's wheelchair empty and on its side, she tried frantically to open the door. It was locked. She anxiously looked through the kitchen window. The scene was the same. The cabinet doors were standing wide open. Plates were smashed on the floor.

Georgia ran back to her car and called 911 on her wireless phone. She stumbled and almost fell twice along the way. She could barely catch her breath as the call was answered.

"This is Georgia Mathis, and I'm at the Carlson home on North Fletcher Avenue near Fort Clinch State Park. Something is terribly wrong."

*The Oval Office, the White House,
Washington DC*
President Wallace and the others were still celebrating the committee vote and preparing for a press conference when President Wallace noticed that Porter was discussing something on his wireless phone.

346

Porter faced President Wallace with an expression that said the conversation wasn't good news. Porter's countenance fell, and he shook his head in disbelief. He turned his back to the group.

President Wallace's smile disappeared. The room fell silent. All present watched Porter as he talked with his hand on his hip. He looked despondent.

"When did this happen?" the president heard Porter say.

Porter pivoted back toward the others. He pointed his face toward the ceiling and closed his eyes, listening. President Wallace watched Porter keenly.

"Are there any leads or suspects?" Porter listened again. "I see. Please keep me posted."

Porter ended the call and faced the group. But he mainly looked at Judge Shelton. "Director Hughes's office patched a call through from the FBI office in Jacksonville. They thought we would like to know immediately. They found Professor Carlson and his wife dead this morning. They'd been murdered." Porter's words were straightforward, but his tone was sympathetic.

Judge Shelton was visibly upset. "What happened?"

"It looks like a robbery. There are a lot of

valuables missing, but the investigation is still under way."

Victoria put her arm around Judge Shelton, and they sat on one of the two sofas in the Oval Office. Judge Shelton buried his face in his hands. Lauren sat beside the grieving couple.

"He was my mentor and friend," Judge Shelton said miserably. "I knew his time was close but never dreamed his life would end like this. And Dot, his wife —"

President Wallace frowned. Things didn't add up. On the very day the committee voted to recommend confirmation of Judge Shelton to the Supreme Court, a dear friend and mentor of Judge Shelton's was murdered. That couldn't be coincidental.

President Wallace walked to Porter and whispered, "Does this have anything to do with Judge Shelton's nomination?"

"I don't know, sir. I immediately thought the same thing, but the local officials are calling it a robbery."

"Make sure the FBI checks that possibility."

"I will."

"And tell the media that the press conference is at least postponed. This is no longer a time for celebration."

Porter left the Oval Office to carry out his

instructions and President Wallace turned back to Judge Shelton, Victoria, and Lauren. Judge Shelton appeared shocked and despondent. They all — and particularly Dunbar Shelton — had gone from a mountaintop experience to the deepest valley in the span of less than five minutes.

President Wallace set his jaw. He walked over and put a hand on Judge Shelton's shoulder. "I promise we're going to find out who did this."

CHAPTER
TWENTY-THREE

The Hart Building, Washington DC

"But I don't want to see Stella," Senator Proctor argued. "It's too early on a Monday to have to see that biddy. You shouldn't have told her that she could come up."

Senator Proctor stood from his executive chair as Cooper finished his conversation with Stella. Cooper put his wireless phone in his pocket and buttoned his coat. Senator Proctor, irritated that Stella had gained entrance to his office so easily, glared at Cooper.

Cooper shrugged as if there were nothing else he could have done. That irritated Senator Proctor more.

"She's already on her way up," Cooper explained. "She said she had something really important to talk to you about."

"What?"

"She didn't say. Just that it's important."

Senator Proctor walked to the other side

of the room. "Let her in. But I'm only giving her five minutes. I mean it. Five minutes, Cooper, and she's out of here."

Senator Proctor poured a cup of coffee and walked around in his opulent office. He didn't sit down. If he did, then so would Stella when she arrived. And if that happened, he feared he'd never get her to leave.

All too soon Cooper opened the door and admitted Stella. She was beaming. She carried two folders and her purse.

Senator Proctor wasn't sure he had ever seen Stella Hanover smile. It was a devilish smile — the kind that didn't come from joy but rather from knowing something no one else knew. Senator Proctor wondered what it was.

He met her in the middle of the room. "What's this about, Stella?"

"Can we sit down?"

"No. I'm in a hurry. I've only got a few minutes. What's this about?"

Senator Proctor stood near Stella, but not too close. He stared and tried to convey the message that he wasn't interested in what she had to say.

Stella only smiled more broadly. "You remember when I was in your office a month ago?"

"How could I forget?"

"Do you remember what you told me?"

"Not exactly, but I'm sure you're about to tell me."

"You said that if I could find anything where Shelton said he would overturn *Roe*, then you would reconsider your position on him."

Senator Proctor rolled his eyes. "Stella, the Judiciary Committee has already voted to send his nomination to the full Senate. There's nothing I can do at this point."

"Sure there is. Look at this." Stella handed Senator Proctor one of the folders she carried.

Reluctantly he opened it. He was still uninterested and simply fanned the pages in the folder without looking at them. "What is this?"

"It's a research paper where Shelton said *Roe* was unconstitutional and should be overturned."

Senator Proctor cut his eyes at Cooper, who raised his eyebrows. Senator Proctor slowly read the document as he sauntered to his desk and sat down in his executive chair.

Stella followed him and stopped in front of his desk. She peered down at him.

The document was twenty-five pages long. He read the first page and a half and looked up at her. "It's too late, Stella."

"It's not too late!" Her smile disappeared.

"He's going to be confirmed by the end of the week. There's nothing I can do."

Stella exhaled angrily. She kept her eyes directed toward Senator Proctor but said, "Cooper, will you please leave us alone?"

Senator Proctor looked past Stella to Cooper. Cooper shifted his weight and shook his head. Stella couldn't see him.

"And don't listen," Stella said.

Senator Proctor smiled at Stella. She was smarter than he gave her credit for being. He waved Cooper out of the room and Cooper left quietly. After Cooper left, Stella handed Senator Proctor the second of her two folders. It was thicker than the first file. Much thicker.

"What's this?" Senator Proctor took the folder from Stella's hand. "Another research paper?"

"Nope. That's my file on you."

Senator Proctor could feel the color leave his face as he thumbed through the contents of the folder. He swallowed hard. There were pictures and memos containing dates, times, and places. Different women appeared in the photographs with him. Some women appeared in more than one photograph. There were pictures of him entering and leaving various hotels around DC with various women. This was bad. Real bad. Stella had done her homework.

"I didn't bring the videos," Stella said.

Senator Proctor closed the folder and slid it across the desk. "All right, Stella. You got me. What do you want?"

Stella left, satisfied, and Cooper returned. He found Senator Proctor sitting dejectedly behind his desk. His head rested against the back of his chair, his eyes were closed, and his face was creased, as if he had a headache.

Cooper sat across the desk from him. "I listened anyway."

"I knew you would."

"She's got one on me, too."

Senator Proctor groaned. "She probably has one on everybody in town."

"You know she tried to have Shelton killed, don't you?"

Senator Proctor opened his eyes but didn't move. "I guessed that was her. She's the only person I know who's that ruthless. But we don't have any way of proving that now, and she's got the drop on me."

"What do you want to do?"

Senator Proctor closed his eyes again. The anguish was apparent on his face. "I don't have any choice. Stella will ruin me if I don't do what she wants. I've got to turn on Wallace."

"That's what I was afraid of."

"Schedule a press conference at one p.m. and start working the phones. Call all the senators in our caucus and tell them that we're pulling our support for Shelton."

The Oval Office, the White House, Washington DC

President Wallace was livid. Porter had never seen him this mad. He was mad, but not this mad, when the Russian president cursed him in Russian because the United States had sided with Israel at the UN Security Council. He was mad, but not this mad, when Congress failed to enact all his tax cuts. This was the angriest President Wallace had ever been. Porter was sure of it.

"He can't back out now! Shelton's already made it through the committee!"

"That's what Cooper said. Senator Proctor's pulling his support for Judge Shelton and will vote against him on the Senate floor."

"Over this!" President Wallace violently waved a copy of Judge Shelton's research paper that had been faxed to his office from Senator Proctor's office.

Porter sat rigidly on one of the sofas and watched President Wallace pace around the Oval Office. He didn't like what had happened any more than the president.

"This is nothing! It's a thirty-year-old research paper, for goodness sake."

"I agree, sir, but —"

"But nothing, Porter." The president's hand slammed down on his desk. "We had a deal, and Proctor's reneging on it. Pure and simple. He was probably planning this from the beginning. He set us up. That's all there is to it."

There was a knock on the door, and the president's secretary admitted Judge Shelton into the Oval Office.

"What's going on?" Judge Shelton asked.

President Wallace could barely look at him. He dropped his head and shook it in disbelief. Porter knew that President Wallace didn't want to tell Judge Shelton the bad news. But he had to. He had to know that his confirmation was likely doomed because of something he'd written thirty years earlier. It didn't seem right to Porter, and he knew it didn't seem right to President Wallace, that a few words written decades ago could have an impact on the current Supreme Court. But they did.

"We've got a problem," President Wallace

said. He handed the fax to Judge Shelton. Porter remained on the sofa. "Senator Proctor's office called and said that he's withdrawing his support of your nomination because of this."

Judge Shelton flipped through the pages, only scanning it as he went. After a few seconds of reading, he looked at President Wallace. "I haven't seen this in years. Where did you get it?"

"Proctor's office faxed it a few minutes ago."

"I only know of one copy of this even existing. The rest were shredded years ago."

"What are you talking about?" President Wallace asked.

"I wrote this when I was in law school. I showed it to Professor Carlson when I finished it. He agreed with my reasoning and kept a copy. It wasn't part of a class. It was just something that I researched and wrote on my own time. After the Robert Bork hearings, Professor Carlson called me and suggested that I destroy any copies of this that I still had."

"If all copies were destroyed, then where did this one come from?"

"I only know of one remaining copy."

"Who had it?"

"Professor Carlson."

It felt as though the air was sucked out of the room.

Porter instinctively leaped to his feet. He could see President Wallace thinking.

The president swiveled toward Porter. "Did Cooper Harrington say where they got this?"

"No. Just that Senator Proctor couldn't support Judge Shelton because of his position on *Roe.*"

President Wallace's previous stomping became a slow, methodical stroll. Porter followed him with his eyes. Judge Shelton lowered the memo to his side and stood quietly beside Porter.

The president stopped and looked through the window behind his desk. "Porter, don't say anything to anybody that links Professor Carlson with this memo. We can't trust Director Hughes, but we must find out who murdered the Carlsons and fast."

Porter knew what President Wallace meant. He didn't care how it was done and didn't want to know what was done. But he wanted it done. President Wallace wanted to know who murdered Myron and Dorothy Carlson, and he wanted to know immediately. Porter was tasked with finding the truth no matter what it took, and he relished the assignment. And just as President Wallace believed he was in the White House for such a time as this in the history of the country, Porter also believed his station in life wasn't accidental. It was handling situations like this one — searching for truth — that gave Porter purpose.

"And if Senator Proctor is hung with it," President Wallace said, "then so be it."

"He's up for reelection this fall," Porter reminded him.

The president frowned. "If he's involved, I hope the penalty is greater than not getting reelected."

"I'm sure it will be. What about the races in Wyoming, Kansas, and Kentucky?" Porter asked.

Without hesitation, President Wallace responded, "Let's get back in those races. Apologize for pulling out and see what we can do to help. If Proctor is reneging on the deal, there is no reason for us to uphold our part of the bargain. Having our folks control the Senate would be huge."

New York City

After her meeting with Senator Proctor, Stella Hanover rode the Amtrak from Union Station in DC to Penn Station in Manhattan. Stella was pleased with herself. The train ride was very relaxing. The ride was about three hours, and she was back in her Avenue of the Americas office in time for Senator Proctor's afternoon press conference.

Stella entered her twenty-seventh-floor office at 12:50 p.m. eastern time, and all of her staff snapped to attention. But she didn't yell at anyone. She didn't bark. In fact, she was rather polite. She was in a good mood. This was the best she had felt in quite some time. She spoke kindly to Valerie before walking into her office and closing the door behind her. She wanted to savor the moment alone.

It was too early in the day for most people to drink, but Stella poured an afternoon cocktail anyway. A celebration like this deserved a little something special. She sat down behind her desk and, with the remote, changed the television channel to CNN. It had the best news coverage, in her opinion.

Soon the screen was plastered with the image of Senate majority leader, Lance Proctor. Stella sipped at her drink and thought about the look on Senator Proctor's face when she'd shown him her file on him. It brought pleasure to her soul. He was easy to blackmail. She had files on practically every member of Congress and most others inside the Beltway. The only one of any consequence she hadn't been able to capture in one of her traps was President Wallace. She doubted she ever would. She increased the volume as Senator Proctor began to speak. There were at least a dozen microphones standing in front of him.

"Some new information has come to light regarding Judge Dunbar Shelton," Senator Proctor said. "And I can no longer support his nomination to the Supreme Court. My office has learned that when he was in law school, Judge Shelton wrote a research memorandum that said *Roe v. Wade* should be overturned. This country cannot have someone with such extreme positions sitting on the highest court in the land."

Stella decreased the volume and finished the last of her drink. She smiled to herself. She was satisfied. She didn't worry about how things had gotten to this point. The end justified the means. The end was that Dunbar Shelton wouldn't be on the Supreme Court. And that was all that mattered to Stella.

CHAPTER
TWENTY-FOUR

James S. Brady Press Briefing Room, the White House, Washington DC

President Wallace's press conference was delayed until Tuesday morning. Porter and his staff had voluntarily disseminated Judge Shelton's research memo following Senator Proctor's press conference the previous day. The press release attached to the memo said that the president only wished the memo had been discovered earlier. He was proud of Judge Shelton's position on constitutional construction. All the networks and cable news channels had opened their Monday-evening newscasts with the memo and pronounced Judge Shelton's nomination dead.

On Tuesday morning President Wallace stood before a bank of microphones in the press briefing room. He had just finished his prepared remarks, which were essentially the same as the press release the previous day. The briefing room was overflowing with members of the White House press corps. Porter stood stage right.

"I'll be glad to take questions," President Wallace said.

Hands went up from every reporter in the room.

"Olivia." President Wallace pointed to Olivia Nelson. He still didn't like her, but she fit perfectly in the plan.

"Mr. President, do you honestly believe that Judge Shelton can still be confirmed?"

President Wallace shifted his weight and leaned on the top of the podium. His face was close to the bank of microphones. "Absolutely. I expect the Senate will confirm him."

There were audible gasps in the room. It was the reaction he and Porter had hoped for.

"But his views are extreme and certainly not close to the mainstream of America," Olivia chided.

"His views are not extreme, Olivia. This memo was written by a law school student over thirty years ago. It addresses constitutional construction, not the morality of abortion or any other societal issue," President Wallace said confidently. "Most jurists in the country think just like Judge Shelton when it comes to constitutional construction. We need men and women like Judge Dunbar Shelton on our courts."

"Don't you think it's time to withdraw Judge Shelton's nomination and nominate someone who won't divide the country?"

President Wallace stood straight and smoothed his royal blue necktie. The press conference was going just like he and Porter thought it would.

"I haven't asked Judge Shelton to withdraw," President Wallace stated, "nor has he asked to be allowed to withdraw. And I don't plan for him to withdraw. Before you even ask, we're not going to relaunch his nomination and present him as something he's not."

"Would you agree that Judge Shelton should at least go back to the Judiciary Committee for additional questioning about the memo?"

Finally the question he wanted. President Wallace didn't like the press, but when necessary he took pleasure in manipulating its members. "Judge Shelton has already answered all of the committee's questions. They asked him about constitutional construction and he told them. The answer won't change if it's asked again. There's no reason for him to appear before the committee again."

And to agitate Senator Proctor so he would take the bait, President Wallace continued, unprompted. "I'll tell you this, though. I think Senator Proctor should resign his seat in the Senate immediately."

The audible gasps rose again, and President Wallace saw and heard pens scribbling on paper. The saber rattling had begun. Instead of being defensive, President Wallace and Porter had decided to go on the attack. Beat Senator Proctor at his own game. If he was going to sabotage Judge Shelton's nomination, then they were going to try to take Senator Proctor down, too.

"What do you mean, Mr. President?" Olivia asked.

"Senator Proctor knew all about Judge Shelton's views before now and he supported the nomination. This memo wasn't a surprise to him. What's changed? I'll tell you what's changed. Nothing. Senator Proctor has always been and will always be a man who can't keep his word. We don't need a man like that in the Senate."

President Wallace paused as the photographers' cameras flashed and the television cameras recorded. His face was full of resolve. "That's all the time I have."

He stepped down from the platform and

Porter followed him from the room. They could hear the cries of "Mr. President, Mr. President!" as they walked down the hall.

"How'd I do?" the president asked Porter.

"Perfect. The senator now knows that we're not going down without a fight."

"But it won't be much of a fight if we can't find out how Proctor got the memo."

Havana, Cuba

Joe Moretti liked Havana. He liked the Cubans' rum and cigars. But he was particularly fond of the high-heeled Cuban women who danced salsa and disco at the nightclubs. They were beautiful, soft, and irresistible.

Joe had been to Havana often when he needed to be invisible for a while. And it was time to be invisible. The Shelton bombing and the Carlson murders required it. Stella had paid him another $50,000 for the box of documents he delivered to her from the Carlson residence. He didn't know what was in the box, but Stella seemed pleased and the job paid well. The latter was more important to Joe than the former.

When he had arrived in Havana early Monday morning via Cancún, Mexico, Joe had plenty of money to flash around. That usually got him whatever — and whomever

— he wanted. When he wasn't chasing women, he liked to eat at D'Giovanni's. It was located near the Marina Hemingway on the north shore of the island country and had the best Italian food of any restaurant in Havana.

Joe sat as his usual table with a beautiful Cuban woman he'd met the previous night. She told him her name was Sofia. He didn't care what her last name was. He wasn't even certain that Sofia was her real name. It didn't matter. She agreed to have dinner with him that evening. He hoped she would also be having breakfast with him the next morning. With her long, curly black hair, dark eyes, and dark brown skin, Sofia was exactly his type.

They were waited on by his usual waitress. The proprietor came by their table periodically to make sure their meal was perfect. Everything was routine and comfortable. He saw some regulars he recognized and some tourists he didn't. There was a Latin American couple sitting two tables away, enjoying themselves. Joe had three glasses of wine and a plateful of linguine. When Sofia touched his hand and peered seductively over her wineglass at him with her dark eyes, he knew it was time to leave.

Joe paid with a crisp Ben Franklin from

Stella Hanover's money and exited the front door. Sofia held his hand in hers.

The Latin American couple exited behind them. The woman hung on to the man's arm, and they laughed and talked in Spanish.

Joe had no idea what the couple said. And he didn't care. He had Sofia on his mind. He lit a cigarette and smiled at Sofia as the couple passed them on the sidewalk. He noticed the uneasy expression on Sofia's face as she looked at the man and woman who were walking a few feet in front of them. It was as if she were listening to their words, and the words troubled her.

It was dusk and the temperature was high. Joe didn't like the hot, humid weather. It wasn't like that in Brooklyn. But he would tolerate it for a while for a girl like Sofia. Some stars were visible in the eastern sky as day reluctantly gave way to night. As Joe and Sofia walked toward his car three blocks away, a man approached them. The man appeared to be an African American and had a thick chest. He wore sandals, Bermuda shorts, and a floral shirt. Joe took him to be a tourist.

"Do you have the time, sir?" the man asked Joe in English.

Joe stopped, released Sofia's hand, and

consulted his watch. "It's almost seven p.m."

"Thank you," the man said.

Joe reached for Sofia's hand again, but it wasn't there. He turned and noticed that Sofia had stepped three feet away from him. Her earlier worried look had changed to fear. But the realization registered too late with Joe.

A four-door car screeched to a stop at the curb beside him. The African American who had asked for the time grabbed Joe around the shoulders and the Latin American couple ran back toward him. Joe struggled to free himself, but the African American was too strong. The woman thrust a nine-millimeter pistol in his face, and the two men shoved Joe into the backseat of the car. The African-American man climbed into the front passenger seat, and the couple surrounded Joe in the backseat. They both pointed pistols at him. As the car sped away, he peered through the rear passenger window to see if Sofia was still standing there, but she had disappeared.

The driver glanced at Joe in the rearview mirror. "We're glad to have you onboard, Mr. Moretti."

Joe flinched. *How do they know my name?*

The driver was a tall man with a mustache and black hair so bushy that it brushed against the ceiling of the car. His voice was American, and he had a large scar under his chin. When he smiled at Joe, a gold tooth glistened beneath his mustache.

"Where are you taking me?" Joe managed.

"Be patient, Mr. Moretti. You'll find out soon enough."

The U.S. Virgin Islands
The jet transporting Porter McIntosh landed at the airport in Charlotte Amalie on the island of St. Thomas just after 8:00 a.m. eastern time on Wednesday. He'd flown on one of Simon's planes so there wouldn't be an official record of his leaving the United States.

One of Simon's men met his plane when it landed and drove him to a safe house near Magens Bay on the north shore of the island. It was there that Porter would meet Joe Moretti for the first time. Even before Porter met the man, he hated him. There were four innocent individuals dead because of Joe Moretti. That was enough to make anyone hate him.

But Porter knew that Joe Moretti was only an instrument. A tool used by someone else to carry out their evil scheme. It was that person Porter wanted. Not the street thug, but the kingpin.

Porter removed his dark sunglasses and entered the safe house without any pomp or circumstance. His driver followed him in and stood just inside the door. Porter nodded at Simon, who met him at the door, then glanced around the room. A Latin-American man and woman stood in the back. The African American, whom Porter recognized from the street in front of Simon's office, stood in the middle of the room. Simon remained near the door.

Joe Moretti was seated in the middle of the room beside the African American. The sight of him initially caused a rage in Porter, but he extinguished it. Now was not the time for vengeance. That would be handled by someone else. Porter needed answers. He walked toward the Mafia man.

Joe Moretti wore a black, short-sleeved shirt and black pants. He was tied to a chair, and his olive-toned face was bruised and bloated. His lips were swollen, and dried blood was visible in the corners of his mouth. His head slumped against his chest. His appearance didn't bother Porter in the least.

"We got here about midnight," Simon said, following Porter from the door. "He hasn't had much to say." Simon smiled.

Right then it seemed to Porter that Simon

relished what he did for a living just a little too much. That made Porter nervous. He was glad that Simon was on his team even if it was only because Porter paid him.

Porter was dressed in a blue blazer, slacks, and a starched white dress shirt. His attire conveyed the message that he was important. "Let's see if he's ready to talk now. I probably have more to offer him than you do."

The African American grabbed Joe by his hair and pulled his head back so Porter could look into his face.

"Mr. Moretti, my name is Porter McIntosh and I'm with the United States government."

Joe peered at Porter through swollen eyes. Porter wasn't certain the guy could clearly see him, but he could hear.

"I'm a U.S. citizen, and I have my rights." Joe's voice was labored and miserable.

Porter knew the man had no idea where he was. The thug certainly didn't know he was in a U.S. territory. And Porter wasn't about to let a murderer think he could use the Constitution as a shield against Porter's wrath.

"The problem, Mr. Moretti, is that we're not in the United States right now, and officially I'm in my office in Washington. So this meeting never took place."

"Who are these guys?" Joe painfully nodded at Simon. "CIA?"

"Nope. They're not CIA, FBI, NSA, or any other agency of the United States government. In fact, these guys don't exist. Officially, they've all been dead for years. But they were hired by me to find you. Do you want to know why?"

"Tell me."

Porter could see on Joe's face that he was beginning to understand the situation, but not completely. Porter rested his foot on Joe's chair, between his legs, and leaned into his face. "Because if the FBI were to find you, then you'd hire a lawyer, have a trial, and get a warm prison cell. And that would be too good for you. If you don't help me and tell me what I want to know, these guys will make you disappear. Nobody will know you're even missing. Because, like I said, they don't exist. It's pretty easy for them to make people disappear. They've had a lot of practice."

"And if I cooperate?"

"If you cooperate, we'll talk about a permanent residence in some place like Budapest or Warsaw instead of you swimming with the sharks."

Porter liked talking tough. He didn't get

to do it often enough. In his day job he had to be polite and make deals. This was more fun. Porter placed his foot on the floor and stood in front of Joe with both hands on his hips.

Joe's head slumped against the back of the chair. "What do you want to know?"

"I want to know who hired you on the Shelton bombing and the Carlson murders."

"I don't know what you're talking about."

Porter stepped away and displayed his back to Joe. "Get him out of here," he ordered.

One of Simon's men held a gun to Joe's head while another began untying him.

"What're they doing? Where're they taking me?" Joe's voice was frantic.

Porter talked with his back to Joe. "I don't know, and I don't care. I'm not playing games, Mr. Moretti. Either you tell me what I want to know or this is your last day on the earth."

"Okay!" Joe screamed. "Okay. I'll tell you."

Simon's men backed away, and Porter turned around.

"But you got to promise that you won't let her near me. Because if I tell you, she'll be after me." There was fear in Joe's eyes.

"I'm not promising you anything," Porter said. "But honestly, Mr. Moretti, are you more afraid of whoever it was who hired you . . . or of these guys?" Porter waved his arms at Simon and his men. "If you help us, we're going to take you to some city in Eastern Europe. Put you up in an apartment, and after that you're on your own. But at least you won't be rotting away in some jail cell or worse."

"Okay, I'll tell you." Joe dropped his head, as if he was afraid to say the words. "It was some woman named Stella. That's all I know. Stella." *Stella Hanover!* The name screamed in Porter's mind. Of all the people in the world, he would never have guessed Stella. He knew she was ruthless but had never known her to be violent.

"Are you sure she said 'Stella'?" Porter asked.

"I'm sure."

"If you're lying, things will be done to you that'll be worse than anything these guys have ever done to anyone else."

"I'm not lying."

Porter studied Joe's face. It was battered and scared, but he appeared to be telling the truth. Porter nodded at the man who'd driven him from the airport, to indicate that it was time to go. Porter stepped toward the door and glanced back at Joe's terrified, swollen face.

"Mr. Moretti, remember that we found you this time. If you're lying or if I ever hear about you again or if you ever set foot back in the United States, we'll find you again. And these guys won't be as hospitable as they were this time."

The Oval Office, the White House, Washington DC

"Stella Hanover," President Wallace said. He spoke into the telephone in his office and didn't ask Porter where he was. The line was secure. "I knew she was cold-blooded, but I would never have thought anything like this."

"All we have at this point is a name. There's still more work to do to pin all of this on Stella and tie Proctor to it. But we're working on it."

"What about the FBI? Can Hughes help us?"

Porter peered at the blue Atlantic Ocean through an oval window in the sleek Gulfstream V jet. He was thirty thousand feet above the Atlantic, somewhere east of Florida.

"I don't think we should say anything to Director Hughes about it. He must be in bed with Proctor somehow. The FBI should've found Moretti by now."

Porter couldn't tell the president that he had just seen Joe Moretti face-to-face or where the guy was going. But Porter was convinced there was simply no reason the FBI shouldn't have already found him. Simon had said it was easy. Joe Moretti had left a bright trail to follow.

Porter knew that the president wouldn't approve of the methods, regardless of the outcome. But Porter also knew that the president wouldn't ask him questions to which he didn't want to know the answers.

"Who are we going to get to investigate Stella and any possible link with Proctor?" the president asked.

"You just let me handle that, sir."

"I think it's time to give Proctor enough rope to hang himself with."

"I agree. It'll be nice to have him out of our way."

As soon as President Wallace disconnected the call with Porter, his secretary ushered Judge Shelton into his office. It was time for the press conference war to continue, with Senator Proctor firing the next salvo. But this time President Wallace was glad to see the senator's face on television. He was doing exactly what President Wallace and Porter wanted: reconvening the confirmation hearings.

"I've asked Senator Montgomery and the Judiciary Committee to reconvene so they can reconsider their vote on Judge Shelton's nomination."

President Wallace and Judge Shelton sat on opposite sofas. Senator Proctor's face was on the plasma monitor across the room from the president's desk. Just looking at him annoyed President Wallace.

"The committee originally voted to recommend confirmation," Senator Proctor continued. "But with these new developments, I think many of the members of the committee would like to ask Judge Shelton some additional questions and consider changing their votes. Senator Montgomery agrees and has scheduled the committee to reconvene on Monday."

President Wallace pressed a button on the remote control and the monitor went black.

"I sure hope you know what you're doing, Mr. President," Judge Shelton said.

"Everything's going to work out fine, I assure you. You just go in there on Monday and tell them exactly what you believe."

CHAPTER
TWENTY-FIVE

Washington DC

Holland Fletcher was at his desk at the *Post* on Thursday morning when he heard over the police scanner about a suspicious death on Thirty-seventh Street. Vice wasn't his beat, but he had a sinking feeling. He left the *Post* headquarters and drove furiously toward Tiffany Ramsey's town house. He could see the flashing blue lights two blocks before he reached his destination, and his heart sank into his stomach.

The parking areas near the curbs were filled with emergency vehicles, so he stopped his car in the middle of the street half a block from the vehicles and flashing lights. He left the driver's-side door open and ran toward Tiffany's home. A couple dozen people were gathered at the yellow police tape that cordoned off the area, and that slowed his progress. He pressed through the crowd and ducked under the yellow tape.

"You can't come in here," a blue-clad police officer yelled. He ran toward Holland and pushed him back under the tape.

"But I'm with the *Post.*"

"I don't care if you're the pope himself. You're not coming in here." The police officer's face was rigid. He moved his body to try to shield Holland from seeing the crime scene.

But Holland had seen enough, and it wasn't good. Employees of the DC coroner's office rolled a gurney with a black body bag through the front door of Tiffany's town house and lifted it into the back of a waiting ambulance.

"Can you tell me who died?"

"We're not releasing the name until the next of kin is notified."

"Is it Tiffany Ramsey?" he asked frantically. He peered over and around the police officer, and the officer moved each time to block his vision.

"I can't say one way or the other."

"Can you at least tell me whether it was the occupant of that town house?" Holland begged.

"Sir, the decedent was an occupant of this residence, but I can't tell you anything further."

Holland ambled miserably back to his car.

His head was down, and he felt like crying. He was scared, too. He sat in his car and watched as the ambulance left the scene unhurriedly. No siren. No flashing lights. He knew that could only mean there was no urgency to carry a lifeless body to the hospital.

Holland recalled his last conversation with Tiffany and the fear in her voice over Senator Proctor. He struggled with whether to go to the police with what he knew. All he could tell them was what Tiffany had told him. The conversation wasn't recorded. He had nothing to corroborate her fears. Would they even believe him over the word of the Senate majority leader? He doubted it.

Holland put his car in reverse and backed into an alley. When he entered Thirty-seventh Street, headed northwest, he almost struck a black Mercedes-Benz S65 sedan that pulled away from the curb. He had seen it before in practically the same location. He tried to pull out and follow it. He wanted to see who was driving or at least memorize the license plate. But his entry onto Thirty-seventh Street was delayed by two other cars that also pulled away from the curb behind the Mercedes. By the time he made it to where Thirty-seventh Street merged with Wisconsin, he no longer saw the Mercedes. He angrily banged his hand against the steering wheel.

By early afternoon the DC Metropolitan Police Department released the name of Tiffany Ramsey. Holland read through the press release and his blood boiled when he saw the cause of death: suicide by drug overdose. *Suicide!* He didn't know Tiffany very well, but he knew her well enough to know that she hadn't committed suicide. Things didn't add up.

He convinced his editor to let him write a small article about Tiffany for the Friday morning newspaper. He didn't mention Senator Proctor or his conversations with Tiffany in the article. It didn't take him long to write it. When he finished it, Holland went home to his apartment early from work.

His telephone rang not long after 6:00 p.m.

"He's killed another one," the woman's voice said.

It was *her,* and Holland didn't feel like talking. He decided it was time to change his telephone number to an unlisted one. "Who are you talking about?"

"Lance Proctor."

Holland lay on his back on his couch and

crossed his feet at the ankles. His body was listless. He didn't have the energy to even sit up. And he certainly didn't want to talk on the telephone.

"The police said it was suicide," he said flatly.

"It wasn't a suicide. It was made to look like a suicide, but it wasn't a suicide."

"You seem to know a lot about it. If it wasn't suicide, how do I know you didn't do it?"

"You don't, but why would I be calling you?"

"To cover your trail."

"All I want is Lance Proctor. I don't care about anything else."

"Why do you hate him so much?"

"Because it's easy to hate him, and he should pay for everything he's done."

"Well, this has gotten way too close for comfort. If Tiffany was killed instead of committing suicide, then whoever did it knows I've been talking to her. And they may be looking for me next. I'm not willing to take that chance."

"You can't give up now," she said.

"You'll have to get Senator Proctor on your own."

With that, Holland pressed the Off button on the cordless receiver without saying good-bye. He tossed the phone to the floor and rolled to his side, facing the back of the couch. All he wanted to do was sleep.

The Hart Building, Washington DC
"Sir, you can't go in there," Cooper Harrington heard his secretary say in the outer office.

He looked up from his desk as FBI Director Leslie Hughes stormed into his office unannounced and unwelcome. It was 8:30 a.m. on Friday. Two of Director Hughes's minions guarded him. His bald head was glowing.

"What's the meaning of this?" Cooper shouted as he jumped from his chair behind his desk.

Director Hughes stomped to the front of Cooper's desk. His bodyguards obediently flanked him on either side. "That's what I was going to ask you!" he yelled at Cooper. "Somebody's sniffing around the Carlson murders, and I want to know if it's you."

"I don't know what you're talking about."

"Don't play games with me, Cooper. You want me to hold off on Moretti while you line up someone else to take credit for finding him."

Cooper spoke defiantly. "I don't know anything about the Carlson murders."

384

"Well, *somebody's* interested in it."

"What are they looking for?"

"They're checking flight schedules in and out of Jacksonville and rental-car records."

"And it's not your guys?"

Director Hughes folded his arms across his chest and sneered at Cooper. "Of course it's not our guys. That's a stupid question. If it were our guys, I wouldn't be in here questioning you about it."

Cooper frowned. "If it's not you, who is it?"

"Somebody's trying to show me up. That's who it is."

"Why do you think the Shelton bombing and the Carlson murders are related?"

"Because Moretti's stupid, that's why. He left a trail to the Carlson murders. It's a good thing we're working it and not the locals. It would be all over the news by now. But we're keeping it quiet because you asked me to." Director Hughes placed the palms of his hands on Cooper's desk and bent his rotund frame toward Cooper. "And if you've got people checking behind me, I'm going to kill you."

Cooper didn't like the thought of that, but he hadn't hired anybody. And he particularly didn't like hearing the name of Joe Moretti. That could only mean one thing.

That Stella Hanover was somehow involved, and that was really bad news.

"Well, I don't know anything about it," Cooper said. "If someone is trying to show you up, it's not me. You're on your own with this one."

Director Hughes looked incredulously at Cooper. He removed a tape recorder from the inside pocket of his coat and pressed the Play button.

Cooper heard his own voice. "I'm just telling you that the senator wants this investigation to go as slowly as possible."

Cooper tried not to look surprised. But in doing so, he was certain he looked like a deer caught in the headlights of oncoming traffic.

Director Hughes was quick to finish the kill. "I'm never on my own, Cooper." His voice was slow and deliberate.

Cooper turned his back on Director Hughes and walked to the window, thinking. He stuffed his hands in his pockets and cursed Director Hughes under his breath. "What do you want?"

"I want you to find out who's going behind my back."

Cooper didn't like the fact that Director Hughes had something on him. But he couldn't do anything about it. His only option was to capitulate, and it infuriated him.

"I'll do what I can," Cooper said. "But you've got to give me that tape."

"Not until I get what I want."

"You've made your point. Now leave."

Cooper didn't turn around. He didn't want to see Director Hughes's face anymore. He was nauseated enough already. It wasn't until after he'd heard the door slam behind Director Hughes and his bodyguards that he faced the interior of the room and began to pace. *Stella had Joe Moretti kill the Carlson couple.*

He dialed Senator Proctor's direct line from the telephone on his desk.

"We've got another problem," Cooper said when Senator Proctor answered.

The law offices of Elijah J. Faulkner, Jackson, Tennessee

Jill Baker went to Eli's office just after 10:00 a.m. central time on Friday. Eli was sitting on the couch in his office, trying to work on something other than Tag Grissom's file.

Jill was excited when she entered the room. "Did you see in the news this morning that a woman died in Washington DC yesterday?"

Eli glanced up when Jill spoke, then back to the set of documents in his lap. "No, but

I suspect that happens often."

"Not just any woman. A Supreme Court law clerk."

Eli looked back at Jill again. "Now you've got my attention."

"The police report says it was a suicide."

"Let me guess. You think there's something else to it."

Jill smiled. "On a hunch I contacted the reporter with the *Washington Post* who wrote the article I read online this morning. His name is Holland Fletcher. Turns out that he knew the woman — her name was Tiffany Ramsey — and he doesn't think it was a suicide either."

"But."

"But he doesn't have any proof that she was killed."

"Does any of this help us?"

"Maybe. Fletcher said that Jessica Caldwell and Tiffany Ramsey were roommates before Jessica moved to Nashville."

"That can't be just a coincidence."

"There's more. Fletcher said that he thinks Tiffany Ramsey knew something about the Caldwell murder."

"Like what?"

"He wouldn't say. He seemed pretty shook up over the whole thing. And there's one more thing."

Jill handed Eli an eight-by-ten photograph and began to pace around the room. Eli thought it was somewhat funny to see Jill pace. He usually did the pacing and she did the listening. This time the roles were reversed. That meant she had matured as a lawyer; she was thinking more and reacting less.

"I got this in the mail today from the Metropolitan Nashville Police Department," she explained. "There was one other ticket issued the night of Jessica Caldwell's murder for running a red light. The surveillance camera photographed this car two blocks north."

Eli studied the photograph. "Government plates."

"The car is registered to Senator Lance Proctor," she announced.

"But you can't see who is driving."

"Right. The camera at this intersection only photographs the car after it's through the intersection. It doesn't photograph any oncoming traffic."

"What time was this photograph taken?"

"One eighteen a.m.," Jill responded.

"And Anna's SUV was photographed at what time? Do you remember?" Eli scratched his head.

"It was time stamped at twelve forty-eight a.m."

"Thirty minutes apart, and both are within the range of time the coroner identified as being the time of death. But we don't have anything that puts this car at Jessica's town house. The photograph was taken two blocks away."

"But it's coming from the direction of her town house," Jill said. "It could've easily been coming from her house."

"What about any other pictures of Anna's car? Any word on that yet?"

"There was another photograph from the same intersection. The police department is sending that one as well. It should be here by Monday."

Eli again considered the photograph of the car belonging to Senator Proctor. It was in the vicinity of Jessica Caldwell's town house the night she'd died. But there was nothing conclusive that would place the occupant of the car at the crime scene. And the reporter in Washington knew something.

"There's the set of fingerprints that the police couldn't identify," Jill reminded him.

He grinned. "Sounds like you just won an all-expenses-paid trip to the nation's capital."

"I thought you might say that. I've already

started checking flights."

After Jill left, Barbara told Eli that Anna Grissom was on the telephone, asking to speak with him. This was the first time he had spoken to either Anna or Tag since he and Jill had discovered it was Anna's car in the surveillances-camera photograph and not Tag's. He decided that he wouldn't tell her about either photograph yet. He sat down in his executive chair behind his desk. He removed the receiver from the base of the telephone and pressed the blinking light.

"This is Eli."

"Eli, this is Anna Grissom."

"It's good to hear from you, Anna. How are you and Tag doing?"

"We're doing fine. Listen. There's a favor I want to ask of you."

"Sure. What can I do for you?"

"Do you remember three or four weeks ago when you talked to Tag and me about Jesus Christ?"

Eli's eyes widened. He gazed across the room at nothing in particular. He couldn't believe Anna had said "Jesus Christ." He'd thought his conversation with her and Tag had gone in one ear and out the other.

"Absolutely," he managed. "What about it?"

"I don't know how to explain it, but I got

this feeling that day that I haven't been able to shake. I've actually been to church the last three Sundays."

Eli detected excitement and awe in Anna's voice as she told him about her church attendance. It lifted his spirits. Somehow Anna knew that telling Eli would be important to him. That meant she must comprehend that Eli cared about her as a person — not just because she was the wife of his client.

He was amazed by how the Holy Spirit worked. All this time he'd thought the words he'd spoken to Tag and Anna about Jesus Christ had fallen on deaf ears, but they hadn't. The Holy Spirit had been working on Anna all this time!

Sara had been right. God moved in his own time.

"Good for you," he said joyfully. "Which church?"

"It's a church here in Brentwood named New Hope Baptist. I like the preacher. I don't understand everything that he says, but I like him."

"What don't you understand?" Eli asked.

"He says the same thing you said about needing a relationship with Jesus Christ. I'm not sure what that means. How do you have a relationship with somebody who's dead?"

Lord, give me the wisdom to say the right words. "It begins with asking Jesus Christ to come into your heart. But he's not dead, Anna. Far from it. The Bible says that if a person believes that Jesus is Lord, that he died to save us from our sins, and that God raised him from the dead, then that person will be saved and Jesus will be in him."

There was a pause on Anna's end of the phone. "It sounds too simple."

"It is simple. Accepting Jesus Christ as your Lord and Savior is very simple. Even a child can do it. But it alters your life forever."

"Every time the preacher at New Hope invites people to go to the front of the church to talk to him, I have this feeling I can't explain."

Eli knew exactly what she was experiencing. It was the Holy Spirit moving her to accept Jesus Christ. "Why don't you just go talk to him?" Eli urged.

"I don't know. Tag got mad at me for even going to New Hope. I don't know what he would say if I told him I actually talked with the preacher personally." Her voice dropped. "Which brings me to my favor."

"What is it?"

"Tag's decided he wants to go to New Hope with me on Sunday to see what all the fuss is about."

"Really."

"Yeah. I think it's more out of curiosity than anything else. But he wants to go, and that's a start. And he can't go with the monitor on his leg. Can you get permission for him to leave the house on Sunday to go to church?"

Eli was even more surprised than before. *Tag Grissom wanted to go to church.* It didn't matter to Eli what Tag's motivation was. If Tag wanted to go, then Eli would move heaven and earth if he had to in order to make that happen. Two souls depended on it.

"I can certainly try. I'll get a conference call with the DA and Judge Blackwood later today and see if I can get it approved."

"I appreciate it. Call me back later when you know something."

"I will. And, Anna?"

"Yes."

"I'll be praying for you and Tag."

"I know."

Eli replaced the receiver and sat behind his desk for several seconds in stunned silence. He would never have guessed, in a million years, that Anna, much less Tag, would be attending church. Joy welled up inside Eli just thinking about it. The seed that God had used him to plant had been watered and cultivated by the Holy Spirit. He hoped that the harvest was soon.

"Barbara," he called out through his open office door.

Barbara stuck her head in the room.

"I need to get a conference call scheduled with Judge Blackwood and Randy Dickerson as soon as possible. It's really important."

Barbara left to make the arrangements, and Eli dialed home. He had to share the good news with his prayer partner. Sara answered after the second ring.

"You won't believe who I just talked to," Eli said.

"Who?"

"Anna Grissom. She and Tag are going to church together on Sunday."

"Eli! Honey, that's great news!"

CHAPTER
TWENTY-SIX

The Hart Building, Washington DC

"Cooper, you're so stupid!" Senator Proctor screamed. "Stella had two people killed to get Judge Shelton's research paper, and we didn't know it before now. I've been out waving it around like a checkered flag since Monday!"

The two of them stood in the middle of Senator Proctor's office. The senator's face was blood red, and he was seething. Cooper stood like a coward in front of him. And for good reason. Cooper always did exactly what Senator Proctor wanted, but sometimes he had no common sense. And it was on those occasions — just like the one they were discussing — that Senator Proctor wanted to rip Cooper's head off.

"But I just found out from Director Hughes ten minutes ago that he was looking at the possibility that Joe Moretti was involved. He isn't certain yet," Cooper tried.

Senator Proctor cursed at Cooper. The words he said would have made a sailor blush. But Cooper just continued to stand there before him, wincing with each verbal assault.

"Hughes may not know it yet, because he's an idiot like you, but I know it. Stella hired Joe Moretti to kill Shelton. And when that didn't work, she decided she had to at least kill his nomination. Professor Carlson and his wife were just in the way."

Senator Proctor was so mad he wanted to hit Cooper, or worse. Instead he kicked a leather chair until it toppled over and then kicked it until it broke. Then he stomped on it twice more to make sure it was dead.

Cooper shivered and sweated.

"And I've already called for the Judiciary Committee to reconvene!" Senator Proctor yelled. "They're questioning Shelton again on Monday."

"Can you stop it?"

"No, I can't stop it. It's too late."

Senator Proctor stomped around his office some more before he slowly managed to gain control of his anger. Even though his anger subsided, he still blamed Cooper for the predicament in which he found himself. The room was eerily quiet. He noticed that Cooper was hardly breathing.

He still looked scared.

Senator Proctor plodded around his office for several more minutes, thinking and planning. "We've got to distance ourselves from Stella," he finally said. "It may already be too late. And tell Hughes if he knows what's good for him, he'll keep my name out of it. But we've got to distance ourselves from Stella regardless."

"The FBI may not be the only ones investigating," Cooper murmured.

Senator Proctor swiveled toward Cooper. "What are you talking about?"

"Hughes told me that someone else is sniffing around the Carlson murders."

"Who? Newspaper reporters? Local police? Who?"

Cooper's answer was faint. "He doesn't know yet."

"Who else could possibly care?"

Cooper drew a breath. "You don't think President Wallace knows anything, do you?"

"It can't be. He's not that smart. And it's not his style. He wouldn't have anyone sneaking around investigating a murder." Senator Proctor shook his head violently. "It can't be him."

"I don't know then."

"Stay on top of this, Cooper. We're in damage-control mode, and any misstep could be disastrous. I want to know what Hughes knows before he knows it. You understand what I'm saying? I want you that on top of the situation."

"I understand." Cooper left without another word.

Senator Proctor stood quietly in his office. Things were in a tailspin. He saw his political life flash before his eyes. He had never had a situation that he couldn't control, but this was one such situation. He felt helpless . . . and he didn't like the feeling.

Washington DC

The president's black bulletproof limo screamed along the Capitol Beltway en route to a speaking engagement in Falls Church, Virginia. The limo was sheltered by the other vehicles in the protective presidential motorcade. President Wallace had to continue to look presidential even in the midst of the storm swirling around Judge Shelton's nomination. No appearances were canceled, but he wouldn't allow questions from the media.

President Wallace and Porter sat deep in the back of the limo. The sky was dark, and streetlights flashed through the windows as the limo sped past each one. The events of the last few days weighed on the president's mind. He was certain they were weighing on Porter's as well.

"Are we doing the right thing, Porter?"

"What do you mean, sir?"

"I mean, is it the right thing to continue to push the Shelton nomination?"

"I think it is. If we quit now, Stella Hanover gets exactly what she wants, and Senator Proctor escapes unscathed."

"But this is not about winning. It's about people's lives. When I nominated Dunbar, I never dreamed any of this would happen. And now four people are dead because of it. Because of my decision."

"Nobody could've predicted what Stella would do. You can't blame yourself for her actions," Porter said. "She'll have to answer for them herself one day."

"You're right. But if we pull the nomination, then we don't risk anyone else getting hurt, or worse."

There was a pause.

"Mr. President, are you still convinced that God has you in the presidency for decisions like this one?"

That was one thing of which President Wallace was certain. He *was* where he was for such a time as this, and he had complete peace about that fact. He knew it to be true just as well as he knew his own name. He looked at Porter and nodded confidently. "Absolutely."

"And are you still convinced that Dunbar Shelton was the right nominee?"

"More than ever."

"Then I don't think we have any choice but to press on. Like you told me when you decided to nominate Judge Shelton, the stakes are too high for someone other than Judge Shelton to sit on the Supreme Court."

It was sage advice, President Wallace thought. He had never felt more in the will of God than right now. He really believed that Judge Shelton's nomination was inspired by God. He also believed that only God knew his ultimate plan — and that God could even use tragedy for his purpose. Pulling Judge Shelton's nomination would mean that four lives would have been lost in vain.

President Wallace shook away the doubts that had crept into his mind. God had a plan. All he had to do as president was to stay in it. "You're right, Porter. We don't have a choice. Let's move full speed ahead."

He saw Porter's smile when a streetlight briefly illuminated the interior of the car. President Wallace breathed deeply and relaxed. It felt good to have the inner peace that God was fully in control.

Eli had obtained permission late Friday afternoon for Tag to leave the house to attend church. That excuse was gone, but Tag came up with several others. Anna brushed them all aside.

"You're going," Anna said. "Eli went to all that trouble to get permission for you to leave the house. So finish getting dressed. You're going."

Tag muttered as he finished dressing and wished he had never told Anna he would go in the first place. He didn't need to go to church. It didn't have anything to offer him. But there was something different about Anna every time she came home from attending church. He couldn't put his finger on it, and she couldn't explain it. His curiosity had finally gotten the better of him, and he'd told her that he wanted to see what all her excitement was about.

That simple statement was all it took. She had been on the phone with Eli five minutes later.

Unlike Anna, Tag had attended church often as a child. His mother had insisted on it. He knew the church routine well. But that was all it was to him — a routine. As a teenager he'd been rebellious, and his mother had had a hard time making him comply. By the time he was in college, he had completely stopped attending any church . . . anywhere, anytime. And his life-style had reflected that choice. As the years progressed, it had become easier and easier — particularly after his mother died — to choose not to go to church. In fact, the thought of going to church hadn't entered his mind in years . . . until Anna started going to New Hope Baptist Church.

He was finally dressed — brown slacks, blue blazer, white shirt, loafers, and no tie. Leaving the bedroom, he found Anna standing by the door that led to the garage, tapping her foot. She wore a red sleeveless dress with white polka dots, and white, medium-heeled shoes. He could hear her foot tapping as he approached.

"Hurry up," she said. "We're going to be late."

"I'm ready."

"Let's go then. I'm driving."

Anna darted down the steps into the garage and was in the driver's seat of her Infiniti SUV before Tag was completely in the garage. She had the engine running by the time he sat down in the passenger seat. She backed out of the garage and drove fast toward New Hope.

"Slow down," Tag ordered. "You're going

to get us killed."

"The service starts in ten minutes, and I don't want you to miss any of it."

All the traffic lights they encountered were green. Tag barely had time to fasten his seat belt before they were in the parking lot of the church. Anna exited the car while Tag took his time.

"C'mon, Tag," Anna said from ten steps in front of him. "Can't you walk any faster?"

He quickened his stride slightly and Anna waited for him at the front door of the church before entering. When they entered, Anna spoke to and shook hands with several people who stood in the foyer. It seemed as if she had been friends with all of them for a long time. She introduced Tag to them, and he grudgingly shook their hands. Then Anna took him by the hand and dragged him through the double wood doors that opened into the church sanctuary.

"This is my usual seat." Anna pointed to a pew in the middle section about one-fourth of the way down.

Tag and Anna sat in the middle of the pew, and again Anna spoke to the people nearby as if they were her best friends. She introduced Tag to each of them, and he forced a polite smile.

"Do you know all of these people?" Tag

whispered.

"I don't know everyone in the room. Just the ones who sit close by. Be quiet and listen." Anna pointed toward the front of the church. "The service is about to start."

Tag looked to the front of the church as the choir entered the choir loft. He hadn't seen anything like it in years. When the music director asked everyone to stand and sing, it seemed to Tag that Anna was the first one out of her seat. He unwillingly stood as well. But although Anna sang, he refused and stood there with his arms crossed.

He couldn't recall ever hearing Anna sing and noted with surprise that she had a pleasant voice. She seemed very happy singing, too. The congregation sang a total of three songs, and then the choir sang one song. When some of the men began to distribute brass offering plates, Tag remembered the ritual of collecting money. He noticed that Anna placed something in the plate that passed by them and leaned over to her.

"What'd you put in there?" Tag whispered. He hoped it wasn't money. He hadn't worked in quite a while and wasn't willing to simply give some away without anything in return.

"Just a card with our names and address on it. That's all. It's a visitor information card. I found a blank one lying in the pew."

He frowned. "Why'd you do that?"

Anna shrugged. "I don't know. I just wanted to. It can't hurt anything."

"But now they know where to find us." Tag glared at Anna in disgust.

Anna ignored him and focused her attention on the front of the church again. After the offering plates were collected, a man who had been sitting in a chair on the stage approached the podium.

Anna bent her head near Tag. "That's the pastor," she whispered. "Dr. Graham Frazier."

Tag nodded his understanding of her words but kept his arms folded across his chest. He refused to allow himself to become too comfortable. Dr. Frazier was a nice-looking man. Tall and professional in appearance. He had dark hair and wore a nice suit. Tag tried hard to block out the words that were spoken by Dr. Frazier. He tried to think about anything other than what Dr. Frazier said.

But the more Tag tried to block out Frazier's words, the more he found himself listening. It was a weird phenomenon. After ten minutes without success, Tag gave up.

He lowered his hands to his lap and simply listened.

Dr. Frazier referenced a passage from chapter seven in the book of Matthew. Tag contemplated searching for the passage in the Bible that rested in the rack on the back of the pew in front of him, but he refrained.

"Friends, we're all going to face God one day," Dr. Frazier said, walking from one side of the stage to the other with an open, leather-bound Bible in one hand. "And he's going to ask us why he should allow us into heaven. Some are going to respond by saying they did great and wonderful things for mankind while they were on the earth. Others will say that they kept God's commandments and followed all the rules. And still others might say that they were in church every Sunday."

Dr. Frazier stopped walking and gazed over the crowd in the direction of Tag and Anna.

Tag shivered. It seemed that the preacher was looking directly at him.

"And God's response to all of these will be, 'Sorry, you can't come in because I never knew you.' "

Dr. Frazier rested his right hand on the podium. His expression turned sympathetic as he scanned the crowd again. "Friends, listen to me closely. There's only one way to get into heaven, and it's not hard. In fact it's very easy and simple. And that's to ask Jesus Christ to come into your heart as your Lord and Savior."

Dr. Frazier's words resonated with Tag. He had heard them before as a child but had never really understood them. As an adult, he had refused to believe them. He had wanted to go his own way. Do his own thing.

And now, he still refused to believe those words. What Dr. Frazier said wasn't logical, Tag told himself. There couldn't be only one way — one door — into heaven. That didn't make any sense.

As Tag rationalized, Dr. Frazier concluded his sermon. The congregation stood and sang again.

A few people walked to the front of the church and whispered with Dr. Frazier. He noticed Anna fidgeting beside him. She rocked back and forth and gripped the back of the pew in front of her. She looked pale.

"What's wrong with you?" he whispered.

Anna took a deep breath and swallowed hard. "I'm fine. I just want to go down there and talk to Dr. Frazier."

Tag was surprised by her response, and it made him nervous. *I won't allow it.* "Are you crazy?" he said aloud. "You can't go down there! And if you did, you'd leave me here by myself. And you can't do that."

Anna stopped rocking and released her death grip on the pew in front of her. The color returned to her face. A minute later Dr. Frazier prayed and the congregation began leaving.

"We hope you'll come back again," two or three people said to Tag and Anna as they exited.

"We will," Anna replied, but Tag nodded politely and kept walking. Soon they were back in Anna's car and she was driving. The pace of the vehicle wasn't as hectic and dangerous as it had been during the trek to the church. *At least they'd make it home safely,* he thought wryly.

"What'd you think?" Anna asked. They were approximately halfway between New Hope and their house.

"It was okay, I guess. But I don't think I want to go back. I saw what it was about and it's not for me."

Tag saw the dejection on Anna's face. Her being down in the dumps had never bothered him before, but this time he felt a little wrench in his gut.

"But you keep going," he said quickly. "You seem to like it."

"I'd like it a whole lot more if you went back with me. Will you at least think about it before saying no?" she pleaded.

"I'll think about it."

He didn't tell her that, frankly, he'd thought about it all he was going to. He was never going back to that church.

CHAPTER
TWENTY-SEVEN

The Hart Building, Washington DC
Porter McIntosh was back in his seat in the front row of the gallery area in room 216. It was 9:00 a.m. eastern time on Monday, the last week of July. When he'd left this room ten days ago, he'd hoped never to return — at least not for another confirmation hearing. And he certainly didn't expect to be back here regarding Judge Shelton's nomination. Things simply happened in Washington.

But this time was different from the last. He and President Wallace had a different plan from the one they'd had when Porter was here before. Previously they were exclusively focused on getting Dunbar Shelton confirmed to the Supreme Court. The new plan was more ambitious, and extremely risky. But if everything worked exactly right, they could change the landscape of not only the Supreme Court, but

411

of the Senate for years to come.

Before he entered he looked for Stella Hanover on Constitution Avenue, in front of the Hart Building. He knew she would be there. The street was blockaded again. The various news organizations reported that thousands of pro-choice activists were expected to rally in front of the building. As was often the case, the news media was wrong. Dead wrong. There weren't merely thousands, but tens of thousands of protestors. And Stella was leading them.

The pro-life supporters came back as well en masse. Porter estimated that there were fifty thousand people stretched for blocks on Constitution Avenue in either direction. The chanting and shouting from both sides could be heard inside the building.

Porter wore his best suit, fresh from the dry cleaner's, and a Columbia blue tie with red stripes. He refused all requests for an interview. It was like breaking a picket line to get into room 216 through all the reporters. It was just as thick inside. Porter was pleased. The more reporters present at the hearing, the quicker Judge Shelton's testimony would be disseminated to the nation and the entire world.

Judge Shelton sat alone at the mahogany table in front of Porter. Victoria — still wearing her cast — and the handlers were on the front row. The room overflowed with news reporters, photographers, and TV cameramen. There was barely room to walk. And the noise was indescribable. Hundreds of camera shutters clicking at the same time and hundreds of people talking simultaneously made it nearly impossible to think. But Porter noticed that it didn't seem to bother one person in the room — Judge Dunbar Shelton.

Judge Shelton always looked very stoic, but Porter was particularly impressed with him that day. Porter knew that Judge Shelton had recently served as a pallbearer at the double funeral for Myron and Dorothy Carlson. That day had to be difficult for the judge, Porter thought. Certainly Judge Shelton must have run the gamut of emotions — from anger to sadness — the day of the funeral.

But today the judge was focused on the task at hand, with all his personal emotions laid aside. Such resolve and discipline impressed Porter immensely.

Behind the dais were the righteous senators. All eighteen of them and their respective staffs. Their demeanor was much less pleasant than it had been two weeks ago when this process had started. Their attitudes and scowling faces didn't bother Porter in the least. He was anxious for the new session to begin.

At last Senator Montgomery banged his gavel and the noise in the room fell to a low murmur. Porter shifted in his seat and crossed his legs as the hearings reconvened.

Senator Montgomery spoke first. "As you all know, we're here today to reconvene the confirmation hearings on the nomination of Judge Dunbar Shelton to the United States Supreme Court." Senator Montgomery's voice was worked up and angry. His scalp appeared red beneath his thinning white hair. He stared at Judge Shelton.

"We're here because of this memo," Senator Montgomery said. He waved what had become known around Washington and in the national media as "the Shelton Memo." "And particularly what you, Judge Shelton, said in this memo. Do you understand that?"

Judge Shelton was calm and unflappable. He sat tall and proud in his chair.

"I do, Senator. And I'll be glad to address that now, if you would like."

"You're going to get plenty of opportunity to talk about this memo, I promise you. But first I want to talk about where I think we are."

Here we go, thought Porter.

Senator Montgomery began a five-minute monologue that would ultimately lead to a question. He droned on about how very important the precedent of *Roe v. Wade* was, and that it shouldn't he overturned under any circumstances. He talked about how the Constitution clearly contained an absolute right for a woman to have an abortion.

Porter grew tired of the senator's monologue. He shifted in his seat again and crossed his legs in the other direction. He studied Judge Shelton, who never flinched. If anything, he appeared more resolved.

Finally Senator Montgomery asked his question. "Judge Shelton, do you understand that you are still under oath?"

"I do, Senator."

"I've read your memo. Several times, in fact. I've read the constitutional provisions you cite and the Supreme Court cases you referenced. And I must say that I disagree completely with your conclusions. Please explain to me how you arrived at the conclusion that *Roe* is unconstitutional."

"Let me first say that I wrote that memo over thirty years ago when I was in law school. They are the words of a student. But what the memo demonstrates is that my philosophy has always been that the Constitution should be strictly construed."

"But do you now believe that *Roe* should be overturned?" Senator Montgomery asked impatiently.

"As I said in my earlier testimony, I believe it would be inappropriate for me to answer a question like that. I cannot provide hints, forecasts, or previews —"

Senator Montgomery angrily cut off Judge Shelton in midsentence. "Stop playing games, Judge Shelton." His voice roared through the room. "You cannot hide behind the Ginsburg rule when you've already written on the subject. Even Justice Ginsburg conceded that point. Now answer the question. Do you believe that the Constitution contains the right of a woman to have an abortion?"

Judge Shelton sat on the edge of his seat and bent forward to where his mouth was very near the microphone. Very deliberately he spoke, as if he wanted to make sure no one misunderstood his words.

Porter held his breath as the historic words that no Supreme Court nominee since 1973 had had the courage to utter were spoken eloquently by Judge Dunbar Shelton.

"Senator Montgomery, I do not believe

that the Constitution contains a provision for the right of a woman to have an abortion. In fact, I'm convinced of it. And if I get the opportunity, I will vote to overturn *Roe v. Wade*."

Even though the place was overflowing with people, Porter could have heard a pin drop in room 216. It was precisely the moment he and President Wallace had hoped it would be. The die had been cast, and President Wallace and Porter didn't fear the consequences.

Arlington, Virginia

Jill Baker's flight from Nashville touched down at Reagan Washington National at 1:27 p.m. eastern time. She rented a white Ford Taurus and checked into the Hampton Inn on Jefferson Davis Highway in Arlington. There were two double beds in the room, and she tossed her luggage and her laptop on the one nearer the door. She decided to sleep on the other. Then it was time to get to work.

Jill's first order of business was to find Holland Fletcher. She located a large telephone book for Metropolitan DC in the bottom of the nightstand and called the *Washington Post* headquarters from the telephone in her motel room. The operator

417

at the *Post* connected her to Holland Fletcher's extension.

"Fletcher," he said.

Jill sat on the edge of the bed that contained her luggage. Both beds were covered with floral bedspreads. When she sat down, she realized that the bed wasn't comfortable. She hoped she could quickly get what she needed from Holland Fletcher so it would be a short stay.

"This is Jill Baker. We spoke last week about Jessica Caldwell."

"Ms. Baker. Yes, I remember. What can I do for you?"

"I'm in town and wondered if we could get together."

There was a pause. "You're in DC?"

"Flew in this afternoon."

"All the way from Tennessee?"

"All the way. It's part of the United States, you know. We do have airline service in Tennessee." When Jill heard Holland laugh out loud, she smiled at her own wit.

"I know," Holland said. "I wasn't trying to be funny. I just wasn't expecting you."

"Can we get together? I want to ask you some questions about Jessica Caldwell and Tiffany Ramsey."

"I'm not sure how much I can answer for you, but I'd be glad to meet. Where are you

418

staying?"

"I'm in the Hampton Inn near Reagan Washington National."

"I'm familiar with the area. There's a Subway restaurant on Crystal Plaza Arc not far from there. I haven't had lunch, and I'm starving. You think you can find it?"

"I'll ask the front desk."

Holland entered the Subway on Crystal Plaza Arc at 3:30 p.m. The establishment was decorated with yellow paint, yellow tables, and wallpaper depicting an old New York City subway scene. It looked the same as any other Subway restaurant he had seen. He looked around for a woman who might be Jill Baker but didn't see anyone. There were only a few people in the restaurant at this time of the day, and they appeared young enough to be high school kids.

His stomach dragged him to the counter and he ordered a club sandwich on white bread with everything. He paid for his meal and sat in the booth in the back of the room. He was midway into his sandwich when he saw an attractive, slender, black-haired woman enter through the front door. She looked about his age and he guessed she was Jill Baker. And if Tiffany Ramsey was an eight, then Jill Baker was at least a nine. Maybe a ten. She scanned the crowd and their eyes met. She started walking toward him.

"Are you Holland Fletcher?"

Holland covered his full mouth with his hand. "Sorry. I just took a bite before you came in. I'm Holland," he said and extended his right hand.

"I'm Jill," she replied and shook his hand.

"Are you hungry?"

"No, I've already had lunch, but I'll get something to drink."

Jill glided to the counter and Holland watched her. Faded blue jeans, tennis shoes, and a loose-fitting T-shirt. She was probably five feet eight inches tall. Her sleek black hair was pulled back into a ponytail, making her beautiful face all the more visible.

Holland hurriedly stuffed the rest of his sandwich in his mouth and chewed fast.

Jill returned with a bottle of water and sat across from him. Holland wadded the wrapping paper from his sandwich into a ball and slid it and his tray to the back of the table.

"So, you're a writer with the *Washington Post*."

Holland sucked on the straw in his extra-large disposable cup and tried to chase down the last of his sandwich. He swallowed hard. "*Investigative* reporter."

Jill's eyebrows rose. "Investigative reporter. Really. That sounds interesting."

"It can be. Obviously you're a criminal-defense lawyer."

Jill sipped from her water bottle. "I work for a lawyer in Jackson, Tennessee. I do whatever he needs me to do. This case we're working on is a criminal-defense case, but that's not all we do."

"Cool. You're a part-time criminal-defense attorney."

When Jill smiled, Holland thought it was one of the prettiest smiles he had ever seen. And she liked his bad humor.

"So, what do you want to ask me about?"

"First, I want to make sure none of this will appear in your newspaper."

"I promise. You're interrogating me. Not the other way around. This is completely off the record as far as my end is concerned. I do hope that at some point you'll let me write a story."

"We'll see. Tell me about Ms. Ramsey."

Holland didn't have any idea where to start because he didn't know much about Tiffany Ramsey. But he draped his arm across the back of the booth and told Jill Baker what he could. "I met her once and talked to her on the phone two other times.

She was attractive and nice."

"You said she lived with Jessica Caldwell."

"That's what she told me. That they lived together for about a year."

Jill took another sip from her bottle. "What did she know about the Caldwell murder?"

She's good, Holland thought. She got right to the point. And she didn't appear to be searching for questions to ask him. She knew exactly what she wanted and focused on it intently.

"I don't think she knew anything for sure. She just had a feeling."

"A feeling about what?"

Holland hesitated and rolled his drink cup between his hands. Tiffany had shared her thoughts with him out of fear. She didn't ask him to keep their conversation confidential, but did he have an obligation to do so anyway? He struggled momentarily with whether to tell Jill or not. But she raised her eyebrows as if she expected him to answer without complaint.

After another minute of struggle, Holland decided to reply. Maybe Jill Baker could help him discover what had really happened to Tiffany Ramsey.

"That Jessica Caldwell and Senator Proctor were having an affair." Holland noticed a strange expression on Jill's face. "What?" he asked.

"Nothing. That fits with something else, but I can't talk to you about it. Why did she think that?"

"Because she caught them together one day."

Jill nodded thoughtfully. "That would convince me."

"And they lived in a town house owned by Senator Proctor," he added.

Holland studied Jill's face. She was obviously pondering her next question. "Interesting. A couple of people the detectives interviewed said something about Ms. Caldwell acting distraught when she returned to Nashville from Justice Robinson's memorial. Did Tiffany say anything like that?"

"Tiffany said she tried to talk to Jessica at the memorial service but that she left too hurriedly. She saw Jessica get into a taxi with a man but said that it wasn't Senator Proctor."

"Did she know him?"

"No, but she described him to me. I was going to try to find him, then Tiffany died."

"You don't think she committed suicide, do you?" The question was blunt . . . almost a statement.

Holland wasn't certain what he thought

anymore. He had no proof otherwise, but it didn't seem right that Tiffany would commit suicide. "I didn't know her very well," he said thoughtfully, "but I never saw anything that made me think she was troubled."

"When's her funeral?" Jill asked.

"It's tomorrow in New Jersey. I'm not going. I can't." But even as he said the words, Holland felt guilty. He wondered if there was anything he could've done to prevent what had happened to Tiffany Ramsey. He hoped Jill couldn't see it on his face. She didn't seem to.

Jill turned her water bottle up, drank the last of it, and screwed the cap back on the empty bottle. "You've been very helpful." She slid out of the booth and stood to leave.

"Where're you going?"

"I've got some more things I need to check out while I'm in town. I'm scheduled to fly back out on Wednesday."

"Why don't I go with you?"

She appeared incredulous. "Back to Nashville?"

Holland laughed again. "You're quick. I meant go with you to check out the other things you mentioned."

"That's not necessary." Jill shook her head. "I can handle it by myself."

"C'mon. You don't know your way around town and I do. And it'll be just like I'm working. I might find something I can write a story about."

"I don't think that's a good idea."

"I insist. I'll follow you back to your motel and you can ride with me. We'll go anywhere you want to."

"You win," Jill relented. "It'll probably be easier to do what I need to do with a chauffeur."

They left the Subway and Jill exited the parking lot in her rental. Holland lagged behind and hurriedly cleaned out as much trash as he could from inside his ancient Camry. He chucked the rubbish in a large trash can on the sidewalk in front of the Subway and ran back to his car. He dusted off the passenger seat as best he could with his hand.

"That'll have to do," he muttered.

Holland caught up with Jill as she entered the parking lot of the Hampton Inn. She parked in a space in front of the motel, and Holland stopped, perpendicular, behind her parked car. Jill walked around the front of his car, sat in the passenger seat, and closed the door.

"I have a Camry, too," she said. "Except mine's a little newer and cleaner, but still a

Camry." She ran her index finger through the dust on the dashboard.

Holland smiled. "It's not usually this dirty."

"I'm sure," she said and brushed her hands together.

"Where do you want to go?"

"Let's start at their town house."

The faded, camel-colored Camry exited the Hampton Inn parking lot and Hal Crowder trailed from a distance in his dark green GMC Yukon. Hal was a DC area private investigator who didn't advertise. He had closely cropped brown hair and a tattoo on his left forearm. His reputation preceded him, so he had all the jobs he wanted. The DC Metropolitan Police Department knew him well, too. Hal operated barely inside — but inside nonetheless — the law. The DC police were always looking for a reason to bring him in.

"I'm following him now," Hal said into his wireless phone. "He's got a dark-haired woman with him."

"Do you know who she is?" Cooper Harrington asked.

"Not yet. I took at least thirty digital photographs of her, and we're tracking the license plate on the car she's driving. It's a rental, so it shouldn't be hard to find out who it was rented to. I should know something soon."

"Stay with him," Cooper said. "I need to know everywhere he goes and everyone he talks to. And let me know as soon as you find out about the woman."

Cooper Harrington hung up and Hal tossed his wireless phone on the passenger seat. His attention then focused exclusively on the Toyota Camry in front of him.

CHAPTER
TWENTY-EIGHT

The Hart Building, Washington DC

Porter glanced at his watch: 4:37 p.m. The day's session was nearing completion. Porter wondered whether tomorrow the committee would resume the reconvened confirmation hearing on Judge Shelton's nomination or whether one day was enough. Other than Senator Montgomery, six other senators pontificated that afternoon for the evening news and asked Judge Shelton virtually the same question Senator Montgomery had. And each time the answer was the same.

"No, Senator. The Constitution of the United States does not contain an absolute right to have an abortion."

Porter saw all the eye rolling and head shaking from the committee members each time Judge Shelton provided the answer. It made Porter mad, even though he expected such antics. But Judge Shelton never appeared angry or upset, and that made Porter proud. The country needed someone like Judge Shelton on the Supreme Court.

Throughout the afternoon Judge Shelton never seemed to be bothered by the stares and jeers and questions from the members of the Senate Judiciary Committee. He was comfortable in his position — whether anyone else in the room agreed with him or not — and never wavered. Judge Shelton explained time and again that his position had absolutely nothing to do with the morality of an abortion, but was rooted exclusively in the plain language of the Constitution.

After the seventh time of Judge Shelton providing the same answer and the senators shaking their heads with their mouths gaping open, Senator Montgomery banged his gavel. His scalp, which was visible through his wispy white hair, was as red as it had been when the session started.

"I think we've heard enough, Judge Shelton," he said. "It's clear to me that your views are completely outside mainstream America. I wish we'd had this clarity two weeks ago. Having heard your testimony today, I don't see any way that I can support your nomination. I also don't see a need for any further testimony. The committee will stand adjourned. We will reconvene on Wednesday to reconsider our vote on whether or not to recommend confirmation to the Senate. I suspect the vote will be overwhelming the latter."

Senator Montgomery forcefully banged his gavel again and glared at Judge Shelton before darting for the exit door to the side of the dais.

Porter met Judge Shelton and Victoria behind the mahogany table. "You did great," Porter said. He patted Judge Shelton on the back.

"I said what I believe, and you know what? I'm glad I did. I don't like having to dance around an issue."

"It does feel good to call a spade a spade, doesn't it?" Porter grinned.

Judge Shelton nodded. "And now it's completely out of our control. If it's meant for me to serve on the Supreme Court, then God will have to make it happen."

"That's exactly what President Wallace told me."

Washington DC
Holland steered his Camry to the curb across the street from Tiffany Ramsey's town house. He put the transmission in park and left the engine running.

Holland pressed a button on the armrest in his door and the driver's-side window lowered into the door. "That's it," he said, pointing across the street at Tiffany Ramsey's town house. Yellow crime scene tape still dangled from around the front door. Jill leaned across the console and peered through the open window. Holland could feel her nearness and smell her perfume. He pressed his shoulders against the seat to give Jill an unobstructed view through the window.

"You think we could go inside?" Jill asked.

"Are you crazy? That'd be breaking and entering. Even I know that, and I'm not a lawyer."

"Only if we get caught. And we'd only be in there for a few minutes. I just want to look around."

Holland shook his head. "I'm not going in there."

"C'mon, we'll only be a minute. We might find something useful." Jill nodded thoughtfully.

"Look." Holland's voice was stern. "I'm not going in there, and you're not either. Two women who lived there are now dead. If someone were to see us go in or found out we'd been in there, we might be next. I've got enough problems already."

"What are you talking about?"

Holland pressed the button on the armrest again, and the window rose back to its original position. Jill returned to her seat and twisted her head to look at him. He placed both hands on the steering wheel and relaxed his shoulders.

"I keep getting calls from a woman who feeds me information, but won't tell me her name. One of her delivery guys stuck a gun in my back at the Fourth of July fireworks show."

"Who is she?" Jill's brow was furrowed.

"I don't know, but she's after Senator Proctor. She doesn't seem concerned with anything else."

Holland put the Camry in drive and pulled away from the curb. He glanced around but didn't see the black Mercedes he had seen the two previous times he'd been on that street.

"I guess we're not going in," Jill said.

"I told you we weren't. It's too risky. And I'm not into risky."

Jill bit her lip through a crooked smile before commenting. "An investigative reporter who doesn't like to take risks. That's got to make your job harder."

Holland didn't respond. "Where to next?"

"You said you were going to find out who

got in the taxi with Jessica after the memorial service. That would be important to me, too. How were you going to check on that?"

"Let's go to the *Post* headquarters and see if we can find some photographs. I know we covered it."

Cooper Harrington sat in a booth in one of the three bar areas of the Hawk 'n' Dove Bar on Pennsylvania Avenue SE. It was only a few blocks from the Capitol Building — in the opposite direction from the White House. A twentysomething woman with long blond hair, long tan legs, and a short skirt sat beside him. Her name was Mona, and Cooper didn't care what her last name was.

Another couple sat across the table. They were Mona's friends. He knew neither and had no intention of finding out who they were. He was polite to them and hoped that would be enough to keep Mona happy well into the night. Perhaps Mona and several stiff drinks could help him forget about Stella Hanover and the problems she had caused. Nothing else had.

Just then his wireless phone vibrated on his hip and the LCD screen indicated the call was from Hal Crowder.

"Her name is Jill Baker," Crowder said

when Cooper answered. "She's a lawyer from Jackson, Tennessee."

"What's she doing in town?"

"I don't know, but her boss — a guy named Elijah Faulkner — is representing the guy accused of killing that former Supreme Court law clerk in Nashville."

Crowder's words caused Cooper to stand up and walk away from the table. He walked into a hallway that led to the kitchen and leaned his back against a wall. "Where are she and Fletcher now?"

"They just pulled away from the front of a town house on Thirty-seventh where a woman named Tiffany Ramsey was found dead last week."

Cooper closed his eyes tightly. Crowder's report worried him immensely. "What were they doing there?"

"They just parked, looked at the front of the town house, and drove away. They never got out of the car."

"Crowder, you need to stay within eyesight of both of them. Get one of your other guys involved if you have to, but I want to know where both are at all times. You got that?"

"I got it, and no problem."

Cooper closed his wireless and slipped it into the breast pocket of his jacket. He ran his hand through his blond hair and returned to his seat beside Mona.

"What was that all about?" Mona asked.

"Senate stuff that I can't talk about."

The Washington Post, *Washington DC*

Holland showed Jill his cluttered, metal home away from home before they went to the photo-archive room. Jill commented that his desk looked a lot like hers, but she actually had four walls separating her from the rest of the office.

The photo-archive room was on the third floor of the *Post* building. Jill wanted to take the stairs, but Holland insisted on using the elevator. He knew that otherwise he would be out of breath by the time he reached the second flight of steps.

As they rode in the elevator, Holland explained that few photographs were actually printed anymore. Most of the digital photographs were archived onto a computer server and only accessible with the appropriate password, he said.

When the elevator reached the third floor, Holland and Jill exited and entered the photo-archive room. The printed photographs were cataloged by date in filing cabinets on the left side of the room. Holland located the correct cabinet, and he and Jill began reviewing the photographs from the date of Justice Robinson's memorial service.

"If we don't find anything here," Holland said, "then we'll check the JPEG files on the server."

"How will we recognize him from these photos?"

"Tiffany said that the man was handsome, with blond hair and a tan, but that's all she remembered."

They studied each photograph, twenty-five in all. Finding nothing, Holland logged onto the computer system at a terminal across the room from the filing cabinets. He sat in a chair in front of the computer, Jill looking over his right shoulder. Just like in the Camry, he could feel her close to him. It made his heart flutter, but there was work to be done. He breathed deeply to calm himself and hoped that Jill didn't notice.

There were 150 JPEG photographs filed under the date of the memorial service. Holland scrolled the cursor over the first one and began opening them in order.

"That's a shot from the back of the cathedral looking toward the front," Holland narrated. "And this one is from the balcony."

They went through the first fifty photographs fairly rapidly. Holland provided narration for each one even though Jill never asked for it. "There's President Wallace and the First Lady sitting with the Robinson family. And this one shows a row of senators who attended."

"What about that guy in the fourth row — the row behind the senators?"

Jill placed her left hand on Holland's shoulder, bent toward the computer, and tapped the man's face on the computer screen with the index finger of her right hand. Her hand on his shoulder caused Holland's heart to quiver again.

"I don't know him," Holland replied.

"I'd say that he's blond and handsome."

"You think so? I don't think he looks very handsome."

"Women have a different eye for things," she explained. "If I were describing him, I'd say he was handsome. And he has a tan."

"If you think he fits the description, then I'll print it out. In the morning we'll start trying to find out who he is. Let's see if there are any others."

Holland and Jill scanned the balance of the remaining digital photographs. They didn't find any other photographs of men that fit Tiffany Ramsey's description. The whole time they were together Holland wondered whether Jill thought men with red hair and no tan were also handsome.

The Oval Office, the White House, Washington DC

The West Wing was never completely empty and never completely quiet. But by 8:00 p.m. on Monday, much of the staff had gone home. Porter remained behind and met with President Wallace. He let himself into the Oval Office unannounced and found President Wallace sitting behind his desk.

The president looked up when Porter entered the room. "It's nice outside tonight, Porter. Let's take a walk."

President Wallace and Porter exited the Oval Office through French doors onto the West Wing colonnade. Two Secret Service agents came to attention and followed President Wallace and Porter as they strolled along the colonnade. Porter loosened his red necktie and stuffed his hands in his pockets. President Wallace had left his suit jacket in the Oval Office. The night sky was crystal clear and stars glistened overhead. The two old friends enjoyed walking and talking.

"Sounds like Dunbar made quite a splash today," President Wallace said.

"It was exactly what we wanted. By tomorrow morning there'll be no doubt in anyone's mind in the country — perhaps the world — that Dunbar Shelton is a pro-life, strict constructionist."

"Good. That's good."

"And the committee will vote eighteen to zero against recommending confirmation."

"That's fine. By the time the full Senate votes, this whole thing will have reversed course again. What're you hearing about the Carlson murders?"

"No doubt Stella was there, in the area. She flew into Jacksonville on Tuesday of that week and rented a car. She stayed at the Ritz-Carlton on Amelia Island Tuesday night and flew back to New York on Wednesday."

President Wallace stopped walking and turned to Porter. Porter stopped walking as well.

"But they weren't murdered until Thursday night," the president said.

"That's where Joe Moretti comes in. You remember him?"

"He's the guy Les Hughes said was involved in the attempt on Dunbar and Victoria."

"Right. We traced his movements that week. He took a circuitous route but ended up in Jacksonville before Stella departed."

"And she told Moretti where to go and what she wanted," the president surmised.

"That's our theory."

President Wallace resumed walking and Porter fell in beside him. They circled around and walked toward the Oval Office. When President Wallace folded his arms over his chest, Porter could tell that he was thinking.

"And Proctor?" the president asked.

"We don't think he knew anything about the Carlson murders beforehand but was an accomplice after the fact. When Moretti returned to New York on Sunday — he took a very circuitous return trip also — he went directly to Stella Hanover's office. She was on the first train Monday morning to DC, and her one and only stop was Proctor's office."

"She hand-delivered the Shelton Memo to Proctor."

"And then Cooper Harrington faxed it to your office."

President Wallace and Porter stopped on the colonnade outside the Oval Office. The office was still illuminated, and three Secret Service agents stood nearby.

"You've got documentation — dates, times, places — to back all of this up?" the president asked.

"We've got it all ready to go. You just say the word."

"Let's wait until after the committee votes

on Wednesday. Thursday would be a good day for it to be released. Maybe Friday. Let me think about it."

"You're the boss."

President Wallace frowned. "Why hasn't Hughes uncovered any of this?"

"We don't know for sure, Mr. President, but the only logical answer is that he's been told or asked to back off. If he'd found Moretti after the attempt on the Sheltons, then the Carlson murders would never have happened. And Moretti wasn't that hard to find. We were able to find him fairly quickly."

"You think Proctor told him to back off?"

"He's the only one among the players I mentioned with enough political weight to cause Hughes to listen to him."

"You're right," President Wallace said.

Porter studied the president's face. He could sense the gears grinding behind it.

After a couple of minutes President Wallace gave Porter additional instructions. "I want Hughes gone as soon as possible."

A Secret Service agent opened one of the French doors and President Wallace and Porter reentered the Oval Office. President Wallace walked with Porter across the room to the door that exited the office.

Porter could tell that President Wallace

was still thinking about something. He waited quietly for the president's words to emerge.

"Porter," the president said thoughtfully, "you keep using the word 'we.' Who are you talking about?"

Porter examined President Wallace's inquisitive face. It made him uncomfortable. But now wasn't the time to tell him about Simon Webster. If things went terribly wrong, then the president could plausibly deny any knowledge of the covert investigation by Simon, and Porter himself would take the fall. He also knew that President Wallace trusted him implicitly.

"Mr. President, if you order me to tell you, I will. But I don't think it's best for you to have that information. At least not right now. Maybe later. But for now I would suggest that you don't need to know."

President Wallace pursed his lips and nodded slightly. "It can wait."

Arlington, Virginia

Holland returned Jill to the Hampton Inn on Jefferson Davis Highway just after 10:00 p.m. They had eaten supper at a Mexican restaurant on the return trip, where they had compared notes further about Jessica Caldwell's murder and Tiffany Ramsey's

442

death — both agreeing it had to be a homicide — then spent the rest of the meal getting to know each other.

Jill waved good-bye and slipped the plastic key into the electronic door lock. The small light on the door flashed green and she twisted the doorknob to gain entry to the room. She looked back and saw the taillights from Holland's Camry exit the parking lot.

Once inside the room, she locked the door behind her, then added the dead bolt and the sliding chain. The floor lamp in the corner, the double lamp on the wall above the nightstand, and light from the bathroom illuminated the tiny motel room. Jill sat on the edge of the uncomfortable bed on which her luggage and laptop lay and called Eli's wireless phone from hers. She knew it was an hour earlier in Jackson, Tennessee.

Eli answered on the second ring.

"We're trying to identify a man who got into a taxi with Jessica Caldwell after Justice Robinson's memorial service," Jill said.

"Who is 'we'?"

"Holland Fletcher and me."

"Oh, yeah. The newspaper reporter. You think you can trust him?"

"I think so. He's nice enough. He also said that Jessica Caldwell lived in a town house owned by Senator Proctor, and he thinks they were having an affair."

"Who told him that?" There was amazement in Eli's voice.

Jill untied her tennis shoes while she talked and kicked them off at the foot of the bed. She then lay on her back and stared at the ceiling. "The Ramsey girl, who died recently. But we need some corroboration, since obviously she can't testify."

"There's something there, Jill. Senator Proctor was having an affair with Jessica Caldwell, and his car was in the vicinity of her town house the night she died. We're close."

"I know, and that's why I may need to stay a couple of extra days."

"That's fine. Stay as long as you need to. It's important that you chase down every lead up there."

"Did you get the other photograph of Anna Grissom's car?"

"I did. It came in the mail today."

"And?" Jill bolted upright and sat on the edge of the bed.

"And it's exactly like we thought. Anna's driving, not Tag. That means Anna was in the proximity of Jessica Caldwell's town house during the time frame the coroner said she died."

"So Tag's fingerprints were inside the

444

town house; Anna was photographed nearby; and Senator Proctor's car was in the vicinity. All at approximately the same time."

"And Tag's DNA matched the skin fragments from under Jessica's fingernail," Eli added.

She sighed. "This case gets more confusing every day."

"I know," Eli said. "I'm going to see Tag and Anna this week sometime. I just don't know when yet. I'm waiting for the DNA results from the fetus because I want to talk with them about that and the surveillance photo at one time."

"Call me after you talk to them. I'd be interested to hear their explanation."

"I will. You be careful there. If Senator Proctor was involved with Jessica Caldwell, we may be playing with fire. He's very powerful."

"I'll be careful, don't worry," she promised.

Jill disconnected the call and watched a few minutes of television. She connected her laptop to the high-speed Internet port in her room and checked her office email. She yawned and stretched her arms over her head. She was exhausted from her flight and from running around town with Holland. By 10:30 p.m. she was in bed, asleep.

CHAPTER
TWENTY-NINE

Arlington, Virginia

The ringing of her wireless phone awoke Jill Baker at 7:00 a.m. eastern time. Her body was still on central time, and 6:00 a.m. was much too early to be awakened. She removed the phone from its resting place on the nightstand and mumbled, "Hello."

"I know who he is," an excited voice on the other end of the phone said.

"Holland, is that you?"

"Yeah, it's me. And I know who the guy in the photograph is."

Jill rolled onto her back and propped her knees under the covers. She could see daylight barely slipping around the edges of the thick curtain that covered the only window in her room.

She shook the sleep from her voice. "What time is it?"

"It's seven a.m.," he reported.

She groaned. "I thought you told me you

weren't a morning person."

"I'm not, but I haven't slept much. Too many things on my mind. I couldn't sleep and got up at about two. So technically I'm not waking up early. I've stayed up late."

"If you haven't slept, what have you been doing?"

"Investigating. That's what investigative reporters do. We investigate. I was online most of the night and I know who he is."

"Who is it?"

"I can't tell you over the phone. I'll be there in thirty minutes to pick you up."

Jill's eyes opened wide and she sat up in the bed. "Thirty minutes! I can't be ready in thirty minutes."

"You have to be. Time's a-wasting. If we're going to solve this crime of yours, then we need to get started. I'll be there in thirty minutes, and we'll talk about it over breakfast."

Jill closed the wireless phone and ran to the bathroom. As she started the shower, she didn't believe there was any chance she could be ready before Holland arrived.

Holland gave Jill five extra minutes before he banged on her door. When she opened the door, she was fully dressed, with not a hair out of place. She wore blue jeans, a red pullover short-sleeve shirt, and tennis shoes, and her hair was pulled back in a ponytail again. She was as beautiful as she had been the day before.

"You're late," she said.

"You said you couldn't be ready in thirty minutes, so I gave you five extra," he said defensively.

She jammed her fists onto her hips. "You said thirty minutes, and I was ready in thirty minutes. If you meant thirty-five, then you should've said thirty-five."

Holland loved her feistiness. "Okay, okay. I'll know next time. You like promptness."

"And don't forget it. Now, where're we going?"

Jill had won, Holland knew. And she had set him straight. But he didn't care. Now that conversation was over it was time to get down to business.

"There's an IHOP three blocks away. Let's get some breakfast and I'll bring you up to speed."

"And you haven't slept all night?"

Holland fumbled his car keys and dropped them beside the car. Retrieving them, he peered over the car at Jill. "Not much."

"How much coffee did you drink?"

"Two pots, and I just finished a grande café mocha from Starbucks."

Jill looked at him over the top of the car and smiled before getting in. It was the lovely smile that he remembered from the previous day and the one that he had thought of several times during the night.

"You're going to crash this afternoon and you'll be worthless," she claimed.

Holland sat in the driver's seat and closed the door. "I'm fine," he said confidently. "I won't need to sleep until tonight."

"You could've at least changed clothes."

Holland hadn't thought about that. He glanced at his face in the rearview mirror. His eyes looked watery and glassy. He hadn't showered or shaved. It was a good thing his red hair was short, he thought. At least that didn't look too bad. Then he grasped that this wasn't the best way to impress an attractive woman.

"Maybe after breakfast I'll run home and take a shower," he suggested.

"I think that would be a good idea."

Ten minutes after leaving the Hampton Inn parking lot, they were sitting in a booth in the back of the IHOP. Jill ordered a ham-and-cheese omelet with hash browns and a cup of coffee. Holland had two eggs, fried well done, with pancakes and a side order of bacon. Jill suggested that he'd had too much coffee, so he ordered a glass of orange

450

juice instead.

"So who is he?" Jill asked after the waitress disappeared to retrieve their orders.

"His name is Cooper Harrington. He's Senator Proctor's chief of staff."

"The Senate majority leader's chief of staff? That seems important."

"I've heard his name before but have never met him. Word around town is that he does Senator Proctor's dirty work and that he's something of a playboy."

"What do you think he was talking to her about? The witnesses in Nashville said she was pretty upset when she returned."

"I don't know, but I had a great idea at about four thirty this morning." Holland smiled, as if he had discovered electricity for the first time. "Why don't we just call and ask him?"

She laughed. "Just like that. Just call him and say, 'What were you talking to the dead girl about before she died?' "

"Sure. What's wrong with that?"

"Because we won't know if he's telling the truth or not."

The waitress reappeared with a large tray containing their plates of food and drinks. She served them and vanished again.

"But we'll never know that," Holland said. "Only she and he know what they talked about. And she can't tell us."

"What about the cabdriver?"

"We'll never find out which cab company, much less which driver drove the car they got in."

Holland sipped from his glass of orange juice. Neither he nor Jill spoke for a few minutes. They each took several bites of their meals. Holland could tell Jill was running through the possibilities in her head, just like he had overnight. And he hoped that she would come to the realization, as he had, that talking to Cooper Harrington was their only real option.

Jill raised her coffee cup to her mouth and blew on the steaming brown liquid before taking a sip. From the way she peered at Holland over the top of the cup, he could tell she had made a decision.

"You're right. Let's call him. I don't think we'll learn anything that we don't already know, but it can't hurt."

The Hart Building, Washington DC

It was 8:15 a.m. on Tuesday, and Senator Proctor and Cooper were alone. The senator sat in his executive chair behind his desk, and Cooper slumped on the sofa across the room. Cooper looked terrible. When his eyes were open, they were bloodshot and glassy. He primarily lay with his head against the back of the sofa and with his eyes closed.

"You got a headache, Cooper?"

"Pounding," Cooper whispered. "Don't talk so loud."

Senator Proctor had no sympathy for Cooper. He blamed Cooper for putting them in the spot they were in. It didn't matter that he himself was the one Stella Hanover had blackmailed into turning on Judge Shelton. It was still Cooper's fault, no matter what. So the senator drank from his coffee cup and stared angrily at Cooper.

"Wake up, Cooper," Senator Proctor said in a voice loud enough that he knew it would make Cooper's head hurt. "You should've taken two aspirin before you started drinking last night and you wouldn't be so hung over."

Cooper sat up on the couch.

Senator Proctor buzzed his secretary through the intercom in his telephone. "Bring Cooper some coffee — black. We've got a lot of work to do, and he needs to wake up."

Quickly the secretary appeared with a cup of black coffee and handed it to Cooper. He took one sip and winced.

Senator Proctor smiled with satisfaction

and began talking. "What are you hearing from Les Hughes about the Carlson investigation?"

Cooper held the coffee cup in both hands. He talked slowly as he began, but the pace and volume of his words increased as he continued. "Clearly Joe Moretti was involved. They traced him to Jacksonville, Florida, and back to Manhattan. And Stella was in Jacksonville two days before the murder."

"Where's Moretti now?"

"The FBI can't find him. Stella probably has him hiding out somewhere."

"Hughes is more of an idiot than I thought if Stella has Moretti hidden where Hughes can't find him. What about the other investigation? Does Hughes know who is doing that yet?"

"He has no idea. They've interviewed all of the witnesses again and were told that whoever else was investigating had official credentials but they couldn't recall what type. The FBI reviewed surveillance tapes from airport security cameras and saw images of some of the other alleged investigators but couldn't match them. It's like they don't exist."

"That's impossible, Cooper. They're not CIA?"

"Not CIA, NSA, or any other federal agency."

"I don't believe it, Cooper. Either Hughes is lying to you, or he's a bigger imbecile than I thought. He should be able to identify these other people and find them. He's doing neither."

Senator Proctor stood and walked to the front of his desk.

Cooper sat upright and crossed his legs. He took another sip from his coffee, and winced again.

Senator Proctor understood the excruciating pain Cooper felt; he'd been hung over plenty of times himself. But he had no sympathy for Cooper. The gravity of the situation wouldn't allow it. "This is bad, Cooper. Really bad."

"I know."

"You tell Hughes that I want to know by the end of the day who these people are, and I mean it."

"I'll tell him."

"Good. Let's talk about the Judiciary Committee. I wish I had never changed my mind about Judge Shelton, but it's too late for that now. We have no choice but to defeat his nomination. I want you to get with Senator Montgomery's people and make sure the committee votes eighteen to zero against confirmation."

Cooper stood and walked toward the door. "I'll get right on it."

"And, Cooper."

"Yes."

"Don't talk to Stella anymore." The threat was barely veiled but from the expression on Cooper's face the senator knew the message had been received.

Cooper Harrington left Senator Proctor's office and handed his coffee cup to the senator's secretary. "I don't want any more of this."

The secretary took the cup from Cooper. "I'll get rid of it. And you have a call from a reporter with the *Washington Post* on hold. Do you want to take it?"

"What's his name, and did he say what he wanted to talk about?"

"Judge Shelton's confirmation hearing, and I've forgotten his name."

"I'll take it in my office."

Arlington, Virginia

Holland and Jill were finished with breakfast, and their table was cleared. Jill had a notepad and pen that Holland had retrieved from the backseat of his cluttered Camry. Holland held his wireless to his ear. He had been on hold for five minutes.

He was surprised when Cooper Harrington finally took the call.

"Mr. Harrington, this is Holland Fletcher with the *Washington Post.* I want to ask you some questions about the confirmation hearings."

"Did you say your name is Holland Fletcher?"

Holland detected hesitation in Cooper's voice.

"That's right, Holland Fletcher. I'm with the *Post.*"

Holland mouthed the words "He doesn't know me" to Jill.

"I don't think we've ever met," Cooper said. "You're not one of the senior reporters with the *Post,* are you?"

"Still working my way up the ladder. That's why I hope you can help me with this article on the confirmation hearings."

"I'm listening. Go ahead."

Holland asked Cooper several bland questions about why Senator Proctor had changed his position on Judge Shelton and about what Cooper thought would happen next. Cooper gave benign responses. Holland savored the cat-and-mouse game.

Jill doodled on the notepad while Holland and Cooper bantered back and forth. Finally she motioned with her hands to Holland. "Hurry up," she whispered.

Holland nodded his understanding. "Mr. Harrington, I appreciate your time. I have one final question, and I'll be finished. Did you know a young lady named Jessica Caldwell?"

There was silence from Cooper's end of the phone and Holland shot a look at Jill. It didn't sound like Cooper had disconnected the call — only that Cooper wasn't talking. In fact, Holland couldn't even hear Cooper breathing.

"Mr. Harrington, are you still there? Did you know her?"

"I never heard of her," Cooper stated flatly.

Holland narrowed his eyes. Clearly Cooper had been surprised by the mention of Jessica Caldwell's name. He pointed at the phone and mouthed "He knows something" to Jill.

"She was a Supreme Court law clerk for Justice Robinson," Holland explained, "and after she moved to Nashville, Tennessee, she was murdered. You sure you didn't know her?"

"I'm sure I've never heard of her," Cooper said. "What's she got to do with the confirmation hearings?"

"Nothing. I'm working on another story and thought you might know something. That's all."

"Well, I don't." The pace of Cooper's words was short and crisp, the tone terse.

"Last question, I promise. Then I'll leave you alone. Would it surprise you to know that someone saw you getting into a cab with Ms. Caldwell after Justice Robinson's memorial service?"

Again there was dead silence from Cooper.

"Mr. Harrington, would that surprise you?" Holland pressed. "I mean, if you didn't know her, why would you be sharing a cab?"

"I don't know what you're talking about. I said I didn't know her and that's the end of it. This conversation is over."

There was a loud slam in Holland's ear, and he jumped in his seat. "He's hiding something," Holland told Jill as he closed his wireless.

She smiled wryly. "I could tell."

The Hart Building, Washington DC
Cooper stared at the phone after he'd violently hung up on Holland Fletcher. He was mad. He was so mad that his body trembled. Fletcher knew something, and that troubled Cooper. He wasn't certain

what or how much Fletcher knew, but it was enough to make Cooper nervous. And something had to be done about it — about Fletcher. He finally dialed the number for Hal Crowder.

"Where are you?" Cooper asked.

"I'm in the parking lot of an IHOP in Arlington. Why?"

"You see Fletcher and the woman?"

"I can see them through the window, and one of my men is inside. Fletcher and the Baker woman have been in there a long time."

"Fletcher just called me."

"He what? He just called you? What about?"

"I can't tell you that, but your assignment just changed."

CHAPTER THIRTY

The Fletcher residence, Washington DC

As promised, Holland went to his apartment for a shower and a change of clothes after he and Jill left the IHOP. It was just past 11:00 a.m. when they both arrived at his apartment complex.

Jill went inside with him and sat in the den while Holland disappeared into his bedroom and closed the door. She was a little uncomfortable being in the apartment of a man she had known for less than twenty-four hours. But Holland appeared harmless, and he was rapidly growing on her. It was as if they had known each other for years. And besides, Jill knew she could take care of herself.

Holland had warned Jill before they entered about the condition of his apartment. He was a bachelor and lived like a bachelor, he said, and he washed clothes only when he absolutely had to. When she entered, Jill discovered that Holland's apartment was messier than his Camry.

It resembled a fraternity house more than the apartment of a junior-level reporter. Three empty pizza boxes covered the scuffed coffee table. Two mostly empty soda bottles sat on the end table beside the worn couch. And the kitchen table was barely visible beneath the pile of newspapers and mail.

It was in stark contrast to her own apartment. Clearly, Holland's apartment needed a woman's touch.

"I'm going to use your computer," Jill called out.

"Help yourself," Holland replied from behind the closed bedroom door. "I've got an unlimited broadband connection."

Jill sat in front of the computer on a cloth-covered secretarial chair that swiveled. She heard the water from the shower start as she clicked on Holland's Internet connection. A Web browser opened. She typed the name *Cooper Harrington* into the search engine, and dozens of links popped up. She clicked on a few and read some articles about Cooper. She thought about how to uncover his connection with Jessica Caldwell, but nothing readily jumped out at her. *What had Cooper said that upset Jessica so much?* Jill wondered.

She also remembered that a car registered to Senator Proctor was in the vicinity of Jessica's town house the night she died.

"I wonder if I can find Senator Proctor's itinerary for May," she said to herself.

Jill found Senator Proctor's official government website but couldn't find a link for archived travel itineraries or appearances. The website only listed future events. She went back to the search engine and searched for Senator Proctor and any reference to Nashville, Tennessee. After a few tries, she found an archived article in the *Tennessean* newspaper in Nashville. As Jill began to read the article, she heard Holland turn off the shower.

"Holland, come in here as soon as you can. I've got something to show you."

Two minutes later Jill heard Holland enter the den from his bedroom. She swiveled in her chair. His red hair was still damp, and he'd shaved. His feet were bare. She could tell his clothes were clean, but they looked similar to the ones he'd had on previously.

Jill scanned Holland from head to toe. "Is that all you own? Polo shirts and khaki pants?"

Holland stretched his arms out from his sides, studied himself, then looked back at

Jill. "What's wrong with the way I'm dressed? It's comfortable."

Jill thought Holland needed a new wardrobe but decided it wasn't her place to say something. "Forget it. Come here and look at this."

Holland walked to where Jill was sitting in front of the computer. "What'd you find?"

"This article from the *Tennessean.* It's dated the day Jessica Caldwell's body was found. You recognize anybody in that picture?"

Holland narrowed his eyes. "Yeah. Senator Proctor and Cooper Harrington. Who's the woman?"

"The caption says that it's Senator Proctor's wife, Evelyn. They were all in Nashville, attending a fund-raiser for Senator Proctor, the night before Jessica's body was found."

Holland straightened his back. "But what does any of that mean?"

"I haven't told you this before, but my boss and I found a traffic surveillance photograph of a car registered to Senator Proctor taken near Jessica Caldwell's town house within the time frame the coroner said she died."

"And you don't know who was driving?"

"Not yet." Jill studied the photograph

again and nodded confidently. *But I'll find out.*

"So it could be any of the three?"

"Right, but which one would have a motive to kill her?"

Holland walked away. Jill swiveled and stared at his back.

Holland verbalized his thoughts without turning around. "We know she was pregnant, so any of the three would have a motive to keep that under wraps. The question is, did any of them know about the pregnancy?"

"My guess is that Cooper knew," Jill said slowly, "and that's what he was talking to her about after the memorial service that made her so upset."

Holland lay down on his couch and crossed his feet. He stared at the ceiling. "So our theory is that she and Senator Proctor had an affair, and she got pregnant. Proctor tells Cooper about it. Then Cooper said what to Jessica? That she needed to have an abortion or what?"

Jill stood and began walking around Holland's den. She was careful not to step on, or trip over, anything lying on the floor. It was a difficult task.

"Probably," Jill responded. "Or that she had to keep it quiet. Give the baby up for adoption. Or something like that. He might even have threatened to hurt her in some way."

"And Jessica refused to do what he said, so one of them killed her?"

"That's the theory."

"That seems like a stretch to me, but I'll bite," Holland said. "Which one? Cooper or Proctor?"

"Don't forget about Mrs. Proctor," Jill reminded him. "She was in Nashville that night, too. Maybe she found out about the affair or the pregnancy or both and didn't want the competition."

Holland closed his eyes. "I can't imagine that she got upset over it enough to kill Jessica Caldwell. There've been rumors about Senator Proctor's infidelity for years. This can't be the first affair he had."

"Yeah, but is it the first time the other woman got pregnant?"

Holland's silence told her she'd made a good point.

Jill continued to pace around the room and Holland remained horizontal on the couch, face up. Jill had convinced herself that one of those three — Senator Proctor, Cooper Harrington, or Evelyn Proctor — was responsible for Jessica Caldwell's death and not Tag Grissom.

Then she remembered Anna Grissom's SUV in the surveillance photograph. That made four suspects besides Tag Grissom. She decided to exclude Anna from the mix, since the possibility that Anna Grissom was the culprit couldn't be investigated from Washington DC. So she focused her attention on the other three.

How do we determine which one killed Jessica Caldwell?

Jill halted by the doorway that led to Holland's kitchen. She looked back at him, lying on the couch. He was lying very still. She couldn't see his face, but he wasn't moving and hadn't spoken in a couple of minutes. "Holland," she called.

No response.

"Holland," Jill said again. When she moved closer to where Holland lay, she heard soft snoring.

"I knew you would crash," she mumbled in Holland's direction. "I just thought it would be at least after lunch."

Jill decided to let Holland sleep for a while. She walked to the window in the den that overlooked the parking area below. There were only a few cars scattered around, and she assumed that most people were at work at this time of day on a Tuesday.

Then she noticed a dark green GMC Yukon parked in front of the adjoining building. A brown-haired man was sitting in it. He was close enough that she could see a tattoo on his arm but couldn't make out the design.

I think I've seen that vehicle before . . .

The James S. Brady Briefing Room, the White House, Washington DC

It was 1:00 p.m. on Tuesday. President Wallace was back in the briefing room and doing the one thing that he hated more than anything else — talking to the White House press corps. It was a job hazard, he knew. But that knowledge didn't make it any easier. Porter was in his customary position stage right. President Wallace glanced briefly at his notes as he began his remarks.

"Today I have accepted the resignation of Leslie Hughes as director of the Federal Bureau of Investigations after ten plus years of public service. My office will now begin the process of interviewing potential candidates and will hopefully make a nomination to fill the vacancy within the next two weeks."

President Wallace addressed the crowd of reporters. "I'll be glad to take any questions."

A hand immediately went up from the front row of the press corps. It was Olivia Nelson, as always. President Wallace intuitively knew the question that Olivia would ask. It was the standard first question anytime there was a resignation from a member of the presidential administration.

"Yes, Olivia," President Wallace said.

"Mr. President, was this a voluntary resignation by Director Hughes or was he asked to resign?"

President Wallace shifted his weight from one foot to the other and grinned at Olivia. "Olivia, I met with Director Hughes this morning and expressed some concerns I had. He decided that it was best if he simply resigned."

"What concerns did you express?"

"I told Director Hughes that I was concerned about why the FBI had been unable to apprehend the person or persons who attempted to assassinate Judge Shelton and his wife. Particularly since it's now been over six weeks since that attack and the FBI is no closer to arresting anyone than it was then. I was also concerned about why the FBI hasn't made an arrest in the murders of Myron and Dorothy Carlson."

President Wallace recognized another reporter in the back left section of the room.

"Do you have any potential candidates for the position?" the male reporter asked.

"I don't have any at this point. Assistant Director Phillip McFarland will serve as interim director until a new director is confirmed, and he's very capable." President Wallace glanced at Porter, who signaled that it was time to end the press conference. "That's all the time I have for questions," President Wallace said.

He stepped down from the platform, and he and Porter exited through the door in the rear of the room.

"If Hughes was in bed with Proctor," President Wallace told Porter, "then we just cut off his information supply line."

The Hart Building, Washington DC

Cooper Harrington yelled and cursed at the television screen that carried President Wallace's image exiting the James S. Brady Press Briefing Room. He used the remote to disconnect the power to the television in his bookcase and phoned Les Hughes.

"Of course the president forced me out. I wouldn't quit on my own."

"Did you find out who else was investigating the Carlson murders?"

"Never did. You're on your own with that one."

Cooper grimaced. He knew Senator Proctor would have his head on a silver platter. "What about my tape recording? Where's that?"

"I've still got that, Cooper. And I'm keeping it in case I need it in the future."

Cooper disconnected the call with Les Hughes and banged his hand on the top of his desk. He knew that without Les Hughes providing information, he would never find out who else was investigating Stella Hanover and Joe Moretti. And that meant Senator Proctor would be extremely angry. Cooper could feel the headache he'd had that morning returning. His problems were compounding more quickly than he could resolve them. Stella Hanover was a problem. Holland Fletcher was a problem. And now Leslie Hughes's resignation was a problem. There was no end in sight.

Disobedient to Senator Proctor's orders, Cooper dialed the number for Stella Hanover. "Stella, this is Cooper. Are you watching the news?"

"You mean the Hughes resignation?"

"Exactly. You realize that's a problem, don't you? It was Hughes who was running interference for you on Moretti."

There was silence on the other end of the phone, then, "I don't know what you're talking about, Cooper."

"Don't give me that, Stella. You know you asked me to speak to Les Hughes for you."

"I don't remember anything like that, Cooper. You must've dreamed that. I would never have asked you to interfere with an FBI investigation. That'd be obstruction, and I wouldn't do that."

Cooper could feel Stella smiling on the other end of the phone. He had violated the cardinal rule of Washington politics. He'd failed to cover his own back. He had no proof — no tape recording, no letter, no nothing — of Stella asking him to talk to Les Hughes.

He sat upright in his chair. "Where's Joe Moretti?" Cooper growled.

"I don't know who you're talking about."

"I'm not going down by myself!" Cooper yelled.

He slammed the phone down — he was getting good at doing it — and yelled and cursed again. He stood and paced around the room, thinking.

Come on, Cooper, you can find a way out of this one. You always do.

But this time his world was crashing in around him.

The law offices of Elijah J. Faulkner, Jackson, Tennessee

The DNA results from the tissue samples of Jessica Caldwell's fetus arrived at Eli's office from River City Laboratory mid-afternoon on Tuesday by express courier. Upon their arrival, the receptionist immediately delivered the envelope to Eli in his office. He sat behind his desk and ripped open the envelope. He unfolded the single sheet of paper and began to read.

"Wow," he said out loud.

The results were unexpected and captivating. He stared at the sheet of paper for several minutes and read through it three times to make sure he saw it correctly.

"Wow," he said again and then called out to his secretary, "Barbara, can you come here, please?"

Barbara appeared in the doorway of his office.

"Can you please get me Tag and Anna Grissom's telephone number?"

Barbara disappeared and, in less than one minute, reappeared with the number. Eli removed the receiver from the phone on his desk and dialed the Grissom residence.

Anna answered after the third ring.

"This is Eli," he said. "How was church?"

"It was great," Anna replied. "But I still

473

don't understand everything that I hear."

"Maybe we can talk about it tomorrow. Do you and Tag have time for me to visit? The trial is three weeks away and we need to discuss a few things."

"Sure. What time tomorrow?"

"Is ten thirty in the morning convenient?"

"That's fine. We'll be here."

"Great. See you then."

Eli replaced the receiver and locked his hands behind his head. He had two things to talk with Tag and Anna about: the enlarged surveillance photo and the DNA results. He knew that both would startle Tag and Anna.

CHAPTER
THIRTY-ONE

The Fletcher residence, Washington DC
Jill allowed Holland to sleep for two hours.
He snored softly but often.

While Holland slept, Jill repeatedly peeked
through the window at the parking lot. Each
time, the man in the green Yukon was still
there. His presence began to concern her,
but she decided she wouldn't tell Holland
when he awoke. Maybe she was worried for
nothing.

Finally she shook Holland's shoulder.
"Holland," she murmured. Then louder,
"Holland." At last she nearly shouted his
name: "Holland!"

Holland's body jumped from the sudden
awakening and his eyes flew wide open. "I
must've dozed off."

She chuckled at the understatement.
"Yeah, for like two hours."

"I've been asleep for two hours?" Holland
sat up on the edge of the sofa. "Why didn't

you wake me?"

She crossed her arms defiantly. "Because I knew you needed to sleep. But now it's almost two thirty. We need to get going."

Holland shook his head, trying to chase the sleep away. "Going where?"

"Back to my motel. I've got things to do, and my flight leaves early in the morning."

His shoulders drooped. "I thought you were staying a few days longer."

"I was, but we — you — figured out that it was Cooper Harrington who got in the cab with Jessica Caldwell and then I found that article. I've done about all I can do here. I've got to get back to the office. The trial is less than three weeks away."

Holland didn't want her to leave, she knew. Dejection was written all over his face. But duty called and she had to go.

It was strange. She'd just met the guy, but even she hoped they would stay in touch.

"You've got my wireless number if anything comes up," Jill told him.

"Yeah, but I was hoping you'd stay a couple more days." His expression was hopeful.

"I wish I could, but I can't. I really need to go back to Jackson. There's too much to do before the trial starts."

Holland went to his bedroom and retrieved his shoes. They were soon out the door and bounding down the flight of stairs from Holland's second-story apartment. When they emerged into the parking lot where his Camry was, Jill glanced in the direction of the green Yukon. It was gone.

Maybe I was just being paranoid, she thought.

Holland was quiet for most of the drive to Arlington. He only spoke when Jill prodded. They ate an early supper — they hadn't eaten since breakfast at the IHOP — at the same Mexican restaurant as the night before. Holland was noticeably quiet during their meal. Jill decided he was pouting and thought it was cute. He really didn't want her to leave, and she'd begun to appreciate that it wasn't just because of the investigation.

On the ride from the restaurant to her motel, Jill was trying to press more pieces of the puzzle together.

"The police detectives found an unidentified set of fingerprints in Jessica Caldwell's apartment," Jill said. "They ran it through the FBI database. If it belonged to Cooper or Senator Proctor, I wonder why there wasn't a match?"

Holland shrugged. "Doesn't the FBI database only contain fingerprints of people arrested?"

"I thought all federal employees were fingerprinted and identified."

"They are, but I think that's through the Office of Personnel Management, not the FBI," he added. "That's part of a presidential directive from a few years ago."

"So if we need to compare the prints with ones from Senator Proctor and Cooper Harrington, then we'd have to do that through the Office of Personnel Management?"

The Camry turned onto Jefferson Davis Highway. "That's my understanding," Holland replied as the car merged into traffic. "But I'm not positive. I just remember seeing something about it when the president's directive came out. But that doesn't cover Mrs. Proctor."

"I'm not worried about her," Jill said. "I'm convinced it's not her. But if we can't get a match, then I can still subpoena her."

Jill glanced at her watch. It was 7:45 p.m. eastern time. She knew Eli wasn't in the office, and it would do no good to call him at home. He'd have to go to the office to look at the file and what she needed could wait until she returned. She'd be back in Jackson after lunch the next day and they could strategize about the fingerprints then. She glanced at Holland's profile as the Camry entered the Hampton Inn parking lot. He was still frowning. The car came to a stop behind Jill's rented Ford Taurus, parked in front of the door to her motel room.

"I do hope you'll call sometime," Jill said. "And you have my email address."

Holland faced her and finally smiled. "I will. And I hope you win your case."

"Do you think you have enough for a story even without any information from me?"

"I don't know yet. I've got to talk to my editor. But above the fold would be a feather in my cap."

"Well, good-bye, Holland."

"Good-bye."

Jill smiled at Holland again and exited the car. She waved as he drove away, then entered her room.

The Grissom residence, Brentwood, Tennessee

Anna Grissom was alone in the den on Tuesday night when she heard her doorbell ring. It was almost 7:00 p.m. central time. She and Tag had finished a light supper thirty minutes earlier. He was in his study reading or on the computer or something. Anna didn't know what. She had been watching television alone — as always.

Anna opened the front door to the house and was surprised to find Dr. Graham Frazier standing on the porch. He was taller than she expected but otherwise looked the same as he did on Sunday mornings. He even had on a suit.

"Mrs. Grissom," Dr. Frazier said kindly. "I'm Graham Frazier from New Hope Baptist Church. I hope I haven't caught you at a bad time. May I come in?"

Anna smiled. She was glad to see Dr. Frazier and opened the door wider. "Certainly. Please come in. I'll see if I can find my husband."

Anna and Dr. Frazier walked into the den just as Tag emerged from his study.

"Tag, this is Dr. Frazier from New Hope. You remember him from Sunday, don't you?"

Anna saw the startled look on Tag's face. Dr. Frazier extended his hand, and Tag took it reluctantly.

"Nice to meet you," Dr. Frazier said and glanced back and forth between Tag and Anna. "Did you say your first name is Tag?"

"Todd Allen Grissom, but most people call me Tag. It's nice to meet you as well," he said stiffly.

"Why don't we sit down?" Anna waved at a leather chair for Dr. Frazier to sit in. Anna and Tag sat beside each other on the sofa.

"I saw you visited our church this past Sunday."

Tag flung his "I told you that you shouldn't have put that card in the offering plate" look at Anna. She grinned meekly.

"Was that your first time to visit?" Dr. Frazier asked.

"I've been there several times," Anna replied. "But it was Tag's first."

"We're glad to have you. Is there anything I can tell you about our church?"

Tag and Anna both shook their heads.

"I think we know enough," Tag responded.

"Good. We hope you'll come back again."

"We will," Anna said before Tag could say anything else. "I enjoy your service very much."

"I'm glad you do and glad you plan on attending again. Well, I've taken up too much of your time. I just wanted to visit with you for a minute since you've visited with us."

"We appreciate your coming by," Tag said.

Anna could tell from his tone that he was trying to hurry Dr. Frazier to the front door.

"But before I go, may I ask each of you a question?" Dr. Frazier gestured with his hands. His face seemed inquisitive, as if he wanted a response from Anna and Tag before saying anything further.

"Sure," both Anna and Tag replied almost simultaneously.

"Are you both Christians?"

Anna saw Tag recoil. She could feel him putting up the same defenses — the same walls — as he had when Eli had asked a similar question.

Anna's heart began to race. Her hands turned clammy. It was the same feeling she'd had when Eli had talked to Tag and her. It was the same feeling she'd had on each of the past four Sundays. She took a deep breath and exhaled quietly. She could tell that Tag was about to give the same speech that he gave Eli.

But before he could start, Anna looked directly into the eyes of Dr. Frazier. "I'm not sure," she said.

"Anna!" Astonishment rode on Tag's words. "We can talk about this later."

"Would you like to be certain?" Dr. Frazier asked. He gazed right back at her.

"More than anything." Anna's voice was hopeful.

"I don't believe this." Tag glared at Anna and stood abruptly. "And I'm not listening to any more of this."

Dr. Frazier tried to get Tag to stay in the room and listen. He apologized several times for upsetting him. But Tag simply said he wasn't upset, though Anna knew he was. Tag claimed that he just didn't want to listen to what Dr. Frazier had to say. But if Anna wanted to listen, then that was fine with him.

Tag went to his study, leaving Dr. Frazier and Anna alone in the den.

Dr. Frazier moved from the leather chair and sat beside Anna on the sofa. "I'm sorry I upset your husband."

"He'll be fine."

Anna saw compassion in Dr. Frazier's eyes. Despite Tag's rude departure, she still felt a yearning inside. The fluttering heart and clammy hands had not gone away. The disruption had not distracted from her thirst — her desire — to hear more from Dr. Frazier.

"Tell me how to become a Christian," Anna whispered.

So Dr. Frazier began to explain gently to her what it meant to be a Christian. He explained that she had to recognize that she was a sinner, because no one was pure in the eyes of a righteous God, and that God's Son, Jesus Christ, had died on the cross for *her.* That without accepting the sacrifice of Jesus's life for her, personally, she would be forever separated from God when she died. If she accepted his sacrifice, she would live with him in heaven. If not, she would go to hell, the place of torment and separation.

"Jesus is waiting for you to accept him," Dr. Frazier said. "He loves you. He longs for you to walk into his arms. All you have to do to become a Christian is to ask him to come and live in your heart."

Anna was drawn by the love in Dr. Frazier's eyes. "It's that simple?" she asked.

"It's that simple. Would you like to do that?"

Without hesitation Anna nodded and softly said, "Yes."

Dr. Frazier's smile grew wider. "I'm glad, and so is Jesus Christ. He sees you right now and is smiling down from heaven. Will you pray this prayer with me?"

Anna and Dr. Frazier bowed their heads and closed their eyes. Dr. Frazier said the words and Anna repeated them. She acknowledged that she was a sinner and that Jesus Christ had died on the cross to save her. She thanked him for his sacrifice. Tears streamed down her face as she comprehended the magnitude of what Jesus Christ had done for her. A chill ran over her body, but at the same time warmth stirred inside. And she felt as if she were talking directly to God because she *was* talking directly to God! For a moment it was as if Dr. Frazier wasn't even there. Anna relaxed, and her arms fell limply in her lap. She released the tension in her neck and turned her face toward heaven.

"And, Jesus," Anna said without any prompting from Dr. Frazier, "please come into my heart and be Lord of my life."

"Amen," Dr. Frazier said.

"Amen," Anna repeated.

Anna and Dr. Frazier smiled at each other, and Anna wiped tears from her cheeks. The fluttering heart and clammy hands were gone. She felt full inside. She could tell that something was different. She'd never felt like this in her entire life!

"You're glowing," Dr. Frazier said.

"I can't stop smiling."

"You've been redeemed, Anna. Jesus Christ now lives inside you. He wants to build a strong personal relationship with you."

"That's what I want, too."

Dr. Frazier and Anna visited for several more minutes. Dr. Frazier explained that Anna needed to grow in her faith in Jesus Christ. Two things she could do were to attend church consistently and study her Bible regularly. They discussed the need for Anna to publicly declare her faith in Jesus Christ and what it meant to be baptized.

They became so engrossed in their conversation that before they were aware of it, the clock read 8:00 p.m.

"I really need to be going," Dr. Frazier said.

"I know. I'm so happy you came by."

"Me, too, and I'm glad you accepted Jesus Christ as your Lord and Savior. You can go to bed tonight knowing that if you were to die, you would go to heaven."

"That's a great feeling."

Anna and Dr. Frazier stood up, and Anna escorted him to the door.

"Good-bye, Anna," he said, pressing her hand warmly. "I hope to see you in church on Sunday."

"I'll be there."

Dr. Frazier left, and Anna closed the door. She rested against it from the inside for several seconds, her eyes closed, reliving the events of the last hour. She felt incredibly wonderful.

For the first time in her life, she knew that she would never be alone again.

Tag stood quietly at the door between the study and the den. He had listened to the entire conversation between Dr. Frazier and Anna for the past hour. His knees and legs ached, but he refused to sit down. He had heard everything. He had heard Anna pray and ask Jesus Christ into her heart.

When she'd done so, he'd felt an inexplicable sensation . . . as if there were a separation between him and Anna that hadn't existed before.

After Dr. Frazier left, Tag eased open his study door and tiptoed into the den. He walked to the foyer and peeked around the corner.

There was Anna, leaning against the door with her eyes closed, smiling.

There's something different about her, he thought. But he didn't understand, and it made him uneasy. His life had taken many twists and turns but none more dramatic than the ones that had occurred in the last several months. Although his marriage to Anna was strained, she had at least remained constant during that time. Now, though, even she was changing right before his eyes. He couldn't stand much more. Dropping his gaze to the floor, he slipped back into his study without Anna seeing him.

CHAPTER
THIRTY-TWO

Arlington, Virginia
Jill Baker awoke unexpectedly in her motel room at 3:30 a.m. eastern time on Wednesday. Her mouth felt parched, and she blamed the Mexican food she'd eaten earlier with Holland. Getting out of bed, she filled a glass of water from the sink in her room. After drinking half of the water, she lay back in the bed but couldn't fall asleep.

Finally she decided to connect her laptop to the high-speed Internet connection in her room so she could check her office email. She responded to three or four emails — she knew the recipients would be surprised to see an email from her at 3:57 a.m. — then lay down to try to sleep again.

Nothing.

After tossing and turning for fifteen more minutes, Jill activated the television and watched it while lying in bed. It didn't take her long to appreciate that the television choices were as bad in Washington at four thirty in the morning as they were in Jackson. The only entertainment was the commercials of lawyers who reminded her of used-car salesmen. She turned the television off, slung the covers back, and rose from bed again. Jill walked to the window and pressed the Power button on the air-conditioning unit, hoping the humming, monotonous sound of the fan would create a better sleeping environment.

After she turned the air conditioner on — and merely out of reflex — she peeked through the curtains. She wasn't looking for anything in particular. She was just looking. But that one look was all it took.

Hastily she closed the crack between the curtains and stood still for several seconds. She forced herself to look again to make certain of what she saw. And she was.

Across the parking lot and directly behind her rental car was a dark-colored Yukon. She couldn't determine with absolute certainty in the black of the night — and with only two quick looks — that the color of the vehicle was green. But she was certain of one thing: there was someone sitting in it.

And that was enough to convince her that it was the same dark green Yukon she had seen from Holland's window the previous afternoon.

Washington DC
It had been five full days since Holland had heard from *her.* He thought — hoped — that she had given up on him or found another avenue to use to attack Senator Proctor. But when his telephone rang at 4:45 a.m. Wednesday, his only thought was that *she* was calling again. He moaned and buried his head under his pillow, hoping she would go away. On the third ring he finally realized that something was different this time. It wasn't his apartment phone ringing. It was his wireless. And *she* didn't have his wireless number.

Jumping from bed, he retrieved the phone from his dresser across the room. He was dressed in his usual sleeping attire — pajama bottoms but no shirt.

"Hello," Holland said. He acted as if he were already wide awake but knew his scratchy voice told the person on the other end of the phone that he had been recently asleep.

"Holland, this is Jill."

Her voice sounded frantic and scared. That immediately caused clarity in his head.

"What's wrong?"

"I hope nothing, but I'm a little scared."

Holland's mind darted to a similar conversation he'd had with Tiffany Ramsey, and his heart leaped into his throat.

"Are you in your room? Is the door locked?"

"I'm okay. The door's locked. But I think someone is watching me from the parking lot."

Holland felt a sudden pain in his stomach at the thought of Jill in peril. "What are you talking about?"

"I should've told you earlier."

"Told me what?"

"That I thought someone was following me — us."

"Jill, you've lost me. When did you think someone was following us?"

"When you were napping yesterday, I noticed a guy sitting in a green Yukon in the parking lot of your building. He was there the whole time you were asleep, but when we left your apartment he was gone. I thought I was just being paranoid."

Holland's pulse began to race. "And now he's outside the motel?"

"I think so. It could be my imagination, but it looks like the same vehicle and the same guy."

"Jill, get dressed, and get all your stuff

together," he ordered. "I'll be there in less than thirty minutes."

Holland heard Jill's protests but ignored them and closed his wireless. In less than two minutes Holland was dressed. He walked to his closet and retrieved a shoe box from the top shelf. From inside the box he removed a silver, semiautomatic handgun that his father had given him when he'd moved to DC. Holland had protested then, but his dad had insisted.

"Son," he'd said, "DC is a different place from Roanoke. You might need this."

Holland had finally taken it, said thank you very politely, and had immediately hidden the pocket pistol in the top of his closet, never to be seen again. But with Jill in danger he decided his father might have been right. He might need it for protection, even though he hadn't fired a weapon in a long time. He slid a clip of ammunition into the magazine, checked the safety mechanism, and stuffed the pistol in his waistband.

Leaving his apartment, he barreled down the stairs from his second-story flat to the sidewalk. He had hardly closed the door to his Camry before he backed out of the parking space and exited the apartment complex's parking lot. He slid the pistol under the driver's seat and glanced in his rearview mirror.

A set of headlights was reflected in the mirror. Holland perceived that the vehicle must have exited the apartment complex behind him.

Not good.

The pace of his heartbeat increased, and he squeezed the steering wheel.

Somebody's following me, too.

He remembered the two other times he had seen a black Mercedes that he thought was following him and believed it was the same vehicle.

Instead of driving south toward Arlington — where Jill's motel was located — Holland steered north and eventually onto Georgia Avenue NW, toward Silver Spring, Maryland. If he was being followed, he didn't want to lead his pursuer to Jill. Georgia Avenue NW was a major north-south thoroughfare through the nation's capital. As in most large U.S. cities, there was plenty of traffic even at 5:00 a.m. It wasn't as dense as morning or afternoon rush hour, but still numerous cars, trucks, and semitrailers crowded the northbound lanes.

Holland merged his Camry into the right-hand lane of traffic and adjusted the speed of his car to that of the other cars on the street. He hoped that if he drove normally, the car following him wouldn't realize that Holland had spotted it. He eventually moved into the center lane. He glanced constantly in his rearview mirror, making sure he knew which set of headlights was trailing him.

Arlington, Virginia
"Going north on Georgia?" Hal Crowder asked.

Hal spoke with Frank Melton — another private investigator — whom he had hired to work the night shift watching Holland Fletcher. It shouldn't have been a difficult assignment.

Hal was confused. "Why would he be going in that direction at this time of the morning?"

Hal sat in his green GMC Yukon in the parking lot of the Hampton Inn on Jefferson Davis Highway in Arlington, Virginia. He had assumed his position at midnight when he'd relieved one of his employees who had handled the surveillance of Jill Baker beginning at 2:00 p.m. the previous day. Cooper Harrington's instructions had been explicit. Hal and his employees were to take Fletcher and the woman to an abandoned building in College Park, Maryland, where Cooper would deal with them personally.

Hal waited in his vehicle, directly across the parking lot from the car rented by Jill Baker. He had an unobstructed view of the door to her motel room. He was waiting patiently for just the right moment to take her while one of his minions sat outside Holland Fletcher's apartment with the same instructions. But now Holland Fletcher wasn't cooperating.

"Don't lose him," Hal said. "Something's up. Everything's quiet here, but Fletcher's up to something. Stay with him."

Washington DC
Holland kept a close eye on the set of headlights two cars behind him and drove carefully. The traffic stopped for a red light at the intersection of Georgia Avenue and Peabody Street NW. Holland's Camry was the second car from the intersection. The weather was overcast, and the stars were hidden behind the low-hanging clouds. Daybreak was over an hour away. The moon's glow was barely noticeable, but the streetlights drizzled brightness on the area around the intersection.

There wasn't a car in the lane to his right, and he nervously glanced through the passenger window of the car to his left. A Hispanic woman was driving, alone, and she never looked in his direction.

Holland's vision darted from one outside mirror to the other and then to his rearview mirror. He saw his shadow two cars behind him and was certain there was only one occupant. But he couldn't resolve whether it was a man or a woman. *The headlights are too high to be that Mercedes.*

The traffic light changed to green and Holland continued north on Georgia Avenue. He occasionally changed lanes to see if the other car would do the same, and it did. When he was certain that he was being followed, Holland called Jill on her wireless.

"Change of plans," he said. "I've got someone following me, too."

"We need to call the police." She sounded even more nervous than he was.

Holland knew from her quick response that she must have been contemplating that course of action since he had spoken with her last. He heard the fear in her voice, but he wasn't ready yet to involve the authorities.

"And tell them what? That we have people following us? The police won't believe us."

"I don't care. I'm calling the police."

"Don't do it yet," he implored. "I might

be able to lose the one who's following me. I'll call you back in a little while."

"Holland, please don't do anything crazy. It's not worth it."

"If they wanted to kill us, they would've already. They're just making sure they know where we are and what we're doing. That's all. We rattled someone's cage, and they didn't like it. I'll call you back."

Holland closed his wireless and tossed it in the front-passenger seat. He gripped the steering wheel again with both hands, glanced in the mirror, and thought about the pistol under his seat. His trailer was still on him, and he began to formulate an escape route in his head. Continuing north on Georgia Avenue past the Emery Recreation Center, he kept his Camry in the middle of the three northbound lanes and met several vehicles in the southbound lanes. A few cars passed him on either side going north, but the pursuit vehicle maintained its position behind him. A lone car behind Holland separated him from his pursuer.

Holland's heartbeat quickened even more. He felt a sensation similar to what he had felt on the Fourth of July night beside the Washington Monument. This time, however, he wasn't as scared. He was more angry than scared. He was angry that someone was following him. But he was even angrier that someone was watching Jill.

Who is it?

It made his blood boil just to think about it. Her safety — perhaps her life — was in jeopardy, and he wasn't going to let anything happen to her if he could help it. He felt as if he had let Tiffany Ramsey down somehow, but he wasn't going to let the same thing happen to Jill.

Holland made up his mind to evade the person pursuing him not for himself but for Jill. Her safety depended on it. He had to escape so he could rescue Jill. It sounded noble and brave — new attributes for him, he knew. But that was his plan, and he was firm about accomplishing it. He had never even received a speeding ticket but decided he would violate every traffic law on the books in order to protect Jill. She was worth it.

In the middle lane, Holland approached the intersection of Georgia Avenue and Piney Branch Road NW. There were two cars in the left lane and slightly behind him. An older-model red Dodge pickup was in the lane to his right. The traffic light changed from green to yellow as he approached the intersection.

Holland accelerated the Camry. The car between him and his pursuer and the vehicles on either side of him slowed for the light. He yanked the steering wheel hard to the left — across the left northbound lane — and maneuvered onto Piney Branch as the traffic light for Georgia Avenue changed to red. The intersection was odd. Piney Branch crossed Georgia at an angle rather than perpendicularly, so Holland's Camry slid into the southwest-bound lanes, almost striking a blue Ford pickup waiting at the light. Horns blew from several directions, and Holland accelerated even more.

He checked his mirror again and didn't see his hunter.

One and a half blocks later Holland veered to the left onto Twelfth Street NW, which ran into Fort Stevens Park. He made another left onto Rittenhouse Street and then a right onto Georgia Avenue, this time going south.

He checked his mirrors again. No cars were near him.

Arlington, Virginia

"You lost him?" screamed Hal Crowder into his wireless. Frank Melton was on the other end of the call. "How could you possibly lose him? He's a newspaper writer — not a race-car driver!"

"He made an illegal turn, and I was pinned in. There was nothing I could do. By the time I got turned around, he was gone," Melton reported.

"You didn't anticipate that he would try to get away?"

"I didn't think he ever saw me."

Hal pounded his fist against the beige leather passenger's seat in his green Yukon.

"Get here as quick as you can," he barked to Melton. "He won't do anything without the Baker girl."

"Yeah, he's still out there," Jill said. "I checked right before you called."

Jill was relieved to hear Holland's voice and even more relieved that he was safe. She had worried terribly from the time he'd called last until now. In the interim she'd paced back and forth across the room and indiscreetly peeked through the curtains. She'd tried to make herself not look at all because she feared the man in the Yukon would see her. But the more she thought about not looking, the more it became impossible to keep from it. She lost track of how many times she'd peered out with one eye at the green Yukon across the parking lot.

Because of the way Holland had acted in front of Tiffany Ramsey's town house, she'd been convinced that he didn't have a courageous bone in his body.

But Holland Fletcher had proved her wrong. He was daring. She was amazed by how gutsy he was. He had eluded his pursuer and was now on his way to help her escape somehow. *But how?*

"Good," Holland replied. "I'm still thirty minutes away because of the detour, but I'm on my way again. Do you have everything packed?"

Holland hadn't described his plan to Jill yet, and she wasn't certain he had one. But plan or no plan, she was ready to make a break for it. She was locked securely in her motel room but didn't feel safe. She felt trapped. Something had to give.

"My bag and laptop are sitting by the door. What do you have planned, Holland?"

"I'll call you back when I get closer. When I do, I want you to double-check to make sure he's still there. Then leave your room very nonchalantly, put your luggage in your car, and drive away like nothing's going on. Don't even look in the direction of his vehicle."

"What're you going to do?"

"You'll see. But you can't go to the airport. They're probably waiting for you there."

"I've thought about that. Where am I supposed to go?"

Washington DC
Holland gave Jill explicit instructions about where to go after leaving the Hampton Inn — assuming his plan worked. He tossed his wireless on the passenger seat again and kept driving. He continued on Georgia Avenue until it changed names to Seventh Street NW at the Florida Avenue intersection. Two turns later he crossed the Potomac River on the Fourteenth Street Bridge and was in Arlington, Virginia.

Although he hadn't calmed down completely, the adrenaline rush he'd felt earlier when he'd eluded his pursuer had subsided. But as he drove west across the Fourteenth Street Bridge his anxiety returned. He breathed deep and exhaled.

Holland glanced at the digital clock in the dashboard: 5:53. Dawn was slowly emerging behind him and the traffic thickened around him. He retrieved the pocket pistol from under the seat and wedged it between his right leg and the seat cushion. He was two minutes from the Hampton Inn, where Jill waited for rescue.

He called her again on her wireless. She must have been holding it in her hand because she answered before the first ring was completed.

"You ready?" Holland held the phone to his ear with his left hand and steered with his right. He'd never felt so nervous but tried to hide his anxiety from Jill. He wanted to appear confident but wasn't certain she was convinced.

"Are you sure we shouldn't just call the police?" she asked again. "At least they'd come and investigate. Maybe the guy would leave if the police came."

"But we don't know who he is or who hired him. Right after I called Cooper Harrington, someone started following us. If Senator Proctor's involved, the police won't help us. We've got to get away from everybody and decide what to do next."

There was a long pause on the other end of the phone. Then a confident reply. "I'm ready."

"You still remember everything?"

"Yes."

"Good. Get started. I'm almost there."

Holland removed the phone from his ear and was about to close it when he heard Jill say, "Holland."

"Yeah."

"Be careful."

Hal Crowder was still incensed that Frank Melton had allowed Holland Fletcher to escape. He'd talked to Melton again ten minutes earlier and had heard the complete story of how Fletcher had slipped away with an elementary school move that any respectable private eye should've been able to prevent. Hal decided that he'd give Melton a good tongue lashing when he got to the Hampton Inn parking lot. Then he'd make sure the guy never got another job in DC.

The sun was beginning to peek over the eastern horizon when Hal noticed Jill Baker exiting her motel room. He glanced at his watch — 5:55 — and back at Jill. He slumped down in his seat and tried to hide below the dashboard.

Jill was leaving early for her 8:45 a.m flight but not necessarily too early. She was likely the type who wanted to arrive two hours early and have coffee and a bagel while she waited to board, he thought. He watched her stash her luggage in the rear seat of the white Ford Taurus and then climb into the driver's seat.

Her Taurus backed out of the parking space and then forward to his left and

504

toward the exit from the parking lot onto Jefferson Davis Highway. Hal turned his head slightly but mainly followed the car with only his eyes. When the car entered the highway, he sat upright in this seat and shifted the automatic transmission of his Yukon into drive. He began to accelerate to catch up with Jill's car.

Out of the blue, there was a burst of movement coming toward him from his right. It startled him. He jerked his head around just as a camel-colored Camry slid to a stop in front of his vehicle. The front of the Camry was beyond the driver's side of the Yukon. The rear half of the car was directly in front of him. He looked through the left edge of the Yukon's windshield at the driver of the Camry and immediately recognized the red-haired man behind the steering wheel.

Fletcher! he screamed in his mind.

Hal slammed the transmission into park and started to exit the vehicle, then thought better of it. At first glance it appeared as though Fletcher was waving at him, but Hal noticed a silver object glistening in the man's hand. Hal's eyes grew wide and he tried to duck beneath the dashboard again. He reached into his shoulder holster for his nine-millimeter pistol. His heart leaped into his throat. He'd worked a lot of jobs but had never had anyone point a gun at him.

He won't shoot me, Hal thought.

But before the thought was completely out of his mind, he heard the *crack* of Fletcher's pistol.

CHAPTER
THIRTY-THREE

Arlington, Virginia

Jill ran to Holland's Camry as soon as it came to a stop beside her rental car in the visitors' parking lot of Arlington National Cemetery. He had told her to meet him there, assuming both of them escaped from their pursuers. He knew the location would be easy for her to find. The entrance to the cemetery was on Jefferson Davis Highway — the same street her motel was on — only farther south.

Jill hugged him vigorously. He put his arms around her slender waist. They didn't speak for several seconds as they recovered control of their emotions, but thousands of words were spoken between the two as they held each other.

"We've got to keep moving," Holland said. "They'll be looking for us soon."

"What'd you do at the motel to get away?"

Holland pushed away from Jill so he could

507

see her eyes but didn't release her from his arms. "I shot his front tire out."

Jill's face turned pale. "You shot his tire out? You have a gun?"

Holland glanced around at the mostly deserted parking lot. "Don't say that too loud. Yes, I have a gun. It was the only thing I could think to do. I knew he couldn't follow you if he had a flat tire."

"Did anybody see you?"

"I don't know, and that's why we've got to keep moving."

"Holland, I'm scared. Let's call the police."

"Not yet. Let's get to some place safe and then decide what to do."

Jill hugged him tightly again. "I'm glad you're here."

Holland gave Jill a firm squeeze and reluctantly released her. He held both of her hands in his and gazed into her warm hazel eyes that were filled with fear and worry. "And I'm glad you're not hurt. I don't know what I would've done if something had happened to you. Don't worry. I'm going to make sure nothing happens to you."

"You're amazing, Holland Fletcher."

Holland forced a smile but knew he and Jill weren't out of the woods yet. They still needed to reach someplace where they couldn't be found.

"We need to go. Follow me."

Jill and Holland returned to their respective cars and exited Arlington National Cemetery onto Jefferson Davis Highway headed south. Holland led and Jill followed, closely. They were soon on George Washington Memorial Parkway and inside the city limits of Alexandria, Virginia.

Things were different between him and Jill, Holland knew. He kept his eye on her car in his rearview mirror and thanked God that she was all right.

Arlington, Virginia

Hal Crowder, steaming mad, was standing in front of his Yukon when Frank Melton arrived. Hal needed Melton now — or he would have terminated his employment. Melton exited his vehicle, crouched beside Hal's Yukon, and examined the ruptured tire. Hal stood with his back to Melton and his hands on his hips.

"What happened?" Melton asked.

"The fool shot my tire out!"

"Who?"

"Fletcher."

"Fletcher's been here?" Melton appeared amazed.

"Yes, he's been here. I just said he shot my tire out, didn't I?" Hal said, glowering. "And I didn't even get my pistol out of the holster."

Melton stood up and walked back to his vehicle. "Did you call the police?"

"No. I don't want them involved. They'll recognize me immediately, then we'll never find Fletcher and the Baker woman."

Hal eyed the shredded tire again. He was mad and embarrassed. Holland Fletcher had outsmarted him and gotten away. The thought that *an amateur* had gotten the better of him incensed him. He didn't know why Cooper Harrington wanted Fletcher and the Baker woman, but he knew that Cooper would be furious when he heard they'd escaped. He dreaded telling him and decided to wait awhile before calling him. Hal hoped that he and Melton would find Fletcher and the Baker woman quickly.

"Did anybody hear the shot or see anything?" Melton asked.

"The motel manager came out, but I told him the tire had exploded from a puncture," Hal said. "I'm not sure he believed me, but at least he didn't call the police."

"What do we do now?"

"We've got to start looking for them. I've got two other guys at Reagan National, waiting to see if they show up there." Hal walked around the front of Melton's vehicle — a red-over-tan Chevy Silverado — and continued talking. "I doubt they will since they know we're on to them, but they might. They went south on Jefferson Davis. Let's go."

Melton jerked his head back toward Hal's vehicle. "What about your Yukon?"

Hal got in the passenger seat, and Melton resumed his place behind the steering wheel.

"We don't have time to repair it now," Hal said curtly. "We've got to start looking. I'll call somebody to come get it. I can't leave it here long before someone gets suspicious and calls the police."

Alexandria, Virginia
They had two cars and had to dispose of one of them. Two cars were easier to spot than one but Holland couldn't decide which one to ditch. Both his car and Jill's rental were identifiable for whoever was after them. All along the short eight-mile trek from Arlington to Alexandria, he thought about how to hide both vehicles but keep at least one close enough in case he and Jill needed it.

Holland exited George Washington Memorial Parkway into the parking lot of a convenience store and parked behind the building. Jill immediately followed his lead in her rental. Before exiting his car, Holland stuffed his pistol under the driver's seat. The barrel was still warm, and as he touched it, he saw a fleeting image of the surprised face of Jill's pursuer.

"We've got to find somewhere to hide your car," Holland said as he and Jill stood between the two cars. He could still see fear on Jill's face.

"Everything's going to be okay," Holland reassured her. "I'm going to see if they have a phone book inside. I'll be right back."

"Please hurry."

Holland nervously entered the store and asked the clerk behind the counter if he could borrow a phone book. He thumbed through the listings for a parking garage and then asked directions. He returned to where Jill was waiting anxiously.

"There's a parking garage six blocks up," Holland explained. "We can leave your rental there. Let's put your bags in my car."

After all Jill's belongings were transferred to Holland's Camry, he led Jill to a parking garage on Roosevelt Avenue. He made sure Jill parked as far in the back of the garage as possible so her car would be harder to find.

When she was safely settled in the Camry with him, he reasoned, "Now we've got to find a place out of the way where we can hide. And turn the power off to your wireless. These people are dangerous, and professionals. They might be able to track us even if we don't use our phones."

After driving around for thirty minutes, Holland finally parked the Camry behind an Amoco convenience store on North Washington Street in Alexandria. He and Jill had circled the block three times to determine the best parking spot, where the car couldn't be detected by street traffic on North Washington. They hardly spoke as they rode from the parking garage to the Amoco and continuously looked in different directions to see if they noticed the same vehicle more than once. Convinced they hadn't been spotted, Holland steered the Camry into the parking lot and stopped precisely in the location he and Jill had identified. It was 7:45 a.m.

"I have an idea, and I'm going to make a quick phone call," Holland said. He left the engine idling and the air conditioner blowing. He ran across the parking lot to a pay phone attached to the back corner of the convenience store. From his wallet he removed a scrap of paper that he had placed there weeks earlier and punched the numbers written on it. The number rang, and Holland glanced back at Jill.

"C'mon, answer," he urged. He twisted back to the pay phone and stared at the key pad.

Two rings.

Three rings.

Four rings.

No answer.

He replaced the receiver, then picked it up again. He slid more change into the slot on the phone and dialed the number again. Two more rings and finally a female voice said, "Hello."

He immediately recognized the voice. It was *her.*

"This is Holland Fletcher," he said.

"Holland Fletcher? What're you doing calling me?"

"I'm working on a story about Senator Proctor. Remember?"

"I thought you'd given up after the Ramsey girl died."

The metallic cord attached to the receiver was three feet long at most, but Holland paced anxiously on the sidewalk beside the pay phone as far as the cord would reach. His eyes darted suspiciously at the cars that entered and exited the convenience-store parking area.

"Given up? Not a chance. But I need your help."

"Will it bring Lance Proctor to his knees?"

"I'm sure of it."

"What do you need?"

Holland told her the abbreviated version of the story, beginning with Jill Baker's arrival in DC up to hiding behind the Amoco convenience store in Alexandria.

"If I can get to my office at the *Post*," he explained, "I can get the story written in time for tomorrow morning's edition. I think I have enough that my editor will run with it. But I can't get there because I'm sure they're looking for my car."

"I know these people, Mr. Fletcher, and I'm certain they'll be waiting for you and Ms. Baker at your office and your apartment. You can't go to either. Can you write the article from another location?"

"I guess so. What'd you have in mind?"

"Are you safe where you are?"

He scanned the parking lot again. "I think so. I'm sure they're searching for us but haven't found us yet. We're doing everything we can to stay out of sight."

"You and Ms. Baker stay put. I'll be there within the hour. I know a safe place where you can go."

Holland hung up the phone and dashed back across the parking lot to Jill and the Camry.

"Who'd you call?" Jill asked even before Holland had completely closed the car door.

"You remember I told you about the mystery woman who'd been feeding me information about Senator Proctor?"

"Yeah."

"Her."

"Her?" Jill's eyes widened. "Why her?"

"Because I know she wants Senator Proctor's head on a platter. And I told her enough of the story to make her help us."

"How's she going to help?"

"I don't know for sure. But she's on her way down here to take us to someplace safe so I can write an article for tomorrow morning's edition of the *Post*."

"What's her name?"

"I still don't know, but we're going to find out soon enough. She'll be here within an hour."

"I hope you know what you're doing. What if she's one of the people chasing us?"

Cooper Harrington repeatedly punched his fist into the gray leather seat of his limousine. It was 8:00 a.m., and he was en route to the Hart Building to prepare for the Judiciary Committee's vote, scheduled for 9:00 a.m. He had just finished speaking with Hal Crowder. All his yelling had been useless. It had been two hours since Holland Fletcher and Jill Baker had escaped, and Cooper knew they could cause him the worst possible trouble.

Why did Crowder wait so long to call me?

Cooper was certain that Crowder and his band of Keystone Kops weren't going to find Fletcher and the Baker woman without some help. He was running out of options and out of time. He only knew one other person who could help. Cooper dialed the number.

"Sure, I still have some friends in the Bureau," Les Hughes said.

"I need to find these two, Les. I'll make it worth your while. They may know something about the Carlson murders and who's investigating them."

Cooper lied to former Director Hughes to get his cooperation. If he had told him the real reason he needed to find Holland and Jill, then Les wouldn't help him. In fact,

Cooper was convinced that Les Hughes would run from the assignment. At least that was Cooper's reasoning, right or wrong. As deep as he was into this crater, one more lie didn't matter.

"I'll see what I can find out," Les agreed, "and I'll call you back in a little while."

Alexandria, Virginia

Hal Crowder and Frank Melton crisscrossed Alexandria in Melton's Silverado looking for Jill Baker and Holland Fletcher. Meanwhile, Hal's Yukon was towed to a service station near his office on K Street NW for repairs. It had been approximately two and a half hours since Fletcher had blasted Hal's front tire.

Hal and Melton hadn't seen hide nor hair of Fletcher or the Baker woman. Hal wasn't even positive that the couple was in Alexandria. That was the direction they had traveled from the Hampton Inn in Arlington, but they could be anywhere. It was like looking for a needle in a haystack.

Hal's men on the ground at Reagan National Airport reported that Jill Baker hadn't yet arrived for her 8:45 a.m. flight and hadn't returned her rental car. Hal directed his men to stay in place and to keep the airport under surveillance. She still might

518

turn up there, he reasoned.

Another man had riffled through Fletcher's apartment, looking for any clue that might direct Hal to the couple's location. He came up empty. Hal had instructed him to wait in the parking lot outside Fletcher's apartment in case he and the Baker woman returned.

Two of Hal's other ruffians sat in a car parked on the curb in front of the *Washington Post* headquarters.

Hal had spoken to Cooper Harrington several times over the previous thirty minutes. Cooper wasn't happy, to say the least. Every time Cooper called, Hal had to tell him that the couple hadn't been found yet but that he and his men were working on it. And after every report Cooper yelled and cursed. But by their last conversation, he had calmed down. He'd told Hal that he had someone monitoring the couple's wireless phone usage — and without a court order. Hal didn't want to know how Cooper was able to accomplish that bit of illegal surveillance.

Hal and Melton flashed photographs of Fletcher and the Baker woman and fake DC police badges at two dozen convenience-store clerks. They finally found a clerk on George Washington Parkway who thought he remembered the red-haired man entering the store and asking for directions to a parking garage on Roosevelt Avenue.

"That's her rental car," Hal said from the passenger seat of Melton's Silverado. They were on the third floor of a parking garage. He exited Melton's vehicle and circled around the rental car. No one was inside, and the luggage he'd seen Jill Baker place in the rear seat earlier that morning was missing.

"They're together in Fletcher's car somewhere," Hal said to Melton as he reentered the Silverado.

Just as Melton guided his vehicle toward the exit from the parking garage, Hal's phone rang.

"Crowder," he said.

"This is Cooper. We have a lead on Fletcher and the girl."

"Where are they?"

"Somewhere near a wireless tower at the intersection of North Washington and Pendleton Street."

"They used a wireless phone?"

"No. But they made the mistake of leaving the batteries in their phones," Cooper explained. "They both registered at this tower a few minutes ago."

"How big a radius from the tower does it

pick up signals?"

"Ten blocks," Cooper reported.

"We're close to that intersection now."

"Get 'em, Crowder," Cooper said. And then slowly, in a growling voice with an emphasis on each consonant, he said it again, "Get them."

Melton stopped the Silverado before entering the street from the parking garage.

Hal closed his wireless. "Go that way," he instructed Melton and pointed toward the north. "A wireless tower at North Washington and Pendleton picked up a signal from Fletcher's and the Baker woman's wireless phones."

Melton accelerated the pickup onto Roosevelt until the duo was traveling northward on North Washington Street. They sped through the intersections with Cameron, Queen, Princess, and Oronoco streets — without obeying the red traffic lights — before reaching the intersection with Pendleton. Melton steered the vehicle into the parking lot of a church on the southeast corner, made a U-turn, and stopped at the edge of the parking lot outlet onto North Washington.

Hal and Melton scanned the area in all directions.

"He said it could be anywhere within a

ten-block radius of this intersection," Hal said.

"That's still a big area to cover."

Hal scratched his chin. "Yeah, but if you were trying to hide, where would you go?"

"Probably some place with a lot of people. Some place out in public. That's what I'd do."

"I agree. Some place with a lot of people. Like a mall or grocery store or something like that." Hal panned his vision up and down North Washington again. "Let's keep going north. I don't recall seeing anything like that in the other direction."

Melton's vehicle reentered North Washington and continued north. The next intersection was Wythe Street.

"I see two gas stations up ahead," Melton said. "Exxon on the right and Amoco on the left."

"Let's start with the Exxon and then we'll cross over to the Amoco."

Melton guided the vehicle into the parking lot of the Exxon and looped the building twice. They didn't see Fletcher's Camry outside, nor did they see Fletcher or the Baker woman through the glass windows in the front of the building. When traffic cleared, Melton maneuvered his vehicle across North Washington and into the parking of the Amoco convenience store.

"There it is!" Hal exclaimed when he saw Holland Fletcher's Camry parked at the rear of the building. Melton accelerated his vehicle through the parking lot and then to a sliding stop in front of the Camry. Hal whiplashed in the passenger seat. The front bumper of Melton's vehicle was mere inches from the front of the Camry.

Remembering Fletcher's silver pistol, Hal drew his own weapon from his shoulder holster and leaped from the vehicle before it came to a complete stop. He sprinted to the driver's-side door of the Camry with his weapon pointed at the window in the door.

CHAPTER THIRTY-FOUR

Alexandria, Virginia

"Mrs. Proctor," Holland said, "I can't believe you're the mysterious woman who's been calling me."

Holland and Jill sat, shaking their heads in disbelief, in the rear seat of a black Mercedes-Benz S65 — the same car Holland had seen on two other occasions. It was moving north on George Washington Parkway and was two minutes removed from the parking lot of the Amoco convenience store on North Washington Street.

Evelyn Proctor sat in the front passenger seat, and an African American with a gravelly voice that Holland hadn't forgotten since the Fourth of July drove the car.

"Why'd you do it?" Holland asked.

Evelyn Proctor peered into the backseat at Holland and Jill. A wicked grin lit her features. "You know what they say about a woman scorned, don't you?"

Hal Crowder peered through the driver's-door window of the camel-colored Camry. There were two wireless phones on the front passenger seat. He slammed his fist like a sledgehammer into the roof of the Camry and kicked the driver's-side door with his foot. Then he yelled and screamed and cursed — both at the empty car and from the excruciating pain in his foot. If a new dent emerged in the side of the car from his blow, it wasn't noticeable among the others.

Hal hobbled back to Melton's truck and rested against the front-right fender. A minute later he phoned Cooper Harrington with the bad news. More yelling and screaming and cursing ensued — all from Cooper — and the only thing Hal could do was grimace and take it.

The Oval Office, the White House, Washington DC

President Wallace, Porter McIntosh, and Judge Shelton gathered in the Oval Office to watch the Judiciary Committee vote. They were dressed in white shirts, silk ties, and dark suits, but President Wallace's suit coat hung in his closet. They looked like they were going to a funeral. All three anticipated the vote to be eighteen to zero, but they wanted to watch, anyway.

President Wallace especially. He knew that the next several days would be one of those points in history where the United States of America would be changed. It was a fork in the road where either America would begin the long journey back to God or she would continue down the path of moral decay and destruction. Regardless of the outcome of the nomination of Dunbar Shelton to the Supreme Court, things were going to change. America would be different somehow. And President Wallace prayed that the changes — a changed America — would be for the better.

President Wallace sat on one of the leather sofas in the Oval Office and Porter and Judge Shelton sat on the other. The plasma monitor across the room from President Wallace's desk displayed the Senate Judiciary Committee hearing. Senator Montgomery was front and center with his wispy white hair and angry face. All the other committee members flanked him on both sides and appeared very solemn. Senator Montgomery banged his gavel and called the meeting to order.

"The clerk will now take a roll-call vote," Senator Montgomery said. "Those in favor of recommending confirmation of Judge Dunbar Shelton shall vote aye and those against shall vote nay."

The clerk was not visible on the monitor but his voice could be heard as he called out each senator's name, beginning with the chairman of the committee, Senator Montgomery.

"Senator Montgomery," the clerk said.

Senator Montgomery sat tall in his oxblood leather executive chair and leaned into the microphone. "Nay!"

"Senator Montgomery votes nay," the clerk repeated.

And so it went. Senator after senator voted against recommending confirmation of Judge Shelton's nomination to the full Senate. President Wallace painfully stared at the monitor and occasionally glanced at Porter and Judge Shelton. Their vision was likewise fixated on the television across the room. After the last senator voted, the monitor switched to a talking head who declared Judge Shelton's nomination officially over and who mused about why President Wallace hadn't withdrawn it before then.

"That's about what we expected," Porter said in President Wallace's direction.

"I'd say it's exactly what we expected."

"What do we do now?" Judge Shelton asked.

President Wallace stood and walked to his desk. He was silent.

It was Porter who responded to Judge Shelton's question. "Senator Proctor is scheduled for a press conference in five minutes to announce when the vote will go to the Senate floor. Once he has officially made the announcement, then we can decide when to take our next step."

"Do you really believe the Senate will confirm me after that vote by the committee?"

"Dunbar," President Wallace began.

Porter and Judge Shelton turned their heads and eyed him.

President Wallace stood tall in front of his desk and set his chin. "This thing is a long way from over. You and I both know that God's in complete control of this situation. That's one reason I nominated you. Because we share the same faith in God. And we both know that we're here for this turning point in the life of our great country."

Judge Shelton gave a nod. "I agree, Mr. President."

"And I have complete faith that you'll be confirmed."

At precisely 9:30 a.m. Senator Proctor appeared on the monitor in the Oval Office. He wore a dark gray suit with pinstripes and smiled widely through his black beard and mustache. He stood before a bank of microphones in the hallway outside room 216 in the Hart Building. He looked smug, but his appearance didn't bother President Wallace. Neither did the venom that spewed when he opened his mouth. President Wallace reckoned that Senator Proctor's day was coming . . . very soon.

"The country has now seen what a complete and utter mistake it was for President Wallace to nominate Judge Dunbar Shelton to the Supreme Court," Senator Proctor proclaimed. "We cannot have an extremist like Judge Shelton on the Supreme Court, and I had hoped that President Wallace would have withdrawn the nomination."

Senator Proctor's corpulent body consumed the monitor, and his voice reverberated through the speakers in the Oval Office. He gestured with his hands as he spoke.

President Wallace generally ignored him and only glanced occasionally at the monitor.

"Since he has not" — here Senator Proctor shook his head, as if in deep regret — "we have no option but to take a vote on the Senate floor. As you just witnessed, the

Judiciary Committee voted unanimously against Judge Shelton's confirmation. I'm confident that the full Senate will do the same, so I plan to schedule a vote as soon as possible."

President Wallace couldn't have cared less about Senator Proctor's prophecy. He hardly watched or listened. But Senator Proctor was finally to the only part of the press conference that interested the president: the date and time of the Senate vote. President Wallace leaned his back against the front edge of his desk and focused intently on the monitor.

"Next week begins the Senate's August recess," Senator Proctor announced, "and I for one want this matter concluded as soon as possible so that the country can begin the healing process. This has been a sad occasion in the life of our nation. An event that never should have occurred. And wouldn't have if President Wallace had done the right thing. He didn't. So I will bring this nomination to the Senate floor for a vote tomorrow afternoon at one o'clock. That should bring an end to this terrible chapter in our nation's history."

"The end to your political career," Porter shot in the direction of the television.

"That's exactly what I was thinking,"

President Wallace said. He pressed a button on his desk and the monitor disappeared. His eyes fixed with intensity on Porter. President Wallace recognized that a historical moment faced the three men in that room, but only he could give the order. Without hesitation or regret he spoke.

"Porter, schedule a press conference for this afternoon, and get everything ready to be released. I want Senator Proctor to be the lead story on the evening news and on the front page of every newspaper in the country tomorrow morning."

"Done," Porter replied confidently. "It'll be the only topic of conversation around the water fountains and coffeepots across the country tomorrow morning."

Then President Wallace looked at Judge Shelton. "The game's on. To the victor go the Supreme Court and the Senate."

Washington DC

The black Mercedes pulled into the driveway of a two-story brownstone in the Montrose Park area of upper Georgetown.

"Whose house is this?" Holland asked.

"Mine," Evelyn Proctor replied.

Jill's mouth gaped open. "This is the safe house?"

"None better." Evelyn Proctor smiled

confidently. "Nobody will think about looking for you here, and the great senator won't be home for hours — if he even comes home."

Holland and Jill shot looks of concern at each other. But this thing had become much bigger than both of them. Holland realized that they had to trust somebody, and Evelyn Proctor's motivation for helping them — although sinister — was still directed at discovering the truth. Holland raised his eyebrows at Jill, seeking approval. She nodded slightly.

"Mrs. Proctor," Holland said, "all we need is a telephone cord. Jill's got her laptop."

"I can do better than that."

En route to Brentwood, Tennessee

Eli had departed Jackson at approximately 8:30 a.m. central time for his meeting with Tag and Anna Grissom at their house in Brentwood. Tag and Anna were expecting him at 10:30 a.m. The traffic was light on the I-440 loop around Nashville, and he was in Brentwood with time to spare. He exited his BMW at 10:20 a.m.

Anna met him at the front door. He was barely inside the door before she announced, "I have some exciting news!"

Eli and Anna moved through the entrance

hall toward the den. He carried a briefcase containing the topics he planned to discuss with Anna and Tag. Anna beamed from ear to ear, but Tag was nowhere to be seen.

Eli studied Anna. She looked different from the last time he'd seen her. She seemed happy. Joyful. He had never seen that trait in her.

And he noticed something else. Anna actually looked pregnant. Her stomach was pudgy, and she wore a red maternity blouse over khaki slacks.

She really is pregnant. At last I know the truth, Eli thought.

They emerged from the hallway into the den and stood near the back of the sofa.

"What's your news?" Eli asked.

Anna smiled even broader. "I became a Christian last night."

Eli rejoiced inwardly. Those were beautiful words! He and Sara had prayed incessantly for the souls of Tag and Anna Grissom, and God had been faithful to his Word. He couldn't wait to tell Sara. "That *is* good news! Tell me all about it."

Eli and Anna sat on the leather sofa, and Anna gave him a verbatim account of the visit from Dr. Graham Frazier. Eli couldn't help but smile as he listened to Anna share her conversion experience. The Holy Spirit had indeed moved in Anna's life. One more lost soul had been rescued.

"That's an incredible story, Anna! Dr. Frazier is right. Jesus Christ will alter your life. What did Tag say about it?"

Her face fell. "We haven't talked about it much. He knows, and I can tell that he doesn't like it. He's been pouting more than usual." She shrugged.

"Perhaps he sees something in you that he doesn't have."

"I doubt that's the case. He wasn't crazy about going to church last Sunday, and he claims he's not going back."

"Maybe he'll change his mind. I'll keep praying for him. And now that you're a Christian, you can pray, too."

"Believe it or not, I've already started."

"That's great," Eli said. "Where is Tag anyway?"

"He's in our bedroom. I'll get him."

Anna left the room and Eli opened his briefcase. It was time to discuss with Tag and Anna the reason for his trip. He removed the photographs — both the original showing Anna's Infiniti SUV and the second of her driving — and the lab report on the DNA testing of Jessica Caldwell's fetus. He placed the photographs and the lab report facedown on the top of his briefcase.

Soon Anna returned to the den with Tag in tow. Tag's hair was messy, and there were baggy circles under his eyes. He wore a white undershirt, blue jeans, and socks — no shoes — and looked as if he'd hardly slept the previous night. He certainly hadn't shaved.

Eli had never seen Tag in such disarray. The contrast between Tag's disheveled appearance and Anna's radiant one was evident to Eli. He and Tag shook hands, and Eli moved to a nearby chair. Tag and Anna perched on the sofa.

Eli jumped into the conversation with both feet. "Tag, I'm sure you recall when we first met that I told you I needed to know everything about this case, good or bad. Do you remember me saying that?"

"I remember," Tag responded.

"The trial is three weeks away, and I think it's time both of you came clean with me." Eli set his jaw so they knew he meant business. He turned his head back and forth to study each of them.

Both appeared alarmed by his directness.

"We have told you everything," Tag said.

"No, you haven't. You didn't tell me the truth about your relationship with Jessica Caldwell, and neither of you was honest with me about where you were the night she died."

Anna covered her mouth and her eyes opened wide.

Tag looked at her, then back at Eli. He ran a hand through his unkempt dark hair. "I don't know what you're talking about."

Eli removed the photograph of Anna's Infiniti SUV from the top of his briefcase and displayed it to Tag and Anna. "Do you remember that you gave me this photograph, Tag?"

Tag nodded, and Anna focused her vision on the photo.

"And you told me that you had received a ticket from the police department for running a red light the night Jessica Caldwell was murdered."

"I never knew anything about this photo," Anna said. Her voice was nervous and sullen.

"I know," Tag replied. "I never showed it to you."

"That's your car, isn't it, Anna?"

Anna nodded.

Eli retrieved the second photograph — the one depicting the driver of the Infiniti SUV — and displayed it to Anna and Tag. "And you were driving it, weren't you?" he asked Anna.

"Don't answer that," Tag directed. He

turned a stern face to Eli. "I was driving."

"I had it enlarged. It clearly shows Anna driving. You want to tell me what really went on that night?"

Tag stood up from the sofa and plodded nervously around the den.

Anna sat in stunned silence.

Tag spoke with his back to Eli. "But she didn't have anything to do with it. I was the one who was there."

Tag's words didn't convince Eli. He couldn't see Tag's face but studied Anna's. It was downcast, and her eyes were teary. She appeared miserable.

Tag seemed to be hiding something. And then it struck Eli.

"I don't believe you, Tag," Eli said firmly.

"I'm telling you the truth," Tag fired back.

Anna's head rose. "No, it's not the truth, Tag." Her eyes met Eli's. "We haven't told you everything."

"Don't, Anna," Tag pleaded. He looked at Eli and Anna over his right shoulder. "Not now."

"I have to, Tag. I can't continue living with this lie." She focused on Eli. "I went to Jessica Caldwell's town house the night she was murdered. I suspected Tag was having an affair and followed him. Tag's car was parked in front of her town house when I got there, but I couldn't get anyone to come to the door. I rang the doorbell and banged on the front door for a while before I left. I was really mad. I drove around for a while, then drove back to her town house. Tag's car was gone. When I got home, Tag was already here."

"But you didn't kill her," Eli said. It was more of a statement than a question.

"I never even saw her that night."

Eli shifted his vision to Tag's back. "But you were telling me the truth when you said you didn't father Jessica's child, weren't you, Tag?"

Tag abruptly twisted. His lips were pursed in astonishment.

Anna also appeared puzzled.

But everything was becoming clear to Eli. He handed Anna the DNA report. He saw Tag's eyes straining to look at the document.

"What's this?" Anna asked.

"It's the lab report on Jessica Caldwell's fetus."

"I don't understand."

"At first I thought you killed her," Tag said, finally breaking his silence. He returned to the sofa, beside Anna. "I was inside her town house with her when you were banging on the front door calling my name. So I knew you had found her place. And then I got the photograph of your car in the mail. It was time stamped well after I left Jessica's town house." His voice trailed off and became a whisper. "I thought you had gone back there again that night . . . and killed her. All because I was messing around with another woman, and you'd caught me."

"You thought *I* killed her?" Anna stared incredulously at Tag.

He straightened his back and cocked his head toward Anna. "Don't look at me like that. You think *I* did it, don't you?" He looked toward Eli, and his tone turned pleading. "I didn't kill her, Eli. I swear to God I didn't and couldn't kill her. But Anna is pregnant. I couldn't let her go to jail for something she did just because she was mad at me. And because I'd fooled around, it was only right that I should be tried in her place."

Anna gasped. "I don't believe this. You thought I killed her and wanted to protect me? You've never acted like you cared that much for me before."

"I loved my mother," Tag said, "but she was taken from me. I didn't want that to happen to you . . . or the baby. It wouldn't be right. So I decided I had to protect you."

But Eli wasn't buying it. "That was your plan initially, right, Tag?" Eli asked. "You were afraid Anna had murdered Jessica Caldwell, so you were willing to face a jury in her place. It sounds very admirable."

"But I didn't do anything," Anna protested. "There was no need to protect me."

Uncomfortable silence ensued as Tag and Anna stared at each other. They searched each other's face for answers, but neither held the complete truth. Only Eli had made all the connections. He spoke with authority to Tag.

"You didn't know that in the beginning, though, did you? And the SUV is licensed to you, not Anna. You had no way of knowing that another photo existed that depicted the driver of the car. So you gave me the photograph, hoping it would further incriminate you. That way Anna would be off the hook. She could have the baby and go ahead with her life without you."

Tag broke his gaze from Anna and shifted his head toward Eli. He nodded slowly.

"And the scratch on your face? How did that happen?" Eli asked.

"The night Jessica died we ended our relationship. She got mad and slapped me. She grazed my cheek. She had been acting weird for about a week anyway. Ever since she came back from Washington. After I was arrested, I was glad she'd scratched me. It directed the police toward me and away from Anna."

The expression on Anna's face showed she was clearly struggling to take all this news in.

"But then, in the preliminary hearing, you saw the HCG notation on the report," Eli said. "And you pointed it out to me."

Tag nodded. "When Jessica told me she was pregnant, I knew I couldn't be the father." He dropped his head. "Our relationship had lasted nearly three months, but we weren't intimate until the last two weeks. I knew that was too soon for her to know she was pregnant from our relationship, so I knew I couldn't be the father. But I still thought Anna had killed her, and I wanted to protect Anna. So the only thing I could think to do that day in court was to lie to you and say I was sterile."

"That's not exactly true either, is it, Tag?" Eli asked.

"What's not true?" Tag's tone was defensive.

"You didn't tell me you were sterile to protect Anna," Eli said slowly. "There was a different reason, wasn't there?"

Tag looked uncomfortable.

Eli went on with his deductions. "And later, in the hearing, when the medical examiner said the fetus was twelve weeks old, you could easily have told me that the fetus was too old to have been fathered by you. The fetus was three months old, but your affair with her was much shorter." He leaned toward Tag. "No, the reason you told me you were sterile was so I would have the body exhumed. You wanted me to find out who fathered her child. Isn't that right?"

"If you're not the father," Anna said in Tag's direction, "then why would it be important to you to know who was?"

Eli continued staring at Tag but talked to Anna. He watched Tag's reaction to his words, and his reaction spoke volumes. "Tag realized at the preliminary hearing that you had nothing to do with Jessica Caldwell's death. He could have ended the entire ordeal right there, but he had some guesses about who the father of her baby might be. The only way to prove it was for the criminal case against him to continue. If the case against Tag had been dismissed, then he wouldn't get the one thing he so desperately wanted. He *had* to know for certain who had fathered Jessica's baby. But to do that, the body had to be exhumed, in order for DNA tests to be run on the fetus. So, you see, Anna, Tag's plans weren't as much about protecting you . . . as they were about convicting someone else."

Eli's eyes met Tag's.

"How long have you known?" Tag asked.

"I've had the DNA results a few days, but just now began to make it all fit together."

"Known what?" Anna asked.

"That Tag's father also had an affair with Jessica Caldwell."

"Tag's *father?*" Anna stared at Tag. "I thought you didn't know your father."

"He knows," Eli said. "It's the same man who fathered Jessica Caldwell's baby."

"I'm confused," Anna admitted.

Eli continued to focus his vision on Tag while he spoke to Anna. "Look at that lab report. It says that Tag and the fetus of Jessica Caldwell were half siblings. Tag and the unborn child of Jessica had the same father."

As Eli continued to study Tag's face, things began to fall into place. Tag wasn't sterile. Eli had confirmed that truth. And that meant Anna hadn't lied to him the first time he'd met with her in his office. She was, in fact, pregnant — she looked it now — and Tag was the father.

The next piece to the puzzle was that Anna wasn't involved in Jessica Caldwell's demise. She was unwittingly complacent in

Tag's claim of being sterile, but that was her only offense. It didn't matter to Eli why she had remained silent in the face of Tag's lie. He decided not to even ask her. Perhaps she was scared or hoped the lie would somehow exonerate Tag. She had said earlier she wanted her baby to grow up with a father. Whatever her reasoning had been, it was irrelevant now. That issue was closed.

But more unanswered questions gnawed at Eli.

"What happened to your mother?" Eli asked Tag.

Tag's expression changed to puzzlement. Eli realized that he was treading in an area of Tag's life that Tag was surprised he'd discovered.

"She died in a car accident. Why?"

"Whether it was really an accident is questionable, isn't it?" Eli asked.

Tag shook his head. "I don't know what you're talking about."

"C'mon, Tag. Her car went over a cliff without any skid marks, and you asked the police to close the investigation? You know something about what happened to her. What is it?" Eli scrutinized Tag's face.

Tag dropped his head. He couldn't look Eli in the eyes. It was as if Tag thought Eli already knew the answer, and he had no option but to reply honestly.

Anna sat quietly, wringing her hands in her lap. She appeared perplexed. Eli sensed that the subject of the conversation between him and Tag was foreign to her.

Tag studied the floor. "I don't have any proof," he said in a low voice. "Only suspicion."

"Suspicion about what?" Eli asked.

"That he was involved."

"Who?"

Tag looked up at Eli and forced the words through his lips. "My father."

"And he told you to leave it alone. He must be very powerful."

Tag's eyebrows rose and he nodded thoughtfully. "To say the least."

"And that was why you wanted to find out the truth about Jessica's fetus. You couldn't prove he killed your mother, but perhaps you could at least find some way to tie him to Jessica Caldwell's murder."

Tag's eyes were angry. He clenched his fists. "He deserves to pay dearly for murdering my mother. She never did anything to him. But if not for her murder, then he needs to pay for something. Without the DNA testing, there would be no way to link Jessica with him. No way to prove that he might be the one who killed her because she was carrying his baby."

"How did you find out that he and Jessica had an affair?"

"She told me. He kept calling her and I saw that it upset her. I asked her who it was and she told me. She had no idea I knew him. The night she told me she was pregnant, she seemed scared. She said something had happened while she was in Washington. But I didn't want to listen. I was ticked off that she was pregnant . . . and hadn't told me before. We got in a fight, and she told me to leave. I was only too glad to do that. I had planned on telling her that night that it was over, anyway."

"So who is it?" Eli prodded. "Who is your biological father?"

"My mother was only a teenager when she got pregnant. It was thirty-five years ago. She told me that he said he loved her but refused to marry her. I guess I should be grateful that he paid for my education, but when I finished medical school, he cut off all financial support. My mother confronted him about it. Two weeks later she was dead."

"Who is it?" Eli insisted.

"When my mother got pregnant with me, he was the son of the governor of Tennessee. Does that tell you who he is?"

CHAPTER
THIRTY-FIVE

The Proctor residence, Washington DC
By noon, Holland and Jill had been working on Holland's article for the *Washington Post* for over two hours. Evelyn did have something better for them to use than Jill's laptop and a telephone line. Holland sat in front of a wide, flat-screen monitor and banged out a rough draft. The irony of using a computer in Senator Proctor's house — in his own lavish study — to write an article about him that might be his undoing wasn't lost on either Holland or Jill.

Jill stood over Holland's shoulder and read every word. She offered suggestions and corrections, and Holland generally accepted them. He reminded her, though, that he was the journalist and she was the lawyer.

"I guess I'm too much of a stickler for accuracy and truth," Jill chided.

Holland snorted and kept typing.

Albert Johnson, the man with the raspy

voice, and his wife, Hazel, waited hand and foot on Holland and Jill. They were treated like favored houseguests. Hazel and Albert prepared breakfast, then lunch, and kept cups or glasses filled. Holland and Jill didn't leave the computer.

At last Jill glanced at her watch. "I better call Eli. My plane landed in Nashville an hour ago, and I wasn't on it. He's got to be wondering what's up by now."

Holland grunted and nodded and kept pecking at the keys. Jill left the study and asked Evelyn Proctor if she could use the phone. Jill and Holland had intentionally turned the power to their wireless phones on and left them in Holland's Camry. Evelyn readily obliged the request.

Jill dialed the number for Eli's wireless. "Eli, this is Jill," she said after he answered.

"Jill? I didn't recognize the number. Where are you? I thought you were due back in Nashville before now." Eli sounded puzzled.

"You're not going to believe me."

"Try me."

Jill told Eli everything that had happened in less than thirty-six hours, beginning with the telephone call to Cooper Harrington and ending with the rescue by Evelyn Proctor.

"Are you safe now?" Eli asked.

"I feel safe, but I'm not sure yet."

A pause, then, "And I guess you don't think Mrs. Proctor was involved anymore?"

"Can't be. She flew back to Washington on a charter after the fund-raiser. Cooper Harrington and Senator Proctor stayed until the next morning. But Mrs. Proctor doesn't know which one was in Jessica Caldwell's apartment that night either."

"The DNA matches Senator Proctor."

"Really? How do you know?"

"Because he's also Tag Grissom's father. Tag and the fetus of Jessica Caldwell were half siblings."

Stunned, Jill fell silent. She studied the carpeted floor under her feet. "Can you have Barbara scan that report into the server and email it to me? I'll log in from here and retrieve it. We may need it to corroborate the story Holland's writing."

"I'll be back in the office in thirty or forty minutes, and I'll have her do it. I'll check on the fingerprint possibility you mentioned, too."

"I've got to go," Jill told Eli. "I need to help Holland. We've got some editing to do with this new information."

"Call me later today. And, Jill?"

"Yeah."

"I've told you this before, but I really mean it. Be careful."

Jill ended the call and returned to the study. Holland was still hunched over the keyboard.

"You've got to do some revisions," she announced. "I have some new information from Eli."

En route to Jackson, Tennessee

Eli worried about Jill as he drove toward Jackson from Brentwood. This murder case now bordered on toppling one of the most powerful men in the country. And Jill was right in the middle of the danger. Eli prayed that God would protect her.

As Eli's BMW traversed the bridge over the Tennessee River that separated west Tennessee from middle Tennessee, he dialed the number for Randy Dickerson's office. Jill had mentioned the possibility that the unidentified fingerprints from the crime scene could be compared against the Office of Personnel Management database to see if they matched a print from Senator Proctor or Cooper Harrington. Eli needed to follow up on that theory, and the easiest and quickest way was through Randy Dickerson's office.

"Has the state lab provided you with the

DNA results on the Caldwell fetus?" Eli asked Randy.

"I received the results yesterday."

"Interesting, isn't it?"

"I'll say. But that doesn't exonerate Dr. Grissom," Randy said quickly. "We can still place him at the crime, and his skin was under her fingernail."

"I didn't expect you to dismiss the charges yet, but that leads me to why I'm calling. I need some additional comparisons on the fingerprints found at the Caldwell murder scene."

"What kind of comparisons?"

"I need the unidentified prints compared against the database for the federal Office of Personnel Management," Eli explained.

"You've lost me."

"I have a hunch — actually it was Jill who had the idea — that perhaps we'll find a match in the OPM database."

"Whose print do you think it will match?" Randy asked.

"I can't say yet."

"I can't help you then." Randy's reply was terse.

"Randy, you know Judge Blackwood will order it done. And he won't require me to tell you who I suspect. I'm just trying to get it done quicker. But you'll know before I do if there is a match."

"You think a federal employee was in her town house?"

"It's possible."

Randy sighed. "I'll see what I can do. It might take a couple of hours."

"Call me as soon as you know something."

Washington DC

Holland worked furiously on the article about Senator Proctor. It covered his affair with Jessica Caldwell, her pregnancy, her murder, the death of Tiffany Ramsey, and the fact that Senator Proctor owned the town house Jessica and Tiffany had shared.

Jill retrieved the lab report via email.

Holland stood from the chair in front of the computer and stretched his arms and legs.

Jill moved into the chair previously occupied by Holland and read the draft on the computer screen. It was 1:00 p.m. eastern time.

"Holland," Evelyn Proctor said. She appeared in the doorway to the study.

Holland and Jill turned their heads toward her.

"You have some competition for the front page."

"What?" Holland stopped stretching.

Evelyn waved them from the room. "The FBI is conducting a press conference right now. You need to see this."

Holland and Jill hurriedly vacated the study and followed Evelyn to the den. The trio stood before a large flat-screen television and watched as the interim FBI director, Phillip McFarland, stepped to a podium in the briefing room of the J. Edgar Hoover Building. Director McFarland was a tall African American with tightly curled black hair tinted with patches of gray. He wore a navy blue suit, red-and-navy tie, and white shirt.

"Good afternoon," Interim Director McFarland said. He read from a report on the podium in front of him. "We're pleased to announce that we have a break in the ongoing investigation of the bombing at Judge Dunbar Shelton's home in Vicksburg, Mississippi, six weeks ago and the murders of Myron and Dorothy Carlson almost two weeks ago. The two events were connected."

For ten minutes Interim Director McFarland described the involvement of Stella Hanover and Joe Moretti with both the bombing and the murders. A chart appeared on the large screen behind him. The chart depicted a timeline of Joe Moretti's travels immediately before the Shelton bombing and of the travels of Stella Hanover and Joe Moretti during the days immediately preceding the Carlsons' deaths.

"We haven't been able to locate Mr. Moretti, but we will continue to search for him. Regardless, the case against Ms. Hanover is airtight. We have agents in New York who are taking Ms. Hanover into custody as we speak. We have probable cause to believe that Ms. Hanover paid Joe Moretti to assassinate Judge Dunbar Shelton and also for the murders of Myron and Dorothy Carlson. But there is one part of the investigation that has not yet been completed."

The screen behind Interim Director Mc-Farland changed. The new chart depicted the timeline of Stella Hanover's travels after the Carlson murders.

"The document that has circulated on Capitol Hill over the last ten days — known as the Shelton Memo — came from the personal files of Myron Carlson. Our investigation has determined that Professor Carlson possessed the only copy of that document. We believe that this was the reason Myron and Dorothy Carlson were murdered. To obtain the Shelton Memo. The graph behind me shows that Joe Moretti arrived in Manhattan on Sunday afternoon a week ago. We believe he was carrying the

Shelton Memo. He went directly to Stella Hanover's office in Manhattan and delivered the memo to her. Then Monday morning Ms. Hanover came to DC. Her one and only stop while in DC was at the office of Senator Lance Proctor."

Holland, Jill, and Evelyn exchanged glances but didn't speak. Their vision returned immediately to the television.

"We plan to interrogate Senator Proctor and his staff as soon as possible." Interim Director McFarland shuffled his report together. "I don't have time for questions. My staff will distribute a press release packet with a copy of the charts behind me as you exit."

Holland, Jill, and Evelyn stared at the television as Director McFarland exited the room and the screen switched to a news anchor sitting behind a desk in New York City.

"I hope they get him for that, too," Evelyn said. There was fire and determination in her eyes.

"We better keep working," Holland told Jill. "And I need to call my editor to make sure he saves some room for my article on the front page. I can't win a Pulitzer if the article doesn't run." He grinned.

Jill and Holland returned to the study. Jill

completed her proofreading of Holland's draft of the article. When she gave it her blessing, Holland dialed the direct number for his editor, Dan Bolding. The phone was cordless, so Holland paced around the study as he talked.

"Boss, I just finished the final touches on an article that I think you're going to like."

"Fletcher, didn't you see McFarland's press conference? I've got everyone working all angles of that one."

"But this story is bigger."

Dan laughed loud and deep. "Bigger than implicating the Senate majority leader in two murders and an attempt at two more? Impossible."

Holland gave Dan the skinny version of the article he'd written. Dan stopped laughing. Holland described how he and Jill had been chased by unknown assailants, but that they were safe. But he didn't tell him where they were.

"Have you corroborated all your sources?"

"Every one," Holland promised.

"And the DNA lab report?"

"I have a copy."

Dan was quiet for five seconds. "Send the article to me and I'll take a look."

Holland pressed the Off button on the cordless phone and set it on the desk in

Senator Proctor's study. Jill stood from the desk chair and Holland resumed his seat in front of the computer. He logged into his *Post* email account. Within five minutes the article and DNA report were attached to an email and sent to Dan Bolding.

The Hart Building, Washington DC
Senator Proctor was livid. He stomped around his office, flinging epithets at Cooper Harrington. They had both watched Interim Director McFarland's press conference and the telephone had been ringing off the wall with media requests for an interview or a comment. At his direction, Senator Proctor's secretary finally stopped answering the phone.

"This is entirely your fault!" Senator Proctor screamed at Cooper.

Cooper cowered in front of him. He appeared frazzled and pale as death. "Everything's going to be okay," he mumbled.

Cooper's voice was detached. Senator Proctor wasn't certain that he was even talking to him.

"You're not very convincing, Cooper. Everything's not going to be okay. How can you say that?"

"The problems keep growing."

"What'd you say?"

557

Cooper looked confused and shook his head, as if he were clearing his mind. His voice became more coherent. "Never mind. All we have to do is deny everything. We didn't know Stella killed the Carlsons to get the Shelton Memo."

"She came to my office as soon as Moretti gave it to her. That looks bad, Cooper. That looks really bad."

"I know, but it'll blow over in a couple of days. Once the press realizes that we were used by Stella, they'll move on to something else. It won't last two news cycles."

"I hope you're right."

"I know I'm right."

Senator Proctor rubbed his forehead. "Let's get a press release out immediately denying any knowledge of Stella Hanover's role in the Shelton bombing and the Carlson murders."

The Oval Office, the White House, Washington DC

Porter McIntosh sat on one of the sofas in the Oval Office. He closed his wireless.

"The press smells blood in the water," Porter told President Wallace. "They're all over Proctor."

Porter had just finished speaking with one of his assistants and received that report from her. He and President Wallace had watched Interim Director McFarland's press conference — a press conference orchestrated by Porter's staff, using the information Porter had accumulated from Simon Webster — on Fox News and continued to watch the events as they unfolded. "And Proctor just released a statement denying any knowledge of Stella Hanover's activities."

"Plausible denial," President Wallace commented from behind his desk.

"Denial, yes, but I'm not sure everyone's buying the plausibility of it yet. And all we need is for the story to continue a couple of days."

"What're you hearing from the Senate?"

"All the other senators are stiff lipped so far. Nobody's said anything yet."

"With Proctor's quick denial, they may all take a wait-and-see attitude. You think this story's enough to turn the tide on Shelton?"

"I hope so," Porter replied. "What else do we have?"

The Proctor residence, Washington DC
"Randy Dickerson had the print run through the OPM database," Eli said.

Jill was using Evelyn Proctor's landline phone again.

Eli continued, "And there's a match."

"Which one?"

"Guess."

"Proctor," Jill said, confident of her answer.

"Nope."

"Cooper Harrington? Really? I wonder if Proctor told him to or if he did it on his own?"

"I don't know. We may never know. But Randy Dickerson realizes we can at least create reasonable doubt with a jury. He may dismiss the charges."

Jill pressed Off on the cordless phone and entered the Proctor study. Holland swiveled the computer chair toward the door when she entered.

"More information," she announced to Holland. "The previously unidentified fingerprint from the Caldwell murder has now been identified."

Holland stared at her, waiting for the answer.

Jill smiled and let him wait several seconds before she said, "Cooper Harrington."

Holland spun back to the computer and started typing again. Thirty minutes later he transmitted a revised draft to Dan Bolding, incorporating the revelation of Cooper Harrington's fingerprints in Jessica Caldwell's town house. It was 3:30 p.m.

Holland waited ten minutes before dialing Dan's direct number. "Did you get the last draft?"

"I got it. I'm talking to the editorial staff and legal counsel for approval. But I like it. Good work. You've scooped everyone in town. And you're right. It may be bigger than the Shelton Memo story. Where are you, anyway?"

"I can't tell you yet."

"Are you and Miss Baker safe?"

"We're safe."

"Call me back in an hour."

Holland and Jill left the study and entered the den of the Proctor house. Through the window they saw a locksmith's box van parked in the driveway. A man was working on the front door. Evelyn Proctor supervised the work.

"What's going on?" Holland asked in the direction of Evelyn.

Evelyn pivoted and faced Holland and Jill with another wicked grin. "I'm having the locks changed."

CHAPTER
THIRTY-SIX

Washington DC

Holland and Jill stayed awake past midnight waiting for the delivery of the Thursday-morning edition of the *Washington Post*. At 2:37 a.m. eastern time, they heard a car pass by the front of Evelyn Proctor's brownstone. There was the *thud* of a newspaper landing in the driveway.

Holland dashed out to retrieve it while Jill waited inside the open door. Holland was breathless when he returned. Under the light in the foyer of the Proctor residence — and with Jill looking over his shoulder — Holland removed the rubber band from around the newspaper and unfolded it. The splash above the fold was an article by Holland Fletcher, investigative reporter.

The White House, Washington DC

Porter McIntosh had the White House staff awaken President Wallace at 5:00 a.m.

Thursday. The president, wearing a burgundy bathrobe, met Porter just inside the main door to the White House living quarters. Porter handed him a copy of the *Washington Post*. President Wallace began to read the article above the fold and moved into a sitting area. Porter followed.

"Did you see who wrote the article?" Porter asked.

"Holland Fletcher."

"That's the cub reporter who wanted confirmation that Judge Shelton was the nominee before we released the name."

President Wallace, his face still in the newspaper, settled into a leather Queen Anne chair. Porter stood in front of him.

"He's come a long way since then," the president said.

"The article about Stella Hanover and the Shelton Memo is on the bottom of the page."

"I didn't think anything would be a bigger story, but this is. I can't believe it."

"Proctor's done for."

"And Cooper Harrington, too," President Wallace said. He looked at Porter. "Get the Senate pro tem on the phone as soon as you can. We still want the vote on Judge Shelton today, even if Proctor's not there. Then start working the other senators. I can't imagine any of them will want to side with Proctor on anything after this."

Interim Director McFarland's press conference and the disappearance of Holland Fletcher and Jill Baker drove Cooper Harrington to the Hawk 'n' Dove Bar again. He arrived during happy hour and drank until after midnight. The bartender called a cab to take him home. He passed out on the sofa, still wearing his tie and suit coat.

At 6:10 a.m. on Thursday he awoke suddenly. The doorbell was ringing, and someone repeatedly banged on the front door.

"Cooper!" a voice yelled. "Cooper, open the door!"

After a few seconds Cooper recognized the voice as being Senator Proctor's. Cooper shook the cobwebs from his head. His tongue felt thick, his head ached, and his eyes burned. He could barely remove himself from the sofa. But he finally stumbled to the door.

He opened it to Senator Proctor's angry face. The senator looked as bad as Cooper felt.

"Have you seen this?" Senator Proctor thrust the morning edition of the *Washington Post* in his face.

Cooper took the newspaper from Senator Proctor's hands and tried to focus his vision. "What is it?"

"Read it," Senator Proctor barked.

Cooper backed away and began to read. Senator Proctor entered and slammed the door. They stood in the foyer of Cooper's Chevy Chase town house. Cooper could hear Senator Proctor's heavy breathing. The more Cooper read, the sicker he became. He stumbled back to the sofa with Senator Proctor on his heels.

"I thought you were going to handle this." Senator Proctor, hands on his hips, stood over Cooper. He peered down at him.

Cooper's face was in the newspaper. He looked up into Senator Proctor's rage. "I was."

"Then how did this happen?" the senator demanded.

"It doesn't matter now."

"I'm not going to jail, Cooper," Senator Proctor yelled. "I'm not going to jail!"

"And I'm not going by myself," Cooper declared. "I did all of this for you. To keep you in the Senate majority leader's office. You're crazy if you think I'm taking the fall by myself."

Senator Proctor gritted his teeth. "This is all you, Cooper."

Cooper struggled to his feet and looked Senator Proctor directly in the eyes. His gaze bore through the senator's rage. Cooper had never stood up to Senator Proctor, but now he was backed into a corner. He had no choice.

"That's where you're wrong, Senator. I covered myself on this one. I've got dates and times and places. I even have you recorded giving me instructions to get rid of Ms. Caldwell. They'll give me a sweet deal to roll over on you, and I plan on getting the best deal I can. No, Senator Proctor, this one's all you."

When it was over, Cooper couldn't believe he'd said it. He thought for a moment that Senator Proctor was going to strike him. But he didn't. He turned and stomped out, slamming the door as he left.

Cooper fell back onto the sofa, his clothes drenched with sweat, and cried uncontrollably.

Washington DC
"I'm going to stay until Sunday," Jill told Eli.

Albert Johnson had taken her and Holland to retrieve their cars and wireless phones. It was 2:15 p.m. eastern time.

"I've renewed my rental and checked back

in to the Hampton Inn. I didn't pack enough clothes, so I'll have to buy some new ones. I hate it."

"I bet you do. Where are you?"

"I'm with Holland. We're heading for his apartment. His editor called and said they've had at least six calls for Holland to give an interview for the evening news. And the Sunday morning programs are after him to appear on their shows this weekend."

"You like this guy?"

Jill eyed Holland and smiled, but Holland didn't appear to notice. He was face forward, driving his Camry, while she sat in the passenger seat. He had waited in the parking lot of the Hampton Inn while Jill showered and changed clothes. It had taken an hour, and he hadn't complained.

"Yeah, I like him. We'll see how things go."

Holland glanced at Jill and raised his eyebrows.

Jill felt her face turn red. "But I haven't told him yet. Ask me again on Monday." Although Jill was speaking to Eli, she was really talking to Holland. "I'll see how he acts this weekend."

Holland straightened his back and came to attention, as if he were signaling that he would be on his best behavior.

Jill laughed at his antics.

"I'll see you Monday then, Jill," Eli said. "Have fun. You deserve it."

"I will. See you Monday."

Jill closed her wireless and exhaled. She contemplated what the next three days would bring . . . and whether they would alter her life forever.

Brentwood, Tennessee

Anna Grissom awoke on the last Sunday in July and found the other side of the bed empty. She glanced at the digital alarm clock: 7:04 a.m.

Eli had called Friday to tell them that Randy Dickerson planned to ask Judge Blackwood to dismiss the charges against Tag. And he'd said the one thing that Tag had longed for years to hear. The great Senator Lance Proctor was being prosecuted for murder — the murder of Jessica Caldwell. But Randy had also promised Eli that he would reopen the investigation into the death of Tag's mother.

Anna had begun to notice a change in Tag almost instantly. It was as if he had a new lease on life.

"Tag," she called out sleepily.

There was no response.

She arose from bed, slipped into a blue satin robe, and walked to the master bathroom. Not finding Tag there, she searched his study, adjacent to the den. It was vacant.

After that she went to the kitchen. There stood Tag, behind the ceramic-tiled island drinking from a white coffee mug. He wore brown slacks. A white, starched shirt. A sports coat. And an anxious face.

"Tag, what are you doing up so early and dressed?"

Tag scanned his clothing, then looked at Anna. "We're going to church, aren't we?"

Anna grinned. "Yes, we are. But the early service doesn't start for another two hours."

"I know," Tag said. "But I don't want to be late."

Anna moved toward Tag, put her arms around his neck, and gazed into his eyes. A solitary tear trickled down her cheek. Anna couldn't recall the last time they had even held hands, much less each other.

"Are we going to be all right, Tag?"

"I hope so," he murmured.

The events of the last few months raced through Anna's mind . . . then disappeared. She trusted that the horrible memories were gone forever. Because for the first time in a long time, she could see love and hope and possibility — visible in Tag's eyes.

EPILOGUE

East Room, the White House, Washington DC
President Wallace concluded his remarks
and stepped away from the podium as Chief
Justice Walters administered the oath of office to the newest associate justice to the
Supreme Court — Justice Dunbar Shelton.
An odd, surreal feeling came over him as he
realized the magnitude of what had tran-
spired.

The Senate had voted ninety-nine to zero
to confirm Justice Shelton, and now he
stood there in the East Room with his left
hand on the Holy Bible that Victoria held
and his right hand in the air. President
Wallace knew that it might not be tomorrow or next month or even next year, but
America would be better, immensely better,
for having Dunbar Shelton sitting on the
highest court in the land. Given everything
that had happened, he could only describe
Judge Shelton's elevation to the high court

as being a divine appointment. Only God could have been in control during all the events that had taken place.

President Wallace's wife, Lauren, stood beside him in a blue dress and white pearls, and gently touched his hand as Justice Dunbar Shelton recited the constitutional oath read to him by Chief Justice Walters.

" 'I do solemnly swear that I will support and defend the Constitution of the United States against all enemies, foreign and domestic; that I will bear true faith and allegiance to the same; that I take this obligation freely, without any mental reservation or purpose of evasion; and that I will well and faithfully discharge the duties of the office on which I am about to enter: So help me God.' "

The Faulkner residence, Jackson, Tennessee
"Eli, come here," Eli heard Sara call out from the back of the house.

Eli was in their den in his brown leather recliner with his feet propped up, remote in one hand, and a glass of sweetened iced tea in the other. He could tell that Sara sounded excited but not panicked. So he was slow to move.

"Hang on a minute," he called. "I'm watching the Braves. It's almost over.

They're up five to four over the Mets in the ninth."

"But this is important. You can rewind the Tivo later. Just come here. Quick."

Again, Eli sensed excitement in her voice.

"Okay, okay," Eli mumbled to himself. He lowered the recliner to its normal sitting position. "I'm coming," he called.

Eli set his half-full glass on a coaster on the end table and tossed the remote into his chair. He backed out of the room, continuing to watch the television for as long as he could before leaving the den and walking fast down the hallway to their bedroom. He wanted to return to the den as soon as possible.

"Where are you?" Eli asked as he entered the bedroom.

"I'm in the bathroom."

"The bathroom? What are you doing in there?"

"Stop asking questions and just come in here."

Eli walked through the doorway from the bedroom into the bathroom.

Sara was standing there with a radiant smile. Tears were streaming down her face.

"What's wrong?" Eli asked.

"Nothing's wrong." Sara pointed at the double vanity. "Look." There was awe in her voice.

Eli looked in the direction Sara pointed. "Is that what I think it is?" he asked, running his fingers through his black, wavy hair.

"Yes. It's a pregnancy test."

ABOUT THE AUTHOR

A graduate of Union University, **Jerome Teel** received his JD, cum laude, from the Ole Miss School of Law. He is actively involved in his church, local charities, and youth sports. He has always loved legal-suspense novels and is a political junkie. He is also the author of *The Election,* another political thriller. Jerome and his wife, Jennifer, have three children — Brittney, Trey, and Matthew — and reside in Tennessee, where he practices law and is at work on a new novel. For more information, visit www .jerometeel.com.

The employees of Thorndike Press hope you have enjoyed this Large Print book. All our Thorndike and Wheeler Large Print titles are designed for easy reading, and all our books are made to last. Other Thorndike Press Large Print books are available at your library, through selected bookstores, or directly from us.

For information about titles, please call:
    (800) 223-1244

or visit our Web site at:
    http://gale.cengage.com/thorndike

To share your comments, please write:
    Publisher
    Thorndike Press
    295 Kennedy Memorial Drive
    Waterville, ME 04901